DRAGON
WEATHER

OTHER NOVELS BY LAWRENCE WATT-EVANS

Dragon Weather

Lawrence Watt-Evans

Misenchanted Press

Bainbridge Island

Dragon Weather

Copyright ©1999 by Lawrence Watt Evans

Published by Misenchanted Press

www.misenchantedpress.com

First Misenchanted Press Edition: March 2021

ISBN: 978-1-61991-028-7

Cover art by Bob Eggleton

Dedicated to Charles Worsley,

an honorable man,

and the man who has made my sister happy.

Book 1:

Arlian

Chapter One

Dragon Weather

The sky to the west was dark with heavy black clouds; Arlian didn't like it at all. He was eleven years old, almost a man by the standards of his village, but right now he felt much younger, and very unsure of himself—his father was away, and the weather seemed threatening and unnatural. He stayed close to his mother as she stood staring down the slope of the mountain, watching the men of the village haul the heavy water wagons back up the winding, stone-paved road.

Oxen would have made the hauling much easier, but the village had no place to graze oxen on the rocky mountainside; what little arable soil they had was all reserved for human needs. That meant that the men of Obsidian had to use their own muscles to fetch water up from the river.

In another year or two Arlian would be big enough to join them, but for now he stood beside his mother and watched.

Arlian's mother fanned herself with one hand, while the other clutched at her black-and-gold brooch, holding her collar open; the air was thick, hot, and stagnant, and her gray dress was soaked in sweat. "I can't stand weather like this," she said. "I'll almost be glad to see winter come this year!"

Arlian looked up at her—though not far up, as he was almost as tall as she, now. He always liked winter, and had never entirely understood why the adults didn't. In winter the mountain was covered in snow—well, except right up by the crater—and he and the other children of the village could go sliding down it; there was plenty of cold, clean water available for the melting, without having to haul it up from the valley when the streams ran dry. He could play outside for hours, then come in and warm up by the fire, and no one would order him out of the way or ask him to help with the chores. Even the adults had less work to do in the winter—so why did they all hate it? Yes, there was less food and it wasn't fresh, and the cold seeped through everywhere, and the fire had to be kept up, but still, Arlian thought that winter was wonderful.

And *anything* was better than this stifling hot, humid summer, when the sun didn't seem to want to show its face and hid behind a thick haze or clouds. This wasn't how summer was supposed to be—there should be bright days and rainy ones, not these endless smothering gloomy days when the clouds hung overhead but the rain never fell. This was ugly and exhausting.

It hadn't rained in weeks, and the crops were suffering—the water the men were hauling up from the river would help, but a good cistern-filling rain, splashing down the mountainside and pooling in the rocks, would have been better.

Those clouds in the west looked even uglier than most of this year's skies. Maybe they would bring storms, and put an end to this nasty heat—but their appearance was not promising, and Arlian didn't trust them.

His grandfather—his mother's father; his father's father was long dead—stepped out on the rocky ledge beside them and looked, not down the slope at the water-haulers he was too old to assist, but out at the clouds.

"Dragon weather," he said with a frown.

"Oh, nonsense," Arlian's mother said. "You've been saying that for weeks. It's just a hot spell."

"Isn't that what dragon weather is, Mother?" Arlian asked. "A hot spell?"

His mother glanced at her father.

"Not just the heat," the old man said. "Look at that sky—hot as a furnace and days dark as night, *that's* dragon weather. You need the heat *and* the dark. If those clouds move in and settle here, that's *really* what we'll have."

Arlian looked straight up at the sky overhead. It wasn't dark as night, but it wasn't very bright, either; the summer haze was thick and foul with the gasses from the smoking peak of the mountain. The fumes had been thicker than usual lately, but whether that had any connection with the weather no one seemed to know. Arlian had heard the adults arguing about it, but the arguments were never settled.

"Why is it called dragon weather, Grandsir?" he asked.

"Because it's the sort of weather that brings the dragons out of their caves," his grandfather replied. "They can't abide cold or light, Ari. In the days when the dragons ruled over our ancestors the world was warmer than it is now, and the great beasts darkened the skies with their smoke so that they could come out by day, as well as night. When the weather's dark and hot now, old and tired as they are, they still stir in their sleep, and sometimes they awaken and come out to feed."

Arlian stared nervously at his grandfather. The old man spoke in a deeper voice than usual—his storytelling voice. It made his words seem more important, and more ominous.

"Don't mind him, Ari," Arlian's mother said, patting Arlian's shoulder reassuringly. "That's just stories. No one's seen any dragons in hundreds of years."

Her father shook his head.

"No, Sharbeth, you're wrong," he said. "When I was a boy I saw a village where a dragon had been not long before. I may be old, but it wasn't hundreds of years ago."

"Tell me about it!" Arlian said.

His grandfather smiled down at him. "Are you sure? They say it's bad luck to talk about the dragons, just as it's unlucky to speak too much about magic."

Arlian nodded. "Tell me about it, Grandsir!"

Grandsir looked up at the sky and frowned, then back down at Arlian, his smile reappearing. "I was a year or two older than you are, and my uncle Stirian had taken me on a trading journey down to Benth-in-Tara, to meet a caravan that was passing through," he said. "We saw the ruins on the way. We'd had a hot summer the year before, weather something like this, and for a few days the smoke from the mountain had been much thicker than usual and had collected in that valley over in the Sandalwood Hills." He pointed over the shoulder of the mountain; Arlian had never been to the Sandalwood Hills, but he had seen them from the crater rim and knew where his grandfather meant.

"The dragon must have come out late that summer," the old man continued, "and no one discovered it over the winter. When we got there in the spring, there was nothing left but charred ruins and bare bones."

"And how do you know it wasn't human raiders who destroyed it?" Arlian's mother asked. "Those bandits in the south are surely bad enough without worrying about dragons!"

"The Borderlands bandits never get anywhere near this far north," her father said, "and human raiders don't leave six-foot claw marks."

"And neither do dragons," Sharbeth said, her hands on her hips, "because the dragons, if there are really any left alive at all, stay asleep in their caves, deep beneath the earth. You must have just *imagined* those claw marks, Father, or misinterpreted sword cuts or wagon ruts."

"They were real, and they were claw marks," her father insisted, but without much vehemence; Arlian realized that the two of them had undoubtedly had this argument many times before, as they had so many others, and had worn the passion out of it. His mother and grandfather argued often, and had done so ever since Grandsir had first come to live with them while Arlian was still a small child. He could barely remember a time when

Grandsir had not been there—or when his mother did not argue with him.

"I'm not going to listen to your nonsense," Arlian's mother said, with no great anger. "I'm going to go see that those men have something fit to eat when they get those wagons up here, something to keep their strength up!" She turned and started back toward the house.

Arlian hesitated. He wanted to stay close to his mother, and help out when the water wagons arrived, but he also wanted to hear his grandfather's story about the ruined village—it wasn't one he remembered hearing before. He wanted to know more about the dragons and what had become of them.

"Are you coming, Arlian?" his mother called. She paused and looked over her shoulder.

"No, Mother," he replied. "I'll stay here for a while, with Grandsir."

"Hmpf." She marched on across the rocky yard, toward their thatch-roofed home.

Grandsir looked down at Arlian. "Eager to see your father and brother back?" he asked.

Arlian nodded. "Tell me more about the dragons," he said.

His grandfather laughed. "That's my boy!" he said. "What do you want to know?"

"Have you ever *seen* a dragon, Grandsir?"

The old man shook his head. "Of course not," he said. "I'm still alive, am I not? There aren't many who see dragons and live to tell of it!"

"There must be *some* people who see them, or how would we know *anything* about dragons?" Arlian asked.

"A fair question," his grandfather said, smiling. He glanced at the water-haulers, judged it would still be a while before they reached the village, and settled down cross-legged on the ledge, into a better position for storytelling. Arlian settled beside him.

"Yes," Arlian's grandfather said, "there have been a few people who saw dragons and lived to tell about it. Most of them were at a safe distance, and the dragons simply didn't notice them, but there have been a few…" His voice trailed off as he looked to the west, at the approaching clouds. He frowned.

"A few what, Grandsir?" Arlian looked, trying to see what his grandfather was staring at.

The old man shook himself. "Nothing," he said. "I just don't like this weather." Then he smiled at Arlian, and said, "Of course, there were a few who got a good *close* look at the dragons. There might even be some of them

4

who are still alive today."

Arlian nodded. "From that village in the Sandalwood Hills, you mean?"

"Oh, no." Grandsir shook his head. "Nothing like that; I saw that village, and there wasn't so much as a rat left alive there, just bones and cinders. But there are old stories, *very* old stories, about dragon venom."

"Venom?" Arlian frowned. As Grandsir had said, most of the adults in the village didn't like talking about the dragons; there were so many superstitions about them that most people thought it safer not to discuss them at all. Dragons were magical, and magic was wicked and untrustworthy, and speaking too much about it could attract misfortune.

Still, Arlian had thought he had a reasonable understanding of what a dragon was, and he didn't remember anything about venom. "I thought dragons breathed fire!" he said.

"Well, they *do,* after a fashion," Grandsir said. "Or so I'm told. But the older stories, the ones from the early days of the Years of Man, say that dragonflame isn't so much fiery breath, as some people would have it, but a spray of burning venom, like a snake's spit of poison. Except dragons somehow set their poison ablaze, and thereby spit flame."

"Ooooh!" Arlian shivered at the thought. It seemed somehow more *real* to know that dragonfire was burning venom, rather than some sort of magical breath. It made dragons seem more like actual beasts, rather than spirits, or illusions like the little images the village sorcerer sometimes conjured up.

"Whether it's the truth or not I can't say," Grandsir continued, "but there are *stories,* very old stories, so old I don't know where they came from, that say that sometimes the venom doesn't catch fire properly. It's still deadly poison, of course, a poison that will burn the flesh from your bones—but supposedly it quickly loses some of its virulence when once it's been sprayed, and a mixture of this dragon venom and human blood is said to bestow long life on anyone who drinks it. *Very* long life. There are tales of men who lived centuries after surviving dragon attacks in which blood from their wounds was mixed with dragon venom and then swallowed—though many of them had been horribly mutilated in the attacks, their faces burned away, arms or legs lost, so that such a life would hardly be a blessing."

Arlian shivered again. He looked at the clouds. The dragons seemed so terrible that it was hard, sometimes, to believe that they were ever real.

Everyone knew they were real, though, or had been once, at least. The dragons had ruled all of the Lands of Man, from the eastern sea to the western wilderness, from the Borderlands in the south to the icy wastes of the north.

5

People had resisted their rule sometimes, fought great wars against the dragons, but to no avail—until one day, about seven hundred years ago, when the dragons had all gone away, leaving humanity free.

Arlian's mother said the dragons had all died, perhaps of some plague, but most people insisted they were still alive, deep in their caverns, and might come back at any time.

And sometimes, according to Grandsir, they *did* come back, briefly.

"That village in the Sandalwood Hills," Arlian asked. "What do you think the people there did to anger the dragon? Why would it destroy them all?"

"I don't think they had to do *anything*," Grandsir said. "The dragon simply felt like destroying something, and they were close at hand."

"But that's so unfair! You mean they didn't do anything to deserve it?"

"Not a thing," Grandsir replied.

Arlian absorbed that unhappily. He didn't like it at all. He knew life wasn't always fair, but he felt, deep in his heart, that it *should* be. He always tried to be fair to his brother, Korian, and to their playmates in the village—even the giggly girls. In the stories his mother told justice always triumphed in the end. Why was the rest of life so messy and unjust?

His father said it was because the gods were dead, and only Fate remained, and Fate had its own plans for everyone.

The village sorcerer—the only person in the village of Obsidian whose name Arlian didn't know, because he said names had power—had said that justice was as much an illusion as any of the little tricks he did to entertain the children.

Arlian wondered sometimes if it might be the other way around—maybe everything *did* work out fairly in the end, somehow, and the apparent injustices were the illusions. He wiped sweat-damp hair away from his eyes and looked down at the approaching wagons.

Maybe the dragon *did* have a good reason for destroying that village. Maybe the dragons were part of Fate's plans.

"Do you really think it's dragon weather?" he asked.

His grandfather put an arm around Arlian's shoulder and gave him a reassuring hug.

"I hope not," he said. "Come on, let's go give your mother a hand."

Together, they turned away from the ledge and ambled toward the house.

Chapter Two

The Coming of the Dragons

The dark clouds hung heavy in the western sky for the next three days, creeping very slowly nearer, spreading across the sky like a stain. The water wagons were brought to the cisterns above the village and emptied into the great stone basins, and water was doled out carefully to each family, enough to keep both crops and people alive, but still thirsty.

The mountain above the village continued to smoke and steam; the air now had a very noticeable sulfurous stench to it, and the sun, when it could be seen through the haze at all, was as orange as a pumpkin.

Despite the oppressive heat and gloom the young men of Obsidian returned to their usual tasks, working the mines, carving the black glass, tending the crops. The women kept house, cooked and cleaned, wove and sewed, minded the livestock and the children. The old men thatched roofs, polished brightwork, and took care of the other less urgent, less strenuous jobs.

And the children ran errands and helped out as required, but still found time to play and explore. On the third morning after the water run Arlian climbed up to the top of the great black rock north of the village; at the top, sweaty and filthy, he settled down cross-legged and looked out over the countryside.

Up here it was just as hot as in the village, but the air seemed not quite so still and thick. From here he could see for miles upon miles, out across the Lands of Man, across fields and forests, from the Sandalwood Hills to the Bitter Lake, from Skygrazer Peak back to Tara Vale, miles in every direction but southeast, where the mountain blocked his view.

To the north, far off on the horizon, beyond the lowering clouds and the pall of mountain smoke, he could see a dull line of blue sky. At one point, to the northeast, that blue was marred by a smudge of smoke; his father had once pointed it out and told Arlian that that was where the great city of Manfort lay, where humans had first resisted, and finally broken, the dragons' hold on the world—Manfort, where the great lords and ladies lived in their stone palaces, in their fine clothes and fancy coaches, with their dress balls and formal duels, amid rumors of secret societies and elaborate intrigue.

Arlian stared at the smoke for a long time, trying to imagine what the city was like.

When he grew up he wanted to travel; he had said so for as long as he could remember. His grandfather had been a traveler in his youth, and Arlian loved to hear him talk about it. He wanted to see all the places Grandsir had described—Blackwater, and Deep Delving, and Benth-in-Tara, and the groves of Nossevier.

And maybe he could even get to Manfort, as Grandsir never had, to see the palaces there, and the old shrines to the dead gods, and the lords and ladies with their swords and horses, and the Duke of Manfort, heir to the great warlords of old. Grandsir had stayed clear for fear of being robbed, or captured by slavers and sold, or killed by some lord he had inadvertently offended, but Arlian was certain he would be able to handle a visit there.

Or he might cross the Desolation to the Borderlands, where, it was said, one could see wild magic flashing across the southern skies, above the wild lands—magic was weak and scarce in the Lands of Man, useful only to trained sorcerers and severely limited even then, but Arlian had heard that in the Borderlands beyond the desert magic was so strong it danced like brightly colored fires in the sky. The intervening Desolation was said to be hot and almost waterless, a wasteland where anyone losing his way would leave bleached bones in the sand, and where bloodthirsty bandits roamed—but caravans still crossed it every year, and Arlian could surely join one.

There was magic beyond the eastern seas, as well, and ships sailed there from the ports of Benthin and Lorigol, and someday Arlian might travel in one.

And maybe he would become a lord himself—he would own a business, perhaps a caravan or a ship or a manufactory, where others would labor on his behalf, and he would carry a sword and dagger on his belt and ride a fine horse.

But wherever he went, Arlian told himself, he would come home at the last, to settle in his own familiar village, just as Grandsir had. Arlian thought he would find a pretty wife somewhere and bring her back here and raise half a dozen children, sons and daughters both, and he would treat them equally and fairly and raise them to be good and just people. And he would tell them stories of his travels at the supper table, just as Grandsir did.

With that thought he realized that it was almost time for the midday meal. Arlian wiped black-tinged sweat from his forehead with his sleeve, then turned away from the distant smoke of Manfort and started back down the jagged side of the black rock.

Later, after everyone had eaten, as his parents headed for the fields, Grandsir beckoned to Arlian.

"Summer can't last much longer," he said, "and we haven't put aside as much for the winter as usual. I want to take a look in the cellars, see what we have and what we need. Come along and give me a hand, would you, Ari?"

Arlian smiled and came willingly; the cellars were usually cool, and any respite from the muggy heat would be welcome. He was not permitted in the cellars without adult supervision; there were too many ways for an active lad to do damage, down there in the cool darkness.

"Bring a candle," Grandsir said, gesturing toward the drawer.

Arlian rummaged through the drawer until he found a good thick candle stub as long as his finger; he lit it with a splint from the kitchen fire, which was kept burning even on days as swelteringly uncomfortable as this.

The candle flared up, and even in the well-ventilated kitchen with its wide-open doors and windows the little flame seemed to brighten the room; the day was darker than Arlian had realized, and seemed to be darkening as he watched.

He took a final glance out the window at the black clouds, then followed his grandfather, trotting through the long narrow pantry, past the tiered shelves to the door at the back.

The rush of air from the cellars when Grandsir opened the door was disappointing, nowhere near as cool as Arlian had expected—apparently the heat had even penetrated into the stone-lined depths beneath the house. Still, it was cooler than anywhere else he might go.

The old man went down the ladder first while Arlian held the candle high; when he reached the bottom the boy handed the light down, then turned and made his own way down the sagging wooden rungs. The rails were slick in his hands, polished to a silky sheen by generations of hands sliding down them, and he had to watch his step closely.

When he stepped off the final rung the stone floor felt warm beneath his bare feet; he glanced down in surprise.

"The mountain is hot," Grandsir said. "I wouldn't be surprised if it erupts soon."

Arlian said nothing, but his eyes widened at the notion. The crater that loomed over the village had smoked all Arlian's life, but there had been no actual eruption for almost fifty years.

The natural path for any lava or ash was down the far slope, well away from the village, but still, an eruption was an exciting, frightening thought.

"Come on," Grandsir said, leading the way down one of the passageways, between dusty shelves lined with earthenware crocks and black glass jars.

Arlian followed, brushing aside cobwebs and soaking in the dimness and the rich musty smells. Somewhere behind him, from the sunlit world above, he heard a distant shriek—probably Kashkar the Stonecarver's three girls playing some silly game, Arlian thought.

A man's voice shouted, but Arlian could not make out any words—probably Kashkar, telling his daughters to go elsewhere with their racket. Arlian paid no attention to the noise, but watched as Grandsir ran a careful finger along a shelf, counting crocks.

"Eighteen pots of the soft cheese," the old man said. "Count the wheels of hard cheese on the bottom shelf, boy, the ones in black wax—my old knees don't want me to stoop that much anymore, and my eyes…"

Arlian squatted and began counting the big drums of cheese—the black wax did tend to fade into the dark background, and he could see how Grandsir might have trouble.

More voices were shouting somewhere in the distance, Arlian realized as he counted—had those girls started the adults arguing?

Then he heard another sound, a hollow metallic booming, and started up so suddenly he almost knocked the candle from Grandsir's hand.

The old man hardly noticed; he had heard the same sound, and was staring at the open door at the top of the ladderwell. From where they stood only a corner of the opening was visible, a triangle of dull gray light in the brown darkness.

They both knew that sound. Everyone in the village knew it. Once a year everyone gathered around and solemnly listened to it, simply so they *would* know it when they heard it. It was the ringing of the great brass warning bell that hung in the otherwise abandoned village shrine.

"Do you think the mountain's erupting, Grandsir?" Arlian asked.

"I don't know," his grandfather replied, taking a step toward the ladder, the candle held high. "It could be. But I don't hear any rumbling…"

Then he stopped moving, stopped talking. People were shrieking again—but this was no game. These were screams of mortal terror, from grown men and women as well as children.

"What's happening?" Arlian whispered hoarsely. He stared at the ladder.

Then a rush of hot air swept down into the cellars, flinging long-settled dust into the air in great swirls; dust stung Arlian's eyes, blinding him momentarily. He blinked frantically, and dabbed at his watering eyes.

Somewhere overhead he heard a tremendous roaring.

"Come on," Grandsir said. "Whatever's happening, we don't want to be trapped down here." He tugged at Arlian's arm.

Still squinting, Arlian came, staggering toward the ladder. The doorway seemed much brighter now—much *too* bright, Arlian thought. He realized with a start that the wind had blown out the candle and he hadn't even noticed at first, so much more light was spilling down from above.

Hot air roiled about them when they reached the ladder. Grandsir gestured for Arlian to wait, and began climbing.

He reached the top and took a step forward, and Arlian did not wait for a signal, but started up the ladder himself.

The minute his head cleared the pantry floor and he could see through the other door he knew why there was so much more light; the kitchen roof was gone, torn away, and the kitchen walls were ablaze. The pantry's stone walls were intact, but the wooden ceiling was beginning to smolder and blacken, and the top shelf on one side was askew.

"What's happening?" he shouted—he had to shout to have any hope of being heard over the immense roaring that now seemed to fill the entire world. Hot whirlpools of smoke and air spilled through the pantry, blinding him anew. "Where's Mother? And Father, and Korian?"

"I don't know," Grandsir said, stepping forward, arms raised to shield his face against the fire.

"Is it an eruption?" Arlian shouted.

Grandsir stopped dead, staring.

"No," he said. "It's not an eruption."

Arlian stared as well; still on the ladder, his waist level with the pantry floor, his vision was limited to what he could see by peering around his grandfather's legs and out through the door to the kitchen. He could see a corner of the kitchen table, a burning fragment of wall, and a wedge of gray sky—and framed in that wedge he saw the dragon.

He could not judge its size accurately, but he knew it was huge. It hung there, flapping its tremendous wings, and Arlian knew that that flapping was what had caused the whirlwinds that had swept through the cellars.

It looked black against the sky, but Arlian could not be sure that was its true color. Its eyes were the color of flame, but perhaps they merely reflected the blazing village.

Its wings swept up in a graceful, gigantic curve, then snapped down, then swept upward again, and between them hung a body as long and lithe as a snake, tail whipping and winding below. Its long neck arched elegantly, and it seemed to be staring right at Arlian.

"Oh," Arlian breathed. The dragon was simultaneously the most beautiful and the most terrifying thing he had ever seen.

Then it turned and soared away, moving through the sky as smoothly and effortlessly as a fish moves through water.

"It's gone," Arlian said.

His grandfather took a cautious step forward, and Arlian hoisted himself up off the ladder, stepping through the doorway into the pantry.

Then they both froze as the second dragon appeared.

This one did not look their way, but simply flew across their field of vision, left to right and angling upward. Its scaled flank caught a gleam of sunlight and shone a dark, rich green, though the rest of it seemed as black as the other.

It was definitely not the same dragon, however. The proportions were different—and the face, even when seen only from the side, was different.

Arlian was startled at how readily he could know that. The dragons, he discovered, had faces as distinctive and as instantly recognizable as people. Why or how it could be so he did not know, but he knew it was.

"Two of them," Grandsir said—he, too, had seen immediately that the two were not the same creature. "*Two* dragons!"

"Are they gone?" Arlian asked.

"I don't know," Grandsir said, stepping cautiously forward. He coughed as a swirl of smoke reached him.

Just then a dragon reappeared—the first one, Arlian was sure. It swept down from the sky toward something Arlian could not see through the burning ruins of his family kitchen, and spat flame.

It was just as Grandsir had said three days before—the dragon opened its mouth and flexed its jaw, and something sprayed out, then burst into flame. The fire never touched the dragon itself; instead a burning mist spattered down across the village below.

Grandsir coughed again.

"Dragons or no, we can't stay in here," he said. "The smoke will kill us both. Maybe we can get to the cisterns—if we hide in there the flames can't touch us."

Arlian nodded hesitantly, and stepped forward—and that was when the third dragon appeared in the kitchen doorway. It was afoot, strolling through the village rather than flying, and had thrust its immense black head into the flaming ruins of the kitchen to see what might be in the depths of the house. It stared into the pantry, directly at Arlian and his grandfather.

Arlian screamed and stepped back involuntarily, back through the door. His foot missed the edge of the floor and he fell backward, hands flinging out in an unsuccessful attempt to catch himself on the doorframe. He tumbled heels over head down the ladder into the cellars and landed, bruised and dazed, on the warm stone floor.

He heard his grandfather shouting wildly; at first he was too stunned to make out the words, but then his senses began to return.

"…our home! May the dead gods curse you and all your kin, dragon—what have you done with my daughter and her husband, and my grandson? You get out of here, back to your caverns! Your time is over! You have no place in the Lands of Man!"

Arlian looked up and saw flames and smoke licking across the pantry ceiling, turning the familiar surface fierce and strange. Still bleary and stiff from his fall but desperate to get out, to not be trapped down here, he struggled to pull himself upright on the ladder.

Then a shadow fell across him and he looked up again to see Grandsir standing on the brink, his back to the cellars, his heels almost over the edge.

"You get away from me!" the old man shrieked, his voice cracking with terror.

And then there was a rush of air, of hot, fetid air laced with a biting acid stench like nothing Arlian had ever smelled before, and a deep, deep sound that was neither growl nor cough nor roar nor rumble nor bellow, and Grandsir let out a scream and fell backward into the cellars, pulling the ladder down with him, knocking Arlian down and landing atop him, the ladder wedged across the passageway over both of them.

Somewhere above, flames blossomed into roaring brilliance.

The boy's head hit the stone, and again Arlian was dazed; pain shot through his head and neck, and he tried to contract his spine, to pull himself inward in self-defense, but he was unable to move.

He lay sprawled on the stone, and Grandsir was sprawled atop him; the back of his grandfather's head was pressing down on his right eye, blocking his vision on that side. With his left eye he could see the burning ceiling far above, now pierced by widening flame-lit cracks, the remaining ceiling black between the lines of fire. Swirls of gray smoke filled much of the ladderwell now and dimmed the light, even though the flames were bright and the ceiling was splitting and crumbling. He could see the left side of his grandfather's face, more or less, but it was so close he had difficulty focusing on it.

Grandsir's weight on Arlian's chest was so much, and the smoke so thick, that he couldn't get his breath to speak—and Grandsir did not speak.

Even if Arlian had been able to speak, and Grandsir to hear, he wasn't sure he would be heard. Above them the pantry and the surrounding village were roaring chaos, a constant hammering of undifferentiated sound—flame and wind and terror.

Grandsir did not move to get up, did not stir, did not raise his hands or shift his feet. He lay still. Arlian thought he might be dead, but that blurry, out-of-focus bit he could see did not seem lifeless—Arlian could see motion, as if Grandsir were blinking, or twitching.

But then he managed to blink the smoke from his eye and get a clearer look, and realized that what he could see was not Grandsir's own face moving, but something *on* his face—something liquid, something that seethed and steamed and roiled.

Arlian desperately wanted to shriek at the sight of that, but he couldn't get enough air; he let out a strangled moan and struggled to free his left arm—his right was too securely pinned under Grandsir's body.

Red and gray fluid was bubbling up where Grandsir's left eye should have been; a bright, sharp stink scorched through Arlian's nostrils, making it even harder to draw the deep breath he desperately needed. Arlian's mouth was wide open as he sucked frantically for air.

He watched in sickened horror as the thick red fluid oozed down Grandsir's cheek.

That was not just blood. Blood would have been bad enough—to have his grandfather lying atop him, perhaps dead, perhaps dying, with blood welling up from his eye socket, would have been terrible enough to give Arlian nightmares for years. But this was *not* just blood; human blood did not steam and bubble, and was never so viscous.

Arlian knew what had happened. The third dragon had looked into the pantry and seen Grandsir there, and Grandsir had shouted defiance. The dragon had listened for a moment, then grown annoyed. It had been unable to reach into the stone pantry with fang or claw, had not wanted to trouble itself with smashing down the stone walls, so it had breathed its fiery venom at Grandsir.

But the dragon had been so close to the old man that the venom would not burn, so close it had not time to ignite; instead it had struck Grandsir full in the face as a toxic spray. Some had burst into flame when it struck the hot ceiling or the back wall of the ladderwell, but the liquid that had hit Grandsir had remained venom, rather than fuel.

And if the stories were right, it was eating the flesh from his grandfather's bones.

Arlian almost *hoped* Grandsir was dead, for his sake—but for his own, he hoped the old man still lived, and might somehow help them both survive.

Survival did not seem very likely for either of them, though. The smoke was growing denser, the roar of the flames louder, and Arlian thought the whole cellar might yet cave in upon him.

And that thick red trickle moved slowly down Grandsir's cheek, and finally dripped down, the first fat drop landing squarely in Arlian's open, gasping mouth.

Chapter Three

Lord Dragon

The shock of that impact on his parched tongue, the indescribably vile taste, the unbearable stench, the corrosive burning that seemed to be tearing the lining from his mouth and throat, the knowledge of what was happening, was more than Arlian could bear; he fainted.

He awoke choking in the dark, coughing up slime, and in his convulsions threw his grandfather's body off him; the ladder that had pinned them both down snapped free and rattled to one side, one rail broken off short.

Arlian rolled over and vomited up everything he could bring up, vomited until his chin dripped with stinking ooze and his elbows rested in a widening pool of acidic detritus. His eyes filled with tears, both from the agony in his gut and the awareness of utter disaster, the knowledge that his home and his family had been destroyed. He pulled himself clear, away from the corruption his body had expelled, away from the ladder and Grandsir, into relatively cool darkness and sweeter air. There he fainted again.

He was awakened again, after how long he did not know, by voices, by laughter. He blinked and lay still, trying to remember where he was, what had happened.

He was in the cellars, he remembered. He could see that he was still in the cellars, looking at the bottom shelf of one rack of preserves. Daylight filtered down from above, daylight thick with drifting dust.

He was alive—the fire had passed over him and the cellars had not fallen in.

He heard footsteps somewhere above, heavy footsteps that crunched as if walking on the black ash the volcano sometimes spewed.

Daylight in the cellars—the roof was gone. Arlian remembered the fire, the smoke, the heat. He remembered the dragons; he remembered the third one's face when it peered into the pantry, its eyes huge and alien and knowing.

It had been the eyes that frightened him into stepping back and falling, far more than anything else. The fangs, the jaws, the dripping venom—he had hardly noticed those. He had seen only those great dark eyes, bottomless and terrifying.

He had fallen; he remembered that now. And his grandfather had fallen.

And Grandsir had been struck by the dragon's acid venom.

Arlian sat up, moving convulsively. He gulped air, choked and gasping, and turned.

Grandsir lay beside him on the stone floor—or rather, Grandsir's corpse lay there.

There could be no doubt that he was dead; the venom had eaten his flesh away, exposing bone in half a dozen places, from a patch of skull where his forehead should be to the protruding parallel curves of bare ribs above the blackened, ruined remains of his chest.

Arlian's empty stomach contracted painfully. He had nothing left to bring up. He moaned, and blinked as his eyes filled anew with tears.

His grandfather was dead. His parents were gone, almost certainly dead. His brother, as well. His entire life had been destroyed, suddenly and swiftly, with no warning—at least, none beyond a spell of bad weather.

Something burned deep within him—not pain, not an emotion, but a strange sensation he had never felt before. He remembered how he had lain trapped while his grandfather's venom-corrupted blood dripped into his mouth.

He moaned again, slightly louder.

The footsteps overhead stopped.

"Did you hear something?" an unfamiliar voice asked—not the voice of any villager, Arlian was sure.

Arlian could hear another voice respond, but could make out none of the words. He looked up, startled, and blinked the tears from his eyes.

Who was up there? He had assumed there were survivors, people he knew—but these voices spoke with an odd lilt, an accent unlike anything he had ever heard. Even the people who lived in the farms and villages down by the river did not sound like that.

The opening at the top of the ladderwell was larger than it should have been; wooden flooring, doors, and ceiling had burned away, and parts of the stone walls had tumbled. Arlian could see hazy blue sky, but not much more than that.

"From that chimney, maybe," the first voice said.

Arlian swallowed, trying to think clearly despite the overwhelming grief and shock that filled his mind. There were strangers in the ruins of his family's home—who were they? What should he do?

Two other voices spoke, and then the footsteps sounded again, moving closer. A moment later a man's face appeared over the top of one of the stone walls, looking down at him.

18

"It's no chimney," the man shouted. "There's a cellar down here! And people, and one of them's alive!"

"Help," Arlian called weakly. "Help me!"

"You wait right there, boy," the man said, grinning down at him.

Arlian stared up at the man for a moment. That grin didn't look quite right, somehow.

Then there was a series of thumps and crashes, and someone was leaning over the ruined remains of the pantry floor, looking down at him. It was a man, a man wearing a sleeveless brown leather coat despite the heat; he held an iron pry bar in one hand. His face and coat were smeared with soot; his hair and beard were black, so the soot didn't show, but they were disheveled.

Arlian had never seen him before; whoever these people were, they definitely weren't from the village. Perhaps, despite their odd speech, they were rescuers from the river towns? Arlian had only been down off the mountain two or three times in his life; perhaps he didn't know as much about the river-folk as he thought.

An almost-cool eddy of air stirred Arlian's hair, and he wondered how long he had lain unconscious; judging by that breeze the long hot spell, the dragon weather, had apparently ended at last. That could happen suddenly, but he feared he had slept for days or even weeks, and been left for dead by his family.

But the dragon weather had passed, and the dragons it had brought were gone; the worst was surely over.

"What's down there, boy?" the stranger asked. "Is there anyone but you?"

Arlian glanced at his grandfather's corpse, then swallowed.

"Just me," he said.

"And what else? Is there treasure? Obsidian?"

Arlian blinked, confused.

"There's cheese," he said. "And preserves, and wine…"

"So you wouldn't starve if we left you, then?"

"Don't leave me down here!" Arlian shrieked.

The man frowned. "It's not up to me, boy," he said. "It's Lord Dragon's decision."

Arlian's jaw sagged, and he slumped back against the shelves. *"Lord Dragon?"* he said.

"Yes, that's what we call him," the man said.

"What we call him." Arlian relaxed slightly; then it was a man after all,

19

and not a dragon. For a few seconds there he had had nightmarish images in his head of one of those black dragons still here in the village, giving these people their orders. He had thought that perhaps all the dragons had awakened from their slumbers and come to reclaim the Lands of Man and restore their ancient empire.

But it was just a man.

Arlian remembered what his parents had told him, how it was the custom many places not to use real names in the ancient tongue, but common words—Lord Stick, Lady Flower, or the like.

But who would dare call himself Lord Dragon?

Just then the man straightened and turned away from Arlian, and spoke to someone Arlian could not see. The boy was unable to make out the words, but the voice answering was cold and deep.

Then the two men, the one in the pantry and the one peering over the broken wall, both vanished. Arlian called, "Hey! Where are you?"

"Shut up, boy," said that cold, deep voice.

Arlian shut up.

If they left him it wouldn't be all that bad, he told himself. He did have plenty of food, and eventually he could get the ladder back in place, or use the shelving to climb out.

Who *were* these men? What were they doing here? They weren't rescuers of any sort, from their behavior.

And then two men appeared where the pantry had been, the man in the brown leather coat and another in a smoke-stained canvas vest; the one in the vest was carrying a coil of rope. They were stepping carefully—Arlian guessed that the pantry floor was largely burned away, and they were wary of falling through.

Then the coil of rope was flung down into the cellars, one end still secured somewhere out of sight; the man in the vest grabbed hold of it and lowered himself cautiously down, carefully avoiding stepping on the gory corpse at the foot of the ladderwell.

At the bottom he stopped and dusted off his pants as he looked around. He grimaced at the sight of Grandsir's remains, then beckoned to Arlian. "Come on, lad," he said. "We'll get you out of here."

Arlian scrambled to his feet. "Thank you!" he said.

The man picked him up and hoisted him, and Arlian stretched out his hands; the other man, the one in the leather coat, caught them and hauled. A moment later Arlian was standing in the ruins of his family's kitchen.

He looked around in horror.

The walls and roof and most of the furnishings were gone save for scorched, fallen beams and drifted ash; the stone floor was strewn with debris. The rest of the village had fared no better; Arlian looked out on a blasted, blackened wasteland, scoured of every sign of life, as dead as the crater at the mountain's peak. No structure still stood any higher than his head; the fragmentary walls of the pantry were among the tallest remaining.

A strong wind was blowing, carrying away lingering dust and smoke and heat. The air was still warm, but no longer thick and hot.

Half a dozen people were moving through the ruins. Behind Arlian, the man in the leather coat was talking to the man in the canvas vest; nearby, the man who had peered over the wall was poking through the crumbled remains of Arlian's parents' bedroom. Three other people, a man and two women, were scattered about the village on foot, and one was seated upon a horse in the little plaza at the center of town, overseeing everything. Over at the head of the path down the mountain stood a wagon, unattended at the moment, with a pair of draft horses in the traces.

Arlian had never seen a horse-drawn wagon before; that established beyond question that these people were not from the vicinity of the Smoking Mountain. Around here wagons were pulled by oxen; no one would waste horses on such a task.

"Where is everybody?" Arlian asked, his voice unsteady. His eyes were wet again, stinging with lingering smoke and tears.

The man on horseback turned to stare at him. Arlian stared back, and started trembling.

This must be Lord Dragon, he realized, and the man's intense wordless stare did indeed remind Arlian of the expression he had seen on the face of the dragon that killed Grandsir.

The horseman was finely dressed in black trimmed with elaborate gold embroidery, from tall leather boots to the dashing, broad-brimmed hat cocked to one side and trailing golden feathers down behind one shoulder. His face was thin and dark, and his right cheek, the one partly concealed by the hat, was heavily scarred—old, ugly scars that looked as if a handful of flesh had once been ripped away and left to heal untreated. He wore no beard, an affectation Arlian had heard of but never seen before, and his mustache was trimmed to a narrow, curving black line. A black scabbard slapped against one of his thighs and the horse's flank, and Arlian realized that the man carried a sword.

21

Arlian had never seen a sword. Only lords and professional guards carried swords, and the village had had neither.

This black-garbed man was clearly an actual lord.

"Come here, boy," the horseman said in a cold, deep voice that Arlian recognized, the voice that had told him to shut up.

Hesitantly, Arlian picked his way across the kitchen floor and out into the village street, until he stood by the rider's boot, looking up at the scarred face.

"Your village is dead," the horseman said. "Don't get your hopes up that your friends or family might still live. Dragons allow no escapes. Unless there are other cellars or tunnels, you are the only survivor."

Arlian could not find a reply.

"We're counting skulls, when we find them," the rider said. "We may miss some, but you'll know that most of them died, at the very least. Take my word for it, boy—they *all* died. One survivor is a miracle; two would be impossible."

Arlian felt tears running down his cheeks, but still couldn't speak.

"Now, do you know where any valuables might be? Where was the chief workshop? I have uses for obsidian back in Manfort. Or perhaps your village sorcerer might have had a few precious possessions?"

"I don't know," Arlian managed to say. His voice was a husky whisper.

The horseman frowned. "You don't know where they worked the black glass?"

Arlian pressed his lips tight to keep from wailing and shook his head.

"Hmph." Lord Dragon looked up and scanned the ruins quickly. Arlian dropped his gaze, and a teardrop rolled down his nose and dropped to the dust at his feet.

His family was dead—his mother, his father, Korian …

And Grandsir, of course. He had seen Grandsir's body and knew beyond question that the old man was dead. The other deaths didn't seem real yet, but he had seen the house, had seen the village, had heard Lord Dragon's words.

And who *was* this Lord Dragon? Arlian looked up again, and as he did caught sight of a sack lying by the horse's front hooves. He turned and glimpsed part of its contents through the open top—and recognized some of the items.

Old Gernian's golden plate, now smeared with wet black ash but still unmistakable. Beronil's crystal cups, handed down in her family for a century or more. The obsidian clock face Kashkar had been working on.

22

They were all thrown in together, and Arlian suddenly realized who Lord Dragon and his men were.

Looters. Human vultures, come to pick clean the bones the dragons had left.

He looked up, and his eyes met Lord Dragon's gaze.

The horseman's eyes were deep and dark, sunken in their sockets, with dark brown iris and almost no whites visible. They were cold and empty eyes that seemed to be studying Arlian as if he were no more than a stone in the path.

"What's going to become of me?" Arlian asked.

"Unless you have rich kin somewhere who might pay a ransom," Lord Dragon replied calmly, "I believe we'll sell you. You look strong enough, and I know a mining company that can always use another strong back."

"But I'm not a slave!" Arlian protested.

"You are now," Lord Dragon replied, in a voice like the boom of the warning bell that now lay broken and half melted a hundred yards away.

Outrage welled up in Arlian's heart. He had done nothing wrong; he had been born free, and did not deserve slavery. "But I'm…"

"You're ours, by right of salvage," Lord Dragon said, cutting him off. "This village and everything in it has been abandoned, and so, by ancient custom, belongs to whosoever first claims it. I am claiming it—and thereby, I claim *you*."

"But…"

"Now, boy, unless you have something to offer me in exchange, I'll hear no more argument. You're mine, and this village is mine." Lord Dragon straightened in the saddle. "*Do* you have anything to offer me? Are there hidden treasures, perhaps? A secret cache in that cellar of yours?"

"No," Arlian admitted.

"But you do know where the workshops were, I'm sure. Now, will you tell us readily, or must we beat it out of you?"

Arlian hesitated, and was suddenly aware that the man in the brown leather coat had come up behind him and was standing not a yard away.

"I'd tell him," the man said.

Arlian hesitated, looking from Lord Dragon to the man on foot and back. He glanced at the bag of stolen valuables, at the horse standing placidly, at the long slim sword on Lord Dragon's left hip and the long heavy knife on his right, and at the merciless calm of Lord Dragon's expression.

"I can show you," Arlian said.

He had no choice.

It was not that he feared a beating, or even death—if Lord Dragon killed him at least it would be over, and he would not be facing the prospect of a life spent laboring in the mines somewhere.

No, it was that if he died, he could never do anything to fix what had been done here.

The dragons had swept in and destroyed everything, slain everyone, for no reason; no one in the village had ever harmed or threatened them in any way. No one there had deserved to die—but they had died all the same.

And this man, this Lord Dragon, had no right to come up here and claim everything as his own. He had done nothing to earn this place, he had taken no risks, he had not sweated and labored to wrench the black stone from the mountain and shape it to human use. He had not sired Arlian, nor raised him, nor even purchased him, yet he now claimed him as mere property.

It wasn't *fair*. It wasn't right. And it was Arlian's duty, as the sole survivor of those who had been wronged, to fix it, to make it better somehow. His parents had taught him that since he was a baby—wrongs had to be put right somehow.

Arlian saw it clearly. Lord Dragon and his looters were stealing, and someone had to punish them for it. The three dragons had killed innocent people; someone had to kill *them* to make it fair. His mother had said there were no more dragons; Arlian wanted to do anything he could to make that belief come true.

He had no idea how it might be done, no real hope of ever accomplishing it, but somehow he knew he *must* do something to fix it all—and he couldn't if he were dead. His job would be harder if he were crippled by beatings.

So, for now, he would do as he was told, and someday he would have his chance. Someday, he would find a way to repair this wrong.

"This way," he said, and he led the man in brown to where the village workshops had stood.

24

Chapter Four

The First Journey

It was surprisingly difficult to walk with his hands tied. Logically, Arlian didn't see why it made much difference, but all the same he found himself stumbling and awkward much of the way down the mountain, and could only attribute it to having his hands bound behind his back, where he could not use them to help maintain his balance.

His eyes stung with tears as he staggered along, and he did not know whether to attribute that to pain or grief or anger—or if it even mattered.

His captors displayed no sympathy for his discomforts, but they were in no great hurry, so he was able to keep up without being dragged, and without being run over by the heavily laden wagon. He wondered whether they would put him in the wagon with the other loot if he collapsed and refused to walk.

One of the looters, a woman called Dagger, glanced at him as he stumbled again. Arlian didn't know whether she noticed his tears, but she deigned to address him.

"You're probably thinking that Fate's been cruel to you, aren't you?" she said. "You being sold into slavery, and all. But look at it this way—if we just left you there, all alone, what would become of you? If you didn't want to starve you'd have to come down the mountain anyway, sooner or later, and beg in the streets—and if you did, you might have been caught by slavers anyway. And it's not all bad. At least slaves know where their next meal will come from."

Arlian stared at her without speaking, his eyes drying.

"And you may think it's hard luck that your family all died," the woman went on, "but *you* survived, didn't you? There's good and bad in everything, lad, if you know how to look."

Arlian didn't say anything aloud, but his thoughts were clear.

Good luck or bad didn't enter into it. The dragons had *chosen* to destroy his village. The looters had *chosen* to scavenge in the ruins. They had chosen to do the terrible things they had done. They could have left the village alone. It wasn't ill chance that had destroyed the village and carried Arlian into slavery; the destroyers did it on purpose.

Fate had not been cruel. The *dragons* had been cruel. *Lord Dragon* had been cruel. The other looters had been cruel.

And if Arlian ever had the chance to repay that cruelty, he would—but for now he would just go on as best he could, in hopes that chance would come. He blinked away his tears and stared silently back at Dagger.

"Not speaking to us, eh?" she said. She shrugged. "Please yourself, then."

They stopped at one of the river towns that night, but Arlian saw almost nothing of it, and had no chance to speak to any of the townspeople. Before they passed the village gate he was gagged, his ankles bound, and he was thrown into the wagon, covered over with a blanket.

He lay there, thinking miserably of his family and the monstrous injustice of it all, and didn't notice when he fell asleep.

In the morning he was too stiff to walk. After he collapsed twice in a dozen yards he was flung back into the wagon and left there, to bounce and bump helplessly as the wagon rattled its way along the muddy road—this stretch was not paved as the mountain road had been. His gag was removed after they had gone a mile or so, and his hands freed, so he could eat. He was given bread and water, which he consumed without tasting it; his hands were then tied again. No further attempt was made to get him to walk.

This set the fashion for the rest of the journey.

On the fourth day they stopped early in the afternoon, and Arlian was hauled out of the wagon and dumped unceremoniously on hard-packed earth. He looked up, and found himself meeting the gaze of a stranger.

He had gotten to know the seven looters by face and voice, and had heard names—though not true names—for all of them; this man was not any of them. He was white-haired, fat, clad in gray wool and white linen with his beard halfway down his chest. He smelled of onions and sweat.

"I'm asking twenty ducats," Lord Dragon's voice said.

The stranger snorted. "Five," he said.

"Shamble, just toss him back in the wagon," Lord Dragon said. "This man doesn't want to be serious…"

"Eight, then."

"Eighteen? Perhaps I might consider that."

"I said eight, not eighteen!"

"Ah, you're still wasting our time with your nonsense. Shamble…"

"And what are you going to do with the boy elsewhere, my lord?" the fat man asked, turning his gaze away from Arlian, presumably to meet Lord Dragon's eyes.

"Oh, I think a handsome young fellow like this would have his uses almost anywhere," Lord Dragon said. "I couldn't possibly part with him for less than sixteen ducats."

"You'll have to haul him a long way to get that much. I'll give you ten."

"Perhaps, as a personal favor, I could settle for fifteen, though you'd certainly owe me a favor in return…"

"Eleven."

"Shamble, look at the boy and tell me whether you think our friend here has gone mad to offer less than fourteen."

"I'm not one to say, my lord," Shamble replied. He was one of the looters—the biggest of them, but not one of the brighter ones, judging by what Arlian had seen of them.

"Eleven, I said," the fat man said.

"Twelve, and that's my final offer." Lord Dragon's tone had shifted, become colder—he had tired of the banter, Arlian guessed. The fat man could hardly fail to notice the change.

"Twelve it is, then," he said, his tone noticeably less confident. "The money's in the strongbox."

"Then let us brook no delay in opening this strongbox," Lord Dragon said.

The fat old man departed, leaving Arlian staring up at the sky—and at a cliff of yellow-brown stone.

He could not move much—his hands and feet were tightly bound, and his neck horribly stiff from his mistreatment—but Arlian turned enough to see that he was surrounded by Lord Dragon's six henchmen while the lord himself accompanied the old man to the strongbox. They were standing easily on stony ground, the wagon at one side. The cliff blocked out almost half the sky, dark against the bleached-out pale blue of a hazy summer afternoon, but Arlian could see no houses or shops, no sign of a farm or village where the fat man might live.

He looked at the looters, trying to memorize their faces so that he would know them someday when he tracked them down.

There was Shamble, big and stupid and vicious, eager to please Lord Dragon however possible.

There was Hide, the man in the sleeveless leather coat who had pulled Arlian from the cellar. He had had little to say on the trip down the mountain to this place, and stood slightly apart from the rest.

Cover, a tidy young man who had worn a vest and climbed down into the cellars, was carefully not looking at Arlian. He seemed uneasy.

Stonehand, who had peered over the wall and first seen Arlian, was grinning at something the woman called Dagger was whispering to him.

And Tooth, presumably called that because so many of her teeth were missing, was staring at Arlian with a crooked, unkind smile on her ugly face.

"I'll remember you all," Arlian mouthed silently.

Then he heard the returning footsteps of the others, Lord Dragon and the fat old man, and he turned his head just in time to see Lord Dragon set a foot in his stirrup.

"Come along," he said.

The six of them came, and a moment later the wagon rattled away amid a flurry of hoofbeats and shouted comments, leaving Arlian alone with the white-haired stranger.

"Welcome to Deep Delving, boy," the man said, prodding Arlian with the toe of a heavy boot. "I'd suggest you look at the sky while you can—you'll never see it again."

Arlian stared silently up at that long white beard and wrinkled face.

I *will* see it again, he promised himself.

Then the fat man grabbed Arlian by one arm and hoisted him upright. Despite his girth he was no weakling; he lifted the boy as if he were made of straw.

"Come on," he said, breathing the smell of onions in Arlian's face. "Let's get you underground where we can take off those ropes without worrying about any silly attempts to escape." Carrying Arlian easily under one arm, the old man marched along the cliff, and then *into* it, through a hidden doorway.

Abruptly Arlian was plunged from the familiar world of air and sunlight into a broad, torchlit stone corridor, awash in shadows and smoke. Memories of the smoke-filled cellar where his grandfather had died flowered suddenly, and he began to struggle and thrash in unthinking panic.

The fat man dropped him abruptly. Impact with the stone floor knocked the wind out of him, and his struggles weakened.

The fat man stared down at him. "What's wrong with you, boy?"

"The torches," Arlian gasped. With one final convulsive shudder he forced the fear away and lay still.

The fat man did not so much as glance at the torches mounted on the walls; instead he kept his attention focused on the boy.

"What about them?" he demanded.

"My family," Arlian said. "Our house burned, and they all died. I was trapped in the cellars." He didn't mention the dragons; he had no clear reason in mind why he should not, but it somehow didn't seem wise.

"And the torches brought it back?"

Arlian nodded.

"Well, that's one fear you'll get over," the old man said. "At least, if you want to eat." He stooped and picked Arlian up again and slung him over one shoulder, almost smashing the boy's head against the stone ceiling in the process. Without further conversation he marched onward, down the long sloping passageway.

Most of the tunnel was dark, with the torches spaced widely enough that at the midpoint between any two there was just barely enough light for Arlian to make out his captor's feet in the gloom. After a couple of hundred yards the torches gave way to dim oil lamps, which were no better, and the darkness seemed to deepen as they descended. The width of the passageway varied; the fat man stayed close to the right-hand wall, where the lights were mounted, and while at times the left-hand side looked almost close enough to reach out and touch, at other times it vanished in the gloom, at least twenty feet away.

Arlian was in no condition to make a close study of his surroundings, but he did notice, when they passed close by the lights, that the walls had not been built, but carved out of the living rock—he was being taken deep into the earth. The walls were rough yellowish stone, with occasional ribbons of gray laced through it. Here and there a bit of quartz glittered faintly in the poor light.

Down into the earth … down where the dragons slept? He shuddered again.

But no, he wasn't being taken to the dragons. Lord Dragon had mentioned a mining company; he must be in a mine, a mine far deeper than the pits where the people of Obsidian had dug out the slivers of black volcanic glass that gave their village its name.

This was no mere pit. This was nothing like the mines Arlian had visited before.

Then the fat man stopped suddenly. From his position on the man's shoulder Arlian could see the tunnel they had just descended, and the broad expanse of the man's back, but nothing of what lay ahead. He had no idea why they had stopped.

"Ho, Bloody Hand!" the man called. "I've got a fresh one for you!"

Then Arlian felt himself being heaved off the fat man's shoulder and tossed; the world seemed to wheel wildly about him, a mad patchwork of light and shadow and glimpses of stone and thick timbers and blackened ropes, and he found himself plunging down into a pit after all …

But only for perhaps a second; then he had landed hard on a pile of rags, knocking the wind out of him.

A young man was standing over him, looking down at him.

"It's just a boy!" he called.

"He'll grow," the fat man's familiar voice called back.

"If we let him," the young man said. He sighed. "You won't get much work out of him at first, you know."

"That's not *my* problem," the fat man replied. "I'll be back when the Gaffer gets here."

Then Arlian heard footsteps retreating up the stone passage.

The young man glared down at him for a moment, then pulled a knife from his belt and reached down to cut the boy's bonds.

Freed at last, Arlian tried to sit up, but found himself too weak and stiff to manage it until the young man grabbed him roughly by one arm and pulled him upright.

"Welcome to your new home," the young man said.

Arlian looked around.

He was at the bottom of a deep round pit, dimly lit by three of the little oil lamps. Two black passageways opened off it, roughly at right angles to one another. The passageway by which he had arrived, however, was not one of them; *that* tunnel was on a higher level. Arlian could see now that he had been casually flung some fifteen feet or more off a ledge; had the huge pile of rags not been here he might well have been killed.

Also at that upper level, in the mouth of the entry tunnel, he could see a complex of ropes, beams, and pulleys, and what appeared to be a large bin of some sort. All the ropes had been carefully tied up out of reach, he saw—there was no way to climb up out of the pit, no ladder, no steps, no dangling ropes.

A row of four ugly little wooden carts stood along one side of the pit, full of gray rock. Somewhere in the distance Arlian could hear a clinking, rattling sound.

"Where am I?" Arlian asked. "Who are you?"

"You're in a mine, half a mile from the town of Deep Delving," the young man replied. "You're here to dig ore. If you dig enough, you get fed; if you don't, you starve. If you cause trouble…" He hefted a whip in one hand, the knife he had used to free Arlian in the other. "I can use whichever of these I think is appropriate to the occasion," the man said. "Or my fists, or a club, or whatever other tool it takes to get the ore out."

"What ore?"

"It's a stone called galena," the man said, waving at the row of carts. "It's gray, darker than the limestone." He then gestured at the walls; Arlian supposed that this meant the pale stone around them was limestone. "When it's smelted it yields lead—and sometimes silver, which is what makes it worth the trouble."

Arlian stared at him for a moment, trying to think what else he should ask. This was all happening too fast, it was all too harsh, to take in properly.

The young man did not wait to hear what else Arlian might have to say, however; he sheathed his knife and grabbed the boy by one arm, then gestured.

"Get that lamp," he said.

Arlian obeyed, and held the lamp high as he was dragged into one of the dark tunnels opening off the pit.

The clinking noise grew louder as the two made their way down the tunnel, through widened areas and past side-tunnels, until Arlian could see light ahead.

Then the man released him and snatched the lamp away.

"Go on and join them," the man said. "They'll tell you what to do."

Arlian hesitated, and the man shoved him forward with the hand that still held the whip. "Go on!"

Arlian stumbled forward into the darkness, and tried to focus on the light ahead. He headed toward it, and finally staggered into a relatively open area lit by several oil lamps, an area where half a dozen ragged, pale-skinned, long-bearded men were working—four of them were hacking at a wall of gray stone with picks, while the other two collected the broken pieces with wooden shovels and dumped them into a wooden cart that stood nearby. A second cart was pushed up against a wall, just below one of the lamps. The clinking Arlian had heard had been the sound of iron on stone.

One of the loaders spotted him as he approached, and stopped his work; the other loader noticed, and stopped as well. In a moment, all six men had turned to stare at Arlian.

"Fresh blood," someone muttered.

"They didn't give him a pick," another remarked.

"Then he's a loader," a third said. "He can do the handwork and push the cart."

31

"He doesn't look strong enough to push it!" a fourth protested.

"Where am I?" Arlian asked.

One man snorted derisively; another laughed.

"You're in the Old Man's silver mine," a third said—an older man who spoke his words oddly, with a singsong rhythm.

"The Old Man? Who's that?"

"He's who owns this mine," the man with the peculiar accent said. "Now you know as much about him as we do."

"Was he the one who bought me and brought me down here?"

The men exchanged glances and grins. "Now, how would we know?" one of them asked. "We didn't see who brought you."

"A big fat man, who smells of onions?" Arlian asked.

"Could be," one miner admitted. "If he's been eating onions."

The others laughed, but Arlian ignored that. "And the one with the whip…" he began.

Expressions turned grim, and one man spat to the side.

"Bloody Hand," one miner said.

"Is that his name?" Arlian asked, and immediately regretted it—how could it be a name?

"It's all the name he needs," the miner replied.

"Why is he called that?" Arlian asked, dreading the reply.

"Because of what he did to poor Dinian," another miner said angrily. "Whipped him until the blood sprayed everywhere. Cut him open to the bone."

Arlian swallowed. "Did he die?"

"Eventually," the oldest miner said. "Not of the whipping itself, but his wounds festered, and he took fever and died. And Bloody Hand didn't do a thing for him."

One of the miners turned away and hoisted his pick.

"You can tell him your stories later," he said, as he swung the pick and bit the point deep into soft gray stone. "If we want to eat tonight, we need to fill that cart, and two more after it, before the Gaffer gets here. The boy'll have the rest of his life to listen to us talk."

The others mumbled agreement and lifted their own tools; one of the shovel-wielders beckoned to Arlian.

"You get the pieces we miss," he said. "Throw them in the cart. Keep the floor clear, so she'll roll. Understand?"

"I understand," Arlian said.

It was simple enough, after all. He could do it; it was honest work, not harming anyone.

There would be plenty of time for escape and vengeance later. He was just a boy. He had his whole life ahead of him.

And he would *not* spend it all here in the mine!

Chapter Five

In the Mines

A rlian hauled on the rope, and the mine cart tipped up, spilling its load of ore into the waiting hopper. Wark leaned over with the rake and scraped out the stones and dust that hadn't slid out on their own; powder swirled up in dark coils that cast shadows on the walls of the pit.

When Wark raised the rake to signal that he was done Arlian let the cart fall back on its wheels; then he unhooked the heavy rope.

"One more," Bloody Hand said.

Arlian and Wark didn't bother replying; Wark was already pulling the empty cart away from the hopper while Arlian crossed to the remaining loaded cart and braced himself to push it into position.

They didn't need to be told what to do; they had been doing it for longer than Arlian cared to recall. He didn't know how long he had been in the mine—years, he was certain. There were no seasons down here, no heat in the summer nor cold in the winter; there were no days or nights. He had not kept count of the shifts worked—and he did not even know whether there were really two shifts a day, as most of the miners assumed, or whether that might vary. Time did not matter to the miners.

But he had grown to man-height here, and was now one of the taller miners, with a respectable beard that reached to his chest, so he knew years had passed. He was sure he must be at least sixteen by now, and feared he was over twenty. He wasn't the biggest man in the mine, by any means—Swamp, named for his foul odor, was a head taller and a handsbreadth wider across the shoulders—but Arlian was tall and strong, and in the prime of life.

Of course, part of that height came from standing straight; many of the men in the mine were bent and stooped from years of labor, or from imperfectly healed injuries. Arlian had been lucky in that regard; he had never yet been struck by a runaway cart, nor injured by flying chunks of ore from a badly aimed swing of the pick, nor suffered any other serious mishap. Oh, he had burned himself with spilled lamp oil or by carelessly picking up a hot lamp, and he'd had his share of cuts and bruises, but he had never broken a bone or lost a finger, and his injuries had always healed rapidly. When the fever had spread through his team he had only had a very mild case and had recovered quickly to help nurse the others.

Not everyone had been so fortunate; Arlian frowned at the memory. Old Hathet had died of that fever. Arlian had been there, wiping the old man's forehead with a wet rag to ease the pain, when it had happened. Hathet had been talking in a thin whisper about his distant and perhaps mythical homeland of Arithei, far to the south, when he had begun coughing, and his mouth had filled with bright red blood, and he had spasmed and choked and died.

Arlian had cried off and on for days after that, even while he tended others who had taken ill; right from that first day, when Arlian had been dumped into the pitshaft and left in Bloody Hand's care, Hathet had been his best friend among the miners, a font of wisdom, guidance, and companionship despite his peculiarities. Hathet had been the one who taught Arlian the systems under which the mine operated, so that he had been able to settle into work right from the start—many new arrivals took days before they learned enough to earn their meals, as only those who met their quotas of ore delivered to the pitshaft were fed. Most of the miners were too busy earning their own keep to help out a beginner, but Hathet had taken the time to show Arlian the ropes.

Hathet had also told any number of stories of his past that Arlian thought were lies, but his instructions about the mine had all been sound.

Arlian had done his best to pass that on to newcomers, as he had tried to use the rest of what Hathet told him. Some of the others—Rat, and Bitter, and Stain—had made fun of Hathet's manner of speech and called him a crazy old man, but Arlian, while accepting that some of what Hathet said was probably nonsense, had found a great deal of wisdom in the old man's chatter, and had taken comfort in his presence. His death had been hard.

Nor was Hathet the only one of Arlian's fellow miners who had died. The old man the others had called Wrinkles had simply not woken up when called for his shift one day. The big, stupid man called Fist had gotten careless in a fit of temper after an argument with Rat and Swamp, and a wild swing of his pick had brought a chunk of tunnel ceiling down on his head, dashing out his brains. Wark's brother Kort had sickened and died, taking a long time about it—Wark was still grateful to Arlian because Arlian had never lost his patience with Kort during that slow decline, had never tried to steal Kort's share of the food and water.

Disease, age, and accidents had killed dozens of slaves, while Arlian had grown from a lost, frightened boy into a man who knew everything there was to know about tunneling, digging and hauling ore, and working the various systems that bounded his life. He had absorbed what Hathet had taught him and learned more on his own.

And through it all he had never once accepted that this was where he would live out his life. Someday he would be free, someday he would hunt down Lord Dragon and his looters, someday he would find a way to punish the dragons for what they had done to his family and the rest of humanity. Someday he would have justice.

Justice—he had learned a great deal about justice in the mines, and about injustice. He had come to understand that the world was not the fair and balanced place he had believed it to be when he was a child; he had heard a hundred stories from the other miners about wrongs left unpunished, courage and goodness left unrewarded. His horror and outrage at the unfairness of it all had faded—but had never died completely.

He had seen events play out in the enclosed world of the mines that taught him by example what the stories of the outside world described. He had seen how a crime left unavenged would rankle, would fester in the victim's heart like a disease, would make the offender harder and harsher, would cut them both off from the tiny society in which they lived. He had seen how just retribution would bring together the miners—except perhaps the criminal against whom the retribution was taken—content that justice had been done. He had joined the others in restraining Rat's worst swindles by stealing back extorted belongings, in keeping Fist from beating miners whose only crime was to be in the wrong place at the wrong time, and he had seen that life was better because these wrongs were prevented or avenged. Even Rat, well after the fact, usually acknowledged as much.

There were rules, and when men understood and obeyed the rules, life was better. That was true in the mines, and true in the outside world.

The world might be an unfair place, but Arlian swore he would do everything he could to make it a little fairer, either here in the mines, or when he once again found his way out. Someday he would punish those who had destroyed and looted his home, and any other wrongdoers he found.

Someday.

He pushed the cart into place and snugged the hook securely into place under the handlebar.

"Ready?" he called.

"Pull," Bloody Hand ordered, his hand on his whip.

His hand was *always* on that whip when he gave orders, but in fact he used it less than Lampspiller, the other overseer. The general opinion was that this was only because he wasn't often given an excuse to use it. Everyone in the mine knew the tale of how Bloody Hand had flogged poor Dinian to death, and nobody cared to risk a similar fate …

Arlian had begun to wonder, some time back, whether Dinian had ever really existed, or whether the tale had been started by Bloody Hand himself, long ago, to cow the workers into obedience. He had asked one of the older surviving miners at the time—Hathet and Wrinkles were dead by then, but Olneor was still around—whether he had actually *seen* the infamous flogging.

"By the dead gods, boy, I did!" Olneor had told him. "'Twas the very first day that red-handed, black-hearted bastard set foot down here. He hadn't yet troubled to tell us his name, just set to ordering us about, and didn't know the first thing about what he was doing. Dinian tried to tell him how the cart rotation works, and Bloody Hand wouldn't hear a word—he ordered Dinian to shut up and do as he was told, and when Dinian wouldn't he said he'd flog him if he didn't get down the tunnel where he belonged."

"And Dinian didn't?"

"Of course not! He didn't have a cart to fill, and he knew he wouldn't get supper if he didn't, so he tried to argue—and Bloody Hand lashed him across the face. That bastard was so mad he was trembling with rage, and Dinian hadn't done anything wrong!"

"Then what happened?" Arlian had asked.

"Then Dinian tried to grab the whip, and Bloody Hand hit him again, and again, and around the third or fourth blow Dinian realized he'd better give up. He went down on all fours and covered his head and tried to wait it out, but Bloody Hand just wouldn't stop—he flogged Dinian's tunic to rags, and then flogged his back to tatters as well, and didn't stop until there was blood everywhere and Dinian was just a heap on the stone."

Arlian had shuddered, and had stayed well clear of Bloody Hand for weeks after that—but with time he had begun to wonder again.

Maybe Hand had been more frightened than angry, alone down here with a score of men who had reason to hate him. Maybe he had misjudged. Maybe he had been too scared to try to do anything for Dinian.

The others all said Hand was a cruel, vicious creature who took delight in the suffering of others, that he'd beaten Dinian to death for fun—but Arlian had never seen Bloody Hand hit *anyone,* despite frequent threats. If he enjoyed tormenting the miners, why had he held off so completely for all these years?

Hathet used to say that there were usually two explanations for everything, the obvious one and the true one; Arlian suspected that this applied to Bloody Hand.

But sometimes the obvious explanation was the only one. For example, whatever Bloody Hand's motives might be, Lampspiller enjoyed hurting people, and made no attempt to hide the fact. His name came from a little game he had invented, not long after the day he had first turned up instead of the Gaffer for the second shift, where he would secretly pour the oil out of a miner's lamp, and then send the man alone down one of the tunnels on some invented errand. The light would go out, and the miner would find himself in utter darkness, unable to find his way back. He would call for help, and Lampspiller would forbid anyone to respond until he heard a satisfactory note of genuine terror and desperation in the victim's cries.

More often than not, it was Lampspiller's laughter that guided the lost miner back.

Several of the miners had felt Lampspiller's whip; he had never flogged anyone to death, but he often used a little sting of the lash to hurry men along. Most of the miners were only too glad to curse both overseers, and to bemoan the day the Gaffer had retired—if he had; no one knew for certain what had happened to the old man. One day Lampspiller had come down the pit instead of the Gaffer, and none of the slaves had ever seen the Gaffer again.

Arguing who was worse, Bloody Hand or Lampspiller, was a popular pastime.

In Arlian's opinion, Lampspiller won easily—but he knew that Dinian's ghost might well think otherwise.

The final ore cart tipped up, and the gray stone spilled into the hopper—or began to, at any rate; the hopper was now full enough that Arlian had to hang on the rope for two or three minutes, holding the heavy cart up, while Wark raked out the ore.

At last it was done, though. Arlian unhooked the cart and pulled it clear; he and Wark stepped back.

"Go on," Hand said, waving them back. He didn't need to explain what he wanted; they knew the rules. No slave was allowed in the pit while the hopper was being raised up and the ore transferred to the waiting wagons.

Wark and Arlian retreated toward the mouth of their home tunnel and watched as Hand signaled to the teamsters on the upper level.

"Hyaah!" someone shouted, unseen, and the two young men heard the crack of a whip, followed by the rattle of chains and the creaking of ropes and wood as the mules began hauling. The hopper shifted, ore clattering and ropes twanging, and began to lift.

Arlian watched as it rose. They didn't have to wait here; it would be a good half-hour before the ore had been transferred and the hopper lowered again with tonight's supper in it. There were empty carts available, and the two of them could easily have returned to work at the rock face in Tunnel #45 and perhaps filled half a cart before returning for their ration. Still, Arlian preferred to watch.

For one thing, if he ever intended to get out of the mine he would probably need to get up that shaft to the entry tunnel. Virtually the only alternative would be to tunnel up to sunlight somewhere without being spotted by the overseers, and Arlian remembered how far down he had come when he was first brought here, and that the entry had been at the foot of a cliff. He was deep inside the earth—he didn't know how far, but he knew it was deep.

The possibility that someday they might tunnel into a natural cave or cavern had occurred to him, but it seemed unlikely—and if it did happen, everyone knew that dragons lived in deep caverns. Much as he wanted to destroy those dragons, he didn't care to face them barefoot and armed only with a pickax.

Up the shaft—that was the only sane way out.

So he watched the lifting operations with intense interest, trying to devise some way that he might get up to that entrance tunnel. The hopper was always carefully stored up at the top, with all the ropes pulled up out of reach; the stone walls were angled inward as they rose and polished smooth, making a climb impossible. The pile of rags used as a buffer for the hopper, and also as a stockpile for the miners' clothing, was too low to be of any real help.

The hopper was almost invisible now, above the area lit by the mine's lamps and not yet into the glow of the torches and lamps used by the wagon crews. Arlian leaned out of the tunnel mouth to peer upward.

He saw the jerk an instant before he heard the snap; one corner of the hopper dropped abruptly, then caught a few inches lower.

Then a second snap sounded, and the entire end of the hopper dropped, swinging down; two of the four cables had broken.

The top layer of ore spilled from the hopper with a thunderous roar that echoed deafeningly from the limestone walls; a hundred jagged head-sized chunks of heavy gray stone poured in a torrent.

And Bloody Hand, who had stepped forward to watch the hauling better, was standing directly underneath.

He raised his arms to shield his head and tried to dodge, but not in time—a stone struck him squarely on the temple, and he crumpled sideways, landing on the rag heap.

Arlian started out of the tunnel, then caught himself.

This was *Bloody Hand,* the overseer, the man who had flogged Dinian to death. And the hopper was still mostly full and swinging about wildly as the teamsters at the top tried to regain control; at any moment the rest of the ore might spill out. Only a tiny fraction had fallen as yet. The remainder was hanging by a thread.

A single chunk of stone the size of a man's chest had killed Fist instantly, and that dancing hopper held several *tons* of ore.

But Bloody Hand was still a fellow human being. Dinian aside, the rumors and stories aside, Arlian had never seen him deliberately harm anyone.

And Arlian had seen too many men die in the mines. He had no desire to see another death, not even Hand's.

He ran forward and grabbed the dazed Hand under both arms, hauling him free of the little heap of scattered stone. Arlian pulled him toward the nearest tunnel mouth, walking backward and dragging Hand along as quickly as he could. He was halfway to the safety of the tunnel's mouth when he heard a twang, and another snap, and saw an avalanche of gray stone pouring down out of the darkness.

Chapter Six

The Price of Mercy

Arlian was coughing, choking on the clouds of rock dust, as he staggered backward; he had dropped Bloody Hand, but the dust in his eyes was so thick he couldn't see where. All he wanted for the moment was to get clear himself, so he could wipe his eyes and see what was happening.

"Ari!"

Arlian recognized Wark's voice. "Here!" he shouted in return.

Other voices were shouting somewhere; Arlian paid no attention to them as he stumbled into a tunnel mouth and cleared his vision.

A few seconds later Wark was there beside him, wiping away dust; Arlian turned and peered out into the pitshaft.

The lamps on one side had gone out, so that great black shadows reared up—and some were moving, dancing, as the now-empty hopper, dangling from one line, swung crazily. A great heap of gray ore covered the rag pile, half obscured by slowly settling black dust. Miners stood in all the tunnels, staring out into the opening, but none had ventured out. Most of the shouting was coming from above.

And then a rope was flung down, and a man came sliding down it, hand over hand—a man wearing thick leather, with a sword on his belt. He jumped free and immediately drew his blade. The sword was shorter and broader than Arlian remembered a sword being, and he had to stop and think where he had ever seen a sword before.

On Lord Dragon's belt, he realized. This was only the second sword he had even glimpsed, and the first he had seen out of its sheath. It gleamed in the dim orange light, and Arlian stared at it, fascinated, studying the way the stranger held it.

"All right, stand back!" the swordsman bellowed. "Where's the overseer?"

Half a dozen voices answered, and several fingers pointed. The man turned and spotted Bloody Hand, lying half covered in dust and rubble.

"What about our dinner?" someone called.

"You'll get your food," the swordsman snapped, as he strode over to Bloody Hand. He knelt, but kept the sword ready and didn't look down as he felt the downed overseer's throat, but instead kept a watchful eye on the slaves in the tunnels.

"He's breathing," the swordsman shouted up the shaft. "I don't see much blood. I think he's all right."

"Can he hold a rope?" a voice called from above.

"Not a chance," the swordsman replied. "Send someone down!"

Arlian watched silently and saw that Bloody Hand was blinking, and trying to raise his right hand free of the rocks. By the time another man had clambered down the rope from the ledge above the swordsman was helping Bloody Hand to sit up.

Arlian and Wark watched as the new arrival helped the overseer to the dangling rope. The swordsman stood guard as the others clung to the rope while it was hauled up; then the rope was flung down again, and the swordsman sheathed his blade and ascended.

Then the rope was pulled up.

For a moment nothing more happened, though Arlian could hear voices. Then the hopper, still dangling by its one corner, was lowered.

"Where's our supper?" someone shouted, and several other voices joined in protest at seeing the hopper descend without the customary contents.

"Wait a moment, will you?" the swordsman's voice called down.

A chorus of angry voices replied incoherently, and at last the miners spilled out of the tunnels into the pitshaft. Arlian saw Swamp shaking an angry fist at the invisible figures in the upper tunnels.

Then a heavy burlap sack came sailing down the shaft, to land with a thump atop the heap of spilled ore. Swamp and the others ran to open it.

Arlian stepped out into the pitshaft, Wark at his heels. The two of them made their way up the mound of ore to where Swamp and Bitter were distributing the usual food from the sack—coarse bread, tasteless dried-out cheese, some dried fruit to prevent scurvy.

Arlian held out his hand, and Swamp started to pass him a slab of bread, when Stain spoke up.

"Not him! He's the one who saved Bloody Hand's life! You don't want to feed *him!*"

Swamp hesitated, and looked at Rat.

Rat, a small man known for his quick wits, looked at Arlian. "*You're* the one pulled him out from underneath, Arlian? Or was it Wark?"

"It was Arlian," Wark said.

"I did it," Arlian admitted.

"Trying to get on the bosses' good side, are you?" Rat snarled. "Couldn't leave well enough alone?"

"You know the rules, Rat," Arlian said—he wasn't exactly slow himself, and had no intention of admitting he had acted out of genuine concern for a fellow human being. "If we don't deliver a live overseer at the end of each shift, we don't get fed."

"You risked your life over one meal, boy?" Rat sneered. "It'd be worth skipping a meal to see Bloody Hand's brains bashed out, if you ask me!"

"Hey, where's Lampspiller?" someone asked before Arlian could reply. "He didn't come down!"

That created a stir of concern—the miners *did* know the rules. Each overseer stayed for a single shift—probably twelve hours each—then was replaced by the other. Bloody Hand had been hauled up, but Lampspiller had not come down for his shift.

And if there were no overseer, there would be no food at the next shift change.

Arlian's saving of Bloody Hand's life was forgotten for the moment as the miners argued and shouted. Arlian ignored the debate and took the bread from Swamp's hand; Swamp didn't resist, but simply shrugged, handed Arlian a wedge of cheese, and went back to distributing food.

Lampspiller did finally descend, by rope, a few minutes later, and promptly laid about himself with his whip, clearing out the pit; Swamp and Bitter hauled the largely empty food sack into one of the tunnels to continue handing out its contents. By that time Arlian had retreated down toward his own sleeping niche in Tunnel #32, gnawing on his bread and cheese.

He sat on the rags he used as a bed, chewing slowly, and tried to think.

Had he done the right thing, saving Bloody Hand? Hadn't the overseer deserved to die for what he did to Dinian?

He had acted almost without thinking, though.

He wondered, for the first time, whether when the time came he would be able to carry out the revenge he had planned for so long. What if someday he escaped the mine, and tracked down Lord Dragon and his men, and then was overcome by compassion and could not bring himself to slay them?

He had never imagined that possibility before, but now that he had saved Bloody Hand's life, at the risk of his own, he had to consider it.

Was he too soft, still a child rather than a warrior?

"Traitor!"

The word was whispered, so he did not recognize the voice, and spoken

45

from behind the shelter of a corner in the passage; Arlian looked up, startled, as an open and lit oil lamp was flung onto his bedding.

The ancient, soiled rags caught, and Arlian hurried to stamp out the blaze as quickly as he could. The smoke affected his already dry throat, and he found himself coughing uncontrollably even after the fire was out. By the time he was himself again, able to take his own lamp and go looking for his attacker, there was no sign that the assailant had ever been there.

He stood in the corridor for a moment, then returned dejectedly to his bedding and settled down cross-legged upon it. He poked idly at the scorched part—he would probably want to replace that, he thought.

The rag pile was under tons of rock, though, so it would have to wait.

Rags and rock and his oil lamp, and a small collection of mementos of dead companions, were all he really owned down here. Some of the miners had managed to make a few things from broken tools or odd scraps, but Arlian had never bothered. He had no paintings on the limestone where he slept, no carved tokens, no knife or spoon or pen; he had spent what little free time he had talking to others, learning everything he could, thinking about ways he might escape and avenge his family.

He had told the others of his plans at first, and been laughed at for his troubles; no one else believed that escape was possible. As for an escaped slave avenging himself against a lord, that was equally absurd, and the idea of killing the dragons went beyond absurd to insane. Even Hathet had sorrowfully told Arlian it was foolish, and Arlian had quickly learned to keep his plans for vengeance to himself—but he had never given them up, and was always alert to learn as much as he could, in hopes of discovering some fact that might show him a way out of the mine.

The owners of the mine provided rags—Arlian didn't know where they came from, but bundles were tossed down every so often, added to the heap in the pitshaft. The miners made their clothing and bedding and assorted other things from the rags—sacks, wallets, wicks, lampshades, and whatever else they could devise. A few miners made a point of collecting white fabric, or when there was no white the lightest colors available, and writing upon it in ink made of charcoal and water—Arlian had never seen much point in that, though he had read a few of the memoirs and stories thus recorded.

Rags, tools, food, water, and lamp oil—the owners sent those down, and the slaves sent back ore. A very simple economy, but one that had functioned smoothly for years.

And there was almost nothing in it Arlian had considered worth saving.

Bitter had a stack of whitish rags a foot high, covered with his rants about how he had been wronged and mistreated, while Olneor had set down his family's history going back four generations, and Verino had written a philosophical treatise on humanity's place in the cosmos; Swamp had covered a wall with surprisingly subtle and beautiful drawings of his home village, while Stain had drawn crude and thoroughly obscene pictures of women in various corners. Rat was reputed to have a stash of food, oil, and knives securely hidden somewhere. Wark had made dolls and other toys out of knotted fabric.

All Arlian had was his collection of mementos.

He had been brought here with nothing at all of his own but the clothes on his back and the ropes he had been bound with, ropes that were promptly stolen by other miners. He had nothing by which to remember his family, and he had quickly come to feel that lack keenly. His life had a hole in it where his family should have been, and he thought that while nothing could ever fill that hole, some memento, some little trinket that would connect his life in the mines to his old life outside, might have helped to cover it, to soften its sharp edges.

When he first saw another miner die, he had resolved that he *would* keep something to remember him, as he had been unable to do for his village, and with each death after that he had added to his collection. Most of the additions were just scraps of cloth—the dead had often been new arrivals who had owned nothing but the clothes they wore.

There were a few other things, though. He had a braided necklace Kort had worn, woven of human hair. He had a chunk of rock stained with Fist's blood. And he had Hathet's purple stones.

They were his most prized possession, and now he reached into the niche in the rock wall and pulled the bag out to look at them.

The miners sometimes found bits of other stone in with the limestone and galena; Hathet had collected one particular variety, a sort of purple crystal he called "amethyst." Hathet had claimed that in his homeland of Arithei, a dream-infested land far beyond the Borderlands in the mysterious and magical realms of the unexplored south, these stones were considered gems and were highly valued. They had, Hathet said, magical properties that could protect their owner.

Hathet had also said Arithei was full of magicians, that dreams became real there and stalked the streets every night, and any number of other absurd things.

Arlian had never believed most of Hathet's stories; even though he had admired the old man, and had taken to heart a great deal of what he said about how a man should live and how the world was best dealt with, Arlian had always thought Hathet was not quite right in the head, and many of his tales were clearly just wishful thinking.

Hathet had claimed that he had been sent to Manfort as the Aritheian ambassador, and was waylaid by bandits on the highway, bandits who had sold him into slavery here—and how likely was that? What sort of bandit could be so stupid as to sell an ambassador as a mine slave, rather than ransoming him?

Hathet's attempt at explanation, involving complicated palace intrigue and high treason, had made no sense to Arlian or the others, and they had concluded that the old man had made it up on the spot. He probably wasn't from Arithei at all. A miner called Brown who claimed to have visited the Borderlands said that the road to Arithei had been closed for years, and all trade blocked, so there was no way Hathet could have come from there. Brown had arrived just after Hathet died, and had then died in a fall himself, so no details were available, but why would he lie?

So Hathet had probably made it all up, and the pretty purple stones were probably just pretty purple stones, of no real value to anyone—but Hathet had collected them carefully, and now Arlian kept that collection. He had counted one hundred and sixty-eight stones, ranging in size from mere specks to the size of his thumb.

He saw no sign that they provided any magical protection, but they were pleasant to look at, and served as a reminder of poor Hathet. Once he got out of the mine perhaps he could find Hathet's family, in Arithei or wherever they really were, and give them the stones as a memento of their lost kinsman.

"Traitor!"

Arlian looked up, unsure whether he had really heard another whispered imprecation or merely imagined it. No lamp followed the word this time.

The threat was there, though. Whether it had been the right thing to do or not, saving Bloody Hand had plainly marked him down as an enemy for many of the miners. Nothing he owned would be safe if left unattended; he still remembered the sick, stricken expression on Elezin's face on that occasion years before when Elezin had returned from working the ore to find his little hand-carved limestone shrine smashed to powder and gravel. Elezin had angered Fist the shift before, and Fist had taken his revenge.

Arlian understood the need for revenge very well indeed, and understood why the others would want to retaliate for his saving of Bloody Hand, but he did not intend to make it any easier to hurt him than it had to be. He gathered up the hair necklace and a few fabric scraps and tucked them into the bag with the amethysts, then twisted a rag into a crude rope belt and tied the bag to his waist. He did not want to come back here in a shift or two and find his mementos gone.

This was normally his off shift, but he was in no mood to rest; he got to his feet, and with the bag thumping against his hip made his way down to the rock face to work off his nerves by digging out ore.

Chapter Seven

The Return of Bloody Hand

Three shifts later the hopper was repaired, and the slaves began shoveling the heap of spilled ore back into it.

Lampspiller was in charge of the operation; his shift was ending, and rumor had it that Bloody Hand was waiting in the tunnel above, ready to return. His previous shift had been taken by a stranger the miners had dubbed Loudmouth, a big brawling man with sun-darkened skin who had disdained the whip and had instead thoroughly beaten Swamp with his bare fists to establish his authority.

The others had watched as Swamp was thrashed for a minor, possibly imagined offense. Had they joined forces they could easily have defeated Loudmouth—but then what? How would they get up the pitshaft to escape? So they had stood by and done nothing as Loudmouth asserted his authority, and they had obeyed Loudmouth's bellowed orders.

Arlian had stayed well out of Loudmouth's way—and as much as possible out of everyone else's way, as well. He had been tripped three or four times while working during the past three shifts; a "mis-aimed" pickax had missed his foot by inches; chunks of ore had been "accidentally" flung at his head. His bedding had disappeared completely at one point, and he had had to dig down through the spill to replace it from the ragpile.

Even Wark was avoiding him—and Arlian couldn't blame him; anyone who was seen befriending the outcast would be outcast himself.

He hoped the others would get over their anger soon. While he had never been the most popular of the slaves, he had always gotten along well enough, and had made no real enemies—until now.

Maybe, he thought as he shoveled, this would mark the end of his harassment. With the hopper back in operation and the spilled ore gone, with Bloody Hand back on the job, perhaps things would return to normal.

Or perhaps when the backlog of ore was gone—every cart in the mine was filled to overflowing, and more ore was piled at the rock face, since there had been no way to haul it up the shaft. Maybe when *that* was gone he'd be forgiven his act of misplaced mercy.

He wasn't counting on it, though; the bag of mementos was still securely tied in place on his belt, and would stay there. He didn't trust anyone at this point.

He glimpsed something moving and ducked as a shovelful of ore flew past his ear.

"Sorry," Bitter said, his tone utterly insincere.

"I wonder if it's occurred to anyone," Arlian said, not addressing anyone in particular, "that if Bloody Hand had died, he might have been replaced by someone even worse."

"And *I* wonder," Bitter retorted, "whether anyone really *could* be worse, and whether Dinian's shade is as angry at the missed chance for vengeance as I am."

"Shut up," Lampspiller roared, "or I'll show you that *I* can be worse than your worst nightmare!"

"My nightmares are about dragons," Arlian muttered.

The whip cracked across his back. "You think I can't be as bad as a dragon?" he bellowed.

Arlian turned and stared at him, ignoring the welt rising on his shoulders. He didn't say anything; he'd been ordered to shut up, after all. He simply looked at Lampspiller.

The overseer faltered, then lifted his whip. "Get back to work!"

Arlian returned to his shoveling. Some of the other miners had paused at the mention of dragons; many felt a superstitious awe of the legendary creatures that had once ruled the world, and Arlian was sure that they thought Lampspiller had just invited evil by his careless retort.

Maybe he had. Arlian had had more direct experience of dragons than anyone else in the mine, but he still knew almost nothing about them. Maybe speaking irreverently of them *could* bring bad luck. Maybe his own grandfather's explanation of dragon weather had brought about the attack on Obsidian.

But Arlian didn't believe that. And even if it were true, it was unjust. He would see the dragons punished someday, or he would die in pursuing it.

"Fill this one right to the top!" Lampspiller ordered. "We've got an extra wagon waiting up above—we'll be making up the missed shipments a little at a time."

"What if the ropes break again?" someone asked.

"They won't," Lampspiller said. "Brand-new ropes all around." He smiled crookedly. "But I won't be standing underneath—*some* of us have more sense than that!"

A few of the slaves smiled or even laughed briefly at that; Arlian did not.

Ten minutes later the hopper was filled to overflowing, and Lampspiller sent the slaves to the tunnels before giving the signal to haul.

He was as good as his word, and backed against the wall of the pit, well clear of the hopper as it rose upward, ropes crackling as they were stretched for the first time, pulleys and timbers creaking under the heavier-than-usual load.

The slaves waited and watched, eager for their next meal and curious about whether the new ropes would, in fact, hold, and whether or not Bloody Hand would be returning.

The hopper ascended into the darkness. Then at last came the old familiar sound of the support arms turning, swinging the hopper over to the ledge to be unloaded.

The ropes hadn't broken. Arlian heard shovels and rattling ore as the crew up above began transferring the ore to the waiting wagons.

The other slaves began chattering among themselves, but Arlian stood apart, farther down the tunnel than the others.

Eventually the ore was gone, and a series of quick thuds could be heard as supplies were tossed into the hopper. The slaves, who had been resting against the walls or sitting on the stone floor, stood up and awaited the signal.

The hopper began its descent, the rigging creaking anew—though less than before, since its new cargo weighed far less than the load of ore.

Arlian peered out of the tunnel mouth and watched the huge iron tub creep downward.

Bloody Hand was standing on one edge, steadying himself with one of the cables and watching everything as he was lowered down into the mine.

That answered *that* question—Hand was back, and although he wore a bandage around his head and his face displayed a few cuts and bruises, he did not seem to have suffered any permanent damage from his misadventure.

The injuries he had received were hardly enough to equal Dinian's, Arlian knew that, but perhaps they would help to appease the other miners.

Were they enough to salve his own conscience, though? Why *had* he saved Bloody Hand, instead of letting Fate collect the debt owed to Dinian's shade?

Then the hopper was down, and Bloody Hand and Lampspiller signaled to the nearest slaves. A moment later Rat and three of the others were heaving out the two barrels of water, the keg of lamp oil, and the sacks of food that would keep the miners alive for another day or so.

Then the slaves were banished from the pitshaft again as Lampspiller rode the hopper up out of sight.

The hopper was never left at the bottom for so much as a minute except under the direct supervision of one or both of the overseers, and only when there were men in the upper tunnel; the owners feared that slaves might climb the robes and escape. At the end of each shift the procedure was the same—the hopper was lowered empty, and then filled; ore was hauled up and loaded into the wagons, and then provisions, adjusted according to how full the wagons were, were sent down, attended by the incoming overseer. The departing overseer then rode the empty hopper up, and made sure it was safely stowed.

Several of the bolder slaves had argued that it would be more efficient to lower the provisions and incoming overseer *first,* and then haul the ore up, so that only one round trip would be needed, but when the overseers bothered to reply at all the response was obvious: The slaves would fill the hopper faster if they knew the food would only arrive when they were done.

When the hopper was gone Bloody Hand stood alone in the pit, looking around.

The pile of rags was still there, but sprinkled with dust and gravel; torn scraps of rope lay piled against one wall, the last remnants of the old, worn-out rigging that had been responsible for the accident. The water barrels and oil keg had been shoved to one side, as well.

And two dozen slaves were slouched in the tunnels, sharing out their newly delivered meal.

There were four other men in the tunnel with Arlian, with one sack of food; he waited while they each took what they wanted.

One of them, Rumind, looked at Arlian, then at his companions, Wark, Olneor, and Elbows.

"That's all of us, isn't it?" he said.

Arlian straightened up.

"Oh, give him his food," Wark said. "The overseer won't like it if we don't."

"Oh, yeah, I forgot, Arlian's the Hand's special friend, isn't he?" Rumind said with a sneer.

Arlian held out a hand, and Rumind threw the bag at his face; Arlian was able to duck the throw, but not catch the projectile. He had to retreat down the tunnel to fetch it.

As he picked it up Rumind shoved roughly past him.

"Excuse me," Rumind said. "We've got work to do, and I don't care for the company here."

Elbows jabbed at Arlian with his namesake joint as he passed; Olneor didn't touch him, but muttered, "Thought you might have some potential, boy. Guess I was an old fool."

Wark simply walked past without comment.

Arlian stood, the food sack in his hand, and watched them descend until they turned a bend in the passage and vanished. Then he sighed, settled to the floor, and opened the bag.

He had just pulled out a heel of black bread and a handful of cheese crumbs when a shadow obscured the lamplight.

"You," Bloody Hand said, "Get up."

Arlian got up.

"Your name's Arlian, something like that?"

"It's Arlian."

"You're the one who pulled me out before the whole thing came down, are you?"

Arlian nodded.

"You expect me to be grateful?"

"No." Arlian couldn't really see Bloody Hand's face, as the light was behind the overseer, but he thought he saw the man frown.

"You made life harder for yourself, saving me, didn't you?"

Arlian shrugged.

"Why did you do it?"

"It seemed like a good idea at the time."

"You know about Dinian?"

"I've heard," Arlian said. "I wasn't here at the time."

"You saved me anyway?"

Arlian shrugged again.

"You didn't make *my* life any easier, either, you know. *Longer,* yes, but no easier."

Arlian didn't even bother to shrug in response to that.

"It doesn't look good, owing my life to one of the slaves. It's trouble all around. I'd like to know why you did it."

Arlian hesitated; then he raised his eyes and looked directly at the shadows of Bloody Hand's face.

"I'd like to know why you killed Dinian," he said.

Bloody Hand snorted.

"Would you?" he said. "Haven't the others told you?"

"They told me you killed him because you're a heartless bastard," Arlian said. "But I've been thinking about it. If you really were as heartless as that, you'd have been freer with the whip all these years I've been here. I don't think that's it."

"Maybe I tried it and decided I didn't like it."

"Or maybe you didn't mean to kill him at all," Arlian suggested. "Maybe you just panicked."

Bloody Hand stared at him. "You think so?"

"I don't know," Arlian said. "I would like to *know* why you killed him, instead of guessing."

"So would I," the overseer said. "It just happened. It wasn't anything I decided to do. I was young and scared and needed to prove I was in charge, and once I started hitting him I couldn't stop—I was too *scared* to stop."

"You think about it often?" Arlian asked.

"Every night," Bloody Hand said. He let out a sound half snort, half laugh. "The funny part is that it was wrong, it was evil, it was the *worst* thing I could do, killing an innocent man who was just trying to teach me something—and everything that's come of it since has been good for me. It gave me that name I hear you men whisper. It frightened you all so much that I've never had to really beat a man since, and my shift still outproduces the other. There's no justice in this world, Arlian, you know that?"

"I know that," Arlian said, his heart suddenly pounding as he remembered the sight of his village, burned and desolate, his family destroyed at the whim of three heartless monsters. "Not unless we *make* it."

"But you had your chance to make it," Bloody Hand said. "You could have let me die for what I did to Dinian, and you didn't. *Why not?*"

Arlian hesitated again. He could have given all the explanations he had made to Rat and the others over the past three shifts, all the reasons it was better to keep Bloody Hand alive than to risk an unknown new overseer or tighter precautions in the mine, how he hadn't wanted to miss even a single meal—but that was all lies, and right now he didn't want to lie to this man, who had admitted what was unmistakably the truth about Dinian's death, who had clearly been troubled by that death for years.

"You were in danger, and I could help you," Arlian said. "Who you were didn't matter."

Arlian could see Bloody Hand's brow lower at that, could almost hear him growl. The overseer's hand lashed out and grabbed him by the beard,

56

pulling Arlian forward.

"It *does* matter," he hissed. "You've seen that it matters! You saved someone's life, and what did it get you? I killed a man, and what did *that* get? It's a sick, unjust world, Arlian, and it *does* matter who we are!" He released his hold and Arlian tumbled backward, catching himself against the tunnel wall.

For a moment the two men stared silently at one another; then Bloody Hand turned on his heel and marched back out into the pit.

"Get to work, slave," he called back over his shoulder. "There's ore to be mined!"

Chapter Eight

Into the Light

Arlian was asleep in his niche when a booted foot kicked him awake. "Get up, slave!" Bloody Hand shouted. He stood over the sleeping miner, lamp in hand, boot ready to kick again.

Arlian rolled aside and struggled mazily upright.

It was his time off, his sleeping time—he had dug and carted his share for this shift, and was entitled to a few hours' rest. He knew better than to argue, though.

As he stood, Bloody Hand leaned forward, his mouth close by Arlian's ear, and whispered confidentially, "If there's anything you prize here, bring it."

Astonished by this sudden change in manner, Arlian blinked at him, then quickly snatched up his bag and belt. He reached for his lamp, but Bloody Hand shook his head and knocked his hand away from it. "Leave it," he whispered.

Arlian left it, and waited for orders.

"It's time I settled with you once and for all!" Bloody Hand bellowed, stepping back, reverting to his usual bullying self and astonishing Arlian anew. "Come out and take it like a man!"

Confused, still half asleep, Arlian staggered out of the niche and up toward the pitshaft, Bloody Hand close behind, shoving him forward every time he slowed or stumbled. He tied his belt in place as he walked. Other than the belt he was wearing only a tattered pair of breeches, and he wondered whether there was anything else he should have grabbed while he had the chance.

Well, it was too late now.

"What do you want with me?" he asked.

"I'm going to ensure that you never lay hands on me again!" Bloody Hand roared. He snapped his whip.

Arlian was baffled. He had saved Bloody Hand's life; was a flogging to be his reward? Perhaps it was what he deserved for aiding a murderer, but he hadn't expected it. Was this Bloody Hand's way of showing Arlian that there was no justice in the world?

It was hardly necessary; the dragons had done that long ago.

Then they were in the pitshaft—and Arlian was surprised to see that it was almost totally dark. All the lamps had been put out; only the one Bloody Hand held remained to provide illumination.

A faint glow came from above, as well, but Arlian wasn't sure whether that was anything out of the ordinary or not. Perhaps there was always a light up there, and it simply wasn't usually visible through the glare of the lamps.

"Now!" Bloody Hand barked, as the two of them reached the base of the rag pile. He blew out the lamp he carried, plunging the already shadowy pit into near total blackness. Only the glow from above alleviated the gloom.

Arlian heard the sound of a rope uncoiling, and a thump—but it wasn't the Hand's whip. The sound had come from the other side.

He turned and found something dangling close beside him, faintly visible, dull gray in the darkness.

A rope.

For a moment he couldn't move; he stared at it in shock. The almost invisible rope seemed so out of place to his sleep-clouded mind that at first he had trouble accepting it as real, and wondered whether he was still asleep and dreaming this entire episode.

He reached out and hesitantly, ready to snatch his hand away at the first sound from Bloody Hand, touched it.

The rope was real. He could feel its rough texture clearly. He was awake.

No rope should be there. No ropes were permitted except during the shift change, when the hopper was lowered and raised. What was this one doing there?

Bloody Hand snapped his whip, and Arlian jumped.

"Darkness for dark deeds," the overseer said loudly. He laughed. Then, in a whisper, he added, "I can't have you down here anymore."

"What?"

"Keep your voice down!" Bloody Hand hissed.

Arlian whispered, "What?"

"I can't have you down here," the overseer replied, in a whisper so low Arlian could barely hear it. "It's bad for everyone. The others hate you for what you did. You make me look weak—you remind them I'm human and mortal. You remind *me* I'm mortal—and how can I abuse the man who saved my life, and treat you like just another slave? You can't stay."

"But I *am* a slave…"

"Do you *deserve* slavery?"

"No, of course not," Arlian said, confused.

"As far as the others are concerned, I'm going to kill you, just as I did Dinian, for your effrontery in trying to help me. And if you don't climb that rope and get out of here, I *will* kill you, I swear by the dead gods."

"Climb…?" Arlian grabbed the rope, a sudden rush of hope rising in his breast.

"There's a guard at the top, but he's my brother, Linnas—he's 'accidentally' lowered the rope, and in a moment he'll throw down a bundle of rags I'll say is your dead body and throw in the hopper at the end of the shift. When you slip past him he'll be away from his post, relieving himself. After that, Arlian, you're on your own, and we'll be even—I'm paying for my life with your freedom, and just as you might have been killed if the ore fell sooner, if I'm discovered at it I'll be killed or enslaved."

"I don't … I mean, thank you…" Arlian began.

Bloody Hand cut him off. "You said there's no justice unless we make it. I'm making my bit. Climb!"

He cracked the whip against the rag pile, and Arlian, with sudden inspiration, screamed. He flung himself up the rope, clinging desperately with hands and knees—he had never climbed a rope before, although he had seen it done often enough.

He managed to haul himself upward, little by little, as Bloody Hand flogged the heap of rags. A louder thump sounded from one side that Arlian guessed was the promised imitation corpse—and then Arlian felt the lash across his own legs, and shrieked.

"Good," Bloody Hand said. "Yell if you want, you poxy fool!" Then he stepped closer and whispered, "I need blood on the whip and rags if I'm to be believed. I'm sorry."

"Don't be," Arlian whispered back, though the pain in his legs was intense. "Thank you, Hand."

"My name is Enir," the overseer whispered back. "Go!"

Arlian went. He panted with the effort of pulling himself up the rope toward the light, trying to match his gasps for air with the beating of the whip on the rags. Every so often he moaned or wailed.

Then his hand struck stone, and a moment later he was scrambling up onto the ledge at the mouth of the entry tunnel, a tunnel lit by two bright lamps.

A man was standing there, a man not in the rags of a miner or the leather apron of an overseer, but in a bright tunic, green worked with gold, over black velvet breeches. He wore a sword on his belt, and after a few seconds of confusion Arlian recognized him as the swordsman who had come down into the pit when the hopper lines broke.

"I'm Linnas," he said, holding out a hand and smiling. "You understand that we never saw each other, that if anyone asks I'd had a bit too much beer and stepped away from my post?"

Arlian nodded warily, and took the proffered hand.

"I wanted to thank you for saving Enir," the swordsman said, as he grasped Arlian's hand. Then he released it, stepped back, and lifted one of the lamps down from its place on the wall. He handed it to Arlian and said, "You'll need this. Now, go on! Get out of here!"

"Thank you," Arlian gasped as he accepted the lamp. Then he staggered past Linnas and headed up the passage, limping on his sore, bleeding legs.

When he had been brought down, years ago, the passage had been lined with lamps and torches, but he knew now that that had been in preparation for a shift change—the mules that pulled the wagons didn't like the dark. He didn't know just what time it was now, but it was clearly the middle of a shift, when no one would normally be in this tunnel.

His legs ached, and he wished that Hand … no, Enir … that Enir hadn't insisted on real blood. He had had plenty of practice in working while sick, exhausted, or injured, though, and trotted on despite the pain.

His lone lamp cast huge, flaring shadows as he made his way up the tunnel. Now he could see, as he had not as a boy, that the passage was an old part of the mine itself, that it followed the course and shape of a great seam of ore that had been dug out; he could see the marks of picks on the walls, the traces of galena too thin to be worth removing, the thick layers of smoke on the ceiling above niches where lamps had been placed over and over.

Seeing it thus was strange, almost dreamlike—he had lived for so long in the same slowly expanding network of deep, branching tunnels that a new, unfamiliar place didn't seem entirely real.

If it were a dream, he told himself, he didn't want it to end; he wanted to be out of the mine, out in the sun and open air, free again, to lead his own life, make his own way, and in time find his revenge upon Lord Dragon and his looters, and upon the dragons themselves.

There were places the passage narrowed enough that Arlian wondered how the ore wagons ever fit through, but even so, it was always wider than most of the mine tunnels, and he already felt as if the world were opening out around him.

And then he was at the top, at the end of the passage, and a heavy wooden door blocked his way. He hesitated. What if there were another guard on the other side? He had no weapon of any kind, not even a rock. What if that horrible fat old man who had carried him down the mine so long ago was out there?

His mouth tightened. If that fat old man was there, Arlian would wring his neck bare-handed. He was no scared child anymore.

He had to stop and think for a moment to remember how to work the latch—he hadn't used one in so long! There were no doors in the lower mine. It was simple enough, though, and he swung the door open.

Blinding light poured in; he fell back, momentarily terrified. The brightness was so intense he thought he might go mad. He flung an arm across his eyes and squeezed them shut, and still the world was flooded in bright red light.

He was seeing the inside of his own eyelids, he realized; the light outside the door, whatever it was, was so bright that it was shining right through his flesh.

But his eyes were adjusting, and after a moment he dared to open one a crack.

The light was the sun. He knew that. He had been down in the darkness of the mines for so long that his eyes were far too sensitive to handle the ordinary light of day.

If he wanted to escape, though, he would have to face it, to venture out into that glare and find his way safely away from the mine before anyone realized he was gone. He stepped forward, his arm still up.

The air moved about him, and felt somehow *wrong.* His skin crawled, and he shivered.

That was *wind,* he realized—just the cool wind blowing. That wrongness was *cold*—he had been so long in the mine, where the temperature was constant year-round save for where the lamps heated the air, that he had forgotten the sensation.

He moved forward, and tried to look around, while still shielding his eyes from the sun's glare.

Everything looked washed out, almost white, the colors faded and thin, but he could see the great yellow cliff towering above him, and wagon tracks in the dirt at his feet, and ahead the slope of a hill covered in lush green grass, falling away into a valley. Sunlight blazed down from almost directly overhead, so there were few shadows.

To his left was a small cluster of buildings, low structures of stone and thatch—the mine headquarters, surely, where Lord Dragon had sold him to the mine's owners. If someone were to look out one of the half dozen visible windows he would be spotted instantly, and could hardly be mistaken, given his ragged condition and pale skin, for anything but what he was, an escaped miner.

He had to get away from those windows as quickly as possible. The wagon tracks led to the left, past the buildings, then down a dirt road cut into the slope, down and away from the cliff.

That meant he didn't want to go left, nor straight ahead. He turned right and began walking—he did not want to tire himself out too soon, so he didn't run. He stayed close to the cliff, hoping to blend in with the stone, and found himself climbing slowly.

Before long he had reached the end of the cliff, and stood shivering on a steep slope amid scattered young trees; he paused and turned around, his arms clutched around himself in a futile attempt to keep warm.

He had not been sure whether it was early spring or late fall until he had noticed freshly fallen leaves scattered here and there, but now he knew it was autumn. He also knew it was definitely colder than he liked.

And the world was so strange, so *intense*—the wind on his skin was a constant rippling of alien sensation, the light was so painfully bright, the colors so glaring and vivid; unfamiliar smells were filling his head, bringing back odd bits of childhood memory he hadn't known still remained anywhere within him.

It was harsh and bright and cold and uncomfortable, the world almost *hurt,* but he never wanted to give any of it up, ever again. He thought he would rather die than go back down into the mine.

And he intended to do everything he could to ensure that he never went back. That meant thinking, planning, not just wandering on aimlessly. He had to see where he was and decide where to go.

To his left, as he stood there, was the forested top of the cliff, rising up to a peak and showing no signs of human habitation; to the right the land fell away from the cliff's base in open fields, and he could see thatched rooftops in the distance. The sun had moved slightly, and appeared to have descended somewhat from the zenith, which meant it was in the west—and he had, he judged, been walking northwest.

Although there was no sign of pursuit, he wanted to put as much distance as possible, and as many other barriers as possible, between himself and the mine. He thought that if he now turned due north, that would provide the ideal balance—no one would find him among the trees, and the cliff itself would be in the way of any search. Since the forest to the north appeared uninhabited, there would be less chance that he might be seen by anyone who would report a runaway slave. It would also be easier on his still-suffering eyes—the trees had lost most of their leaves, but they would still provide some shade, and shelter from the biting chill of the wind.

Accordingly, he headed north.

Hours later, when his eyes had adjusted and he barely had to squint even when looking west into the setting sun, he paused and looked around. He had put several miles behind him, across completely unfamiliar terrain; he had stayed clear of roads, houses, barns, and cultivated fields as much as he possibly could, and had seen other human beings only from afar. The outside world was still wonderful, but already beginning to lose some of its intensity and strangeness.

Now he was on a rocky hilltop, and it was time to stop and plan again. He had to do more than flee aimlessly. He was free of the mine, well clear of it, and it was time to choose a place to go *to,* rather than one to flee *from.*

He scanned his surroundings, and saw little but bare trees and empty sky—the day was cloudless, the sky brilliantly blue, a color brighter than anything he had ever seen in the mine.

He had crossed streams and taken a drink or two, but he was thirsty again, and hungry, and cold; winter was coming, and he had no coat, not even a shirt. He had no food, no shoes—his feet had been toughened by years of walking on stone, but the sharp twigs and pebbles had still been hard on him as he fled.

And he knew he must look terrible. His hair had not been cut or combed in years; his beard had *never* been trimmed. His skin was either woefully pale or starting to redden from the sun, but certainly unhealthy.

He needed things only other people could provide—but he also feared that anyone who saw him would instantly recognize him as a fugitive. He had no money, no family, his only possessions a crude bag of worthless mementos.

And he had no idea where he was.

His mouth quirked into a smile. By any practical measure he had been better off down in the mine, where he always knew exactly where he was and where his next meal would come from—but he would not have given up his freedom for anything. He would rather die of exposure this very night, he told himself, than live to be a hundred as a slave.

But he had no intention of dying, in any case. He intended to live, to make a life for himself, and to somehow avenge his family.

Water was not a problem, as these hills produced plentiful fast-running little streams; the summer did not appear to have been dry. Food—he could go for days without food if he had to, he was sure, and had heard tales of people surviving on tree bark and insects.

Clothing and shelter, though—he needed to find those before the weather turned any colder. Perhaps he could take shelter in a barn somewhere, steal a jacket …

But where would he find a barn, or any other human habitation? He turned around slowly, taking in the endless parade of gray, leafless trees.

And saw smoke. A thin line of distant gray smoke was rising in the east.

For a moment he thought it might be the smoking crater of his own native peak; then he thought it was more likely to be just a hearthfire in some nearby home.

Either way, though, that smoke meant people, and perhaps shelter.

Well, then, he told himself, that was where he must go. He would, he promised himself, walk until he found what he sought, or until he could walk no more.

And he set out to prove it.

Chapter Nine

Sanctuary

The night was moonless, and after he had walked into branches half a dozen times and stumbled a score, Arlian admitted that he could walk no more—painful as the bright light of day had been, he needed it to see where he was going. Even his dark-adapted eyes could not deal with the forest at night, so he dug himself into a pile of dead leaves for warmth and huddled there until morning.

He did not sleep well in the cold and unfamiliar surroundings, and awoke before dawn had turned the eastern sky from gray to pink. He wasted no time in getting himself moving once again, and was pleased to see that the line of smoke he had followed the previous evening, until darkness had made it impossible, was still present—though it seemed no closer than before.

Around midmorning he came upon a homestead, a house and three small barns set upon a few acres of fields; watching and listening carefully for any sign of the occupants, he crept into one of the barns and used the sharp end of an old hoe he found there, struck against a whetstone, to hack his beard down to a more reasonable length. It was still ragged and unkempt, but he had been working his fingers through beard and hair almost constantly as he walked, and he thought he might now look merely disheveled, rather than completely wild. He used a discarded bit of leather to tie his hair back—it wasn't a proper braid, by any means, but it was better than nothing.

He looked at his reflection in a half-filled trough and thought that if he had had a blouse and sandals he would be willing to allow himself to be seen.

There were no shoes or shirts to be found in the barn, though. He did fish a handful of dried corn from the bottom of an abandoned trough and carry it away, nibbling it one or two grains at a time.

That first homestead was not an isolated outpost in the wilderness; rather, Arlian realized when he crept out of the barn and looked squintingly eastward, it stood at the end of a narrow road, and other small farms adjoined it. He had crossed back over the line between the forested wilderness and civilization.

He hoped that he had put enough distance between himself and the mine that this would be entirely a good thing. He didn't dare use the road openly, as yet, but instead crept along behind the houses and barns and smokehouses.

Staying close to the buildings also served to shelter him from the worst of the cold winds that seemed almost constant.

He fed himself from livestock feed as he went, stealing a handful of grain here, a few dried fruit there; he resisted the temptation to break into a smokehouse or creamery for anything more substantial. He had eaten no meat since the day his parents died, and the scents that drifted from the smokehouses were almost overwhelming, both tempting and nauseating, driving him to hurry past as quickly as he could.

He made his way onward, eastward, for another several days, sleeping in barns or woodsheds, living on animal feed and drinking from untended wells, perpetually cold and hungry, shivering as he walked. Several times he saw people, and a few times he was seen; whenever that happened he veered away but kept walking, so as to appear an ordinary traveler. Twice someone called to him, but on both occasions he ignored the hail and kept walking, and both times the other decided against pursuit.

He passed villages occasionally, but skirted well around them.

On the fourth day after his night in the woods he came across laundry hung out to dry, and took a man's linen blouse, promising himself that someday he would pay the rightful owner back. When it had dried it provided some significant comfort against the cold, but he still dared not let himself be seen—after all, not only was he still suspiciously shaggy and barefoot, but the shirt's rightful owner might recognize it.

On the fifth day he could no longer resist temptation, and stole a ham; he was sick that night as his stomach rebelled at the unfamiliar food.

The next morning there was frost on the fields, and between that and his upset digestion he was somewhat slower than his usual in setting out. He took the time to study that column of smoke that he had followed for so long.

That was no mere chimney, nor even a village, he realized, but the smoke of a great city.

Manfort, almost certainly.

He had always wanted to see Manfort. What's more, if he wanted to find Lord Dragon, to avenge the desecration of his village, Manfort was the logical place to start looking—but he could hardly walk all the way into that famous city in his present condition, wearing nothing but ragged breeches and a stolen blouse so close to the onset of winter.

Well, it was still some distance away, he was certain. He was well clear of the forest now, making his way across gently rolling hills where one farm blended into the next and the next and the next for as far as the eye could see, where the road led from one village to another at intervals never exceeding twenty miles and often crossed or joined other roads in the process, but it was still countryside, and he had yet to glimpse a single watchtower or turret.

Still, he could hardly proceed in his current manner indefinitely; some time before he reached the walls of Manfort he would have to find a way to clean himself up and obtain proper clothes. Then he could present himself at one business or another, looking for honest work, to get himself a living before he began his pursuit of revenge.

He gave the matter some thought as he rambled onward, past farms and villages.

Perhaps, he thought late one chilly afternoon as the sun was reddening behind him, he could simply present himself as a traveler down on his luck, one who had been beset by bandits but escaped, and offer to work for his keep at an inn. He had no special skills, but he had learned to swing a pick in the mines, and he thought that he could use that experience in splitting firewood.

He remembered Grandsir saying that bandits never came this far north, but he could hope that either the old man was wrong, or times had changed while he was in the mine, or whoever he approached might not know as much as his grandfather had.

He blew on his hands to warm them and rubbed the palms together, and decided that the time had come to try. He would have to rejoin the human race eventually, and this seemed the right time.

He was approaching the biggest town he had seen yet, one so large that it could scarcely be called a village, much larger than his own childhood home. He was also nearing Manfort; that thin line of smoke had become a broad tapestry streaking up the eastern sky, and on those rare occasions when he caught an unobstructed view to the east he thought he could see the tops of towers in the distance.

He was not about to march on into the city, but this town seemed suitable. He decided to risk inquiring somewhere within it—but he could not yet bring himself to walk openly down the main streets. Instead he crept into the town through the alleys, skirting the denser areas, looking for the back of an inn—he thought that if he presented himself in the stableyard he might be more acceptable than he would be at the front door.

Then, when he had circled almost halfway around the town's heart, he saw a building some three stories in height, of dressed stone trimmed with carved wood and all roofed in tin, with a dozen curtained, well-lit casement windows. A coach stood by the side door, with four horses yoked to it and a driver sitting impatient at the front, clearly waiting for someone who had gone inside. The yard behind the main building held more horses, rather than oxen or mules, and the whole complex was off to one side of the main highway, outside the town itself.

That was surely an inn, and a very respectable one from the look of it. He crept toward it. He did not want the coachman to see him yet, so he circled around toward the other side, and at last emerged between the stable and a woodshed into a muddy yard.

The inn's back door was closed and dark. He frowned, and looked up at the windows.

As he did, a casement on the second floor swung open, the curtains were pulled aside, and a young woman leaned out, flapping one hand as if to drive away an unpleasant odor.

Arlian stared.

Except for a few quick glimpses from a distance over the past few days, he had not seen a woman since he was a boy of eleven. Many times over the years in the mines, as he grew to manhood, he had been very much aware of this lack, but he had been in no position to do anything about it; since his escape he had been too busy, too concerned with other matters, to give it any thought.

Now, though, all those years of deprivation caught up with him at once, and he stared open-mouthed.

The woman's features seemed impossibly delicate to him, her eyes huge and alluring; her dark hair was long and elaborately curled, hanging in graceful curves around her face. Her arms were bare and slender, her skin fair.

And she was naked—or at least, all he could see of her was. Her exposed breasts were plainly visible in the pinkish glow of sunset, the nipples large and dark.

Arlian's breath caught in his throat; his clothes suddenly seemed to constrict, strangling him.

Then she stopped waving and closed her eyes for a moment, tipping her head back and taking a deep breath of the cool outside air. Her hair fell in sliding coils down her back and flowed around her shoulders, shining in the lamplight that spilled out around her, and Arlian swallowed hard. He was feeling sensations he had no name for, things he had never felt before. He took an uncertain step forward.

As he did the woman opened her eyes and looked down into the stableyard. Arlian froze, but it was too late; her gaze locked with his, and her eyes opened wide in surprise.

Arlian stood, rooted by terror and shame and lust, his thoughts buried in a conflicting tangle of fierce, unfamiliar emotions.

For what seemed forever the two of them stared at each other. Then the woman smiled down at him—not just a smile, but a *grin*. She made no move to cover herself; instead she cast a quick glance back over one shoulder, then leaned out farther and beckoned to him.

Arlian took another step forward, then hesitated—what was he doing? Who was this woman, displaying herself so brazenly? Could she really want him to approach? An urge to turn and run began to build—but at the same time he couldn't tear his gaze away from her.

"Come on," she called down to him. "Do you like what you see?"

His mouth opened, but nothing came out. He tried to swallow, but his throat was suddenly too dry. His hands clenched into fists.

She was just a person, another human being. He had spoken fearlessly to women as a child; why should it be a struggle now?

Of course, none of the village women had been naked, and so far as he could recall none of them had been so beautiful.

"I like it," Arlian managed to croak, and he took another step.

"Then can you climb? If you can get to the window I'll let you in, and you can look all you want. You can do *more* than just look!"

Arlian was utterly confused now, but for a moment the desire to get closer to her, and the desire to get out of the cold, completely overcame his shyness and uncertainty; he trotted across the yard and flung himself atop a handy barrel, then jumped for the sill of the open window. His fingers caught the edge, but could not hold, and he slid back down, missed his footing on the barrel, and fell to the ground.

The woman laughed, a musical, watery sound that filled him with a great swelling urgency and a ferocious embarrassment. He leaped to his feet and looked around the yard. He didn't dare look at her; he was certain his face was bright red with shame, and that the tightness of his pants was obvious and offensive.

"I'm sorry," she called from just above and behind him. "I shouldn't laugh. *Can't* you find a way up?"

He turned and looked up at her. He licked his lips, then cleared his throat and tried to speak.

He got a strangled noise out, then had to stop and cough. He looked down to collect his wits, then back up.

"I take it I can't use the door," he said, actually getting the entire sentence out cleanly.

"Oh, no!" she said, her smile vanishing. "Not dressed like that! They'd beat you half to death."

"Ha!" he said, though even then he could not possibly have explained why he would react to such a threat with bravado instead of caution. The possibility that he might be doing something foolish and dangerous occurred to him, but it simply didn't matter; he desperately wanted to get in that window, get at that woman.

At the same time he wanted to run away, but he fought that impulse down. He looked around for something he could use to mount the wall.

Inspired, he ran to the unlocked woodshed and pulled out a good-sized chunk of unsplit firewood, hoisting it up on his shoulder—he realized after he had it up that it was solid oak, or perhaps ironwood, and must have weighed at least fifty pounds, but nonetheless he hauled it across the yard and thumped it down onto the barrelhead, standing it on end. Then he leapt up on the barrel, stepped up onto the log, and thrust himself upward at the window.

This time he was able to get his chest onto the windowsill and his arms through the casement, his fingers clutching at the inner edge of the sill. The woman had moved back at the last possible moment to avoid his lunge, but now she leaned forward and grabbed the back of his stolen shirt, helping him haul himself upward and into the room.

She was not totally naked after all, he saw as he tumbled in, but clad in a lacy white skirt slit up the front, and a golden girdle wrapped around her waist. She was kneeling on a windowseat. An elegant glass and brass lamp on a wall bracket was burning brightly, lighting her face beautifully.

He was lying on a fine parquet floor, looking up at her and at gauzy curtains behind her. The air around him was warm, and thick with a cloying, sweetish smell—and with a confusion of other scents as well, including lamp oil and sweat and several he didn't recognize.

"Where am I?" he asked.

"You're in my room," she said, with an impish, irresistible smile. She settled into a sitting position, her legs tucked underneath, and looked down at him. "Now, who are you? What sort of desperate creature have I just invited in?"

"My name is ... is unimportant," he said, staring hungrily at her, almost in awe of this gorgeous creature. He had caught himself at the last moment; his name would probably mean nothing to her, but he did not want to risk it. Word of an escaped slave named Arlian might well have spread this far.

She was so small, he thought as he stared—smaller than any of the miners, even Rat. He had forgotten that women were so small and delicate looking. And her skin was impossibly smooth and soft, her face and chest utterly hairless.

She laughed at him.

"Ah, then, Unimportant," she said, "welcome to my humble home! Might I call you something shorter, perhaps? Trivial, or Minor?"

"Not Minor," he said. It was too close to terms he did not want to be associated with. He was vaguely aware that he ought to come up with a name for her to use, but he couldn't think clearly enough to suggest one.

"But Trivial is acceptable? Or just Triv?"

"Triv would be fine," he said, as he untangled himself and sat up. He was breathing heavily, and not entirely from the exertion of getting in the window.

He shifted, but his breeches remained uncomfortably tight.

She shifted her own position, as well, and his breath came out in a shudder.

"Tell me about yourself," she said.

"I don't…" he began. Then he asked, "Where am I? Is this an inn?"

"An *inn?*" She laughed again. "Not exactly, no."

Just then he heard a shout from outside, and the rattle of harness—that coach at the side door was leaving. She looked up, and out the casement.

"Did you see any other horses out there, or coaches?" she asked.

"There were horses in the stable."

"How many?"

He blinked uncertainly. "I didn't count."

She frowned slightly. "Did you see any other coaches, though?"

"No," he replied, puzzled.

"Good. Then we should have some time." She swung the casement shut and latched it, and dropped the hooked-up curtain back in place.

Arlian watched her breasts bob as her arms moved, and had to struggle to keep his hands on the floor, rather than in his breeches or on her—though he wasn't sure he would have had the nerve to touch her.

Then she turned back to face him, and swung her legs out, so that she was sitting upright on the windowseat. Arlian saw with a shock she had no feet—both legs ended at the ankle in neat pink stumps.

"Now," she said, "what am I going to do with you? Am I going to get a straight answer out of you?"

"I don't…" Arlian began. Then he stopped and swallowed hard, staring at her.

It was too much. He could no longer find words at all. He was too tangled up in confusion and lust.

She laughed.

"*I* think," she said, "that you're too distracted to tell me anything. And I *also* think that I know how to solve that. If you'd just carry me over to the bed, I'm sure we can take care of the problem." She pointed over his shoulder.

"Bed?" he gasped. He turned, and saw a great pink featherbed atop an oaken frame; a pink silk coverlet lay askew atop it, and pink lace bedcurtains hung from a pink silk canopy. Round silver mirrors were set into each corner of the canopy, angled to face the center of the bed. Another glass-based oil lamp stood on a bedside table amid a clutter of fancy bottles and jars, casting a warm glow across the entire arrangement.

He made a wordless noise.

"Please?" she said, holding out both her delicate arms, palms turned up beseechingly.

He rose unsteadily to his feet, reached hesitantly for her—and then, when he felt her soft skin and saw her welcoming smile, his reservations faded away; he snatched her up in his arms, whirled about, and plunged with her into the waiting bed. Before he had even gotten both his feet off the floor she was untying his breeches.

And then he was lost in an unfamiliar but delightful sea of perfume and flesh and sensation.

Chapter Ten

Sweet

He let his breath out in a long, contented sigh and lay a moment longer, staring at the ceiling. Then he turned to look at her grinning, heart-shaped face as she lay propped on one elbow beside him.

"Where am I?" he said. "Who are you?" He wanted to ask why she had seduced him, as well, but couldn't think of any decent way to phrase it.

"You're in the House of Carnal Society," she told him.

"The *what?*" he asked.

She giggled. "It's a brothel, silly! Hadn't you guessed?"

Arlian looked at her in embarrassed confusion. "What's a brothel?" he asked.

"Oh, my dear…where are you *from?* Well, never mind, you'll tell me that in a moment, I'm sure. A brothel—well, among other things, men come here to pay for what you've just had as a gift."

Comprehension finally burst upon him—he had encountered the concept in conversations in the mines, under a cruder name, but had had no idea how numerous such institutions were, or where they might be found. Certainly there had been none in his home village.

Apparently they did exist here, wherever he was. "Ah!" he said. "And you…"

"I live here," she said. "I'm called Sweet." She grinned and tilted her head entrancingly. "You can judge for yourself whether the name fits."

He smiled back at her. He was warm for the first time in days, and feeling just fine in other ways, though he was still dirty and underfed. "I'd say it does."

"Well, good. Thank you. Now, who are *you,* and how did you get here?"

Arlian hesitated. "I'm from a village on Smoking Mountain," he said.

She looked puzzled. "There's a village on Smoking Mountain?"

"Well, there *was,*" he said. "But dragons destroyed it, and my family was killed."

"Oh, you're from Obsidian?" she exclaimed. "But that was seven years ago, and I thought *everyone* there was killed! Were you away when it happened?"

He shook his head—and his voice shook as well as the memories poured back. He had not spoken of the disaster, or his family, in years—not since Hathet died. Some of the other miners had mocked him whenever he mentioned his past, refusing to believe that he had survived seeing dragons, sometimes refusing even to believe he had ever been free, or knew who his parents had been, and in time, to avoid their mockery, he had stopped speaking of his former life.

But this woman knew about the attack, knew his village's name—and knew it had been seven years.

Seven years in the mines. So he was eighteen, then?

"I hid in a cellar," he said.

"And you *lived?* The dragons didn't find you? How wonderful!"

He looked at her face, at the sincere interest and pleasure he saw there, and realized that Sweet was younger than he had first thought—she was perhaps no older than he, not much more than a girl.

"But how did you get *here?*" she asked. "What have you been doing all this time?"

"I was … I was working in the mines, in Deep Delving," he said. He didn't see any need to mention that his stay there had been involuntary. She might already know that the mines were worked by slaves, but he did not care to be the first to mention it.

"Oh—that's why you're so pale, then, where you aren't burnt?" she asked.

He nodded.

"But you left?"

He nodded again. "And came here," he said.

"To Westguard? But why?"

He shrugged. "It seemed as good a place as any."

"I suppose," she said doubtfully.

"You don't like it here?"

She snorted derisively. "Oh I just *love* my work, of *course!* Catering to every sick whim of any man who can pay the fee…"

"Oh," he said, his warm comfort suddenly vanishing. He sat up and looked at her. "You're not here by choice?"

"Of course not!" she said angrily, pulling away from him. "We're all slaves here; didn't you see that?" She lifted one leg and pointed at the stump of her ankle.

"What happened to it?" he said stupidly, unable to stop himself even as he realized what must have happened.

"They don't want us to run away," she said bitterly. "So they cut our feet off. They couldn't do that if we were free. Now I not only can't get away from the customers, no matter what their demands, I can't run *anywhere*—even if I had somewhere to run to, which I don't. I'm not fit to make my living any way but as I do. *That's* what happened."

"I'm sorry," he said, well aware of the inadequacy of his words. A tight knot had formed in his gut.

How could anyone have deliberately maimed anything as beautiful as this woman? How could anyone do something like that to *anyone?*

"There's no justice in this world," Bloody Hand had said, and here was more proof of his bitter words.

"I'm sorry if I hurt you," Arlian said. "I'll go if you want me to."

"Oh, *you* didn't hurt me," she replied. "You didn't know any better, I guess—though I don't know how anyone could be so naive."

"I just spent the last seven years in a hole in the ground," Arlian said wryly. "I'm sure there are thousands of things you take for granted that I've never heard of."

She nodded. "You were a miner?"

"I was a slave," he said. "Like you. Except if they'd cut our feet off we couldn't have dug the ore, so they just kept us down a hole, where we couldn't see the sun or feel the breeze. More than a score of us."

The words caught in his thoughts for a moment— "see the sun and feel the breeze." The breezes he had felt the last several days had been cold and biting, but he still cherished them.

"You escaped?" Sweet asked.

He nodded.

Enlightenment widened her eyes. "So *that's* why you were out there barefoot in the cold, with no coat!"

He nodded again. "I just got away a few days ago. You're the first person I've talked to since I left the mine."

"You did more than *talk,*" she said, smiling again.

"You're the first woman I've seen since my mother died, seven years ago," he said apologetically.

Her mouth opened in surprise; then she grinned again, and flexed her body. "I hope you like what you see," she said.

"Very much," he said. He reached a hand out to stroke her shoulder; she allowed it, and pressed her cheek against his hand.

"Why did you invite me in?" he asked a moment later.

"A whim," she said. "I wanted a little fresh air—my last customer *reeked,* and splashed perfume everywhere on top of it—and when I opened the window and saw you there, staring at me, it tickled my fancy to invite you in for a closer look. They're so determined that only the paying customers will see us that I like to show myself to anyone I can." She shrugged. "And I was curious—we don't often have dirty, ragged strangers wandering the streets here. The guards don't allow it."

Arlian felt suddenly cold again. "Guards?"

"Well, of course—the lords and ladies post well-paid guards in all the major towns around Manfort, to keep the peace and make sure no one interferes with their investments. You're lucky they didn't catch you."

"Oh," he said, looking at the window—which was tightly closed, a fact he found somewhat comforting.

"Of course, if Mistress or one of the lords finds you in here with me, that might be even worse for you," Sweet said thoughtfully. "Sending you back to the mines would be the *least* they would do. Feet aren't the only thing they've been known to cut off."

"Oh," Arlian said again, and again he glanced at the window—but this time he was considering it as an escape route.

"Oh, don't worry," she said. "I'll hide you. There's a closet, or you could squeeze under the bed. And we can get you cleaned up so you'll pass for a respectable citizen when you go; the guards won't bother you then."

"But why would you … *we?*"

Sweet grinned at him. "Of course, 'we'," she said. "I think the other girls would be very pleased to meet you."

Just then someone knocked on the door.

"Ten minutes!" a woman's voice called.

"Oh, dear," Sweet said. "A customer. Help me straighten things out a bit, would you? Then I'm afraid it's into the closet with you."

Arlian blinked at her. "Are you…"

But Sweet wasn't listening; she was looking around the room.

"It's not bad," she said. "Lord Drisheen wasn't interested in anything but me and the bed and his horrible perfume. Could you straighten those curtains, and give me a hand with the coverlet?"

Arlian hurried to the window to adjust the curtains, still slightly askew from his entry; he turned to find Sweet on her knees atop the pillows, pulling the disarrayed coverlet into place. He hurried to assist her.

"Hand me my jacket, would you?" she said, when the bed was

reasonably straight. She pointed at a little heap of white satin on the carpet by the bed. While Arlian fetched it Sweet took a brush from the bedside table and, with the aid of a handheld mirror, began fixing her hair. The table held an assortment of cosmetics, and between brush strokes Sweet tallied the little bottles. "Kohl, rouge, talc…"

Arlian cleared his throat.

She looked up at him, and for a moment he was overcome by her charm, the delicacy of her face, and could not speak.

"Yes, Triv?" she asked.

"The closet," he said. "I don't want to open the wrong door."

"Oh!" She pointed to a panel upholstered with pink silk. "It's right there. There's a stool, so you won't need to stand; you must be tired."

Arlian started to ask why there was a stool, then thought better of it and hurried to the closet door.

In his past experience, which had been limited to one mountaintop village, "closets" were small, rough storerooms; his family had had none, but the two largest homes in Obsidian had boasted one closet apiece, off the master's chamber. Arlian was rather startled to discover that Sweet's closet was another matter entirely.

It was small, not much more than a cupboard, and made to seem smaller still by the gowns and robes hung on hooks on either side. The rear wall held half a dozen large drawers.

And everything, the walls, the drawers, the inside of the door, even the ceiling, was covered in rich red velvet; the floor was hidden by the smallest, thickest carpet Arlian had ever seen, woven in a floral pattern in a dozen shades of red. Two fine white tapers, unlit but half burned, were mounted in golden sconces on the rear wall, to either side of one of the drawers.

And as Sweet had promised, a stool stood in the center of the tiny room—a stool upholstered, like the walls, in red velvet, its black wooden legs adorned with golden filigree.

Arlian stared, trying to imagine why anyone would waste such appointments in a windowless storage compartment, then remembered himself and stepped inside. He turned to close the door, and stopped dead.

The closet was not entirely windowless after all. The door had a window set into it, a little window completely hidden from the outside by the pink silk covering.

Sweet glanced up just then and noticed his puzzlement.

"Sometimes we have customers who just want to watch," she explained.

"Oh," Arlian said, blinking as he tried to absorb this completely unfamiliar notion. He found it troubling; he settled slowly onto the stool and pulled the door shut.

He found himself looking out through the silk, with a good view of most of the bedroom; Sweet and the bed were in the center of his field of vision. The filtering silk gave everything a pinkish cast, as if seen though a rosy mist, and the pink bedclothes consequently tended to fade into the background while Sweet's pale skin and black hair stood out sharply.

She smiled at him, then tugged her satin jacket into place, gave her hair a final pat, and sat waiting on the bed.

Arlian thought she was heartbreakingly beautiful there, dark curls spilling over her shoulders, wearing only the light jacket, lace skirt, and golden girdle.

And then the door opened and a man stepped in, a man dressed in fine clothes, with rings on his fingers and plumes in his hair; Sweet bowed her head and murmured, "My lord."

The man backhanded her cheek. "I gave you no leave to speak," he said.

Arlian started from his seat at the sound of the blow, but caught himself. He clenched his fists and forced himself to sit back down.

Sweet did not speak again while her customer was there; the customer addressed her only to give curt orders that she hastened to obey.

Arlian watched what followed in sickened amazement—or sometimes could not bear to watch and turned his head aside, eyes tightly closed, trying not to hear the sounds from the bedchamber. He bit his lower lip until it bled to keep himself from shouting out in protest; his fingernails dug into his palms, his knuckles white.

He found himself praying to the dead gods that it would stop. Had Sweet called for help he knew he would have been out of the closet and upon the customer in an instant, even if it meant his capture and execution.

But she did not call out, and eventually it was over. The customer tied his breeches, straightened his velvet jacket, and left without another word.

And Arlian fell out of the closet and staggered to the bedside, desperate to do what he could to comfort Sweet after such abuse. He struggled for words and could find none as he reached out to touch her cheek.

She sat up, startled, and looked at him dry-eyed.

"He hurt you," Arlian said.

"No more than usual," she replied calmly. She picked up the mirror from the bedside table to study the shallow scratches on her face, left by the man's rings. "Mistress isn't going to like that," she said. "She'll probably charge him extra." Then she looked at Arlian and saw the expression on his face.

"Oh, Triv!" she said, "you look so *surprised!* What were you expecting?"

Arlian could see her struggling not to laugh at his stricken appearance. She seemed so utterly untroubled by what she had just been through that he began to doubt his own memory of what he had seen.

"Did you *enjoy* that?" he asked.

She snorted. "Of course not," she said. "If I had, he wouldn't need to pay for it, would he?" She smiled at him. "You poor boy," she said. "You *do* have a lot to learn. I didn't like it at all, but I'm not as delicate as I look."

"So I see," he said, struggling to control the seething tangle of emotions he felt.

She stared at him for a moment, and tears started in her eyes. "You're so *sweet,* to worry about me!" she said. "*You* should be Sweet, and *I* should be Trivial!"

"Never," he said. "You could never be unimportant."

"Oh, you're silly!" she said. She blinked away her tears and gathered herself. When she was composed she said, "We should have a little while now, at the very least, before anyone else comes in, and we may have all night—let's see about getting you cleaned up!"

Chapter Eleven

Rose

There were sixteen slaves in sixteen rooms on the upper floors of the House of Carnal Society; crippled as they were, and kept busy by customers, they ordinarily saw little of one another.

Arlian's presence changed that. On the very first night he was there, long after midnight, after the lanterns by the coach door had been doused, after the lamps in the hallways were out, after the guards had taken their nighttime post and the dreaded Mistress had retired to her ground-floor chamber, Sweet threw her arms around Arlian's neck and had him carry her out into the hallway and up the stairs to the first door on the third floor. "I could walk," she said, "on my knees—that's what I usually do. It's hard work, though, and slow. It's much more fun this way."

They moved slowly in the dark, and Arlian tried to be as quiet as he could; fortunately the stairs were stone, and did not creak. Sweet did not seem to be particularly concerned about maintaining silence, but she wasn't trespassing, and she was valuable property. If they were caught she could claim to have been carried off against her will.

They were not caught; they reached the door Sweet had indicated, and Sweet took one hand from Arlian's shoulder. She knocked, and then knocked again.

The motion unbalanced them, and yielded no reply. Finally, at Sweet's whispered insistence, Arlian took over the task and rapped on the polished wood until a voice from within called, "At *this* hour?"

"It's me, Rose," Sweet called. "Let me in!"

"Sweet? Why?" Rose asked sleepily, but a moment later the door swung open, spilling light.

At first Arlian stared right over Rose's head; after a moment's confusion he remembered that of course Rose would be female and therefore shorter than himself to begin with, and unable to stand because her feet were gone. He looked down and found her kneeling in the doorway—a redhead, a little taller and older and plumper than Sweet, with an oval face and green eyes, wearing a gauzy nightgown. She held a candle.

"Who's this?" Rose asked.

"Rose, this is Triv. Triv, this is Rose, my best friend here and the only person I'm absolutely sure we can trust," Sweet said. "May we come in, Rose?"

"What's he doing here?" Rose demanded, but she moved aside and let Arlian step inside and deposit Sweet on the bed.

Where Sweet's room was decorated in pink silk, Rose's was decorated in dusky red velvet; where Sweet's room held four glass lamps, Rose's had fat candles perched in a dozen places. Arlian took a quick glance around, then asked Rose, "Shall I give you a hand?"

"You're not a customer, are you?" Rose asked, looking up at him. "Nor a guard, dressed like that." She didn't answer his question, but raised her arms toward him, the candle foremost.

Arlian took the hint. He placed the candle on a nearby table, then carried Rose to the bed, setting her beside Sweet—who immediately leaned over and gave Rose a hug.

"It's been so *long* since we had a chance to talk!" Sweet said. "Why did they ever move you up here?"

"What's he doing here?" Rose asked, ignoring Sweet's question. "Is he a friend of yours?"

Arlian decided that more light would be a good idea, and began lighting more candles from the one Rose had provided.

"I was looking out the window, and I saw him in the stableyard," Sweet said. "I invited him to climb up, and he *did!*" She giggled.

Rose turned and eyed Arlian appraisingly. "You know, if they catch you in here you're in serious trouble."

"I'm in serious trouble anyway," Arlian said, looking up from his third candle.

Rose looked questioningly at Sweet.

"He's an escaped slave," Sweet explained. "From the mines in Deep Delving."

Rose frowned. "If anyone asks, he broke in here uninvited, right, Sweet?" she said. "And we poor helpless crippled women couldn't do a thing to stop him."

"Of course!" Sweet agreed, nodding enthusiastically. "Oh, absolutely. We couldn't even scream for help, with the thick walls—no one would hear us. He was unstoppable. And he raped me, too." She giggled again.

Rose threw Arlian a glance. "Did he?"

"More the other way around," Sweet said.

"Not that I minded," Arlian added, as he put a fifth candle back in its place and decided that would do.

"Anyway," Sweet said, getting down to business, "I thought we could clean him up, give him some real clothes, so he won't have to hide all the time."

"We could," Rose admitted.

"And maybe somehow I can help you, in exchange," Arlian said, setting down the candle he had started with.

Rose snorted. "Help us?" she asked. "Help us *how?* Unless you're a wizard who can grow us new feet, what can you do?" She shook her head. "No, we'll be here until we're too old to please the customers, and then we're dog food."

Sweet bit her lower lip. "Don't say that," she said.

Arlian stared at the two women. "Dog food? You don't mean that *literally,* do you?" he asked.

"I don't want to think about it," Sweet said, clapping her hands over her ears.

"It's one possibility," Rose told him.

Arlian stood staring stupidly at her, unable to think of anything he could say to such an outrage. For a few seconds no one spoke.

Then Sweet recovered herself and said, "Let's start with his hair."

Rose hesitated. "Sweet," she said, "letting him in here is one thing. We can say he forced us. But fixing his hair? What if someone finds us?"

"Then we'll be dog food that much sooner," Sweet said. "What's the difference, if that's how we'll wind up anyway? Come on, it'll be fun!"

Rose frowned at Arlian.

"Why would anyone check on us?" Sweet asked cajolingly. "They never do—that's the whole point of cutting our feet off! The guards only watch for people breaking in, they don't see what we do in here."

"Mistress does."

"She's asleep downstairs! And Triv's here, and we can't just send him out into the cold the way he is! If we hear someone coming he'll hide."

"Where?"

"Wherever you like. Under the bed, in the closet…"

"In the attic?"

Sweet blinked. "There's an attic?"

Rose pointed at a panel in the ceiling of her room, its edges hidden by gilt trim. "That lifts up," she said. "Mistress was thinking of putting in a peephole, but decided against it." She looked at Arlian. "Think you can get up there?"

"I think so," he said, gauging the height of the ceiling carefully. "If I have something to stand on. That chair would do." He pointed.

"Well, put the chair where you need it, just in case," Rose said.

Arlian nodded and moved the chair; while he did the two women whispered together. When he was satisfied with the chair's location he turned back to them.

"Come on," Sweet said. "We're going to fix you up. When we're done you'll be the most beautiful man in Westguard!"

"At least," Rose agreed. "Give me a hand, would you?"

Rose, Arlian discovered, did not have the same small bedside table Sweet did; instead one corner of her room was equipped with a vanity table, two stools, three mirrors, and a huge quantity of cosmetics, as well as a pair of brass lamps to provide steadier illumination than candles could. Arlian set one woman on each stool, then knelt between them.

Rose untied his scrap of leather and began vigorously brushing out his tangled hair; Sweet was more direct and snatched up a pair of scissors.

"I liked the way Lord Inthior wore his, didn't you?" she asked.

Rose looked up from Arlian's tangled curls and frowned. "You mean swept back in the center and cut short on the sides? I don't know…" She studied Arlian, took his chin in her hand and tilted his face up.

Arlian had no idea what they were talking about, of course. He had never heard of any Lord Inthior, and had little concept of hairstyling. He was hardly inclined to resist, though; being alone here with two beautiful women, in these warm and perfumed chambers, was so wonderful he could scarcely believe it was really happening. If he just had something to eat, and no concerns about discovery, he thought this would be complete perfection.

Rose turned his head and he found himself staring up into her intense green eyes.

She was beautiful, no question, but he found himself looking critically at her face, noting all the tiny ways in which Sweet's was preferable.

Then Rose smiled at him. "Inthior's style it is," she said. "I think you'll like it, Triv." She turned to the table and found a metal comb, which she handed to Sweet.

Sweet had already started clipping at Arlian's dangling locks, but she accepted the comb and began tugging it through the tangles. Rose, meanwhile, found another comb and scissors and attacked Arlian's beard.

In time Rose traded her scissors for assorted cloths and powders and began cleaning Arlian's face, while Sweet continued working on his hair. It took an hour, and much fussing and fraying of tempers, before the two women declared themselves satisfied and sat back.

"Take a look," Rose said, gesturing at the biggest of the three mirrors.

Arlian looked.

The face that confronted him was one he could hardly credit as his own. His beard had been trimmed, shaped, and slicked down with some unfamiliar waxy substance, and was now reduced from the chest-covering chaos he had seen reflected in windows and ponds to a short, almost triangular affair that reached a graceful point just an inch or two below his chin. His hair had been cut away and swept back from his forehead, leaving a point at the center of his forehead that seemed to echo the beard, and showing bare skin at either temple. Dark curls wrapped neatly around his ears. Wax and powder had concealed his sunburn, and his complexion was now unnaturally smooth and clear.

And the face thus adorned was straight and strong, with clear dark eyes and firm, full lips surrounding a long and elegant nose—a nose like Grandsir's—eyes like his father's, and his mother's mouth.

The result was nothing like the face of the village boy he remembered; he looked instead like an aristocrat.

"That's amazing," he said.

Sweet leaned over and kissed him on the now exposed temple. Rose just smiled.

"Now," Rose said, "I think it's time to get some sleep before they wake us for breakfast."

"Should I go, then?" Arlian asked, gesturing at the window.

"Must you?" Sweet asked.

Arlian hesitated. "I don't want to be caught," he said.

"Then you don't want to leave yet," Sweet said. "If you go walking the streets with a lord's head above a farmer's best shirt and that filthy pair of workman's breeches and your own bare feet, the guards will be very curious about who you are and what you're doing in Westguard." She pointed at the attic and asked Rose, "He can sleep up there, can't he?"

"Go ahead," Rose said resignedly.

Sweet smiled. "And tomorrow we'll see about fixing you up *below* the neck!"

Arlian smiled back at her.

This was wonderful, being here; the tin-roofed attic would surely be at least as comfortable as the barns and sheds he had been sleeping in, and the risk of discovery would be less. These women were providing him with what amounted to a perfect disguise—no slave-catcher searching for an escaped miner would bother a man with his hair trimmed and oiled and his face powdered.

And being around women was a pleasure he had never before experienced—just enjoying their company, quite aside from Sweet's unorthodox welcome. That welcome, of course, was another, and much more intense, pleasure he had never known until tonight.

If only he had something to eat … but surely Sweet would think of that in the morning, and they would manage something. Maybe he could slip out long enough to find something, then return.

Or if necessary he could simply wait until his disguise was complete. He was hungry, but not starving.

"Go on, then," Rose said. "Take Sweet back to her room, and then get up there."

Arlian, perhaps inspired to extra courtesies by the lordly image he saw in the mirrors, rose gracefully and essayed a bow. Then he picked Sweet up.

"He's a strong one, isn't he?" Rose remarked, upon seeing how easily Arlian lifted her friend.

"Seven years hauling ore," Arlian explained as he held Sweet in one arm and opened the door with the other.

A moment later he had deposited Sweet back in her own bed; then he turned away and hurried back up the stairs.

In his last glimpse of Sweet's face he had thought she looked somehow disappointed, but he couldn't think why she would be—perhaps she'd noticed some flaw in his appearance? He didn't dare take the time to think about it, though; he wanted to get safely into hiding in the attic.

He had left Rose's door open; now he strode briskly in, closed it behind him, climbed up on the chair, and lifted the attic trap.

A jump, and his elbows caught the edges of the opening; then he hauled himself up, trying not to kick anything as he did. At last he tumbled into the attic.

It was dark, and much cooler than the room below, but still nowhere near as cold as the outside world. Immense beams ran across it, dividing it into bands; he lowered himself carefully into one of these troughs and found himself on rough planking. He could see nothing of what he sat upon, as the faint light that leaked up through the open trap did not reach that far, but a brief exploration with his hands found what seemed to be solid wood—and also a band of stone, presumably the top of the wall between Rose's room and the corridor.

"Close it!" Rose called.

Arlian started, then hastened to obey, lowering the trapdoor back into place, closing himself in and shutting out the light.

That done, he sat alone in cool, silent darkness.

He feared that his concealment might not be perfect; if he stepped on the wrong board it might sag visibly below, or even break, sending him tumbling through someone's ceiling. The beams, wide as they were, were not so wide that he could lie down upon one to sleep. Accordingly, he settled onto that band of stone, bracing himself against the beams on either side. He lay there, intending to review his situation and make plans for the future.

But then, despite the cold and the dark and his awkward position, exhaustion overcame him and he fell asleep.

Chapter Twelve

Decisions

Arlian awoke in utter darkness, and for a moment thought he was back in the mines, that his escape had all been a dream. Then he shivered with the cold, and knew he was outside—the mines were never so chilly. He reached out and touched wood instead of stone, the rough wood of a heavy beam, and remembered where he was. He raised a hand to his head and felt his neatly cut hair, then stroked his short-trimmed beard.

The events of the previous night had been real, then. He was hidden in the attic of a whorehouse.

He winced at the word, one he had learned in the mines; it was so harsh! And he couldn't bring himself to think of Sweet or Rose as "whores." It was unquestionably an accurate description, but it simply didn't seem right. Sweet's own word, "brothel," was not much better.

He sat up, and found that the windowless attic's darkness was not absolute; faint sunlight seeped in through the eaves, enough to make out dimly the massive beams, the sloping rafters overhead—and not much else.

He couldn't guess at the time; the trace of light was far too diffuse to show him the sun's angle. He hesitated, trying to think what he should do.

He was hungry—hungry and *thirsty*—but where could he find food or water? He frowned.

Food could wait, he told himself, but he needed water soon.

And a chamberpot or privy would be welcome, too. He didn't dare simply use a corner of the attic; it might seep through, and even if no one found that suspicious it might send someone up for a look at the roof.

He could scarcely just open the trap and drop down, though; what if Rose were with a customer?

He clambered cautiously over the intervening beam, knelt, ran his fingers along the boards until he found the edges of the trap door, then put his ear to the wood and listened.

He heard voices—one he thought was Rose, but he didn't recognize the other.

Whoever it was, Arlian knew he would have to wait. He sighed and sat up on the beam.

He remembered that before going to sleep he had intended to make some plans, but had dozed off; well, now he was awake, and not going anywhere. It was time to give some serious thought to his future.

He was free of the mines; if the women carried through on their plans to dress him, once his disguise was complete no one would ever recognize elegant young Triv as the escaped slave Arlian. Escape, his first goal, was largely accomplished. He need merely cooperate with Sweet and Rose and avoid being spotted by the brothel's guards or the dreaded Mistress, and he would be free to move on wherever he chose.

Ensuring his continued survival had to be his next priority; he needed food and water, and some way to earn a living. He was a healthy young man, big and strong—surely he could find work.

That would require some thought, though. Perhaps the women would have some useful suggestions.

And his third goal was justice—vengeance for the murder of his family and the destruction of his village, vengeance for the looting of the ruins and his own enslavement.

And the mine—was that just? Was it right that a score of men led such a miserable existence as that he had fled? Was it right that Lampspiller and Bloody Hand had power over them?

His thoughtful frown deepened. There were undoubtedly many injustices in the world; he could scarcely hope to end them all.

But surely, he had to do what he could. As he had told Bloody Hand, people could make their own justice, and he was obliged to at least try.

Below him even now, he realized, was a massive injustice; what could Sweet or Rose or the others possibly have done to deserve being crippled? Did they really face the possibility of someday, when they ceased to be profitable, being murdered and fed to the dogs?

That couldn't be allowed. He would have to find some way to prevent it.

But how? And how could he find the looters, or the dragons? How could he destroy the dragons? He was just a man—scarcely more than a boy. He knew little of the world; obsidian carvers and silver miners had no need to know of much beyond their own limited surroundings. He had no weapons, and no money; even his clothes weren't fit to be seen on the streets.

He had his little bag of keepsakes, but that was all—a few scraps of fabric, a crude necklace, and a handful of pretty stones. What sort of justice could that buy?

Hathet's stones … might they really be worth something, beyond the Borderlands in far-off Arithei?

Was Hathet really even *from* Arithei? Did Arithei even exist?

If it did and Hathet was genuinely Aritheian, Hathet might have family there, people who had been wondering all these years what had become of him. Perhaps they would appreciate word of their lost kin.

Arlian swallowed, wishing his throat weren't quite so dry—and that his bladder weren't quite so full.

He had intended to go to Manfort, in part to track down and confront Lord Dragon—for surely, even if Lord Dragon did not live in Manfort, most of the great lords and ladies did, and they might know who dared to use the name "Dragon."

Now, though, Arlian had second thoughts. He was just a youth, with no friends, no family, no funds—how could he hope to destroy a lord, a man who could casually buy and sell men and women? He remembered what that man had done to Sweet the night before, and how Sweet had not dared to resist or even speak, and how he had simply watched, not daring to act. He was not ready to fight such men. Perhaps he should go seeking Arithei to find Hathet's family …

Or perhaps he was afraid.

He bit his lip. Was that it? Was this simply cowardice?

All those years in the mines he had dreamed of the day when he would be free, and could confront Lord Dragon and strike him down. In the few days since his escape, though, he had learned a little more of the ways of the world, and of himself—he had not even dared confront ordinary farmers. Even now he was hiding in an attic, lest he be seen by mere guards.

He had told himself that because right was on his side, in the long run he could not fail—but was that true? Perhaps justice must triumph in the end, as he very much wanted to believe despite all he had seen and heard, but need he live to see it? Had Fate, or the gods, told him so?

If he were to head to Manfort and march boldly into Lord Dragon's home, did he really think that he would be able to kill Lord Dragon? Wasn't it more likely that Dragon would run him through with the sword he carried? Or simply laugh, and call a dozen guards, who would deal with this intruder?

And that assumed he could even *find* Lord Dragon's front door.

But his memory of the looters pawing through the wreckage of his home, the memory of being hauled to Deep Delving and sold as if he were a bolt of cloth, would not allow him to give up the idea. He *must* avenge himself somehow!

He would need to work at it, to find some way other than simply walking in the front door.

He needed to know more about Lord Dragon. He needed to know more about Manfort. He needed to know more about everything.

And the women here might know a few things. They might know of Lord Dragon; he might even be a regular customer. He would, at the very least, want to ask them a few questions before he left and went on his way toward Manfort.

And he might want more than that, if the women could provide it. There were many things he needed to learn about the outside world.

Just then he heard a voice call, "Triv? Are you awake?"

"Rose?" he called back quietly.

"It's clear!" Rose replied.

Arlian hastened to dig his fingernails into the crack around the hatch and lift the trap open; then he lowered himself down until he hung from his hands, and let himself drop the last foot or two.

Then he looked up at the black square, and hurriedly fetched the chair, climbed up on it, and slid the door back into place.

Then he turned to Rose, who was sitting up in her bed, eating breakfast from a tray on the bedside table. The room was dim, lit only by what light filtered through the drawn curtains, but otherwise just as he remembered it. He stepped to the bedside.

"Care to join me?" she asked.

"In a moment," he said; he felt along the side of the space under the bed with his toes, and found a chamberpot. Then he stood awkwardly for a moment, looking at Rose.

She looked at his face, then down. Then she pointedly turned her back.

"I won't look," she said.

She didn't, and a moment later, when the chamberpot was safely stowed away again, he was nibbling a sweet roll and drinking cider, sharing Rose's cup.

The food was excellent, but there wasn't much of it. Rose noticed Arlian gazing hungrily at the empty plate and said, "They don't want us to get fat; most of the customers like their women rounded, but not fat."

"Oh," Arlian said.

"We probably eat better than most slaves," Rose said. "Maybe Sweet has more."

Arlian was at a loss for how to reply to this until Rose added, "Why don't you go see? Careful going out in the hall, though—make sure no one's collecting the trays yet."

Arlian nodded. He crossed to the door, opened it a crack, and peered out.

The hallway appeared deserted. He slipped out, crept down the stairs and along the corridor to Sweet's door, and knocked.

"Come in!" she called.

Like Rose, she had saved a portion of her breakfast for him; between bites he thanked her for her thoughtfulness.

"Oh, don't be silly," she said, reaching up to pluck a cobweb from his hair. "Look at this! You've gone and messed up all our work. We'll have to teach you to take better care of yourself!"

"I'd like that," he said. "Perhaps there are other things you can teach me, as well."

"I'm sure there are," she said, putting her hand in his lap and leaning her face toward his; he started, scattering crumbs across the bedside table.

She giggled, and slid her hand in the waistband of his breeches. "I told them I wasn't feeling well," she said. "Unless someone asks for me specifically and won't take no for an answer, we should have at least an hour. And you've *already* mussed your hair."

Half an hour later, as they lay side by side on her bed, he remembered himself enough to ask, "Have you ever heard of someone named Lord Dragon?"

"Not by that name," she said, running a finger across his chest. "Why?"

"I need to kill him," Arlian told her.

Sweet propped herself up on one elbow and stared at him. "Could you explain that, please?"

Arlian explained; in fact, once he began talking he found it hard to stop, and he poured out everything—his happy childhood on Smoking Mountain, the long, hot months of dragon weather and their horrific end, his discovery by the looters, his years in the mine, his long conversations with Hathet, his rescue of Bloody Hand and the overseer's repayment, his dreams of vengeance and justice.

It took more than half an hour, but Sweet made no move to stop him; she listened intently to all of it.

He ran through all of it, his life story to date, then began to fill in bits he had skimmed over at first. When he described lying trapped under Grandsir's corpse, Sweet shuddered and asked, "You swallowed his blood?"

"I choked on it," Arlian answered.

"Was there venom in it? They say dragon venom is powerful magic."

"What kind of magic?" he asked. For years, he had tried not to think about that horrible moment; now he suddenly tried to recall every detail.

And he remembered what Grandsir had told him, that human blood and dragon venom were supposed to bestow long life. Did that mean that he could expect to live a century or more? Somehow, in seven years in the mines, he had never really given the matter much thought—time and age didn't seem important down there in the dark.

Sweet shrugged. "I don't know," she said. "We hear stories about dragons sometimes, though—some of the lords like to talk, and sometimes they talk about the dragons. They seem to admire them." She shuddered again. "What does *that* say about them, that they admire monsters?"

And what did it say about Lord Dragon, Arlian thought, that he had taken his very name from a monster?

And what did it say about him that his face was so hideously scarred? That was no clean cut left by a sword stroke, nor the marks left by pox.

"Have any of your customers here had a scarred right cheek?" he asked. Perhaps Sweet knew Lord Dragon by another name.

She laughed, a high, sweet sound. "Oh, *dozens* of them are scarred!" she said. "At least one in ten, perhaps one in five. And the right cheek is as common a place as any."

"Oh," Arlian said, disappointed and confused. Several of the men in his home village had been scarred, but most commonly on the hands or legs or chest, rather than the face.

"I'm sorry I don't know who your Lord Dragon is, Triv," she said. "But we'll fix you up, and teach you everything we can, so that when you go looking for him you'll have a better chance."

"Thank you," Arlian replied. "I wish there were some way I could repay you."

She waved that away. "Just knowing there's someone out there trying to right some wrongs is enough for *me*," she said.

"I'll do my best, then." He sat up and looked at his clothes, lying bunched up at the foot of the bed. "What were you planning to do with those, wash them? I don't know if those breeches will ever come clean…"

"Those?" Sweet kicked at them with the stump of an ankle. "We'll give those to the first beggar who asks, and make you some *real* clothes!"

Arlian blinked, startled. "*Make* me clothes? Today?" It took more than a day to make a decent suit of clothes.

She laughed. "No, not today, silly!"

"But I thought I'd leave today or tonight…" Arlian began, puzzled.

"Have you looked out a window?" Sweet asked, grinning.

Arlian looked at her playful expression, then got up wordlessly and crossed to the window, where he pulled back the curtains to reveal a dim world of gray and white—gray skies, drifting white flakes, and white ground.

He blinked and stared. "It's snowing," he said stupidly.

"So Eahor told me," she said. "When he brought my tray. I made him open the curtains so I could see."

"But I could still go," Arlian said.

"You'd freeze," Sweet said. "And more importantly, you'd leave tracks, and tracks go both ways. You are *not* going to leave a trail back to my window, Lord Trivial! I'm in no hurry to meet those dogs Rose mentioned."

"You want me stay until the snow melts? But that might be days!"

"It might be until spring," Sweet said, smiling wickedly. "And that wouldn't bother me at all."

Arlian turned to stare at her. "You think you can hide me here until spring?"

"I think it will be fun to try!" Sweet told him.

Book 2:

Triv

Chapter Thirteen

Departure

Arlian fluffed his pillow, settled down onto his bedding, then blew out his lamp. He groped for his coverlet in the dark, started to pull it up, then hesitated.

The attic was warm tonight, almost uncomfortably so; he didn't need the coverlet. He left it folded at his feet.

He might never unfold it again. This was to be his last night here in the brothel's attic. The snows had finally melted, and he had been planning his departure for several days now, discussing possible destinations with Sweet and Rose and the others—he had been introduced to all fourteen of the other whores in the House of Carnal Society, one by one, over the course of the winter, and all of them had heard his story and made suggestions about what he should do with himself after he left.

After considering and discarding several other possibilities, from Arithei to the Eastern Isles, just about everyone had finally agreed that he should go to Manfort, at least at first. The great city was less than a full day's travel to the east.

Arlian intended to set out the next day and head in that direction.

Sweet was still trying to talk him out of leaving so soon, claiming that footprints in the mud would be just as bad as footprints in the snow and that there was still too much he didn't know, but Arlian was resolved; he couldn't stay here, the pampered pet of a dozen or so whores, forever. He needed to make his own way in the world—and to avenge the injustices visited upon him and his family.

Besides, Mistress, the dreaded manager of the House, had almost caught him the other day. He had barely gotten the closet door closed when she had marched in with the guards behind her and begun upbraiding Sweet for being too openly unenthusiastic about Lord Jerial's fancies.

Arlian had seen the marks Lord Jerial had left; he had had to fight down the urge, unarmed as he was, to leap out and defend Sweet.

Sooner or later, if he stayed, either someone would discover him accidentally, or he would give in to one of his impulses to confront those who abused the occupants of the House of Carnal Society. In either case, he was likely to be killed without accomplishing anything.

In the morning he would leave; he would slip out a window and be gone, bound for Manfort. It shouldn't be too difficult for a charming, well-dressed, well-muscled young man to make his way there. The girls had spent the winter making his wardrobe, teaching him etiquette, explaining everything they knew of human nature, training him out of his rural accent, and educating him in many other ways, as well, in preparation for whatever he might encounter in his search for revenge on Lord Dragon.

His strength had been built up by years in the mines, and he had kept his arms and back strong by carrying the poor crippled women hither and yon; he had not let himself go soft despite the luxury of his surroundings.

Even his attic was luxurious now; obtaining bedding that was deemed too stained to remain in use downstairs had been easy, and his lamp was dented and had therefore been discarded, but was still entirely serviceable. He would bundle it all up and bring it with him, one more small addition to his fortune.

He had a few other additions, as well. Occasionally the whores were given coins or other tokens by their customers, and Sweet, Rose and Hasty had collected a modest sum and bestowed it upon him—as prisoners here, they had nothing they cared to spend money on.

Furthermore, Rose had taken him aside one night and whispered a secret to him.

"Sometimes our customers tell us things," she said. "Many of them come here drunk, after all, and then when they've had their fill of us they're often relaxed and careless." She added bitterly, "And after all, what harm can it do to tell *us?* We're trapped here."

"I understand," Arlian said soothingly.

"Well, one night when Lord Kuruvan was exceptionally drunk and sentimental, he told me he was one of the owners of this place—one of *my* owners—and that if anything ever went wrong, he'd come and get me, and we could flee into exile together. And he said he had money hidden away, so that we could live in luxury even then. And he told me where it is."

Arlian looked at her warily. "I'm not a thief," he said.

"*I* earned that money for him, Triv," Rose said fiercely. "I, and the others here. *He* never lifted a finger for it. And if we can't have it, then I'd rather *you* did."

"*I'd* rather that *you* did," Arlian replied. "After all, as you say, you earned it, not I."

"But I'll never be able to get it, Triv, and someday you might."

Arlian frowned thoughtfully.

"You do what you think is right, Triv," she said. "You always do."

"No," he said, "or I would have left long ago. I owe you all more than I can repay."

"Well, you can repay *me* by taking that money Lord Kuruvan hid!" she said. "He'll probably never even know it's gone. It's in a keg marked 'sour wine' in the northeast corner of the cellars under an inn called the Blood of the Grape, on the road to Manfort."

"I'll remember," Arlian had told her.

He still hadn't decided whether or not he would actually try to find Lord Kuruvan's little cache; he was already so far in Rose's debt that he quite literally saw no way he could ever repay her, and that troubled him. Still, she wanted him to find it …

Well, he would decide once he saw how he fared in the outside world. The money, if it was there at all, had stayed hidden for years; it could wait awhile longer.

With or without that cache, he was ready to move on, but he knew he would miss the women here, all of them—beautiful Sweet with her joyful laughter, practical, motherly Rose, Daub the amateur portraitist who was constantly studying his face, poor bewildered Hasty, moody Sparkle … all of them.

Sweet most of all, of course. The thought of leaving her here, not seeing her again, was painful—his heart ached every time he looked at her and remembered that they would be parting. He hoped he could come back for her someday—but still, he had to go. There were things he had to do if he was to live with himself.

He lay back on the downy bedding, ready for sleep—when a thump and a bang sounded from below, and he snapped his eyes wide, suddenly alert.

He heard Rose complaining sleepily, though he couldn't make out the words through the ceiling and closed trap door; then he heard Mistress's harsh bellow.

"… been hiding someone! At first I thought I was imagining it, but the more I thought about it—bedding is missing, and you've been using up fabric without new gowns to show for it, and food's cost more this winter than it should. So it's been going on for months! And you haven't been sneaking him in and out—I've changed the guards, and there weren't any tracks. So you've been hiding him, but I couldn't think *where* he could be—until ten minutes ago I remembered the attic…"

By the time she got this far in her speech Arlian was squatting on one of the beams, all his belongings gathered into a hasty bundle. He wrapped them in a small roll of canvas Daub had provided out of her painting supplies, and bound them with a pair of leather belts as he considered his options.

"I know he's up there," Mistress shouted. "Is he armed? Tell me!"

Arlian could not make out the words of Rose's reply—unlike Mistress, Rose was not yelling—but he could tell from her tone that she was feigning innocence.

Mistress undoubtedly had at least two of her guards with her. He might be able to surprise them, and in the mines he had learned something about brawling, but they would have swords and know how to use them, and there might be more than two. The brothel employed six at various times, and for something like this Mistress would have summoned all of them.

He would have no chance of defeating six armed men, and even escaping them seemed unlikely.

He could surrender—and be put to death. Even if he was never identified as an escaped slave, he was a thief and a trespasser.

That wouldn't do.

There was a third alternative, however. If he avoided the guards entirely, went *around* them, he might well be able to flee with his skin intact. And he had an idea how he might accomplish that. He rose—not to his full height, which would have slammed his head into the rafters overhead, but to a crouch—and began to move quickly away from the trap door.

Rose was still protesting, but Arlian didn't listen. He was searching.

During the long winter he had spent many long hours, both day and night, hidden away in this attic. He had, simply out of boredom, explored it thoroughly. The walls were solid stone; the roof was good tin over heavy planking; there were no windows. The only vents were under the eaves, and quite aside from the thirty-foot drop they were far too small for him to squeeze through.

The floor, however, had weak spots; it had never been intended as a floor at all, but merely as a ceiling for the rooms below. Arlian had noted them only to avoid them, for fear of detection, but now he deliberately sought out a board that was half eaten by ants and rot. Apparently the roof about it had leaked at one time, and the moisture had done its work. The roof had been repaired; the damaged ceiling had not.

He stepped from beam to beam in the dark, moving by feel and memory, until he knew he had reached the right area. He heard the muffled sound of a blow, and knew someone had struck Rose, knocking her against something; his mouth tightened, but he did not stop. He moved along the beam, pressing his foot on the boards below until he found the rotted one. It was low under the sloping rafters, just where Arlian had remembered.

Mistress was shouting again, but he was far enough away now that he couldn't hear her words.

The trap door flew open and rattled against the beams, and light fountained up. A guard's head appeared, lit from below, scanning the attic. Arlian set both feet on the rotten board, braced his back against the roof and pushed.

The ceiling crumbled beneath him, and he plunged through feet-first, the jagged broken ends of the boards tearing at his clothes and his bundled belongings. His right elbow slammed painfully onto still-solid wood, and he flung his arm upward to free himself, dropping farther into the unlit room below.

Someone screamed, a loud, high shriek of terror.

Arlian's plummeting feet struck the edge of something soft, something he couldn't see in the darkness, and slid off to one side, throwing him off balance; he sprawled sideways, tumbling onto the floor in a tangle.

He rolled free of whatever he had struck and clambered to his feet, still clutching his bundle.

The room's occupant screamed again.

"Hush!" Arlian called. "Where's the door?"

Even as he asked he thought better of it. The moon was up, and the curtained window was faintly visible, a square of dim gray light in the blackness.

"Triv?" a voice asked wonderingly.

Arlian did not bother answering; instead he ran full-tilt for the window, knocking aside a table that happened to be in his path.

He recognized the voice as Sparkle's and now realized that when he fell he had landed on the side of her bed and slid off onto the floor, but he had no time to worry about such things. He could already hear heavy footsteps in the corridor outside her door.

Sparkle's room was at the far end of the corridor from Rose's and faced the street, rather than the stableyard; that was good.

He didn't bother opening the casement; he slammed against it with his bundle held in both fists, and the glass and lead shattered. He shoved the bundle through the opening and dropped it, then climbed up on the windowseat and turned around.

Fists were pounding on the door of Sparkle's room, and he could hear crunching in the attic overhead. He took hold of the windowsill and began lowering himself.

"Good-bye," he called to Sparkle—after all, it could do no harm at this point. "Give the others my love." Then he was hanging by his fingers, his arms stretched to their full length, as far down as he could climb.

He pushed off with his feet and let go.

The fall seemed eternal, though he knew it was probably only a fraction of a second; then he slammed onto the mud of the street, flat on his back.

He lay dazed and aching for a moment, the breath knocked out of him; then he blinked and saw a dark shape leaning out of the now lit square of Sparkle's window.

He forced himself to move; he rolled over onto his knees, groping for his bundle. He found it, grabbed it, and pushed himself to his feet.

His back hurt, and one knee didn't seem to want to work properly, but he staggered on, choosing his direction at random.

The cool night breeze smelled of fresh soil and woodsmoke. The mud was cold between his toes, and he realized for the first time that his feet were bare—but that was hardly surprising; after all, he had been preparing for bed, not for flight. He had a pair of velvet slippers in his bundle—the women had been unable to manage boots—but he was not about to take the time to put them on.

Behind him lights were appearing in several of the brothel's windows, and he heard several voices shouting; he struggled to pick up his pace.

Before him the moonlight showed him the late-night streets of Westguard—shops and houses, porches and wooden sidewalks, and streets of dirt and mud, the only color anywhere the yellow lamplight in a few windows. The town looked lifeless and empty.

The town's hired guards were probably making their rounds, though, and he needed to avoid them. If Mistress decided to make enough of a fuss even the sheds and stables he had used before wouldn't be safe. He had to find somewhere they wouldn't look at all—or some way to keep them from recognizing him when they saw him.

And that might not be too difficult to manage, he realized a hundred yards farther down the street, as he caught sight of a signboard depicting a man leaning heavily on a staff. His pursuers hadn't seen him clearly, if at all; they would probably expect him to look like a vagabond, as he had when he arrived.

Sweet and Rose and the others had spent months making him look instead like a young lord, and he could capitalize on that. He limped up to the closed door below the sign and began pounding on it.

"Ho, landlord!" he bellowed.

The windows were dark, and the door was locked, but there could be little question that the place was an inn—probably the Weary Traveler, which he had heard mentioned a few times.

An upstairs window opened, and a face appeared—but at the same time Arlian heard the jingle of armor and the crunch of boot steps. Fortunately, it came from the right; the House of Carnal Society was to the left. This was simply a guard making the rounds; Arlian ignored the sound and looked up.

"Ho, there!" he called, doing his best imitation of the lordly manners he had observed at the House of Carnal Society. "I know it's late, my good man, but my blasted horse threw me—have you a meal and a bed?" He glanced at the approaching guardsman, but did his best to appear completely casual, as if he knew he could not possibly have anything to fear from a mere guard.

The innkeeper glared down at him. "At *this* hour?"

"Well, it wouldn't have *been* this hour if the confounded beast hadn't run off!" Arlian shouted back, exasperated. "I've been walking for *hours*—barefoot, since one boot caught in the bloody stirrup—will you *look* at the mess it's made of me? Surely you won't turn me out like this!"

The innkeeper still hesitated. The guardsman had come up behind Arlian and was listening closely—though he was distracted by a commotion up the street, in the vicinity of the House of Carnal Society. Arlian turned to him and asked, "He's an innkeeper, isn't he? Doesn't he have to let me in if I ask?"

"That's up to him, sir," the guardsman said.

Arlian glared at him, a glare Rose had had him practice for hours. *"Sir?"* he said.

"My lord," the guard corrected quickly.

Arlian nodded his approval and looked up at the innkeeper. "I'll pay a little extra, if you like," he said.

"Then your funds weren't all on your horse?" the innkeeper asked. "I won't give credit."

"Do I look like a complete fool?" Arlian demanded. Then he held up a hand. "No, don't answer that—I don't want to know what I look like at this point! Yes, I have good coin, if your prices aren't utterly savage."

The innkeeper hesitated for another second or so, then gave in. "I'll be right down," he called.

"Good," Arlian said, as the window closed. Then he turned back toward the brothel, as if just now noticing the noise. Two of the brothel's guards were approaching at a trot.

"Whatever is going on there?" he asked the town guardsman.

"I don't know, my lord," the guard replied.

"Does it have anything to do with that ragged fellow who went running past a few minutes ago?"

The guard was suddenly alert. "What fellow, my lord?"

"How in the name of the dead gods should I know who he was?" Arlian said. "He was a young man in dreadful torn clothes who went running that way." He pointed away from the House of Carnal Society. "His nose was bleeding quite spectacularly. Do you suppose those two are looking for him?"

"I don't know, my lord; they might be."

"Well, why don't you go ask them and see? I'd like to know."

"Yes, my lord," the guard said. He trotted obediently off.

That, Arlian thought, would keep the brothel guards busy for a moment, explaining the situation to their compatriot, and it should give him time to get safely inside the inn.

None of his pursuers had gotten a good look at him, he was certain, and he hoped the women would have the sense to lie about his appearance; his best chance, he was sure, was simply to insist that he was what he claimed to be and had no connection with the intruder in the brothel.

Maintaining his imposture as a rash young lord would not be easy; for all he knew he had already made half a dozen slips. Still, he could not think of any better ruse.

The door of the inn opened, and the scent of stale beer wafted out. Arlian slipped quickly inside.

Chapter Fourteen

Deceptions

Arlian tensed as the inn's door opened again and the town guardsman stepped in. He quickly forced himself to relax, to appear calm, as he took another bite of the slightly stale bread the innkeeper had provided.

His bundle lay at his feet; he had had to open it to pay the landlord in advance, and the price of a bed and a meal had almost exhausted the money Sweet, Rose, and Hasty had given him. The meal before him was simply bread, cheese, a few dried plums, and a flagon of ale—the innkeeper insisted nothing else could be had at this hour, and Arlian had not argued beyond the minimum he felt necessary to stay in character, for fear of wiping out his funds completely if the innkeeper did find something better. He chewed slowly and picked up the ale as the guardsman approached, with a half-formed idea that if necessary he could fling the beer in the man's face and make a run for it.

"My lord," the guard said. "You wanted to know the cause of the disturbance."

Arlian swallowed the bread and washed it down with a mouthful of cold ale. "Yes, I did," he said. "Whatever happened? Was someone murdered in his bed?"

"No, no, nothing like that," the guardsman assured him hastily. "It seems that one of the young women at, uh … a certain establishment was hiding someone from the management. He was discovered, and fled—making quite a mess in the process."

Arlian feigned astonishment. "*Hiding* someone? You mean inside the house?"

"So it appears."

"Well, well." He shook his head in amused dismay. "However did the young woman get this lover of hers inside in the first place?"

The guard shook his head. "I don't know, my lord. I don't think anyone does—except the man himself, of course."

"So you think that might have been the fellow with the nosebleed that I saw?"

"We think it likely, my lord, yes. Ah … could you tell us any more about

109

the man you saw?"

"Of course. He was, oh, about your own height, I'd say…" The guard was easily three inches shorter than Arlian himself. "Thinner, though, with a square-cut beard." The guard's beard was rounded, and Arlian's triangular. "And his clothes were disgraceful—homespun, one sleeve half off. I couldn't tell if they were gray or brown or what, in the dark." Arlian's blouse was fine white linen, his breeches black wool. "Beyond that I really couldn't say—it's *dark* out there, and I was hardly considering asking him to sit for a portrait."

"Of course, my lord. Thank you." The guardsman bowed and retreated, leaving Arlian to finish his meal in peace.

And he did, marveling at how easy the deception had been.

The whores had told him that deception was easy; they had all had plenty of practice, feigning the reactions that their customers wanted, whether it was love or fear, pleasure or pain. "People see what they expect to see," Rose had told him.

"People see what they *want* to see," Sweet had corrected her. Arlian felt a pang at the memory; he had seen her just an hour or two before, and already he missed her.

He wondered what was happening back at the House of Carnal Society. Was Mistress taking some sort of retribution against Rose? Had she realized that *all* the whores were involved? She knew it wasn't just Rose, from what she had said.

She couldn't punish *all* of them. The women would be well enough, Arlian was sure.

After all, they knew how to deceive. They had taught him, and here he was, safe in an inn, playing the lord.

They had had him practice, play-acting various roles he might need if he wanted to move freely in Manfort and find ways to confront Lord Dragon. Here he had left the brothel less than an hour ago, his heart was still beating fast from the exertion of his escape, and he was already putting those lessons to good use.

Fate was being kind to him—or perhaps merely playing with him; after all, where was the generosity in allowing his discovery mere hours before his intended departure? Might he be on his way to some delightfully ironic catastrophe?

He sat holding the flagon, sipping at the last of the ale, smiling to himself at his own foolishness. No one could know what Fate had in store, but the last few months had certainly been interesting, and he was not dissatisfied with where he was now.

He finished the ale and made a face.

He had never drunk ale before; it was odd stuff, strong-flavored, cool and burning at the same time. He wasn't sure whether he liked it. In the mine he had drunk only water; in the brothel he had drunk a variety of beverages, including juices and watered wine, but never any sort of beer or ale. Mistress had considered it inappropriate for her charges.

He would have to get used to ale, though; every young man of good fortune was expected to drink it in large quantities. He would also have to learn to tell good ale from bad; he hoped the innkeeper hadn't expected any comment on what Arlian had just drunk.

There were so many things he still needed to learn! His education so far had been, to say the least, unorthodox, and he was painfully aware that while he knew far more about the uses of pickaxes and cosmetics than most men, he was woefully ignorant of ordinary things. Ale was just one trivial example.

Well, he would have plenty of time—especially if his grandfather's stories were true, and dragon venom mixed in human blood extended life.

That was a strange prospect, and one he had sometimes faced with dread, on those rare occasions he thought of it at all—the idea of living a century or more in the mine or as a fugitive had held very little appeal.

Now, though, his life seemed to hold some promise—thanks to the finery and the training in deception that the girls had provided, he was now giving orders instead of taking them. He put down the empty flagon and called, "Innkeeper! Where's that bed?"

The innkeeper showed him the way upstairs. Arlian's room was small, tucked up under a gable on the third floor, but that hardly troubled him; it was equipped with niceties that he had done without since childhood, such as a window and a real floor. The bed was small and hard, the sheets rough—but Arlian really didn't care, and settled into it blissfully.

He slept late, and took his time in dressing—not because he had many choices to make, but simply because he wanted to do it well. He had three pairs of breeches and four assorted shirts to his name, counting those sorry specimens he had been wearing when he first arrived at the House of Carnal Society, but the night's adventures had ruined one blouse and left one pair of breeches sadly in need of cleaning and repair, reducing his circumstances farther. He had no mirror, and the room did not include one, so he had done the best he could with his face and hair using the windowglass—fortunately, he did have some of Sweet's castoffs, including a sparsely toothed comb and a thinning boar-bristle hairbrush.

And he had two pairs of hose and his velvet slippers. It was a pleasure to slip them on—but one of his first purchases would have to be a pair of boots.

He had a fine coat with silk facing, as well, one that Sweet had labored long and hard over, but he was not going to wear that recklessly; it was too precious to risk in everyday use. When the need arose, though, he would be able to look every inch a lord.

By the time he was satisfied with his appearance the morning was well advanced, and most of the inn's other guests already departed; Arlian had to make do with cold pastries for breakfast. He was finishing his third and brushing the crumbs from his lap, vaguely aware of the innkeeper talking to someone in the hallway, when the door of the common room burst open and Mistress marched in.

Arlian looked up, and struggled to hide any trace of recognition—although he had seen her through veils and peepholes several times, she had never before set her eyes on him, not even during last night's flight.

He wanted to ask her what had happened, whether Rose and Sweet and Hasty were all safe, but he knew he mustn't. He said nothing at all.

She glared around the room, and then at him.

"Who are you?" she demanded.

He blinked at her with exaggerated nonchalance. "Are you addressing me?" he asked.

"Yes!"

"Then I will thank you to do it politely," he said coldly. He dabbed at his mouth with his napkin, fighting not to tremble. He felt cold just seeing her like this, with no concealment, nothing but his wits to protect him.

She bit her lip, still glaring; he could see her forcing herself to hide her anger. He wondered whether she had slept at all since yesterday.

"I beg your pardon," she said. "Could you tell me please who you are?"

He flung the napkin on the table and stood up.

"My name is Lanair," he said. "My family's holdings are in orchards between Deep Delving and the Smoking Mountain, and I employ some eleven freemen in my own name, so I trust you will address me accordingly. Now, who are *you?*"

"I am Madam Ril, of the House of Carnal Society," she replied, only belatedly adding, "my lord." Arlian nodded an acknowledgment, and she continued, "You are the man who arrived here late last night, after the inn had closed?"

"I am," Arlian replied.

"I understand you saw a man running in the street last night."

"I did," Arlian acknowledged.

"Lord Lanair, it is absolutely *essential* that this man be found," Madam Ril said. "Can you tell me anything that might help?"

"I gave a description to a guardsman last night," he said. "I have nothing to add to that. Why is it of such importance?"

Madam Ril—Mistress—was visibly struggling to control herself.

"Because if we do not find who he was, and how he came to be there, the House will have to be destroyed," she said.

Arlian had to swallow hard before he could say, "Oh? Why?" He hoped she would think he was getting down the last of his meal, and not see how concerned he was.

If the House was destroyed, what would become of the women? Rose's phrase "dog food" echoed in his memory, and Bloody Hand's statement that there was no justice in this world.

"Because my clients expect safety and privacy in their visits there," Ril replied. "If we cannot guarantee that, if there might be spies or assassins lurking … you understand, our clients are peculiarly vulnerable. We cater to the wealthy, the powerful…"

"I know," Arlian said. "I believe my cousin Inthior has patronized your establishment."

She nodded at the name. "Yes, then you must surely see—these are men with enemies. If I cannot assure their safety, I cannot operate."

"Indeed," Arlian acknowledged. "Well, that's most unfortunate, I suppose, but it's hardly my concern. I told that guardsman everything I had to tell."

"A nosebleed, you said."

"Yes."

"We found no blood."

Arlian remembered the long scratch on one calf that he'd received plunging through Sparkle's ceiling and frowned. He had invented the nosebleed because he thought he'd left blood spots here and there, but apparently he had not. "I suppose he managed to catch it all on his shirt," he said. "Really, I have no idea of any details; I merely caught a glimpse. He certainly appeared to have blood on his beard and running from his nose."

"Did you see what he wore on his feet?"

"I'm afraid not. I was more concerned with my own just then; I lost my horse last night, you know, and my boots with him."

"I'm sorry to hear it, my lord. Your sword, as well? The guardsman said you did not have it with you."

"Yes," Arlian said, realizing for the first time that that was a serious flaw in his disguise. A real lord would not travel abroad unarmed. The lords he had seen at the House of Carnal Society had left their weapons downstairs, of course, but undoubtedly they had all carried swords when walking the streets. He had sometimes risked a glance out a window at the streets, and seen as much. The lack of a sword at the breakfast table was unremarkable, but arriving at the inn without one …

Well, his runaway horse was enough explanation for the moment. He should have mentioned it sooner, though, before it was questioned.

"You can think of nothing more that might aid us in finding this man?" Mistress asked.

Arlian shook his head. "Nothing at all," he said. "I trust you will be able to apprehend him without my assistance."

"I hope so," Ril said. "I very much hope so."

She stared blankly at him for a moment, and he realized that the discussion was over; he turned away, dismissing her with a wave of his hand, and headed for the stairs.

As he mounted the steps he frowned and mulled over just what he should do next. He had intended to head for Manfort and look for work after he left the brothel, but he had not expected to be a fugitive, or to be concerned about the welfare of Sweet and the others.

His fugitive status seemed more urgent; surely nothing irrevocable would be done about the women until the escaped trespasser was found. His disguise seemed to be working reasonably well, but sooner or later someone might realize that his arrival, sans swords and boots, at the very same time the trespasser escaped was just a little *too* coincidental.

Madame Ril might already be suspicious.

Furthermore, now he was known here as Lord Lanair—what if he were to reach Manfort seeking employment, and be recognized as Lanair? Would he need to maintain this identity for the rest of his life? He didn't mind the name, certainly—after months of answering to "Triv" he could scarcely object to a respectable name like Lanair—but sooner or later someone might turn up who knew that no such person as Lord Lanair had lived between Deep

Delving and the Smoking Mountain. He might do better to go somewhere else for a while.

Or perhaps he should go back to the brothel and try to rescue Rose and Sweet. Surely, none of his pursuers would expect that!

He continued to think about it as he packed up his belongings and cinched tight the canvas bundle.

By the time he had settled his bill the sun was almost directly overhead. He blinked at the brightness as he opened the inn's front door; his eyes were still more accustomed to darkness than to daylight. He squinted as he looked either way along the street.

Then he stopped and stared.

A crowd had gathered around the House of Carnal Society. Coaches stood at the brothel's two doors and along the wall between them—perhaps half a dozen vehicles in all, each of them large and splendid. Arlian had never before seen so many coaches in one place.

From what he could see of the gawkers around them, neither had anyone else in Westguard.

He had still intended to head east, toward either Manfort or the Blood of the Grape, but now instead he strolled up the street, as casually as he could, to see what the excitement was about.

As he approached he could hear voices arguing, loud, angry voices, both male and female. He could also see things being carried out of the brothel and loaded into the coaches, boxes and bundles of various shapes and sizes, and with a shock he realized that some of those bundles were the women who had lived there, wrapped in blankets. A few struggled and protested; most did not.

A driver shouted a command, and one of the coaches pulled away, the horses straining—they looked tired, and Arlian wondered where they had come from. Had they pulled that coach all the way from Manfort just that morning?

The coach came toward him, gathering speed, and he stepped out of its path. As it went by he glimpsed Hasty and another woman through the windows—the other might have been Kitten, but he couldn't be sure. The passengers also included a well-dressed man and one of the brothel guards.

The House of Carnal Society was being closed down, just as Mistress had said—and so quickly! Arlian had had no idea it would happen so fast.

At least the women were being taken away unhurt—though he worried about *where* they were being taken.

Another coach pulled away but turned down another street, where Arlian could not see who it carried.

He reached the edge of the crowd and tried to push his way forward—but the crowd pushed back, as two more coaches began rolling.

A tall man was standing in the open door of one of the two remaining vehicles, facing the brothel's open door—Arlian could see his back, but could make out no details. Mistress stood beside the door, shouting at him, pleading and threatening—Arlian could not make out her exact words, but the tone was plain enough.

A fifth coach pulled away, leaving only the one where the tall man stood, and Arlian found himself abruptly pushed forward, closer to the scene at the brothel door. He could see two women in the remaining coach—Sweet and Dove, both sitting in terrified silence, huddled against the rear of the compartment. Arlian took an involuntary step forward at the sight of Sweet, then caught himself.

No guard sat in that coach, but the driver was in place, reins and whip ready in his hands. Arlian dared not approach too closely.

Sweet and Dove were alive and well, even if they were scared; he had no need to risk his own life in an attempt to intervene in whatever was happening.

Two guardsmen appeared in the doorway—one wore the uniform of the brothel's guards, while the other was in Westguard's livery. They said something Arlian couldn't catch, and the man in the coach ordered clearly, "Burn it."

The two hesitated, and Mistress screamed in protest.

The man in the coach drew a long, slim sword and repeated his order, steel blade naked in his hand. "Burn it, I said!"

The two guards bowed a hasty acknowledgment and ducked back inside.

Six coaches, Arlian saw, and in each one he had seen clearly there had been two women and one guard, as well as the driver and the coach's owner. That accounted for twelve of the sixteen whores, and all the six guards.

Where were the other four women?

Why had the guards hesitated?

"Oh, gods," Arlian said, suddenly panicking. "Don't let it be true!" He pushed forward desperately, trying to shove his way through the crowd.

He had seen a few great injustices in his life, and he had loathed them, suffered from them; he could not stand idly by as another was perpetrated. He could not quietly allow four women to be burned to death because *he* had been sheltered among them. There must be some way he could prevent it.

"Please, my lord!" Mistress shrieked, stepping toward the man in the coach, arms raised in supplication—even in his distress, a part of Arlian's mind marveled at the sight of the dreaded Mistress so terrified.

"Madam Ril," the man in the coach roared back, "You were responsible for this. You failed in your trust."

The sword flashed, and for a moment the world froze. Arlian could not believe what he was seeing.

Then time started again as Madam Ril crumpled to the ground, blood spurting from her throat; gasps and screams came from the crowd. The swordsman wiped his blade on a handkerchief and sheathed it just as the guards reemerged from the brothel door at a trot.

"Get in," the swordsman told the brothel guard, as he himself bent and sank back into the coach, settling on one of the seats. Now, for the first time, Arlian could see the man's face.

The coach rocked as the guard climbed aboard and slammed the door, but Arlian saw that face clearly—that beardless face with the scarred right cheek, as if something had once gouged pieces away …

"Lord Dragon!" Arlian called, without meaning to—the cry had been startled out of him by the shock of recognition just as Lord Dragon rapped on the coach's ceiling and the driver shook out the reins.

No one had heard, so far as he could see.

Arlian struggled against the crowd—people were backing away in fear and confusion as Madam Ril lay motionless and bleeding on the street and wisps of smoke began to trickle from the brothel doorway.

The coach started moving, and Arlian stared, torn.

He had to stop the coach and get at Lord Dragon, he had to rescue Sweet and Dove, he had to avenge his family and all the other innocents, and even Madam Ril—monster though she was, how could Lord Dragon cut her down in broad daylight, before a hundred witnesses, and expect to get away with it?

But he had to get into the brothel, he had to find the other women.

By the time he fought free of the crowd's press the coach was fifty yards away and picking up speed, and smoke was bleeding from the brothel in a dozen places. The town guard who had helped start the fire was standing in the doorway, his short sword drawn.

Arlian hurried up to him and then stopped dead as the guardsman raised his ugly blade.

"Where do you think *you're* going, my lord?" he demanded.

"I … I thought there might be someone still inside," he said. "I thought I heard voices."

"You didn't hear voices, my lord, and we'll have no looting here. You *did* hear the owner ordered it burned."

"But really, I thought … you're *sure* there's no one inside?"

"No one alive," the guard replied. "There are four dead slaves, with their throats cut, just like this one." He gestured at Madam Ril.

"Oh," Arlian said, stepping back.

The coach was too far away to catch now—and if he had caught it, what would he do? He was alone and unarmed, and Lord Dragon and the guard had swords and clearly weren't afraid to use them. Sweet and Dove might help, but …

No, it was hopeless.

But there would come another time, he swore to himself—he and Lord Dragon would meet a third time, and Lord Dragon would pay for his crimes.

For now, though—could the guard be *sure* the other four women were dead?

"Excuse me," Arlian said, pushing his way back out through the crowd.

A few minutes later he had slipped into the stableyard, just as he had months before.

This time, though, smoke was billowing from the eaves and the windows were blackened, showing occasional flickers of bright orange where the glass was not yet completely obscured. Arlian dropped his bundle, then found a cast-off horseshoe and heaved it at a window.

The glass shattered and flame puffed out.

Arlian broke another, and this time only a swirl of thin gray smoke emerged; he positioned the barrel beneath that one, ran, and jumped. A moment later he was inside, holding his blouse over his mouth as he struggled to see through the smoke.

The room he had entered had been partially stripped—bedcurtains gone, furniture overturned. Smoke was a thick haze, but no flames were visible.

The corridor beyond was like a glimpse into the crater—smoke rolling across the ceiling, flames licking the walls and spilling under the doors, horribly reminiscent of the scene in the pantry of his childhood home as the dragons burned Obsidian. Pushing the memories aside and crouching to stay below the smoke, Arlian hurried to check each bedroom.

He found the first corpse in the second room he checked—Silk, one of the oldest of the women. Her throat had been slit from ear to ear, and she lay in a dried circle of her own blackened blood.

The third room was empty, and he could go no farther down the passage; the rest of the second floor was awash in flame. He turned and made a quick dash up the stairs to the third, where he found one more body.

Rose lay across her bed, naked head flung back, hair dragging on the floor, blood still trickling down her chin.

And the smoke and flame were thickening rapidly; he fled down the stairs and escaped, climbing back out the window and dropping to the barrelhead. The other two were surely beyond hope, as well.

Coughing and weeping, he jumped to the ground, found his bundle and stumbled away, bound for the Blood of the Grape.

Chapter Fifteen

At the Caravansary

Arlian frowned as he looked down at himself. He had put on his fine silk-faced coat, as the day had turned chilly, and that looked as elegant as he might ask, but underneath the coat his blouse was soaked in sweat and streaked with smoke, and his breeches were no better. His new slippers were scuffed. The canvas wrapping on his bundle of possessions, which he had not taken into the burning building, was cleaner than most of his garments, despite having been smeared with mud when he first fled.

He needed to take better care of his clothes, obviously.

He also needed to get more of them. This whorehouse finery was all very well, but not really suited to an active life, and he seemed destined to lead an active life.

He really did need to find employment—or some other source of money. He wished that amethysts really *were* precious—months ago he had shown one of his larger ones to Sparkle, the brothel's resident self-taught expert on gemstones, who had declared it lovely but worthless.

At least in the Lands of Man; in distant, possibly mythical Arithei, who could say?

Lord Kuruvan's gold, on the other hand, would be good anywhere, and Arlian no longer had any compunctions about taking it. Lord Kuruvan had been one of the owners of the House of Carnal Society; that undoubtedly meant he had been in one those coaches, and had carried away two of the women …

But not Rose. He had left Rose lying there with her throat cut.

Perhaps he had had her killed *because* he had told her where his money was hidden; perhaps he had simply tired of her, or liked the other two better.

Or perhaps Rose had been killed because she had hidden Arlian in the attic above her room, and Kuruvan had had no say in it.

It didn't matter. Whatever the reason, Rose was dead, and Lord Kuruvan was an accomplice in her murder.

Arlian intended to collect a blood-price, if he could—if Lord Kuruvan had not thought better of his hiding place and moved the money elsewhere.

Taking that money would be a *start* on avenging Rose.

And there were a dozen women to be rescued, as well—Sweet among them. Arlian was determined to find and free them all—someday. He had no idea where they had been taken; the coaches had left no trails he could see. They were still alive somewhere, though, most probably in Manfort, and in time he would find them and rescue them. The thought of Sweet in Lord Dragon's possession, forced to obey his every whim, haunted Arlian; somehow the idea of a single master abusing her was even worse than the casual mistreatment she had received from so many in Westguard.

Kuruvan's gold might be enough to buy the women free. If possible, Arlian promised himself, he would do that, and see them all safe, before he pursued his revenge.

He *would* have revenge, though.

The dragons that had destroyed Obsidian needed to be punished, but they had been acting within their own nature; looting the ruins was simple greed, and understandable, if reprehensible; but Lord Dragon, Lord Kuruvan, and the others had killed those five women and destroyed the House of Carnal Society on little more than a whim, so far as Arlian could see. Such callousness was beyond his comprehension, and he could not permit it to go unchallenged. The mere thought of it set him trembling. Anything he could do to avenge that crime, *anything,* he would do. Stealing Lord Kuruvan's gold, and perhaps using it to buy the women if he could find them, was all he could see a way to accomplish as yet, but he swore the day would come when he would do more, when he would see each of those six lords suffer for their evil.

If Lord Kuruvan's gold financed that revenge, so much the better. Arlian just wished he had some clearer notion of how that revenge might be brought about. As he neared Manfort he grew ever more aware of the size of the place, and the difficulties he might face in locating and destroying his enemies there; he seemed to see guardsmen everywhere as he drew closer to the city, and was uncomfortably aware that even in his deteriorating disguise as a lord he was still unarmed and untrained, with nothing to support him but his own wits and the guidance the women of the House of Carnal Society had given him.

That hardly seemed enough.

He looked up again as he rounded a bend in the road. Manfort was an immense presence ahead of him now—it was built on a hill, and he could see walls within walls rising up the slopes, a maze of buildings and fortifications, towers thrusting up here and there. A thousand plumes of smoke trailed up into the blue springtime sky, and he could make out, directly ahead of him but still a mile or two away, the tops of the great gray gates.

Closer at hand, though, was a square, a place where the road widened into a broad plaza paved with stone—and that plaza was crowded with a variety of wagons, men, women, and oxen. A babble of voices reached him.

He frowned. Who were all these people? What was this place?

Then between two of the taller wagons he caught sight of a sign at one side of the square—a board on which two crudely sketched green leaves, a black line for a stem, and a score of overlapping red circles represented a bunch of grapes, with red drops dripping from them.

The Blood of the Grape. This was the inn where Rose had said Lord Kuruvan hid his gold. The wagons and oxen were presumably owned by patrons of the inn.

Arlian tucked his bundle securely under one arm, raised his head, and marched forward.

The crowd seethed around him; surely it couldn't *always* be like this here! Something special must be going on. He tried to catch the words of those he passed.

A driver was telling a woman to make sure their daughter stayed clear of certain individuals; two men lifting boxes from one open wagon to another were complaining about the weight of their burdens.

Here was a man in a black leather tunic seated in the driver's place on one of the simplest of the closed-in wagons, talking to a guardsman who stood by the wheel; Arlian slowed his pace and strained to hear.

"... no, really! Do you want to spend the rest of your life rousting pickpockets and helping drunkards home and never get farther than Southwark or Westguard?"

"Well, if I spend my life that way it's likely to be a good bit *longer* than yours," the guardsman retorted. "Sooner or later you'll get a bandit's arrow in the neck, or bad water in your gut, or some ghastly foreign disease in your heart, and I'll be safe at home by my own hearth while you cough out your life in some stinking desert."

"Oh, I won't deny there are a few hazards on the road," the man in the wagon said, "but how many of your comrades have gotten a knife in the back while breaking up a brawl? Life's a risk anywhere, man! Your own wife might go mad and slit your throat while you sleep."

The guardsman snorted. "You'll have to find your men somewhere else," he said. "I'm not going anywhere."

"So I see," the man on the wagon said. "Well, if you know anyone with a soul more adventurous than your own, send them to me—I'll feel better with a few more blades along."

Arlian stopped dead and listened as the two men said farewells, and the guardsman ambled away.

This leather-clad person, whoever he was, was hiring men. Arlian might well need an income; he couldn't be sure Kuruvan's gold was still there. He hesitated, then turned and stepped up to the side of the wagon.

"Excuse me," he said.

The man in black leather had been scanning the crowd, but now he turned around and looked Arlian in the eye. "Yes?" he said.

Arlian frowned, trying to phrase his question; the man in black leather mistook the reason for the frown and added, in a tone a real lord might have considered insolent, "My lord."

Arlian heard the insolence, but he was hardly about to quarrel with it; he was no lord, not really, and this man was not someone he cared to antagonize. The eyes gazing at him were a cold gray-blue, set in a weathered, scarred face between hair pulled back in a tight knot and a beard trimmed unfashionably short. One of the man's hands rested on the hilt of a sword that lay on the seat beside him; the other gripped the hilt of a dagger sheathed on his belt. The fellow appeared ready for anything—but those cold eyes were somehow not hostile; he was looking at Arlian with fair consideration. The youth had the impression that this was a man who really saw what he looked at and listened to what he heard, rather than perceiving what he expected to see and hear.

"I couldn't help overhearing part of what you said to that guardsman," Arlian said.

"My sympathies on your inability," the man said, raising one corner of his mouth sardonically. "I sometimes think the gods erred in not providing a means to close our ears, as we close our eyes."

Arlian managed a weak smile in return. "Am I correct in believing you are hiring men?"

The grip on the dagger-hilt loosened visibly.

"Not precisely," the man said. "I am aware of someone who is, however."

"Ah," Arlian said. "And who would that be? I'd be grateful for whatever you might tell me of this matter."

"Would you, indeed, my lord?"

124

Arlian nodded. "I'm a stranger here," he said.

The man in black considered Arlian for a moment. "It is my understanding," he said at last, "that the caravan master has budgeted for a dozen guards for this trip, and as yet has hired only eight, myself included. For my part, I don't think a dozen any more than adequate and I'd be glad if he found more."

At the word "caravan" understanding dawned upon Arlian; the confusion around him suddenly made sense, and old childhood dreams burst into renewed life. He remembered Grandsir's tales of travel, and his own desire to emulate the old man.

"A caravan!" he said "Of course. And where does it go? What goods does it bear?"

"We go east, to the port city of Lorigol," the man said. "As for what we carry, we carry whatever the investors choose to send—but I'd assume you'll find bolts of cloth, jars of herbs, and the like in these wagons." He took his hand off his dagger and waved in a gesture that took in most of the plaza.

Arlian nodded. "And you need more guards?"

"I'd say so," the man said dryly.

"And … well…" Arlian wasn't sure what to ask next, and the guard took pity on him.

"You're thinking of signing on, then? Seeking adventure in the wide world?"

"Yes, exactly!" Arlian said, smiling. He had intended to go on into Manfort in pursuit of his vengeance and Sweet's rescue, but now he suddenly found himself with an attractive alternative. He was still determined to free the surviving whores, still determined to find some way to strike at the dragons that had destroyed Obsidian, but he was young, he had time, and the world was large and he had seen so little of it. From his mountainside village he had seen the land spread out before him, but most of what he had seen since had been stone walls or a stuffy attic. To get away from his past for a time, to breathe fresh air and see new lands … that would be good for him, he knew it.

And he would make some money, learn more of life as a free man, give himself more of a grounding before he flung himself at his foes in his pursuit of vengeance.

Of course, it meant that the women would remain in captivity somewhat longer—but he had no way to find them, nor means to free them, in any event. Perhaps a few weeks with a caravan would give him time to plan and

125

prepare.

"You'd be willing to serve as a mere guard?" the man in black asked, interrupting Arlian's thoughts. "It's hardly suitable work for a lord."

"My holdings are greatly diminished," Arlian improvised. "I must take what I can find."

"Can you fight?"

"I can learn," Arlian replied promptly.

"Have you your sword? We leave tomorrow at dawn, or as close as we can manage with this many wagons—there's no time to fetch your great-grandfather's blade from the family vaults in Blackwater, or wherever it might be."

"I have no sword," Arlian admitted.

"Ah. Then you aren't fully a lord yet?"

"No." Arlian could scarcely argue with that. His disguise, as he had feared, had a fatal flaw.

"Have you any armor, perhaps?"

"No," Arlian said, seeing his dreams fleeing back into childhood fantasy. "Not so much as a penknife."

The man did not dismiss him, as Arlian had expected; instead he stared at Arlian with those intense blue eyes for a moment. "Could you use a sword if you had one?" he asked.

Perhaps there was hope after all. "I could *learn,*" Arlian insisted.

"My lord," the man said, "If you want to learn swordsmanship, there are schools and tutors—signing on as a caravan guard is not the easiest way. Hasn't your father offered to have you taught?"

"My father is long dead," Arlian said.

"He left you no sword?"

Arlian shook his head. "It's lost."

"And your mother?"

"Dead as well—and my brother with her." That much was true—and if the man assumed that the family's sword had been lost in the same catastrophe, Arlian would not disabuse him of the idea.

"And the family business?"

"Gone as well."

"I begin to understand," the man in black said. "Nothing left but your pride, eh, my lord?" The mockery that had been in his voice whenever he spoke the title before had been replaced by pity.

"A little more than that," Arlian said defensively, remembering

Kuruvan's cache. "I believe I can *buy* a sword and armor—and pay you to teach me their use."

"What makes you think I know enough to teach anyone?"

"You didn't get those scars on your face from a woman's fingernails," Arlian said.

The man in black laughed. "No, *those* scars are on my back," he agreed.

"And I heard what you told that townsman," Arlian continued. "If you have so little fear of bandits, then you must have confidence in your own skill, and you don't look like someone easily deluded, even by himself."

The man nodded. "How much can you pay?"

Arlian hesitated. "I'm not sure," he admitted. The truth was he wasn't entirely sure the money was there at all, or how he could get his hands on it if it was—the innkeeper was not simply going to let a stranger carry a keg out of the cellars, no questions asked. "I still need to settle a few accounts. You'll be here until tomorrow's dawn?" That would give him one night to get what he needed.

The guard nodded. "But the caravan master may hire all the men he needs before that," he warned. "In fact, I hope he does—I hate traveling with overconfident fools and insufficient defense."

Arlian's expression turned woeful, and the man in black smiled.

"There will be other caravans," he said. "They gather here every so often. Perhaps instead of accompanying me to Lorigol you'll find some other teacher bound southward to the Borderlands, or west to the mountain tribes. Go get your sword and armor, and…"

He stopped in midsentence and considered Arlian thoughtfully.

"Do you know how to choose a sword?" he asked. "Or armor?"

Arlian shook his head. "I was only eleven when my father died," he said.

"But you've lasted this long without him."

Arlian shrugged.

The man in black studied him. Then he looked around the plaza. Finally his gaze returned to Arlian.

"Do you have the money with you? Enough for a sword?"

"No," Arlian admitted. "But I should have it by some time tonight."

The man snorted, and gestured at the western sky, where the sun was much nearer the horizon that the zenith. "I can hardly hope to see you equipped by dawn if you don't have the funds until tonight! But I don't know that I like this caravan master that much in any case; he should have had his full complement of guards by now, and I shouldn't have to do his recruiting.

I'll tell you what, my would-be lord—if this caravan doesn't have twelve good men signed on by morning, I'll stay here and take your money and see you properly fitted out, and we'll join the *next* one that comes along, if it's headed somewhere worth going. Would that suit you?"

"I believe it would," Arlian said cautiously.

Indeed, it might prove ideal. If the next caravan did not depart until some days had passed, he might have time to learn some basic swordsmanship from this man, he might be able to rescue the women, and then carry them all away with him when the caravan departed.

He didn't want to commit himself too completely, though; he might not be able to get the money at all, and he did not want to be responsible for costing this man his employment.

The guard seemed confident that he could find another job readily enough, though, and Arlian didn't doubt it was true; certainly, had Arlian been hiring guards, this man appeared formidable and experienced enough.

"Well, then," the man in black said. "Go and settle your accounts, and I'll see you in the morning."

"And what name shall I give when I look for you?" Arlian asked.

The guard smiled. "They call me Black," he said, hooking a thumb under his leather tunic and displaying it. "And you?"

"Lanair," Arlian said—he thought that alias was still safe enough.

"Then perhaps I'll see you in the morning, Lord Lanair," Black said. "Or perhaps not—I may be gone by the time you rise, if all goes well. Or *you* may be gone, if those accounts you wish to settle aren't cooperative, eh?"

Arlian managed a nervous laugh. "The morning, then," he said. He essayed a quick bow, then turned and made his way through the crowd toward the inn.

Chapter Sixteen

The Blood of the Grape

The interior of the Blood of the Grape was as crowded as the plaza. Harried boys and women were carrying trays back and forth through the throng in the common room; every chair was occupied, and most had someone standing behind them, waiting for the present occupant to finish.

Arlian had not anticipated anything like this when he heard Rose describe Lord Kuruvan's hiding place; he had expected a quiet little inn like the Weary Traveler, not a vast and crowded caravansary.

The caravan merchants would surely have made most of their preparations elsewhere—in Manfort, or on their estates, or in the surrounding towns. This was only a final gathering place for the wagons and travelers.

The caravan's personnel had certainly gathered, though, and they were obviously enjoying this chance to obtain food and drink in a civilized setting before venturing out into wilder lands.

Although, Arlian realized, those lands might not be *that* much wilder; surely there were other inns, other caravansaries, on the roads to the east. The route to Lorigol could be peppered with such establishments, neatly spaced, each one day's journey from the last—at least for part of the distance. If the entire route were safe, there would be no need to travel in caravans in the first place.

Arlian knew little of geography beyond what he had been able to see from the Smoking Mountain, or what his grandfather had told him; he had no idea how far Lorigol was from Manfort, or what lay between, or where the ships that sailed from that port might trade. For the first time in his life that ignorance troubled him. He realized he didn't have any very clear idea how long he would be gone if he signed onto a caravan.

Those were all matters he could worry about later, he told himself; for now he needed to focus on getting at Lord Kuruvan's gold. He looked about, trying to think what he should do next.

He had originally thought he would take a room at the inn—though that might have been difficult in any case, since his entire remaining fortune, after settling at the Weary Traveler, consisted of eight coppers and a tiny silver coin of uncertain value—and then sneak out of his room at night, find his way

129

down into the cellars, and carry off the keg. If it was there.

That was clearly not going to work; this place was full of people, and even if he could still somehow get a bed he was sure he wouldn't get a room to himself. He doubted that he could move about the place, even in the middle of the night, without waking anyone.

He found himself a corner in which to stand, dropped his bundle to the floor, and watched the crowds while he tried to puzzle out a plan.

The steps were easy enough to spell out: He needed to get down into the cellars; he needed to find the keg; and he needed to get the gold out of the inn.

He had intended to sneak down into the cellars by night, but it belatedly occurred to him that he might not have been able to do so in any case; the cellars were probably kept locked. If so, his original scheme wouldn't have worked at all; he was vaguely aware that there were ways to open locks without the appropriate keys, but he certainly didn't know any of them.

That might complicate matters.

At present he didn't even know where the cellar door was, but that would be easy enough to remedy—he could just follow one of the servers.

Once in the cellars, finding the keg should be fairly easy—how many kegs marked "sour wine" would there be? But getting it out through a crowd like this would not be so simple. He could not possibly hope to get it out unseen.

For a moment he considered ways he might simply carry it out openly—could he claim to be Lord Kuruvan's representative, come to fetch it?

No. The innkeeper would surely demand at least a letter from Kuruvan, and there might well be a prearranged password, or some other means of verifying his right to the keg.

Could he switch it with another keg, and claim that he was a merchant in the caravan and it was his own property?

No, there would almost certainly be paperwork of some sort. He couldn't expect to get away with that.

Carrying a keg out openly wasn't going to work; someone would want to know who he was and where he was going. It would take an incredibly audacious thief to simply walk in and carry a keg away, but it wasn't impossible that it had been tried. He'd been successfully audacious back in Westguard, but he couldn't rely on it.

Besides, how *big* was this keg? How far could he carry it? Where would he take it? Would the innkeeper notice that it was gone?

Then a thought struck him. He didn't really want the keg at all; he wanted what was in it. Suppose he were to knock the bottom in, take out the gold, and leave the empty keg where it was? A real keg of wine would make a mess, but gold wouldn't leak out on the floor.

He had no tools to stave it in, but there would probably be something down there to tap the barrels of ale, after all.

He prodded his bundled belongings with one toe. He had only a tiny purse, one intended for a woman, that Sweet had given him; that would surely not be big enough for the booty he was after. He had no proper sack or chest, but he ought to be able to find something he could wrap the gold in quickly. One of his shirts, perhaps.

If he knotted the sleeves, then tied the collar shut—or just used the sleeves as sacks ...

That might work. He might not be able to fit all the gold at once, if the keg were actually *full*—but that hardly seemed likely.

Then another, better thought struck him. He had another pair of stockings, in addition to those he wore. He could use those as sacks. They might not hold very much, but then he didn't know how much was there.

He just needed to get into the right part of the cellars, and to be left alone there for a moment or two.

He considered the crowds, then knelt, opened his bundle, found the hosiery, and tucked it into the waistband of his breeches. Then he rolled his belongings back up and replaced the belts.

The next step was to hire an accomplice. He stood again and scanned the crowd. Then he stepped back to the door and looked out at the plaza.

He saw no promising candidates inside, but outside there were several children scattered about, in various attire. Some were helping load wagons, or running back and forth, but a few were merely standing and watching.

Arlian made his way toward a group of these—three of them, two girls and a boy, the oldest no more than ten, all three of them wearing little more than rags. As he drew near one of the girls happened to glance in his direction, and he caught her eye and beckoned.

She quickly slipped away from the others and came near him—but stopped out of reach and looked up at him warily. She was no more than eight, he judged, and woefully thin and dirty.

"Good evening," Arlian said cheerfully. "Would you be interested in earning a little money?" He held out one of his coins.

She nodded enthusiastically.

Arlian knelt, bringing himself down to her level, as he fished two more coins and added them to the first.

"In a few minutes," he said quietly, holding out the coins, "I'm going to go into the inn. After I do, I want you to count as high as you can—can you count to a hundred?"

She nodded again.

"Good. Then count to a hundred, or even more if you like. Then go to the back door of the inn and find someone who works there, and tell him that a man named Lord Inthior wants to speak to the proprietor *right now.* He can't leave his wagon so he hired you to send the message. Do you understand?"

She nodded.

"Can you do that? Can you remember that, and say it?"

She nodded.

"Let me hear you say it, then."

"Lord Inthior's at his wagon and he wants to talk to the innkeeper *right now,* and he's really mad about something!" she piped, in a high, clear voice.

Arlian smiled. "Very good."

"And I count to a hundred first, or more, so you have time to get somewhere."

The girl was clearly not stupid or naive.

"And when the proprietor comes out, you don't see Lord Inthior anywhere, he must be gone."

"I guess he got tired of waiting," she agreed.

He handed her the three coins. "Do this, and you'll have three more later tonight. Fair enough?"

She nodded.

"And in case you're thinking this might be too dangerous and you'd be better with just the three, here's the best part," Arlian said. "If anyone suspects anything and gets mad, you can tell the truth and say I paid you. I'm Lord Inthior's cousin. I'm not going to steal anything; I just want to check something while the proprietor's not looking."

She smiled broadly, obviously relieved—until then her expression had been utterly serious. "Oh, good," she said. "Thank you, my lord; I'll do what you said." The three coins disappeared; Arlian didn't see what she did with them.

"Good," he said, getting back to his feet. "I'm counting on you."

She nodded; he smiled at her, then turned away and headed for the inn.

Once inside it took longer than he liked to find the proprietor of the Blood of the Grape; the staff was busy, and not sure just where their employer was at any given time. At last, though, he found himself face to face with a formidable old woman.

"Lord Kuruvan sent me," Arlian said. "You may have heard about a recent disturbance in Westguard?"

"I might have," the innkeeper agreed.

"Well, there was a disturbance," Arlian said. "And as a result of that incident, my uncle is concerned about his investments."

"Everything's fine here," the woman said. "It's busy tonight because of the Lorigol expedition, but we've had no trouble. You can tell your uncle he'll have his rent on time."

Arlian hid his surprise and quickly revised what he had planned to say; it had not occurred to him that Kuruvan might own the inn, but of course it made sense. What better place to leave his cache than on his own property?

And that explained how Kuruvan could be sure the innkeeper wouldn't get curious and investigate what was really in the keg—Kuruvan had probably brought the keg here himself when the innkeeper wasn't around, and as the owner he would have had free access to the cellars—or anywhere else. The innkeeper probably didn't even know the keg was there, let alone what was in it.

That should make Arlian's job easier.

"Of course," he said. "He was never in any doubt of that. However, he asked me to look around and make certain that everything is in order."

The innkeeper—not actually the proprietor at all, Arlian now realized—frowned. "Look where? At the accounts?"

"No, no—he wouldn't trust me to do that. Just to see that everything here is as it should be. He asked me particularly to make sure that no one's hiding in the cellars—I understand some scoundrel had concealed himself most cleverly in Westguard, and my uncle is concerned lest that be repeated here. If you would permit me to see the cellars for a moment, I can satisfy myself that his fears are groundless and be on my way."

"Hiding in the cellars?" She plainly thought the idea was ridiculous.

Arlian shrugged. "This fellow reportedly hid in an attic for several days in Westguard."

The innkeeper looked him in the eye, then glanced over his clothing. "You're Lord Kuruvan's nephew?"

"Well, yes," Arlian said. "My name is Lanair."

"Do you have a letter, or other credentials?"

Arlian shook his head. "No. But I'm not going to take anything, or look at the accounts; I just want to poke around the cellars enough to satisfy Lord Kuruvan."

She stared thoughtfully at him.

He sighed theatrically. "I know my appearance is a disgrace, and I *should* have a letter," he said. "But I don't. My uncle insisted I come here *immediately,* lest the villain escape."

"Well, come on, then," she said. "I don't have time to argue about it. You'll have to leave that with one of my staff, though." She pointed at his bundle.

"Of course," he agreed.

When that was arranged, she led the way to the cellar door. They had to step aside as a serving wench emerged with a tray of brimming mugs of ale, but then the innkeeper led the way down worn stone steps into the cool, lamplit gloom.

For a moment, as they reached the bottom and stepped onto stone pavement, Arlian felt an unreasoning rush of terror; the stone walls and lamplight were so reminiscent of the mines that on some level he felt himself flung back in time, trapped and enslaved again. Then he recovered and looked about with interest at the barrels that lined either side of a passage ahead.

In addition to wall-mounted fixtures, a shelf mounted between two barrels held four brass lamps similar to those used in the mine, all lit; the innkeeper took one of them down and led the way along the passage between the two rows of barrels. "Beer and ale and cider on that side," she said, waving to the left, where a dozen huge tapped barrels were racked side by side against a stone wall. "Then the ordinary red and white over here," she continued, indicating the right, where nine or ten smaller barrels, only two of them tapped, formed a barrier separating the passage from the unlit remainder of the cellars. Two gaps in the row provided access to that dark space beyond.

Arlian nodded as he maneuvered past a serving maid drawing ale from a barrel, noting that a tap, a corkscrew, a hammer, and a crowbar hung from hooks below the shelf of lamps, each tool on a leather thong. He stooped to glance under the framework supporting the barrels, acting out his ruse of searching for a concealed fugitive.

He had expected the innkeeper to turn to the right and take them through one of those gaps in the line of barrels, into the main part of the cellars, but she did not. At the end of the passage stood a heavy wooden door; the innkeeper marched directly up to it. She transferred the lamp to her left hand and fished a key from her pocket with the right to unlock it.

"The superior wines," she said as the door swung wide.

The room beyond was unlit, perhaps fifteen feet square, with only the single entrance. All four walls were lined with wine racks, most of them full; some of the bottles were clean and new, others gray with dust and cobwebs, and others at every stage between. Wooden cases holding more bottles were stacked chest-high in the center of the room, leaving only a narrow walkway around the sides.

"No one in here," the innkeeper remarked.

Arlian, still acting out his role, insisted on stepping inside and tapping on the walls and floor and several of the boxes; the innkeeper waited impatiently while he played out the charade.

They emerged from the wine vault; Arlian waited while the innkeeper carefully locked it. Then they turned aside, stepping between the wine barrels and into a maze of side passages, past vegetable bins and root cellars. Servers continued to fetch wine and beer, providing a constant background of moving shadows and the sound of footsteps and splashing beverages.

As the search continued Arlian began to wonder whether that little girl had decided to settle for just the three coins after all. He tried to steer toward the northeast corner, but felt compelled by his role to poke at the produce and tap walls at every opportunity.

Then a boy came stumbling down the stairs calling, "Madam Innkeeper!"

Arlian waited politely, a few steps away, as the boy told her that Lord Inthior wanted to see her outside *right now.*

The innkeeper glanced at Arlian unhappily.

"I'll just look around a little more," he said. "I won't disturb anything. And I'll wait for your return."

"Very well," the innkeeper agreed. She followed the boy up the stairs.

There was a temporary break in the stream of barmaids; no one wanted to be in the innkeeper's way as she climbed the stairs. Arlian took advantage of this and snatched the hammer and crowbar from the hooks; he tucked them under his shirt and held them with one hand while he lifted a lamp with the other and made his way quickly back through the line of wine barrels, and through the labyrinth of pillars, bins, barrels, and boxes to the northeast.

At last he reached a dead end, with solid stone walls ahead of him to both the north and the east.

This corner was among the darkest and dustiest he had yet discovered. Three kegs stood along the north wall, one stacked atop the others.

The top keg was open, and held nails; Arlian lifted it off and set it aside.

The others were sealed. One was unmarked; the other had faint lettering, drawn with charcoal. It was too dusty to read, but Arlian thought it *could* say "sour wine." He tipped it, listening closely.

Nothing sloshed, and the weight did not shift like liquid.

He turned it over and attacked it with hammer and crowbar. His mining experience came in handy; he was able to knock in the end quickly.

He thrust in a hand, squeezing it between the broken lid and the side, and grabbed. Then he pulled it out into the lamplight.

Gold coins glittered in his palm.

He smiled, pulled the stockings from the waistband of his breeches, and began stuffing them.

When the stockings were full he tucked a few more coins into his tiny purse, then returned the keg to its place, the open end on the bottom where it wouldn't be noticed as readily.

The keg was still mostly full; he wished he had some way to get the rest out, but could not think of any way to smuggle it past the innkeeper and her staff.

All the same, once he had secured the full stockings he had several pounds of gold hidden under his shirt, and that would have to do. He hurried to replace the keg of nails, then to put the hammer and crowbar back where they belonged.

He was waiting at the foot of the stairs when the innkeeper returned.

"I took the liberty of investigating further while I waited," he said. "I'd say my uncle's fears are groundless, Madam. I congratulate you on the efficiency and good order of your cellars."

She stared doubtfully at him, then looked at the door to the wine vault—still securely closed, of course.

"Would you by any chance have a bed available, or has this throng taken all of them?" Arlian asked.

She laughed harshly. "Oh, all of them and more, my lord," she said. "I could rent you a space on the floor, if you have bedding."

"I think not," Arlian said. "Thank you all the same." He mounted the steps, trying desperately to move just as he had when there was nothing beneath his shirt but himself. The coins were packed too tightly to jingle, but they might shift ...

But they didn't, and a few moments later he was back out on the plaza with his bundle under his arm; a few seconds in a relatively quiet corner had let him transfer the heavily loaded stockings to the bundle.

He had money at last, real money, but all was not yet perfect. The sun was setting behind the rooftops to the west, and he still needed to find somewhere to sleep.

Chapter Seventeen

Black

He slept on Black's wagon, on the rear platform, wrapped in the bedding he had brought from the House of Carnal Society. Black himself slept inside.

"Accounts settled, then, my lord?" the guard had asked him as Arlian had roamed aimlessly about the plaza, trying to think what he should do.

"Why, yes," Arlian had said. "Quite successfully."

"The caravan master's yet to find another man who knows one end of a sword from the other," Black said. "I think I may be able to help you with those purchases after all."

"Excellent!" Arlian had said. "Now, if only you could help me find a bed!"

"Can you pay?"

And it had been as simple as that.

He was awakened not by Black, nor by preparations for the caravan's departure, but by a rude shaking. He opened his eyes to find the little girl standing on the wagon's step, looking down at him. The sky behind her was just turning pale in preparation for sunrise.

"She says you owe her money," Black said from the wagon's door.

"Indeed I do," Arlian agreed, as he blinked sleep from his eyes. "Three-tenths of a ducat, I believe."

She nodded silently.

Arlian sat up and found his purse, and extracted the promised coppers. He was pleased to see gold coins glittering in the morning light, reminding him of the previous night's adventure.

On an impulse, he pulled out the smallest gold coin he could find and gave that to the girl as well.

"Thank you," he said. "Your timing was impeccable."

"And they didn't even ask me anything when they couldn't find Lord Inthior," she said cheerfully. "They believed the whole thing."

"That's just as well," Arlian said. "It keeps matters simple." He patted her shoulder, and watched as she climbed carefully out of the wagon and ran

139

off.

He wondered whether the innkeeper had really believed the story; it might be unwise to let her see him again this morning.

"I take it your business went well last night," Black remarked, watching her go.

"Reasonably well," Arlian agreed.

"If you'll pardon me, I'll go see whether our friend the caravan master was equally fortunate."

"Of course," Arlian said. He squeezed to the side so that Black could descend the step to the ground.

Black locked the wagon's door, then stepped past his guest and headed away. Arlian watched him go, curious as to just where the caravan master was. Black, however, almost immediately disappeared around the corner of another wagon.

Arlian hesitated, unsure what he should do. He looked out across the plaza.

Men and women were rising, going about the business of making their wagons ready; on all sides oxen were being led into position and hitched in place, awnings furled, cargo strapped down. Arlian watched the bustle for a moment, wondering whether he should perhaps ride out with these people even if Black did not—though he had nothing to trade but gold, no skills to offer …

On the other hand, perhaps, whatever Black did, he should just go on into Manfort, in pursuit of Lord Dragon, and the twelve surviving women, and those looters who had accompanied Lord Dragon in picking Obsidian's bones, and the five other lords who had so casually participated in the destruction of the House of Carnal Society and the murder of one-fourth of its inmates.

And information about the dragons themselves. Manfort would unquestionably be the best place to start any attempt to track down and destroy the three dragons that had slaughtered his family.

Sweet was probably somewhere in Manfort. Rose was dead, but Sweet and Dove had been carried off alive.

But finding them, in that great metropolis, and freeing them from Lord Dragon, would take time and skill and whatever other resources he could muster. Perhaps, rather than heading directly into the city, he should stay here and see if he could find a way to get the rest of that gold.

But Black had offered to help him buy a sword and learn to use it, and he shouldn't be hasty in passing that up …

"Stay, then, blast you!" someone bellowed, disturbing the peaceful scene; Arlian saw a dozen people start, and a cat jumped from somewhere and dashed for cover at the sound. "We've nine brave men and true, and that's more than enough!"

Arlian smiled wryly; it appeared Black would not be traveling with the caravan after all. He got to his feet and brushed himself off.

A moment later Black reappeared, frowning slightly. Another man walked beside him—a big, black-haired, bushy-bearded fellow in brown leather, with a sword on his hip.

"My lord," Black said as he approached, "I must ask you to remove yourself from that wagon."

Startled, Arlian gathered up his bundle and climbed down. "Is there a problem?" he asked.

"It would seem that I will not be going to Lorigol with these gentlemen," Black said. "And this wagon is the caravan's property, rather than my own, so I am required to turn it overt to Bonecrusher, here, forthwith."

"Ah, I see," Arlian said, stepping out of the way.

"Do you, indeed?" Black said as he mounted the step. "And they say today's young men have no understanding of the deeper issues." He vanished into the wagon's interior.

Bonecrusher waited on the ground, standing a foot or two from Arlian's side; Arlian looked him over and decided against any attempt at conversation.

Half an hour later the ox-drawn wagons of the caravan were moving slowly out the eastern side of the plaza, one behind another, while Arlian and Black, also headed eastward, walked easily past them. Black's belongings, intended to keep him adequately supplied for the trip to Lorigol, were in an immense pack he carried on his back.

As they walked Black cast a glance backward at the wagon he would have driven had he stayed with the caravan; it had not yet begun to roll. Bonecrusher stood at the driver's seat, exhorting the other guards to get themselves and their possessions aboard quickly.

"I wish them well," Black remarked, "but I can't say I'm impressed. That wagon should be at the *front* of the column. If I were driving it *would* be at the front, and any guards who weren't aboard it, or astride horses, would ride with the master."

Arlian asked, "What does it matter, so close to Manfort? Surely there are no bandits *here!*"

"It's a matter of discipline, lad! You must keep order, or the caravan isn't a caravan so much as a lot of wagons that just happen to be traveling the same direction."

Arlian blinked; he had more or less thought of a caravan heretofore as "a lot of wagons that just happen to be traveling the same direction."

No, he corrected himself, he had thought of it as a lot of wagons traveling *together,* and he now saw that that really wasn't the same thing. Black's distinction was important. He remembered times in the mines when teamwork had been important, when the miners had had to work together, not just in the same place.

"I see," he said. "You want everyone to know his place, and stay in it, so that everyone will know where to be and what to expect if they *do* find trouble later."

Black glanced at him. "You're quick," he said.

Arlian shrugged.

"Or maybe I'm just accustomed to fools," Black said, with a shrug of his own.

Arlian smiled a little to himself. They were passing the lead wagon now, and he asked, "So the guard wagon should be here? Not the master?"

"The master's place is at the back," Black explained. "That way no one can fall behind without his knowledge. The guard wagon goes here to be the first to meet any trouble that might be encountered on the road. There should be at least four men in it, and at least two more in the master's wagon, and horsemen riding up and down on either side of the column, ready to investigate anything out of the ordinary; the master of *this* particular caravan has decided to dispense with the riders. Which means he's dispensed with *me*—I've no horse, but that doesn't mean I don't appreciate their value."

Arlian nodded.

"I understand your horse ran off?"

Startled, Arlian glanced at Black. How had he heard that?

That was a stupid question, Arlian realized; gossip had a way of spreading, and while the story of Lord Lanair's arrival at the Weary Traveler was hardly a very exciting tidbit, it was something that Black could easily have picked up.

He hesitated, then admitted, "Actually, I had no horse to begin with."

"Ah," Black said. "And were you perhaps resident in Westguard for several days, then?"

"Perhaps," Arlian admitted. He eyed his companion warily, wondering if he would need to flee.

"You'll have heard, my lord, that an intruder was discovered at the House of Carnal Society?"

"Why, yes," Arlian said.

"It's a curious thing, that no one has found any trace of him since his escape, in his brown homespun and bloody beard."

"Well, he'd certainly have washed the blood out by now," Arlian said.

"Indeed. And he might well have trimmed the beard, as well. And changed into a good white blouse and black breeches, and grown a few inches."

Arlian studied Black, but saw no sign that the man intended any hostile action. "You think so?" he asked.

"Why, I'd venture that at this very minute, he's on his way to Manfort to buy a sword," Black said. "But I admit to wondering why he *wants* a sword, and why he would head for Manfort, rather than some more isolated area."

"Well, perhaps he intended to elude pursuit by joining a caravan to some distant land, and needs a sword for that. Or perhaps he wants a sword the better to disguise himself as a lord. And where better to find a good sword, and news of a caravan, than in Manfort?"

"You don't think it more likely he'd have headed off in some other direction, where he might buy a sword in some outlying town and join a caravan as it passes through?"

Arlian replied, "I can think of two—no, of three reasons he might have preferred to turn toward Manfort instead." He ticked them off on his fingers. "First, it would scarcely be expected, would it? And to do the unexpected is surely wise when one wishes to avoid pursuit and capture. Besides, where is it harder to find a dropped straw—on the road, or in a haystack? Tracking a man through a crowd must surely be more difficult than tracking him through a forest."

Black nodded.

"Second, perhaps this person has some business to attend to in Manfort, some matter of which we can scarcely be expected to know."

"It's possible," Black agreed.

"And finally," Arlian said, "If this person has never before visited Manfort, what could be more natural in a young man of normal curiosity than to wish to see the great city?"

"I see," Black said. "Then you think our fleeing felon intends to buy his sword, attend to his business, see the city, and *then* join a caravan and depart for places unknown? Is this not a risky course of action?"

"Perhaps this person has been a trifle overconfident," Arlian agreed thoughtfully. "After all, if we can so readily imagine his plans, those who are seeking him might do as well." He turned and looked back at the caravan; they were almost at the fork where the caravan would turn to make its way around the city, while they would proceed on to the gate.

"Do you suppose this young man might have acquaintances who would hide him in the city?" Arlian asked. "Perhaps someone he met only recently."

"And what would induce any sensible person to take such a risk?"

"Why, gold, of course."

"Of course," Black agreed. He smiled.

Together the two men passed the fork and started up the slope toward the city gates.

Chapter Eighteen

Lord Ornisir's Sword

"It should balance about here," Black said, resting the sword across two fingers. "It should be light enough that you can use it without tiring, strong enough to pierce your foe without bending or breaking." He tossed the weapon in the air and caught it in one hand. "The hilt should fit your hand comfortably," he said. "Remember that a good sword is a *tool,* something to be used—it's not just for show. Lordlings such as yourself sometimes forget that." He took the blade in his left hand and passed the sword to Arlian, hilt first.

Arlian accepted it, closing his hand around the grip. He hefted the sword, feeling its weight, then slashed tentatively at the air.

"You realize, of course, that all the blades you see here have been rejected," Black said, waving a hand to take in the entire interior of the swordsmith's shop. "These are noblemen's blades, not the cruder tools customary for an ordinary guardsman like myself. Every fine sword is made to a customer's specifications—but the customer may not be pleased with the results, in which case the swordsmith tries again, and the rejected weapon is sent here, to be sold to the likes of us, who know better than to buy the cheap cutlery some people would palm off on buyers, but who lack either the time or the money to commission our own."

Arlian looked at Black, startled, but before he could reply the swordsmith spoke up.

"And sometimes," he said, "the swords are sent here because the buyers who ordered them never came to collect their purchases—sometimes out of negligence or inconsideration, but sometimes because the buyer suffered a severe reversal of fortune, perhaps died, before the sword was ready." He pointed at the weapon Arlian held. "*That* blade was made for the late Lord Ornisir."

"Ah," Arlian said, looking at the sword.

It had a hilt bound in black leather and silver wire, a bell guard of steel inlaid with petals of mother-of-pearl, a long, slim, straight blade, and a pommel of lead caged in silver. It was indeed clearly a weapon meant for a nobleman.

Arlian glanced at the sword on Black's belt. That, too, was a nobleman's sword, though older and worn—but Black was clearly no lord; he was employee, not employer.

"And who are we to deny that it was made for Ornisir?" Black said sardonically. "Of course, some would consider it ill fortune to purchase a sword intended for a man who was slain in his bed by assassins."

"And they'd be fools," the swordsmith said with a shrug. "Lord Ornisir never set his hand on it, and it's a fine weapon."

"I like it," Arlian said.

"There are a dozen others to inspect before making any decisions," Black pointed out.

"Of course," Arlian agreed.

All the same, an hour later it was that same sword in his hand when they left the shop.

"Do you think it was really intended for this Lord Ornisir?" he asked, as he slid it awkwardly into the new leather loop on his belt. He almost tripped over it before he got the hang of walking with the blade at his side.

Black shrugged. "It might have been; it seems a good blade. Even if it was made for someone else and rejected, that doesn't mean there's anything wrong with it—it might not have fit his hand well, or perhaps he thought the chasings didn't match the color of his eyes. If it suits you, then all's well enough—though you won't know its true quality until you've fought for your life with it."

Arlian nodded. "And your own sword? You've fought with it?"

"Often," Black said.

"Did you buy it here?"

Black shook his head. "I took it off a dead man, years ago," he said. "It's served me well."

Arlian nodded again.

"But of course, a sword is only as good as the man who wields it," Black said. "Or the woman, for that matter, as I've seen a few women who could use a blade as well as most men." He pointed at Arlian's new acquisition. "That's truly a lord's sword you just bought, and a good one, but even if it's the finest blade ever forged I'd rather face you with that sword than a real fighter with a butcher knife any day."

Arlian grimaced. "I know," he said. He looked up the street ahead.

They were in Manfort, and the city was still strange and new for Arlian. It smelled of smoke and sewage and baking bread, and when the wind was right or he walked the right streets he could smell the tanneries and dye

146

houses along the eastern wall. Mangy dogs and wary cats foraged in the gutters and alleys, and crows circled overhead or roosted on rooftops, but except for the overcast sky Arlian thought he was nearly as enclosed in stone as ever he was in the mines of Deep Delving. The bustling streets and squares were all paved, either in cobbles or flags, and lined with shops and houses, two or three stories in height, all built of stone and roofed in tile. Since passing the gate he had seen not a single exposed timber nor thatch, nor anything green and growing.

He had remarked on this, and Black had told him, "Stone doesn't burn. Dragons spit flame. This place was built as our fortress against the dragons. You'll find plenty of wood and other tinder inside, but not out in the open." He had nodded up the hill. "In the Upper City the great lords have torn out pavements and buildings to put in gardens here and there, but the common folk down here are happy with the stone."

Manfort was also vast; the streets wound on as far as Arlian could see in every direction—though that was not far, given the curving streets, high stone walls, and overhanging upper stories. They had stopped at Black's rented room to deposit their belongings, startling the landlady, who had thought Black was gone with the caravan; Arlian had been thoroughly lost by the time they reached the place. The city was a maze, and while Arlian was sure he could learn his way around quickly enough, he knew he was not yet ready to attempt to find Lord Dragon or his captives.

And he knew he was not yet ready to fight Lord Dragon. He remembered the speed and ease with which Dragon had drawn his sword and cut Madam Ril's throat; he thought he could manage something not too greatly inferior against an unarmed foe, but he had the imagination to see that matching the attack was not enough. He saw that he must also defend himself against such attacks, and he knew he could not possibly do so effectively.

"Maybe I should have had a sword made new," he said. Any advantage he could buy, he wanted.

"It wouldn't make much difference," Black said. "It's how you use it that really matters. A new sword would be more expensive and would take at least ten days, probably more—I thought you wanted to find another caravan as soon as possible, and one might form by then. *I* intend to join the first one I can."

"Oh," Arlian said.

"Besides, there's no reason to think one made for you would be any better, and you don't yet know enough to be able to say what would work best for you. Not to mention that the chances are good that if you're serious about learning to use it, that sword will get broken at some point in your training."

"Oh," Arlian said again. Even this leftover sword had cost more than he had ever imagined a simple piece of steel could cost—and now Black was saying it might break?

He obviously still had a great deal to learn.

"Now, most of the lords don't bother with armor," Black said, changing the subject. "After all, if you use your sword only to punish unarmed subordinates, or in formal duels, or to defend against assassins who will have done their best to catch you unprepared, armor really isn't going to be worth the discomfort and expense. However, we lesser mortals, who carry weapons for money, can expect to encounter bandits or other unfriendly folks who are very definitely armed, have no interest in formalities, and who haven't the patience of real assassins. They may be using clubs or cutlasses, arrows or arbalests—their armament tends to be quite varied and imaginative. A well-padded helmet can save your life when escorting a caravan; a mail shirt or breastplate is heavy, but turning an arrow is worth a little weight."

"Of course," Arlian agreed.

"And therefore, let us visit the armorer around the corner here," Black said, taking Arlian's elbow and turning him. Caught off guard, he almost collided with an old woman before getting himself headed the right direction.

The swordsmith's shop had been spare and elegant, the walls draped in cloth, the smith's forge and workshop hidden away in the back; the armorer's shop was a startling contrast, crude and cluttered, with weapons and armor stacked everywhere and a rough wooden workbench standing in the very center.

Arlian was amused to see a rack of swords—surely, these were the "cheap cutlery" Black had mentioned. They were shorter and heavier than the weapon he now wore on his belt, with broader blades; some of them curved. He picked one up and hefted it while Black spoke to the armorer. He felt the blade, tried to flex it.

The feel of the metal was different, with little spring to it; this was clearly inferior stuff. He suspected that it would be easy to notch, bend, or break a sword like this.

"My lord!" Black called, and Arlian started. He put the sword back on the rack and turned his attention elsewhere.

Two hours later the two men finally emerged from the shop, Arlian carrying a bundle that contained a mail shirt, a helmet, a set of greaves, and three assorted blades.

Two of the blades were knives—an ordinary belt knife and a dagger. The third was something Arlian had never heard of before, which Black called a "left hand," or "swordbreaker," though once he had gotten a good look at it Arlian realized he had seen at least one, long ago.

Lord Dragon had worn one on the right side of his belt on that day almost eight years ago, when he had sat astride his horse looking down at Arlian amid the smoldering ruins of Obsidian.

It was, in fact, constructed much like a sword, with a hilt and guard, but the blade was only about a foot long, and there were two four-inch steel spikes parallel to the blade, one on either side.

"Catch a sword in one of those," Black had explained, "and you can just twist your wrist and snap the blade right off."

Arlian had stared at the device in wonder; the maneuver Black described should indeed work.

"Every lord has one now, and those who do any serious fighting know how to use them," Black had said. "I have one myself, though I don't parade it about."

"It just snaps the blade?" Arlian had asked, twisting the swordbreaker to demonstrate. "Just like that?"

Black had laughed at him. "It's *catching* it that's the hard part!"

Difficult to use or not, Black had strongly advised him to buy the thing, and he had.

They returned to Black's room, a stuffy, dim little place high under the eaves of a bakery.

"A good day's work," Black said, as he opened the door at the top of the stair. "At least you're properly equipped now, even if you haven't any idea how to use any of it. Tomorrow we'll start teaching you the basics, and see if there are any caravan notices posted."

"Thank you," Arlian said, as they stepped into the room. "You've been very kind."

Black glanced at him as he closed the door. "I have, haven't I?" he said. "You know, I'm not sure why."

Arlian started to say something, thought better of it, and coughed on his own saliva as the words caught in his throat.

"I think, my lord, that it's time you told me more about yourself," Black said. "Let us start with my suspicion that you have somehow availed yourself of a sorcerous glamour."

Arlian's jaw dropped in astonishment. "What?" he said. He had been expecting questions and suspicions, but not that one. He had seen no magic of any kind since he entered the mine, and had almost forgotten such things existed.

"Well, my lord, you must admit that there's something peculiar about your circumstances," Black explained. "You seem to have been exceptionally fortunate in deceiving your pursuers—I understand that the town patrols in Westguard questioned Lord Lanair, and never once suspected that he might be the fugitive they sought."

"I wasn't what they were expecting," Arlian protested. "A woman taught me that—people see what they're expecting to see." His throat thickened at the mention of Rose, as he remembered how he had last seen her, lifeless and bleeding. He swallowed. "So I made sure I wasn't what they expected," he continued. "They were looking for a fleeing vagabond, not a young nobleman demanding lodging."

"And a good ruse it was, surely…"

"*You* saw through it quickly enough, though, didn't you?" Arlian interrupted, suddenly troubled.

"Indeed. If I were easily fooled I'd have been dead years ago. But on the other hand, my lord, consider that you and I are both here, in my lodgings, when by rights I should be twenty miles east of here on the road to Lorigol, leaving you to make your own way in Manfort. Why is that?"

"Do you think I *ensorcelled* you?" Arlian asked, flabbergasted.

"The thought had crossed my mind—and much later than it should have."

"I haven't," Arlian said. "I know nothing of sorcery."

"Then we have a mystery."

"Perhaps I've just been lucky," Arlian said. "Fate is being kind to me at last."

"Perhaps," Black conceded. "I tend to think it's something more than that, though. There's something in your eyes, and your manner—you have a certain charm about you, and I find myself wondering whether it might be a literal charm, rather than a figurative one."

"If it is, it's none of *my* doing."

Black nodded, and stared at him thoughtfully.

"You know," he said at last, "I've seen it before, I think. In certain of the nobility. There's an air about them, as if they were born to command those around them. It's hard to doubt you, or to deny you."

Arlian snorted. "If you see that, then it's sheerest artifice, and a recent acquisition."

"Oh, I see it," Black said. "No one could doubt your noble birth. It's a strength, a power—in lords or warriors they call it the heart of the dragon, and men who have it make great leaders."

"'The heart of the dragon'?" Arlian's gorge rose as the words suddenly brought back the memory of lying on the cellar floor, pinned beneath his grandfather's corpse, with that blood and venom dripping into his mouth. He could almost *taste* the ghastly brew …

Was there a connection?

"I'm not of noble birth," he said, more to distract himself than anything else. "I was born to a family of freeholders. Tradesmen and artisans."

"Oh?"

"They're all dead," Arlian said. "I was sold into slavery."

"Yet you *look* every inch a lord."

"I was taught to look like one, and act like one," Arlian said. "By women. And *they're* dead now, some of them. Or gone." He thought of Sweet, carried off in Lord Dragon's coach, and wondered where she was—was she somewhere in Manfort? Was she nearby, perhaps?

Would he ever see her again? He ought to be out searching for her—but he needed to know how. He couldn't simply roam about the city at random.

"If that's all it is, then they did a good job," Black said. "I suspect there's more to it than that. And why did these women choose to teach you?"

Arlian shrugged. "A whim."

"You said you were a slave; how did you get free? You must have had help."

"I saved an overseer's life," Arlian said.

"And he freed you, in gratitude?"

"Yes."

"In my experience gratitude is an emotion more common in children's tales than in everyday life."

Arlian frowned and said nothing.

"It seems to me that whatever else may have happened, there is something about you that prompts others to your aid," Black said. "You say it's not sorcerous; very well, I believe you. Nevertheless, call it nobility, or the dragon's heart, or the urging of Fate, I think it's real."

Arlian remembered the taste of his grandfather's blood. "Perhaps it is," he said. "It's not of my choosing, but if it aids me in the pursuit of my destiny I'll not quibble."

"You think you have a destiny, do you?" Black asked.

Arlian glanced at him, expecting to see sardonic amusement in his face, but found only a thoughtful expression.

"Yes," Arlian said. "Or at any rate, I have sworn an oath I mean to fulfill, if it takes all my life."

"And what would that oath be?"

"To destroy the dragons who destroyed my village, and to bring justice to others who have wronged me and those about me," Arlian replied.

Black stared at him silently for a moment. "Dragons," he said at last.

"Yes," Arlian said defiantly. He knew that his oath sounded stupid, a child's overblown fantasy—no one had ever killed a dragon. Still, he intended to try.

"Your home was destroyed by dragons?"

"Three of them," Arlian said. "I saw them."

"You speak our tongue like a native, and you are too young to be from Starn, in the Sandalwood Hills," Black said, "so you must mean Obsidian, on the Smoking Mountain."

"Yes," Arlian said. He swallowed. It was odd to hear that name again after so long.

"Was your family there?"

"My parents, my brother, my grandfather," Arlian said.

"And you? Where were you?"

"I was there," Arlian said. "I hid in a cellar. Looters found me, and sold me to the mines in Deep Delving."

"So you *saw* the dragons?"

Arlian nodded. "I looked one in the eye," he said. "Before I hid."

"Perhaps that's it, then," Black said contemplatively. "You looked Death in the eye and lived; perhaps that's what it is." He frowned. "But I've faced death at times, and while it changed me, I haven't the dragon's heart as you do. Maybe it's the dragon itself that makes the difference…" He sank into silent thought for a moment. Then he roused himself and said, "And you're resolved to waste your life hunting dragons? Then why come to Manfort?"

"Many reasons," Arlian said. "First, where better to go to learn about dragons? This is where men first defied them, isn't it?"

"True enough," Black agreed. "The secrets are still kept secret, though."

"Then I'll still learn them somehow."

Black nodded. "And another reason?"

"I need to know more about *everything,* if I'm to have any chance of success," Arlian explained.

"And where better than Manfort?"

"Exactly."

"You seem to be more concerned with learning the sword than with sorcery, though, and surely magic is your best chance against dragons."

"I'm leaving the dragons until last," Arlian said. "I'm not a complete fool; I know I probably can't kill them. I intend to try, but I know I'll probably be killed myself. So I'm going after the others first."

"Others?"

"The looters," Arlian explained. "Lord Dragon and the six he brought with him." He shuddered at the memory. "They took me from the ruins before I'd had a chance to mourn. They sold me as a slave. They took everything we owned that the dragons hadn't destroyed—the obsidian, my mother's jewelry, even the cheeses from our cellars! They'll pay for that—and payment's long overdue."

"By eight years, or thereabouts," Black agreed. "Now, *that's* a goal I can believe in."

"And Lord Dragon ordered Rose killed," Arlian said, beginning to lose control of himself. "He had Sweet's feet cut off. He had the House burned. He cut Madam Ril's throat. He and Lord Kuruvan and the others..." He gasped for air, and burst out weeping.

He had held it in for so long, but he could do so no more; it was all too much. He had never had a chance to mourn *any* of them properly—not his mother, or his grandfather, or his father, or his brother, or Hathet, or Rose, or Silk, or the two others dead in the brothel. He didn't even know which two they were. He didn't know where Sweet was, whether she was alive or dead, or what had become of all the others. He stood and wept uncontrollably.

Black embraced the youth and let him cry, and the two men stood together for a long time.

No further mention was made of Arlian's supposed sorcery.

Chapter Nineteen

The Merchant Lords

Black stopped dead in his tracks as the two walked down the Street of the Wainwrights, and flung his arm across Arlian's chest.

"What is it?" Arlian asked, startled, as he, too, came to a sudden halt.

Black pointed at the notice tacked to the crazed green paint on a provisioner's door. "At last!" he said,

Arlian looked, and read.

CARAVAN the parchment read in big blue letters at the top. Just below, in smaller print, it said TO THE SOUTHERN BORDERLANDS.

And in black, below that, "Seeking Merchants to Join the Expedition, and Men at Arms to Escort Us." At the bottom were instructions for contacting the caravan masters—three partners' names were listed, with the address of an office on the Street of the Silk Merchants.

Arlian read this with mixed emotions. Black had been seeking employment with a caravan all along; while he accepted the gold Arlian paid him for lessons in swordsmanship, he had made plain that he considered this a stopgap and had no intention of being a mere tutor.

"There are things you won't learn on the practice ground, boy," Black had said one night as they drank ale at the tavern around the corner from Black's room—Black had undertaken to teach Arlian to tell good ale from bad, along with his other tutelage. "I don't know who this 'Lord Dragon' of yours is, but if he's as formidable as you make him sound, you'll need to know more than I can teach you here in Manfort!"

Arlian was not entirely convinced. Lord Dragon was here in Manfort, he was certain; it seemed wrong, somehow, to spend a year or so deliberately going elsewhere—and he now knew that a caravan's journey out and back, with stops for trade along the way and at the end, could easily last a year or more.

But on the other hand, he knew he still had much to learn before he could face Lord Dragon, even if he found him.

He had not had to make a choice before, as no caravans were in the offing—but now this notice meant he would have to decide, and quickly.

"The Borderlands," he said, as they stood before the provisioner's door.

"That's a long way, isn't it?"

Black glanced at him. "Very long," he said. "Could be two years, all told, before we're back here."

Arlian frowned. He was thinking that Sweet might be alive somewhere in Manfort. He had asked a few questions, made a few brief excursions into the broad avenues of the Upper City, where the city's nobles made their homes, but had found no trace of her, nor heard any mention of any lord calling himself Dragon—but they might still be here.

"I don't know," he said. "That's a long time."

"You're young, lad," Black said, as he turned away from the door. "You've plenty of time for your revenge. And you'll learn more about the world this way, not just about swordsmanship; when you come back you'll either be ready to take vengeance or you'll know you'll never be."

"You seem very sure of that," Arlian remarked, turning to follow.

"I *am* sure of it," Black replied, setting a brisk pace. "If it were Lorigol, or one of the other ports like Benthin or Sarkan-Mendoth, or if it were into the western mountains, or if it were any number of other routes, then maybe not. But the Borderlands—you visit the Borderlands, boy, and the lands beyond the border, and you'll come back with a proper respect for dragons, and for the people who took their places."

"Why?" Arlian asked. "What do dragons have to do with the Borderlands?"

Black turned to stare at him as they walked. "You know why they're called the Borderlands, don't you?"

"They're the farthest extent of the Lands of Man," Arlian said. "So?"

"So, my boy, think about it! The Lands of Man are the lands we took away from the dragons, yes?"

"Yes."

"And *all* the dragons are gone, yes?"

"Well, they're sleeping in the caverns," Arlian said. "They aren't *dead*. I *saw* them."

"Then what lies beyond the Borderlands, my young lord?"

Arlian stared at him blankly.

Black sighed as they turned a corner onto the Street of the Coopers. "*Think,* boy! You've just all but said that what lies beyond is the lands ruled by neither men nor dragons. So what do you think *does* rule there?"

Arlian's stare was no longer blank, but shocked. He stopped in his tracks. "I don't know," he said. "Gods?"

"Maybe some places," Black conceded, as he, too, stopped and turned to face his young companion. "Gods here and there, perhaps, and certainly a few magicians elsewhere, but mostly … mostly it's *other* things. Things that neither men nor dragons conquered."

"Oh," Arlian said.

"And what's more," Black continued, "they're things that *couldn't conquer the dragons.* And we're going there to trade with them—or at least with their subjects. When you see what's beyond the borders, maybe you'll see a little more of why I think that's important, and what it says about the dragons."

"I know about dragons," Arlian said.

"You know *everything* about them?" Black asked. "Can you tell male from female? Do they lay eggs or bear their young alive? How long do they live?"

"I don't know," Arlian admitted, taking a step down the sloping street.

"Neither do I," Black said. "No one does, so far as I know. But you said you know about dragons."

"I know enough!" Arlian said angrily, turning away and marching on.

"How do you *know* you do?" Black insisted, pursuing. "Isn't it good sense to know everything you can about your enemy before you go to fight him?"

"All right!" Arlian said, throwing up his hands in surrender. "All right. I'll come with you to the Borderlands—and you'll teach me to fight. Every day."

"Every day," Black agreed. He glanced thoughtfully back toward the notice. "And if you have any sense, boy, you'll take that gold of yours and you'll buy a wagon of your own, and stock it with trade goods, and you'll sign onto the caravan as a merchant, not a guard."

Arlian stopped, thunderstruck.

"I hadn't thought of that," he said.

He had been slightly concerned of late at how fast his supply of gold was dwindling; he still had more than enough to fill any purse, but after arming himself and paying Black's teaching fees he was no longer sure that his stolen fortune would be enough to live on indefinitely.

He hadn't worried about it, really. After all, he could always go back to the Blood of the Grape and fetch out more of Lord Kuruvan's gold, and that would be enough to live on for a very long time.

But if he invested it in a caravan—especially if he took *all* the gold from the broken keg and invested *all* of it …

Everyone knew that caravans were risky, but highly profitable. He might well return to Manfort really *rich,* a real lord instead of a fraud, rich enough to hire men to hunt down the looters, buy the twelve women free, and hire an army to hunt the dragons.

Or if disaster struck, he might return to Manfort penniless—or not at all. Still, if he was going to accompany Black in any case, it seemed worth trying.

He would need to get the gold out of the inn's cellars. He would be able to handle the operation far more effectively this time, since he knew just where the keg was and he had the time and money to prepare properly, but he would still need a distraction.

Black had stopped beside him; now Arlian turned to face the older man. "Tell me," he said. "Do you know much about wine?"

The next night, while Black spent half an hour choosing exactly the right expensive wine for an imaginary occasion, thereby keeping the innkeeper busy in the vault, Arlian told the rest of the inn's staff, "I'll just get my own ale, thanks!" and strolled down the cellar stairs, mug in hand.

No one argued with the impeccably dressed young lord. He wore his hair brushed back in the latest style, his beard neatly trimmed to a point; he wore a beautiful sword on his belt, and had a fine leather pack slung on one shoulder. He simply *reeked* of wealth and confidence.

And if he took a long time fetching his ale, and the pack looked a little heavier when he emerged, what of it? He tipped each of the staff a gold half-ducat, even the pot-boy, and it wasn't as if anything in the cellars other than the rare wines in the vault would be worth such a man's efforts to steal.

On the dusty walk back to Manfort he asked Black, "What should I buy?"

"A wagon and two yoke of oxen, to start with," Black said.

"I know *that,*" Arlian said, nettled. "I mean, what do we take to *sell?*"

Black shrugged. "I'm no merchant," he said.

"But you've been to the Borderlands before, haven't you?"

"Twice," Black acknowledged. "The merchants brought wool and silk and other fabrics, and northern wines, and certain herbs, and traded for talismans, gems, dyes, rare woods, drugs and potions, strange foodstuffs, and for still other fabrics. Oh, and exotic pets—there was a fashion for lizards at the time, though it had all but passed by the time we returned."

Arlian nodded and shifted his pack to a more comfortable position. "And if we were bound for Lorigol?"

Black looked at him, startled. "Why?"

"I'm just curious."

"Wool and silk and wine, and we'd come back with oil and salt and spices, with dyes and pearls and curiosities made from seashells."

"And the western mountains?"

"Well, we wouldn't take wool!" Black said with a snort of laughter. "Theirs is better than ours. We'd take oil and grain and spices, and we'd bring back brass and chalk and dyes and herbs. And other things; I don't know. Merchants are always trying new goods."

"And isn't that where the most money is to be made?"

"Or lost, if you misjudge what people want to buy."

Arlian nodded, thinking hard about gold and what it could buy. The best goods were obviously things that were small, so that more could be fit into a wagon, and cheap to buy but precious at the other end of the caravan's route. And best of all would be something that no one else in the caravan had brought, so that you and the other merchants would not undercut each other.

What gold could buy …

"Do they make good swords in the Borderlands?"

Black looked thoughtful. "No, they don't," he said. "They hardly work metal at all. That's one reason *we* go *there,* rather than their merchants coming to Manfort—they make their wagon fittings of wood and leather rather than iron, and arm themselves with arrows, spears, and slings, and the wagons just don't last that well."

"Then … well, is there some reason no one takes swords and ironmongery to sell?"

"I don't know," Black said slowly. "I believe … well, remember, many of the lands beyond the border are ruled by magical creatures of one sort or another. Such beings are said to dislike silver and cold iron; I know that all the coins in the southern lands are of gold or copper, never of silver. Perhaps iron and silver aren't *allowed* there."

"Then wouldn't that make them all the more precious?"

Black smiled. "Most likely," he agreed.

Arlian was careful not to say anything more on the subject until the following day, at the office on the Street of the Silk merchants, after Black's employment as commander of the caravan's contingent of guards was settled and the contracts signed. Then, when that was irreversible and Black's position secure, he announced what he proposed to sell.

The three caravan masters, seated in a row behind their polished black table, were shocked. "Selling iron is *forbidden* in the magical realms," Lord Drens said.

"Most of them," Lord Sandal, seated on Drens's left, corrected. "Not in Arithei or Stiva."

Arlian, standing before the table, started at the mention of Arithei; this was the first time since Hathet's death he had heard the name spoken aloud. And it was spoken by someone who had been to the Borderlands, and would know the truth. That meant it *did* exist.

It didn't mean any of the rest of Hathet's story was true, though. He was probably mad, not an ambassador at all, and his amethysts were probably nothing but pretty stones.

"But who can *get* to Arithei or Stiva?" Drens retorted. "Not I! The roads are closed, and the native guides are gone, and the only routes are across the Dreaming Mountains. I have no desire to live out my life beset by nightmares, to never again have an untroubled night's sleep!"

"Really, my lord," Lady Thassa, at the right end of the table, said, addressing Arlian directly again, "I would not advise bringing ironwork. Our wagons and swords are not permitted in certain areas as it is; we bring them over the borders only under severe restrictions."

"What about silver?" Arlian asked, pushing Arithei out of his mind.

"Banned in Shei, Furza, and Tirikindaro," Lady Thassa replied. "Out of favor in the neighboring lands and of no use as currency, but not forbidden."

"Is it more valuable there than here?"

Thassa, Drens, and Sandal exchanged glances.

"I don't know," Sandal admitted.

"And what if I were to sell my goods on *this* side of the border?"

"We can hardly object to *that*," Sandal said. "Trade within the Lands of Man is free and open."

Lord Drens started to protest, and Lady Thassa interrupted him; a moment later the three were in the midst of a full-blown argument.

Their clerk sent Black and Arlian away, with instructions to return the next day.

They did, and learned that the vote was two to one in Arlian's favor; Lord Drens yielded with poor grace, but he had yielded.

Now he glared across the table at the troublemaker. "Always remember, Lord Ari," Drens said, using Arlian's latest alias, "that we reserve the right to expel you from the caravan at any time should we decide that your continued presence endangers the rest of us."

"Understood, my lord," Arlian said with a bow.

"And you understand our contracts? That each member shares in the expenses?"

Arlian nodded. The contracts were quite complex, and rather daunting, as they covered any number of possible contingencies, including provisions for what would happen to his goods if he died at various points in the expedition, and how any proceeds would be shared between his heirs (if any) and the other members of the caravan.

Arlian understood this, and since he was going more to continue his education than to make a profit and had no heirs, nor any intention of dying, he was untroubled by the terms.

"They are quite satisfactory," he said.

The three masters nodded, and the papers were brought out for Arlian's signature, concluding the negotiations.

When the caravan assembled in the plaza before the Blood of the Grape two days later, Arlian's new wagon held some three dozen fine swords—the complete stock of four swordsmiths' shops—and hundreds of good daggers. A large part of his wealth had been transformed from gold to silver, as well.

He had also acquired all the usual requirements for a long journey—clothing, bedding, nonperishable foods, extra harness for his four oxen, a huge quantity of grain, water, wine, lamp oil, hundreds of feet of rope, and so on. He had even equipped himself with a bow and a dozen arrows—not that he knew how to use them effectively.

In addition, he brought two pairs of practice swords—low-grade steel with no edge and blunt points, but with the weight and balance of a proper sword.

Although he was a merchant and a full member of the caravan, Arlian was also contracted as a guard in training, an unpaid apprentice, and as such he was assigned the second position, directly behind the lead wagon Black shared with seven other guards; that suited him well. He hired one of the other guards, a man called Quickhand, to teach him to tend and drive oxen, and to drive for him until the lessons were learned.

There were three more guards at the rear, in the masters' large and elegant wagon, and four on horseback who also slept at the rear—fifteen guards in all. That was deemed adequate by all.

The two wagons that were to hold guards—the lead wagon and the masters' oversized conveyance—both had large shutters on either side that could be swung back, opening the sides to let in air and light, or to allow the occupants to survey their surroundings; the other wagons, intended primarily for keeping goods safe, were far more solidly built. Arlian's was little more than a large wooden box on wheels with a platform on either end and a bench seat at the front, all painted a rich blue and trimmed with varnished bamboo.

And on a fine bright day in late spring Arlian sat beside his hired driver as the caravan rolled out of the plaza and headed south, toward the Borderlands.

Chapter Twenty

The Road South

"This is Benth-in-Tara," Quickhand said, as the wagon rolled past a stone marker toward the sprawling town ahead. "We'll be stopping here for a day to trade with the locals."

Arlian frowned at the name; he knew he remembered it, but couldn't quite place it. The long fertile valley of Tara Vale was familiar enough, of course ...

Then it came back to him; Benth-in-Tara was where Grandsir had been headed when he saw the ruins of Starn, the village in the Sandalwood Hills that the dragons had destroyed.

Arlian turned to the southwest, peering into the distance.

Those hills were surely the Sandalwood Hills, then—though he was seeing them now from the other side, and as a result there was little familiar in their appearance. The shadowy spike on the horizon would be Skygrazer Peak, and the distant smoke rising from a humped peak beyond the hills would be from the Smoking Mountain, where he had been born.

When he was in the mine he had often dreamed of returning there, and now, if he chose, he could—who would stop him?

But why should he? Nothing remained of Obsidian but ruins. Sweet had told him, one long night last winter when he and she had exchanged reminiscences, that the village was never rebuilt; a place that dragons had destroyed was considered cursed, forever unsafe.

The thought of Sweet troubled him; he seemed to see her face in the western sky. He felt guilty that he was here, rather than back in Manfort searching for her.

He could never have found her and rescued her as the ignorant naïf he had been before meeting Black, though. He was not yet ready to make his bit of justice in the world, not yet ready to free her and avenge poor Rose. Thinking about Sweet could only distract him from more immediate concerns; he would come back for her in time.

He once more turned his attention to the town they were entering.

So this, he thought, was Benth-in-Tara, where his grandfather had long ago come to trade. And now here he was, following in Grandsir's footsteps—but nobody here would be interested in swords or daggers.

He had not thought of that when stocking his wagon; of course the caravan made other stops on its way south, and he had brought nothing to sell at any of them.

That might be an expensive oversight. He frowned.

"A day here," he said. "What's the next trading stop, then?"

"Jumpwater, I think," Quickhand said.

"And after that?"

Quickhand thought for a moment, then ticked off the names on his fingers.

"Blasted Oak, Sadar, Cork Tree, Stonebreak," he said. "Then we get to the Desolation, and from there there's nothing until we reach the Borderlands, and where we go depends on what road the masters choose."

"There's more than one road?"

"There are at least three routes across the Desolation, and they branch further on the other side."

"And what determines which route we take?"

Quickhand shrugged. "News and rumor in Stonebreak, the weather, any signs or omens we might encounter … whatever the masters hear and see."

Arlian frowned. It all seemed too vague and poorly planned for his liking.

"It's in the southern part of the Desolation that Black and I are going to earn our pay," Quickhand remarked. "That's bandit country, where the roads come down off the high plateau and wind through the canyons."

"Not until then?"

Quickhand shrugged again. "Oh, maybe," he said. "If we weren't here there would probably be burglars and sneak thieves slipping into the wagons in every town, but who would dare tackle a group this size, even if they were just merchants?" He gestured at the long line of wagons trailing behind them. "Even merchants can put up a fight, after all."

"But then how do the bandits in the Desolation operate?" Arlian asked. "How can there be enough to attack this large a group, but few enough that a dozen or so guards can handle them?"

"The canyons," Quickhand explained. "They can block the road, trap the whole caravan, with just a few men, and then starve the caravan into submission. A dozen good fighters can drive them away and keep them away while the others clear the road." He paused, then added, "Usually. They have other tricks, as well—they'll try to split the caravan, or disable a few wagons so they can loot them, or take a few prisoners they can ransom."

"Oh," Arlian said. Just then he caught sight of a curious structure ahead, at the very heart of Benth-in-Tara—a single vast roof supported on a forest of pillars, its sides and interior open. "What's *that?*" he asked.

"The marketplace," Quickhand explained, as he steered the plodding oxen directly toward it.

The caravan rolled into the marketplace and formed up in three lines beneath the roof—one along either side, and one down the shady center. The guard wagon, which had no goods to display, was in the center—and Arlian's own wagon was right next to it.

When they had stopped, as the other wagons were still rolling into position, Arlian leaped to the ground and greeted Black, who had already disembarked.

"Nothing to sell here?" Black asked.

Arlian shook his head. "I didn't think of it," he said. "Foolish of me."

"Ah," Black said. "And here I thought you'd done it deliberately, so I'd have more time to thrash you tomorrow."

Arlian smiled; sure enough, he realized, if he had nothing to trade on trading day, he could devote the time entirely to his swordsmanship.

Word of the caravan's arrival was spreading rapidly through the surrounding farms and villages, and the next day brought hundreds of people flooding into town, eager to see what treasures the caravan might be carrying—even though most of them couldn't afford to buy anything.

Arlian and Black left the crowds behind and found an open field just outside town, left fallow this year and now green with weeds and sprinkled with wildflowers. There Arlian took up a dull-edged practice sword and a wooden swordbreaker, and faced off against Black, blinking in the bright summer sun.

The day after, as the last straggling customers headed homeward and the caravan began rolling again, Arlian was no longer smiling; Black had indeed thrashed him, figuratively and almost literally. They had fought only with blunted practice blades, but Arlian still had a dozen cuts on his chest and arms, all of which had been treated with brandy and bandaged. He also had a scratch across one cheek deemed too small for bandaging, as well as innumerable bruises received not only from the practice weapons, but when dodging had slammed him against a tree or rock, or when he had dodged or parried a stroke of Black's blade only to receive a punch or kick, or when he had fallen to get out of the path of Black's blade.

He had thought he was making progress in his lessons, but the day spent in Benth-in-Tara had shown him how far he still had to go. For the first time Black had moved beyond the basics and a few simple practice moves into real fencing, and he had demonstrated that he was able to cut Arlian at will, while turning aside every assault Arlian attempted.

Arlian overcame his initial resentment at this brutal treatment by reminding himself that Lord Dragon might well be as good a swordsman as Black, or better, and Lord Dragon would not hold back, would not stop his blows as soon as they cut cloth or drew blood. He knew that Black, in his brutality, was really doing him a kindness.

But as he sat on the seat beside Quickhand, the cuts stinging and bandages tugging with every bounce the wagon took, it didn't *feel* like a kindness.

The evening lessons on the road returned to the less-strenuous mode of demonstration and practice, rather than actual combat, but at Jumpwater, six days later, another trading day meant another all-out training session.

Jumpwater had no covered market like Benth-in-Tara's, but a series of three broad terraces on the road that wound down the slope toward the Forest River. The wagons lined up on those terraces above the town, and merchants were able to display their goods to the entire population of Jumpwater simultaneously.

Arlian still had no goods to display. The road out of Jumpwater now led across a sturdy wooden bridge, but Black took Arlian down to the rapids, and they fought on the stones that had once been the only way across the river and which had given the town its name.

Arlian's only consolations were that he received significantly fewer cuts and bruises, and two of the three times he fell in the water he was able to pull himself out before Black could come to his aid.

Ten days after that, at Blasted Oak, while the merchants did their business in the great central square around the shrine that supposedly sheltered the stump of the blasted oak itself, Arlian met Black in a field behind the brewery. There he actually managed to counter one of Black's lunges and draw blood from the back of the older man's hand—whereupon Black announced that Arlian was getting too familiar with his opponent's style, and set the other guards to taking turns in sparring with Lord Ari when they weren't occupied in keeping order at the caravan market.

None of the others attacked as fiercely as Black, but Arlian discovered that Black had been right—several of the others were able to get past his guard by making moves that Black had never tried.

As he lay on the thin mattress in his wagon that night, wishing he had paid the money for a featherbed at the local inn so that his bruises wouldn't hurt quite so much, he began to wonder whether he would ever be a real swordsman. There was so *much* to learn! How could anyone ever learn to counter every possible move, in every possible style? Black insisted that wasn't necessary, that there were patterns he could learn, but Arlian did not yet see them.

At Sadar he began to see them.

Sadar had no true marketplace, and they were out of the forest once more and onto an open plain; the caravan simply lined up along the road south of town. Black led Arlian out onto the empty plain to practice amid the tall grass.

Summer was just past its peak, and the weather had grown steadily warmer as they moved further south, so the fighting there was done bare-chested and dripping with sweat. Arlian found that this made defense easier; he could see his opponent's muscles start to tense before the sword itself moved.

Perhaps that was the extra bit of information he needed, or perhaps something simply fell into place, but he found himself moving his own sword to parry his opponent's before he was consciously aware that Black had attacked. It simply felt right.

Up until now exchanges had mostly been quick—typically feint, parry, thrust, parry, and then a touch or a break. Now, though, Arlian found himself launching into sustained bouts, where his blade and Black's would dart and clash for minute after minute before one of them left an opening or stepped back to regroup.

Arlian received only a single cut after that, and few bruises.

A fortnight later, at Cork Tree, while the merchants did what business they could in pouring rain, Arlian and the other guards fought in dripping shirts in the yard behind a slaughterhouse. At midafternoon, Arlian left a red welt on the side of Black's neck.

Black smiled at him. "If you'd been using a real sword I'd be dead or dying," he said. He touched Arlian's forehead with the tip of his own mock weapon and flipped a lock of wet hair aside. "See why I keep mine short?"

"I'll cut it later," Arlian said with an exhausted grin.

At Stonebreak the caravan set up along the base of the cliff, and the masters demanded that the guards stay close by, and maintain a careful watch—while this wasn't yet bandit territory, the locals were not entirely trustworthy. Arlian and Black were therefore only able to manage an hour or two of practice, no more than on most evenings when the caravan was traveling.

Black and Quickhand were now working together, so that Arlian could practice fighting multiple opponents; after all, bandits didn't usually stage formal duels.

From Stonebreak the caravan made its way up the ravine, into the Desolation. Rumors passed up and down the chain of wagons as to which route the masters would choose when they emerged onto the plateau.

Everyone agreed that the direct route, the straight line across the high desert, would not be safe—the summer had been fairly dry, and the Midway Waterhole would almost certainly be empty, which would mean dead oxen and disaster.

That left the Low Road, around the western rim of the plateau, safe but slow, and the Eastern Road, much shorter and reasonably well watered but through rough country.

Arlian hoped for the Eastern Road; he was impatient to get back to Manfort. He knew that he was now at least an adequate swordsman—still no expert, but adequate—and wanted to get on with his plans for rescue and revenge.

The trail up the ravine was hardly a road at all, Arlian noticed; there were no wheel ruts to be seen, nor any sort of marker. It was simply the route where there were no rocks in the path big enough to stop a wagon. He commented on this—he had to speak loudly to be heard over the wind that howled overhead, above the ravine.

Quickhand shrugged. "Well, there's nothing up here but the Desolation," he called back, "and nobody goes through the Desolation except the one or two caravans a year bound for the Borderlands. That's not enough to make a real road."

"And the roads across the Desolation…"

"They're like this. The Low Road has a few markings so people won't lose the path; the Desert Road doesn't. I've never been on the eastern route."

Arlian nodded. They rode on, until they finally emerged from the top of the ravine and Arlian saw the Desolation.

He stared out at it in dismay.

For as far as he could see there was nothing ahead of them but brown stone and golden sand; the thin stream that had cut the ravine was hidden in its stony bed, showing only as a black line across bare stone. Not a single blade of grass, not a single speck of green, could be seen anywhere. Hot wind swept across it, stirring the sand.

Arlian leaned to the side and looked back, past his own wagon, past the caravan. The ravine's curves hid the route they had followed to reach this height, but he could see across the stony plateau to the cliffs.

Beyond those cliffs the world below was still green; he could see green faintly through the summer haze. That was a comforting reminder.

He turned forward again.

Black had stopped the guard wagon by the crack in the stone, and was climbing down. Quickhand directed Arlian's own wagon to stop beside him.

"We'll want to top off every water barrel," Black called. "And while we're doing that the masters can settle our route." He turned and squinted at the wasteland. "Doesn't seem *too* bad," he said. "I've seen it worse."

Arlian swallowed; his throat was suddenly dry. "How could it be worse?" he called.

Black looked up at him. "The wind could be stronger, the sun brighter, the air hotter. If we'd been here earlier, at midsummer, I'm sure it would have been worse."

"Oh," Arlian said.

"It's a tricky matter, timing a southbound caravan," Black remarked. "Too soon, and the summer heat will kill you. Too late, and the streams will have dried up and you'll die of thirst. I think we've hit it about right."

Arlian looked out at the aptly named Desolation.

"Oh," he said again.

If this was *right,* he hoped never to see wrong.

Chapter Twenty-One

The Eastern Road

They took the Eastern Road.

Arlian thought calling it a "road" was sorely misleading; "taking the Eastern Road" just meant circling around the utterly barren sands at the heart of the Desolation on the eastern side until they reached one of the defiles leading down from the plateau.

This route would bring them to the eastern Borderlands; a few of the merchants grumbled that they'd have made a better profit to the west, but most were pleased. Arlian didn't know enough to have an opinion either way.

Navigation on the Eastern Road was simple enough, even though there were no markers; keep the sands always on your right, and stay on bare stone. Boulders, rockslides, and breaks in the stone too wide for a wagon wheel to cross—and all three were numerous—meant detours. In several places the "road" led across immense, tilted slabs of rock; some of the upward-sloping examples of these were steep enough that the oxen couldn't manage them unaided, and the riders had to get out and push. A few were so extreme that oxen had to be shared and the wagons hauled up the slope in shifts. On downward slopes the wheelbrakes were used to keep the wagons from running away and running into their own oxen, and riders would walk alongside, ready to grab if the brakes started to slip. When anyone spotted a hole in the stone the entire caravan would come to a halt while buckets dredged up the trapped water.

Arlian wondered how these holes had formed, but no one had an answer. They were simply part of the Desolation; each spring the rains filled them, and until they dried out they made it possible for caravans to get across without dying of thirst, and without hauling insanely huge quantities of water up the ravine from Stonebreak. The limited water supply was the reason only a single caravan each year could rely on safely crossing the Desolation by each of the three routes.

The caravan traveled as far and as fast each day as the oxen and the terrain would allow; there was no reason to linger in this ghastly wasteland. By day the sun and hot wind baked them dry; by night the wind was cooler, almost pleasant, and most of the caravan's personnel slept out on the rocks, under the stars, rather than in their stifling, overheated wagons.

It never rained in the Desolation in the summer. The more experienced travelers laughed at the very idea. Rain fell heavily enough in the cold months, sometimes flooding dangerously across the stone and turning the sand into treacherous muck, but in the summer the Desolation was always utterly dry.

The sun beat down relentlessly from the cloudless sky, and despite the heat Arlian began wearing a broad-brimmed coachman's hat to shade his face from that withering glare. He had bought the hat back in Manfort, at Black's urging, but had never expected to use the thing; now he found it indispensable. As usual, Black had been right.

As the days passed the terrain grew even worse, and more detours were required; they passed broken stones that Arlian thought might be ruins of some sort—but who would ever have built anything here, in the Desolation?

He also found odd marks in the stone on occasion. At one point he noticed a set of three parallel grooves, almost like claw marks—though they were too large for claw marks, and what could claw solid stone?

Other than dragons, of course.

Some of the waterholes were not mere holes, but caves, reaching deep into the stone beneath their feet. One day, as they were pulling water up from one of these, Arlian remarked, "I wonder if any of these connect to the caverns where the dragons sleep?"

Black threw him a sharp glance. "I doubt it," he said.

Another guard, a smaller man who went by the name Stabber, pointed to the east. "The *big* caves are over there," he said. "I saw some of them once when I was with a caravan that got off course in a sandstorm."

Arlian looked where Stabber pointed, then noticed Black staring at him.

"Don't worry," he said. "I'm not going to go dragon hunting yet." He returned his attention to hauling water.

After that, however, every so often he found himself gazing eastward.

Some of the oxen, which had plodded on all this way without protest, began to weaken as the journey across the waste stretched on; a few became too feeble to continue pulling, and were unhitched and allowed to walk behind the wagons on ropes. Most of these recovered their strength; a few did not, and were butchered, cooked, and eaten, thereby extending the human food supply while conserving the grain the oxen ate—and incidentally providing the only meat most of the people aboard the caravan had had since leaving Stonebreak.

Arlian's own team of four was reduced to three; he rotated them, two pulling and one ambling alongside, thereafter.

A guard's horse stumbled on the stone and broke a leg, and that, too, provided a brief addition to the supply of meat while conserving grain. The guard was transferred to the masters' wagon, leaving only three horsemen to ride alongside.

One of the older merchants died in his sleep, and was buried beneath a cairn of stones before the caravan rolled on. As required by contract his goods were divided among the survivors, with the masters taking the largest share and the wagon itself. His heirs back in Manfort would receive a refund of his initial investment, plus the proceeds from the sales he had made so far at the various stops along the way, plus a percentage of whatever profit the masters eventually wound up with.

Arlian had lost count of the days when at last he saw Black pointing at something ahead. He shielded his eyes with his hand and stared, trying to see what Black was indicating.

The horizon was very slightly nearer than it ought to be, Arlian realized. They were finally within sight of the southern edge of the plateau.

They were almost out of the Desolation, and the water and food had not run out.

They celebrated that night, roasting another of the dead oxen and consuming a case of the dead merchant's wine. Divided among the forty-two surviving merchants, the three masters, the fifteen guards, and some fifty assorted drivers, servants, and family members, that came to little more than a few sips for each, but it was the spirit that counted, not the quantity, and no one was inclined to waste any more of their trade goods in such a manner.

Besides, they were all tired and ready to sleep, and most of them still had to inspect the wheels and traces to make sure nothing needed repair before the next day's journey. Any wagon that delayed the caravan to replace a broken wheel would be fined by the masters.

At midmorning the next day Arlian was sitting beside Quickhand at the front of his wagon when one of the horsemen, a fellow called Knobs, rode up alongside.

"Ho, there!" Arlian called. "How goes it?"

"Well enough, my lord," Knobs called back. "I think I see another hole in the rock ahead." He pointed.

Arlian leaned out to see where Knobs was looking—just as something dark whipped out of the opening in the stone. Knobs gave a wordless cry of surprise and pain and clapped a hand to his shoulder.

Then Knobs, Arlian, and Quickhand were all staring at the black wooden shaft that protruded between Knobs's fingers.

"Whoa!" Arlian bellowed, yanking at the reins.

The arrow was as long as a man's arm, bearing two black feathers and one red, and had struck Knobs just below his left shoulder. The tip now made a visible bulge in the back of his shirt, and red was beginning to stain the white fabric—Knobs had not been wearing any sort of armor in the fierce heat of the Desolation, still miles from where anyone had ever encountered bandits.

"By the dead gods," Knobs said thickly, as he stared at the wound.

Arlian stared as well, sick with horror, but even so he did not permit himself to be shocked into inaction. "Get down!" he shouted. "You're a target there!" He stopped his team and set the brake, then snatched off his hat—it could only get in the way—and flung it back into the wagon; then he grabbed for his sword.

Another arrow whickered past, brushing Knobs's horse on the flank before smacking against the side of the next wagon back and glancing off; the horse shied, and Knobs swayed drunkenly in the saddle.

"Shouldn't we keep moving?" Quickhand asked, as he groped for his own weapons. "A moving target … and Black didn't give an order…"

"*I* gave an order!" Arlian snapped. He'd found his sword; now he drew it, tossed the sheath back into the wagon, and leaped to the ground. Another arrow buzzed past him and thumped into his own wagon, burying its barbed metal head in the wood.

"But you're not even a guard!" Quickhand protested. Arlian ignored him.

The lead wagon had stopped as well, and Black was also on the ground, sword in hand—and swordbreaker in his left; Arlian had not taken the time to find his, and his left hand was empty.

"Keep apart!" Black shouted. "Come at him from different sides!"

"Where *is* he?" Arlian bellowed.

Another arrow flew, and this one caught Knobs's horse in the flank, behind the left foreleg; the animal reared, and Knobs, already dazed with pain, tumbled from its back to the stone.

The desert air was full of shouts and screams now, as the rest of the caravan became aware of the attack; some wagons stopped, but others turned out of line and kept moving in various directions. Some were trying to loop around and turn back, away from the ambush; others seemed to be trying to charge forward.

One of the other horsemen was approaching at a gallop, and Arlian had to dodge aside to avoid being trampled.

A fifth arrow missed the galloping horse's face by inches, and it veered aside; its master struggled with the reins and spurs, trying to regain control.

Knobs's mount, wounded, was galloping off across the stony ground, its saddle empty.

Arlian now knew where the archer was, though; he had seen the last arrow emerge, as if from the earth itself. Their attacker was hiding in one of the waterholes, popping up only long enough to aim and loose.

A moment later he and Black knelt over opposite sides of the yard-wide opening, peering down into the darkness, ready to kill the archer if he dared rise to fire again.

He didn't.

"Get a lantern," Black ordered.

"Quickhand!" Arlian shouted. "A lantern! *Now!*"

Quickhand had been helping Knobs to his feet; still supporting the injured man, he turned and bellowed, "Somebody get a light, blast you all!"

A moment later Stabber hurried over, lamp in hand.

Black and Arlian looked at each other.

"He could be waiting for us," Black said.

"I know," Arlian replied. "Give me the lamp."

Stabber obeyed after only the briefest glance at Black. Arlian got down flat on his belly on the hot stone and crept toward the opening, sword in one hand and lamp in the other, until he was close enough to lower the light down into the hollow in the stone.

Nothing happened, and he saw nothing but bare stone. He crept closer, until he could lean down and stick his head down into the cave.

He found no one—but it was obvious that someone *had* been here. The hole in the stone was roughly spherical, and about fifteen feet in diameter; it smelled unmistakably of human sweat and urine. In the center was a rough wooden platform, perhaps ten feet high, with a ladder up one side—plainly, the now vanished archer had stood atop this to fire at the approaching caravan.

But the platform was by no means the only man-made object in the cave. Looking past it Arlian saw a bedroll lying open on the stony floor to one side of the platform's base, a blanket bunched at one end; an empty wineskin lay beside it, and an earthenware mug atop the wineskin. Half a dozen candle stubs were perched on irregularities in the cave walls, and the stone above each was streaked with smoke stains, and half a dozen more were set on the framework supporting the platform. Orange rinds and crumbs of bread and cheese were scattered everywhere. Even a chamberpot stood in one corner—all the comforts of home, Arlian thought.

He peered a bit more intently into the gloom, and noticed something he hadn't seen at first—two of those black arrows were thrust point-down into the chamberpot. He grimaced in disgust; *that* was a nasty touch!

It was no mystery where the archer had gone; a wide opening gaped in the south wall of the little cave, about six feet high and three feet wide—and Arlian, after seven years in the mines, knew at a glance that that opening was not natural.

"There's a tunnel," he called. "He's gotten away."

"Can't you go down after him?" Stabber asked.

Arlian lifted his head back out, and had to squint against the sunlight; he momentarily regretted leaving his hat in the wagon. He glanced at Stabber, then at Black.

"He knows the tunnel and we don't," Arlian said. "He can hear us coming, and his eyes will be better adjusted to the darkness. And he may have friends down there—he didn't cut that tunnel single-handed."

Black nodded. "It would be suicide," he agreed.

"We can cover the opening, though," Arlian said.

"With what?" Stabber asked.

"Anything," Arlian said. He happened to look between the wagons and glimpse Knobs's horse just then; it was out on the sand, weaving unsteadily, head bobbing up and down, the arrow still projecting from its flank. "A dead horse, maybe."

Stabber followed his gaze. "She's not dead," he protested.

"Not yet," Arlian said.

"She's not going to be! We can fix her up well enough."

Arlian opened his mouth, intending to describe the contents of the chamberpot in the cave, then saw the expression on Stabber's face and thought better of it.

"Some junk, then," Arlian said. "An unused chest, maybe." He peered back down the hole. "And we'll want to wreck that platform, while we're at it."

In the end, Arlian was lowered down into the cave with a rope about his chest, ready to be snatched back up if anyone emerged from the tunnel. He collected the bedroll, blanket, and wineskin, snapped the two arrows in half, then flung the contents of the chamberpot—he judged it as at least two days' accumulation—as far down the tunnel as he could.

Then, with the aid of ropes and several willing helpers, he disassembled the platform and framework and hauled the pieces out of the cave. Once out, he and the others rebuilt the platform over the opening, sealing it up.

While he had been doing this, others had captured the wounded mare and had tended to her injuries. Knobs, too, had been carefully ministered to.

For Knobs, the shaft was broken off short and pulled out through the back of his shoulder to minimize the damage the barbed head would cause. For the unfortunate horse no such method was possible; the barbs had to be cut out of the animal's flank. She screamed and reared wildly as this operation was performed, despite the efforts of a dozen men restraining her.

"It's all no good," Arlian told Black quietly when he had emerged from the cave and had seen what had been done. "The arrows were poisoned."

The two men were walking beside the caravan, seeing that all the wagons were back in line.

"You're sure?"

Arian felt ill as he nodded. "Smell them," he said. "You'll probably be able to tell."

As it happened, the arrow that had glanced off one of the wagons lay on the stone not far from where they were walking; Black stooped and retrieved it. He held it gingerly as he sniffed the head.

"Ah," he said. "I see. Simple, but probably effective in the long run."

Arlian nodded again. "Slow, though."

"Knobs is a strong man," Black said as he tossed the arrow aside. "He may survive it."

"I hope so," Arlian said. He swallowed, sickened by the memory of that shaft through Knobs's shoulder and the spreading stain on his shirt. They took another few steps, and then he added, "I take it we can expect more of this."

"Maybe," Black said. "I don't know; I've never heard of anything like it. *Tunnels* through the stone?"

"Then it's not the usual method?"

"Not at all. Usually there's no trouble at all until the wagons start down the slope at the southern rim; then you'll have rock slides, deadfalls, anything they can do to slow us down, maybe cripple a wagon so it has to be left behind." He looked thoughtfully at the nearest wagon, a gaudy red-painted construction trimmed with gilt. "It's almost as if they want us to turn back.

"But we can't," Arlian protested. "There's no water—not if we follow the same route. We used it all."

"I know," Black said. "And they probably know it, too. So they know we won't turn back, but they're trying to discourage us."

"To convince us to surrender without a fight?"

"Probably," Black said. "He aimed for a horseman—he was after guards, not merchants."

"And the poison … that's to slow us down, too. Burden us with sick companions."

Black nodded. They were nearing the rear of the caravan. "I think a few words with the masters are in order," he said.

"I'll come with you," Arlian said.

Black put a hand on Arlian's chest to stop him. "You're not a guard yet," he said. "You're a merchant, and a very junior one."

"My wagon's at the front of the caravan," Arlian said. "I think I have a right to express my concerns to the masters."

Black looked him in the eye, then shrugged. "Have it your way," he said, dropping his hand.

Chapter Twenty-Two

The Bandits Strike

The caravan finally began moving again around the middle of the afternoon, inching forward cautiously. People who had previously walked alongside, chatting easily with one another, now huddled in their wagons; the two remaining horsemen did not continue their regular trots up and down the caravan's length, but instead dodged about, scouting for sinkholes or other hazards and staying much farther from the wagons than the norm.

Everyone knew now that they had lost the first round of the gamble every caravan faced. Bandits had found them. They were walking into an ambush—but what choice did they have? They couldn't turn back. To the west lay mile upon mile of empty, lifeless sand; to the east the terrain grew ever more rocky and broken until it ended in immense cliffs above the Ocean Sea, where waves twice the height of a man smashed relentlessly against the jagged stone.

Bows were strung, oilcloth bundles of arrows unwrapped, swords polished, swordbreakers readied, helmets and breastplates donned, and maces brandished.

Arlian was annoyed to discover that his hat would not fit over his helmet, and the helmet provided no shade for his eyes. After some debate he settled on wearing the helmet.

As the others readied themselves, poor Knobs lay on his bedding in the masters' wagon; his mare followed wretchedly behind, at the end of a long tether. Every trace of the previous evening's jubilation was gone.

They trudged on much later than usual as the sunlight faded in the west, in an attempt to make up for lost time; there would be no chance to practice swordsmanship unless Black wanted to see what his pupil could do by firelight.

Arlian scanned the horizon, shading his eyes with his hand, when the call to stop was finally passed forward from the masters. "Where do you think that tunnel comes out?" he asked Quickhand.

The guard looked at him blankly. "I don't know," he said. "Does it have to come out somewhere?"

"Well, of course..." Arlian began.

Then he stopped. What if it *didn't* come out anywhere? What if it were just long enough for the archer to hide in? They might have trapped him, had they known.

But no—that made no sense. Who would have built such a trap?

But where could the tunnel go? Not the southern slopes, surely; the bandits couldn't have burrowed under ten or fifteen miles of stone. The archer must have come out somewhere not far from the caravan—yet they had seen no sign of him.

Arian frowned. He didn't like any of this. These bandits were being altogether too clever.

He slept in his own wagon that night, despite the heat; no one was inclined to risk bedding down on the stone. It took him an unusually long time to doze off.

He was awakened in darkness by a shout and the bellow of a wounded bull; he knew instantly that dawn had not yet come, yet he heard voices calling. He climbed to his feet and made his way out of the wagon by touch.

The moon had risen while he slept, and its light was eerily bright on the sand to the west; to the east the occasional patches of drifted sand shone palely against the dark stone, and shapes were distorted and hard to recognize in the maze of light and shadow, but he could see someone running.

Then the running figure vanished, just as two more figures appeared, pursuing the first.

Arlian leaped down, sword in hand.

The two figures slowed to a walk, moving forward cautiously; Arlian could see that they, too, held drawn swords. They came to a stop near the point where the first had vanished and conferred inaudibly, then turned and headed back toward the caravan.

"What happened?" Arlian called quietly.

One figure veered toward him, and he recognized Black.

"The bastard picked off two of our oxen," the head guard said in disgust. "The sooner we get off this plateau and out of these rocks and meet these blackguards openly, the better I'll like it."

"Another tunnel?" Arlian asked, pointing toward the spot where the fleeing figure had disappeared.

"So it seems," Black said. Then he realized who he was addressing. "Go back to bed, my lord," he said. "We should reach the southern slopes tomorrow afternoon, and that's when we can expect to face something more than a few arrows. You'll want to be rested."

Arlan looked at the colorless landscape, at the black emptiness where the bandit had vanished. There was nothing useful he could do; reluctantly, he obeyed Black's command.

He awoke at dawn, as usual, and the caravan was rolling again before the sun had cleared the horizon. One ox was bandaged but mobile; another was dead, and was unceremoniously dumped atop the opening where the archer had vanished.

The ground was sloping downward now, and treetops were visible in the distance—but trees unlike any Arlian had ever seen before, with long, slender trunks supporting clusters of immense fronds. They grew steadily nearer as the day wore on.

The rough stone turned gradually into something resembling a real road as the morning progressed—they were moving down a gravel-bedded wash between two stony ridges. The sand was no longer visible to the west.

Around midday a man appeared, strangely dressed in a flowing robe, strolling easily across the gravel toward them; Black beckoned for a horseman to go meet this new arrival and report back.

The rider conferred briefly with the stranger, then rode back to report. Arlian handed the reins to Quickhand, jumped down from his own wagon, and ran forward to hear what was said—not merely for his own information, but so he could pass the word to the other merchants while the rider reported directly to the masters.

"He's offering us safe passage," the horseman explained. "For one-fourth of everything we carry."

Black nodded. "Go tell the masters," he said. The rider saluted and rode off.

"*One-fourth?*" Arlian exclaimed, shocked, still walking alongside the guard wagon.

"That's the point of those archers," Black replied. "If we'd come this far unmolested we would have just laughed at such a demand. Now at least some of us will want to consider it."

"*I* won't," Arlian said.

"And of course that settles it," Black said. "I hadn't realized you were the caravan master; when did that happen?"

Arlian flushed, and said nothing more. Instead he turned and began walking back, calling out the news to each wagon as he passed.

At last he came to the masters' wagon; the side shutters were open, and the masters were arguing in the center. Knobs lay abed at the rear; two guards were on the rear platform, and two—one of them driving the oxen—on the front bench.

"I've passed the word," Arlian said.

Lord Sandal turned to look at him. "And what are the sentiments of our fellow merchants?"

"I don't know," Arlian admitted. "I didn't take time to ask." He hesitated, then added, "*I* don't want to give in to extortion."

"That's one," Lady Thassa said.

"Out of forty-two," Lord Drens said. "It proves nothing."

"Are you proposing we take a vote?" Sandal demanded.

"No, of course not," Drens said. "But it would do no harm to know what the merchants think."

"Might I remind my lords," Arlian said, "that my cargo is primarily fine weaponry. Turning one-fourth of it over to outlaws does not strike me as wise."

"I *told* you we shouldn't have allowed him to bring those things!" Drens exclaimed.

"Sometimes," Thassa said angrily to Drens, "I wonder why we brought *you*."

"As the voice of caution, as I recall," Sandal said wryly.

"A role I do my best to fill," Drens retorted, "since neither of *you* seems to have any sense of self-preservation!"

Sandal sighed. "I had hoped we would be able to preserve the appearance of unity," he said, "and present everyone with a unanimous decision. I take it, however, that this isn't going to be possible."

"Not unless the two of you suddenly regain your sanity," Drens said. "One-fourth of our goods is not worth my life."

"You put little faith in Black and his men," Sandal said dryly. "Not to mention our own capabilities with missile and blade."

"I *know* my own abilities," Drens said. "And one of those abilities is the ability to die if struck through the heart by one of those arrows!" He gestured at Knobs.

"And you seem far more able than I to trust these bandits to keep their word," Thassa replied. "Why should they settle for a fourth, when by a simple betrayal they can have all? These are men who have already fired upon us from ambush, after all. I vote to refuse."

"As do I," Sandal agreed.

"Shall I tell Black?" Arlian asked.

"That's my job," called a horseman. He urged his mount forward.

By the time Arlian reached his own wagon Black and the other guards in the lead vehicle were in their full armor, helmets, breastplates, and mail, their weapons at ready. Out ahead of them the bandits' representative was walking, pacing the advancing caravan at long bowshot.

"Give him our reply," Black ordered, pointing.

Half a dozen men raised bows, and half a dozen arrows flew.

"But he's unarmed!" Arlian protested—too late. The outlaw fell, screaming, with an arrow in his thigh.

"By all the dead gods!" Black exclaimed. "You *hit* him! Good shooting!"

Arlian ran up alongside the lead wagon. "But he was just a messenger!" he called.

"He's a bandit," Black said. "Besides, I just thought we'd scare him away—I didn't expect a hit at this range!" He marveled again at the sight of the wounded bandit lying on the gravel, clutching his leg.

"He can't take our response back to the bandits now," Arlian said.

Black turned to stare at him. "And you think that's *bad?*" he said. "You *want* them to be warned?"

Arlian opened his mouth, then closed it again. He stopped walking, letting the wagon pull away.

Black turned to the horseman, ignoring Arlian. "Go see if he wants to surrender," Black ordered. "And kill him if he doesn't."

"Should I retrieve the arrows, if I see them?"

Black shook his head. "You'd have to dismount. We'll get them when the caravan reaches them."

Arlian's own wagon came alongside him, and he jumped aboard. He hesitated, and then instead of seating himself next to Quickhand he ducked inside and found his helmet and mail.

The bandit surrendered and was lifted aboard the lead wagon, where Black questioned him intently—but quietly; Arlian could not overhear anything of the discussion.

Word was passed, though.

"They'll attack tomorrow," Stabber told Arlian and Quickhand. "He swears he doesn't know exactly when, but Black says it'll probably be right after dawn, before we get out of this defile into open country. They've got plans to trap us and disable the wagons, but this boy didn't know any details."

Arlian nodded, and Stabber moved on to the next wagon in line.

Quickhand sighed with relief. "Tomorrow," he said. "That gives us time to prepare a little."

Arlian nodded—but frowned.

When the messenger didn't return, wouldn't the bandits realize their man might have been captured alive? Would they really expect him to have kept his mouth shut?

Arlian knew that had he been the bandit leader he would have had an alternate plan. He would attack *tonight.*

But Black and the others must surely have thought of that.

For the next half hour they rode on in silence, but the thought that they were riding into a trap nagged relentlessly at Arlian, and finally he could stand it no more. He dropped to the ground and ran forward to catch Black's wagon.

Black listened calmly to Arlian's concerns, then nodded.

"You may be right," he said. "But if they're planning to *trap* us, then they must have set it up well beforehand, and I doubt it could readily be moved. Still, we'll want to be very careful tonight."

That did very little to allay Arlian's worries, but he reluctantly returned to his own wagon. He couldn't tolerate doing *nothing,* though, so despite the sweltering heat he again donned his mail shirt and helmet.

It was less than an hour later, while the sun still hung high above the western ridge, that the trap was sprung.

The gravel road had turned into the bed of a steep-sided canyon, sloping steeply downward between jagged, uneven stone walls; even with brakes set the wagons tended to slide forward on the loose gravel, and the oxen were holding the wagons back as much as pulling them, squalling unhappily about it. The animals could undoubtedly be heard for a mile in either direction, Arlian thought—and perhaps that had been what allowed the bandits to carry out their attack with such perfect timing.

Arlian had been watching his own oxen struggling to keep their footing, and keeping an eye on his wagon to make sure it wasn't going to slide out of control, when he happened to catch sight of a rock on the canyon wall that appeared to be moving under its own power.

He started to say something, to call a warning or a question, but then the rock tumbled free and a rope sprang up from beneath it, snapping taut.

More rocks tumbled, and more ropes appeared, and the gravel ahead of Arlian's oxen suddenly showered upward as an immense net burst up from concealment—*between* Arlian and the lead wagon.

Even as the oxen struggled to turn aside before plunging into this unexpected barrier, and the wagon slewed sideways on the gravel, Arlian saw what the bandits had done. Heavy ropes had been run up either side of the canyon, hidden behind outcroppings, stuffed down into crevices, or covered with loose stone, and on cue these ropes had been pulled, hard, snapping them up out of their hiding places.

And these cables supported a gigantic rope mesh extending the entire width of the canyon; when the ropes were pulled the top of the net sprang up to a height of ten or twelve feet, while the base remained hidden in the gravel. This net had been completely buried under the loose stone of the road, impossible to detect until it was too late.

On the other side of the net most of the guards had leaped from their wagon, which Black was struggling to stop; now they ran up to the net, blades naked in their hands.

But on the north side, where Arlian was, bandits had appeared along the ridgetops, arrows nocked, bows raised and ready—at least a score of them, all in those flowing red-and-white robes.

"Get down!" Quickhand barked, ducking back into the wagon. Arlian barely heard him over the lowing of frightened oxen and the shouting of angry men.

One of the bandits was making his way carefully down the slope toward the caravan; he appeared to be shouting something, but Arlian couldn't distinguish his voice over the din.

On the other side of the net Black was standing in the open-shuttered and now halted guard wagon, holding the wounded captive upright by the front of his shirt.

"You *lied* to us, you little bastard!" Black bellowed, in a voice that somehow carried clearly to Arlian over the chaos.

The prisoner said something in reply, but Arlian couldn't hear it.

The other guards were hacking at the huge net, but making little progress; the ropes were as thick as a man's forearm and tarred with something that stuck to sword blades. That, and the springiness, made it almost impossible to cut through.

Arlian jumped to the ground, sword ready. He refused to hide in his wagon.

Someone farther back in the line was shouting for quiet, and the voices, both human and ox, were dying away as the caravan came to a full stop, the situation became clear, and the confusion began to fade.

"Surrender!" the bandit on the slope called. "We'll take half your goods as toll, and then you're free to go!"

"Half?" Arlian wasn't the only one to shout that back angrily.

"You have until I count ten, and then my archers will loose!" the bandit spokesman cried down.

Arlian ignored him, and turned to the net.

Trapping seven of the guards on the other side was clever—but not *that* clever. "Climb over!" Arlian shouted. "Two of you hold it steady for the others, then two steady it from this side for the last two!"

"Do as he says!" Black called.

"Five!" the bandit shouted.

"Quickly!" Arlian screamed. "And dive for cover when you're over! Under the wagons!"

"Eight!"

Arlian suddenly realized that he should take his own advice—but if he ducked inside his wagon he would be trapped there, pinned down.

He would take his chances, he resolved. Perhaps whatever Fate had propelled him this far from Obsidian and Deep Delving would protect him—Fate, and the armor he wore.

"Ten! Loose!" the bandit cried—diving to the ground himself as he did. Bowstrings snapped, and a hail of arrows soared down into the canyon—but none fell near Arlian.

That made sense, he realized as he watched the shafts rattle off wood and stone; there were perhaps thirty archers, at most, shooting at forty-five wagons—forty-four, if the lead wagon wasn't included.

The guards were still struggling with the net—climbing it was apparently far more difficult than Arlian had realized, since men on the ground could not steady the top few feet. "Up the slope!" Arlian called, waving frantically. "It's not as high up there!"

The bandits, having fired, were advancing down the slope as they drew fresh arrows from the quivers on their backs; each took two or three steps before nocking the next shaft, and then two or three more before drawing. At that rate they would reach the caravan after another half dozen volleys—which was undoubtedly the idea.

"If we have to come down there and fight," the bandit spokesman called, "we'll show no mercy!"

A bowstring snapped, and an arrow sailed past the spokesman, missing by several feet. *Someone* intended to resist, at any rate.

Arlian thought his own bow was still somewhere in his wagon; he had no idea how to use it and knew it, so he had no intention of going back for it. Instead he intended to use his sword—if he could get close enough to the bandits.

They were moving down the slopes on either side, but they were also converging toward the center of the caravan, several wagons back from Arlian's own position; he began to run and dodge up the sloping road, changing his direction sharply whenever he heard a bowstring.

An ox bellowed as an arrow struck meat.

The bandit strategy was becoming clearer; they were using the arrows to keep the merchants cowering in their wagons while they were collecting into a group that would attack the central wagons one by one. The guards, isolated at either end of the line, might be unable to reach them in time.

Arlian wasn't about to allow them to attack unhindered, though; he might be just one man, but he could do *something*.

And he saw now that he wasn't alone—at least two of the guards from the masters' wagon were on the ground and moving down the road to meet the bandits, and one of the horsemen was charging, sword drawn, up the canyon side toward the approaching marauders.

The bandits shouted to one another, and the next ragged volley of arrows was concentrated on the horseman; his mount suddenly stumbled and went down, a shaft projecting from its neck.

One of the faster-moving bandits had reached the side of the caravan; he dropped his bow and pulled a heavy mallet from beneath his robe and ran up to the nearest wagon's rear wheel, mallet swinging.

Arlian understood that tactic well enough; the bandits wanted to cripple some of the wagons so badly that the caravan would abandon them, trade goods still aboard. With a wordless yell, Arlian ran at the hammer-wielding southerner with his sword raised in an overhand attack.

At the last instant the man dropped his mallet and turned; at the last instant the horror of what he was doing suddenly registered in Arlian's mind; but it was too late. His sword plunged forward and down, into the unprotected hollow at the base of the bandit's throat. His forward motion pushed the blade deep and thrust Arlian up against the bandit, so close he could smell the man's stinking breath.

The bandit's eyes flew wide, his mouth sprang open as if to vomit, but nothing came forth but a sort of choking gasp.

Then Arlian heard a sound behind him; he whipped his blade free and turned, and the bandit tumbled forward, blood spurting, to land at his killer's feet. One hand slapped limply against Arlian's shin.

But another bandit was upon him, this one with a wooden spear in hand, and Arlian was too busy to think about the man at his feet.

It was only later that he realized that for the first time, he had killed a man.

He could kill if he had to. When the time came, he could strike Lord Dragon down.

Somehow, that knowledge failed to cheer him.

Chapter Twenty-Three

Aftermath

The fight was long and bloody; the caravan guards were outnumbered, but better armed and better trained. The merchants for the most part proved to be useless as fighters; most were unable even to defend themselves.

Arlian was the exception; he fought side by side with the guards, doing his part to even the odds. In the chaos of wielding sword and swordbreaker against spears and clubs, so completely different from the one-on-one sword fights of his practice bouts, he was unsure whether he killed anyone after that first assault. He knew that he drew blood many times, but beyond that he could not be certain just what effect his blows had.

He shouted for the merchants and their families and hirelings to come out and fight, did everything he could to urge them to join in their own defense, but to no avail. Most remained huddled in their wagons and were completely useless even there.

This was demonstrated several times by one of the bandits' favorite tactics, which was for half a dozen men to charge into a wagon with clubs and spears and slaughter everyone aboard, then to use the wagon as a miniature fortress against the guards. The guards, outnumbered as they were, could not defend the entire long line of wagons at once and were unable to prevent these captures.

It was Black who came up with the counter—station a man at each end of the captured wagon with orders to kill anyone who set foot outside. Two men could bottle up half a dozen bandits this way, and in fact roughly one-third of the entire raiding party was trapped in this fashion.

Another third was killed or incapacitated.

And the final third, realizing that their attack was a failure, fled up the slopes into the gathering night, dragging those of their wounded who were unable to walk.

Some of the wounded bandits who were not dragged were barely able to limp away, and could easily have been caught and killed, but Black called out to let them go. "Let them be a burden to the others!"

Three guards had been slain outright, as well, and two more seriously wounded. Black took a gash on the side, but insisted it wasn't serious and refused to relinquish his command of the caravan's defenders. One horse was killed by a spear, and several oxen received minor injuries.

Five merchants and their families had been butchered in their wagons.

When the fight was over the guards turned their attention to the three wagons still occupied by bandits. Black stood, holding one hand to his injured side while his sword dangled from the other, staring at the first of the wagons.

Lord Drens came up, a lantern in his hand, looking worried. He had already set merchants and drivers to repairing broken wagons and smashed wheels, Arlian noted with approval, and was now coming to attend to the remaining bandits. "I think we had best…" he began.

"Shut up," Black barked at him. "This is *my* business still, not yours."

Drens stopped in his tracks, shocked; he looked at the blood seeping through Black's fingers, at the guards standing around him spattered with blood and dirt, their swords still in their hands, and decided against making any protest. "As you say," he agreed.

"What are you going to do with us?" a bandit called from the wagon.

"You might as well let us go," another added. "We won't bother you again."

"And if you don't, we'll wreck everything in here!" a third called.

"What do *I* care if you spoil someone else's property?" Black bellowed in reply. "You already killed the owner, you murdering bastards!"

"You can't kill us in cold blood!" the first voice said.

Several of the guards muttered in reply to that, and Arlian knew all of them were thinking the same thing he was: Why not?

But his gorge rose at the thought. He didn't want any more deaths.

"Who said anything about killing you?" Black called back. "We aren't going to kill you if you come out peacefully, with empty hands raised above your heads."

"You'll let us go?"

"I didn't say that, either—but I'll release you, most of you, under certain conditions."

"What conditions?"

"No, no," Black said. "You don't hear the conditions until *after* you surrender."

Utter silence fell for a moment as the bandits considered that; then one called, "Go feed the dragons!"

"Maybe someday I will," Black retorted, "but I assure you we won't feed *you.*"

"But there's plenty of food stored in there," Arlian whispered to Stabber, who stood nearby.

"*They* may not know that," Stabber whispered back.

They could all hear what happened next—the bandits argued quietly among themselves, and then came the sound of a blow, and a body falling.

"I surrender!" called a voice, and the first bandit came out, hands up.

A moment later the entire wagon was empty of bandits; at Black's direction each was securely bound.

A similar scene was then played out at each of the other two disputed wagons, until ten bandits huddled on the ground, hands and feet tied, surrounded by the caravan's guards.

"Now," Black said, "we will let you go, one by one—but first we'll make sure none of you can draw a bow against peaceful merchants ever again." He pulled the first bandit up, and with four other guards holding the man securely in place and using a wagon's end platform as a chopping block, he used an ax to amputate the man's left hand.

The other bandits—and Arlian—stared in horror as the crippled marauder screamed and the guards struggled to bandage the bleeding stump.

"I hope you weren't left-handed," Black said. He raised his voice and called to the others, "Are any of you left-handed?"

One man, weeping with terror, barely able to get the words out past his tears, said that he was. Black took him next, so as not to risk forgetting, and removed his right hand.

Then the others, one by one, were dragged to the improvised chopping block.

Black chased away any member of the caravan who came to either watch or protest, insisting that they should attend to their own affairs—including getting the caravan ready to move. He also sent four guards up the canyon walls to cut the ropes holding the net.

When each bandit had been dealt with and each fresh stump had been bandaged, that man was given a push and sent scrambling as best he could up the side of the canyon; most collapsed, moaning or screaming, a few yards away.

When the last had been shoved away Black turned to the ashen-faced Lord Drens and announced, "The threat has been dealt with, my lord, and we'll have that inconvenience"—he gestured at the net—"out of your way shortly. Might I suggest that despite the darkness, we press on for another mile or so?"

Arlian stared at the two men in the lamplight and realized that *both* of them were unnaturally pale. Drens was uninjured, so his color was surely just from his reaction to the attack and its aftermath, but Arlian feared Black's pallor was due to loss of blood.

"As you say," Lord Drens agreed.

It took another twenty minutes to straighten out the mess and finish minimal repairs. The bodies of the dead members of the caravan were hastily wrapped in sheets and loaded aboard wagons; the bodies of dead bandits were flung out on the roadside. Guards took charge of the five wagons that no longer had living drivers.

By the time they began rolling, with lantern-bearers on foot walking ahead to light the way, Black had collapsed into the lead wagon, slumped against one side, while a volunteer from one of the merchant families set about cleaning and bandaging the gash in his side.

By the time they reached the mouth of the canyon, less than a mile from the site of the ambush, Black was unconscious. Stabber took charge and chose their campsite, on a level, sandy area by a stand of those strange southern trees.

Arlian slept late the next morning—but so did almost everyone. He arose and climbed out of his wagon to see a new and wondrous landscape spread out before him.

They had camped atop a long slope, below the broken cliffs that marked the southern edge of the Desolation. Now Arlian had a clear view down that slope, past groves of unfamiliar trees—not the tall ones bare for most of their height, but almost normal ones, low, spreading trees bearing orange fruit—to a town of yellow brick and red tile, gleaming in the sunshine. Green leaves and bright flowers were everywhere, and the air was thick with the sweet smell of ripe fruit.

After the stark and ugly terrain of the Desolation, this lush display of beauty and color was overwhelming. Arlian stared wordlessly for a long moment, drinking it in.

"The Borderlands," Quickhand said, appearing beside him. "Beautiful, isn't it?"

Arlian nodded. "Where are we?" he asked. "What town is that?"

Quickhand squinted, then shaded his eyes with his hand and peered at the collection of buildings at the foot of the slope. "I don't know," he admitted. "The Eastern Road shifts somewhat with the sands, and we could have come down any of at least three different canyons. That *might* be Sweetwater."

"The name's in our tongue?"

"Oh, yes," Quickhand said. "We're still in the Lands of Man. The border is at least three days farther south." He pointed at the southern sky. "Look at the clouds."

Arlian looked, then closed his eyes. He rubbed them, then opened them again.

It didn't help; the clouds above the distant horizon were still impossible to see clearly. Arlian glimpsed purple and a sort of pinkish gold moving through gray masses, but he could not make out details, and after a second could no longer be sure he had seen what he had thought he saw.

There were things flying through those clouds—not birds, nor even dragons, but vast dark shapes and flashes of bright color, all somehow indistinct, more so than mere distance could explain.

"It's magic," Quickhand said. "You don't want to study it too closely."

Arlian remembered how Grandsir, long ago, had told him that in the Borderlands one could see wild magic flash across the sky. He had not realized just how literally the old man had meant it.

"Is it *always* like that?" he asked.

"No," Quickhand told him. "Sometimes it's worse, but usually there are just clouds." He smiled crookedly. "It's *never* entirely clear, though." He pointed to the spot where the clouds were thickest. "I'm told there's something down there that doesn't like the sun, and has the power to do something about it."

Arlian glanced to the east, at the golden southern sun, and asked, "If it doesn't like the sun, why does it live here, instead of in the north?"

"Because the dragons drove it from the north, thousands of years ago," Quickhand replied.

"But the dragons are gone," Arlan said. He grimaced. "Mostly," he added.

Quickhand said, "Maybe it hasn't noticed that yet."

"What *is* it?" Arlian asked.

Quickhand shrugged. "I don't know. It lives in Tirikindaro, and the people there are its slaves—and now you know as much about it is as I do."

"Does it have a name?"

"Not that anyone dares speak aloud—unless its name is Tirikindaro. Really, my lord, that's all I know."

Arlian nodded, and after staring a moment longer turned his attention back to the town. "And that's Sweetwater? We should be there by midday, I think."

"It *might* be Sweetwater," Quickhand corrected him. "I'm not sure. But yes, I'd say we can be there by midday."

Arlian leaned to the side and peered back at the other wagons. "Is there a market?" he asked.

"If it's Sweetwater or Orange River there is."

"So we've reached our destination? We'll be trading everything here?"

Quickhand shook his head. "No, my lord. It's just another way station, like Stonebreak or Cork Tree." He pointed at the horizon. "It's down there, at the border or beyond, that the *real* money is made. Around here … well, we're still in the Lands of Man, even if we are past the Desolation."

Arlian considered that.

Quickhand hesitated, then added, "By the way, my lord—don't be surprised if you see some one-handed farmers in the orange groves, or if you meet one-handed townspeople with the bandages still fresh."

Arlian turned to stare at him.

"Well, where did you think those bandits came from? You can't really make a *living* off banditry," Quickhand said. "Not the sort you'd rely on to keep a family. It's a sideline, a risky way for the rowdy young men in the area to take a chance on maybe getting rich."

"But they'd come openly into the town while we're still there?"

"Why not? What are we going to do? If we try to accuse them, who do you think the locals will side with—the rich strangers, or their own friends and neighbors?"

"But … but how can we trust anyone here, then?"

Quickhand shrugged. "We can't, really. But they don't want to drive us off entirely; they don't want the caravans to stop coming, and they don't want to anger the lords in Manfort enough to send an army down here. They won't bother us in the towns or on the main roads; it's only in the badlands that they'll try to steal everything we have."

"But last night we were fighting them," Arlian protested, trying to grasp the situation. "We were fighting to the death! I *killed* one of them!"

"I wouldn't say anything about that in town if I were you. You might be talking to one of his relatives."

Arlian blinked in amazement. "It's insane!"

"It's the way it is." Quickhand hesitated, then added, "I did have another reason for mentioning this."

"My cargo," Arlian said.

Quickhand nodded. "This wouldn't be the best place to sell it," he said.

Arlian looked at the open-sided wagon ahead where Black lay, still unconscious. Sell swords and daggers to the men who had wounded him, the men who had killed three of the guards and slaughtered five merchants?

In fact, he was beginning to wonder whether he wanted to sell those blades *anywhere* in the Borderlands. He wished the masters had brought this up back in Manfort, when they had tried to convince him to carry a more conventional cargo.

"I agree," he said. "I agree entirely."

Chapter Twenty-Four

The Borderlands

The town was indeed Sweetwater. While most of the merchants traded with the townsfolk, the three masters debated what route to take from here.

With Black in no condition to move, let alone fight, Arlian was concerned that the masters might be excessively timid—or might do something foolish. Leaving his own wagon securely closed, locked, and guarded, Arlian tried to eavesdrop on the masters' conversation, but with limited success. The shutters of their wagon were closed, and guards were posted, so that he could not put his ear right to the side.

But their words were audible through the cracks, all the same. Arlian had always had good ears, and now he put them to use.

"Tirikindaro does not appear safe at present," Lord Sandal admitted, even before Lord Drens could bring up the question. "We might wait it out, or we might head east to Pon Ashti."

"The Blue Mage is said to be unusually quiet just now, though," Lady Thassa pointed out. "If the other powers are quiet as well, there are any number of possibilities. Even the road to Arithei might be open."

Arlian, who had been slouched comfortably against one of the strange trees he now knew were called "palms," jerked upright at that. His hand fell to the pouch he still carried on his belt, the pouch that held Hathet's purple stones. He had thought of the possibility that the caravan might try for Arithei, but had decided it was too much to hope for.

The next thing he heard confirmed that.

"Arithei?" Lord Drens protested. "Are you mad?"

"Optimistic, perhaps, but scarcely mad," Thassa replied. "Travelers have made the passage sometimes—I met the Aritheian ambassador at one of the Duke's banquets a few years back, and he assured me the hazards are exaggerated—real, but exaggerated. He seemed eager for trade."

"The old road is closed," Drens said. "The native guides no longer venture into the Borderlands. Sahasin came through before that happened, and I doubt he's been home since—he's as much an exile as an ambassador."

"That wasn't my impression," Thassa said. Before Drens could argue further, she admitted, "But it was years ago that we spoke."

"Arithei lies beyond the Dreaming Mountains," Drens said, "and *I* have no intention of crossing that range without a known route and a magician as escort. You may not be mad now, but you most likely would be by the time you returned thence."

"Arithei is too risky for me," Lord Sandal agreed.

"Why do we need to cross the border at all?" Drens asked, his tone wheedling. "Why not simply work our way along the border towns, and leave the realms beyond alone?"

"Because beyond the border is where the real wealth lies," Sandal replied. "You know that as well as we do—beyond the border we can trade for *magic,* real magic, magic you can't get anywhere in the Lands of Man. Why else come here?"

"For the exotic fruits and strange wines and rare woods, the sapphires and emeralds, the bright dyes," Drens replied. "We have our own sorceries back in Manfort; why should we meddle with the unnatural forces beyond the border?"

Sandal and Thassa exchanged glances. "Our little sorceries are hardly the same as southern magic," Thassa said.

"Perhaps we should split up," Sandal suggested. "I have no wish to drag Lord Drens places he'd rather not go."

"Divide the caravan?" Drens said, shocked.

"Only temporarily," Sandal assured him. "We would regroup here in Sweetwater in, say, two months' time, and head north together. I've no more desire to go up that canyon into the Desolation without sufficient numbers than you do—maybe those men can't draw bows anymore, but they probably have cousins eager for revenge."

"What would we do for wagons?" Drens asked. "We share this one."

"We have six left unmanned," Sandal pointed out. "By contract those are ours, to dispose of as we see fit, once the goods within have been dealt with."

Drens nodded thoughtfully.

"Is it safe enough even here in the Borderlands?" Thassa asked. "After all, we've lost almost half our guards, either dead or wounded."

"I'd say so," Sandal said. "After all, divided even three ways, if we each take a different route, we'd still have more than a dozen wagons apiece. We can hire locals as guards."

"I wouldn't *trust* locals as guards," Drens said. "But I don't expect any trouble so long as I stay in the border towns." He nodded. "If you two are determined to cross the border, and the merchants are willing, then we'll split up."

Thus it was settled, and the word was passed to the merchants. That evening the destinations were announced—Lord Drens would proceed to the southwest and visit the border towns from Redgate to Skok's Fall; Lord Sandal would head east to Pon Ashti, then return—by way of Tirikindaro, conditions permitting. The wounded and ill, or those too timid to venture further, could stay in Sweetwater; accommodations were being arranged.

And Lady Thassa would venture south, to the foothills of the Dreaming Mountains, choosing her exact course only when she knew more of the situation beyond the border.

"To Arithei?" Arlian called.

Lady Thassa shook her head. "No," she said. "Without a full complement of guards, or a hired magician, that's too dangerous."

Arlian did not argue—but he also did not give up. After overhearing the masters' plans he had spent the rest of the day talking to the townspeople, inquiring about Arithei. He had no way of knowing how much was exaggeration, how much outright lies, but there were certain points of universal agreement.

Arithei lay to the southeast, but to reach it one first had to head southwest, as the only road circled around the west of Tirikindaro before turning eastward across the Dreaming Mountains. The hazards along the way were trivial—the road avoided the various magical demesnes—until reaching the mountains.

The Dreaming Mountains, however, were haunted, awash in magic—not the feeble controlled and regulated magic of the northern sorcerers, or the limited spells of the human magicians to the south, or the personal power of the godlings and spirits like the one that ruled Tirikindaro, but feral, chaotic magic. There were *things* dwelling in those mountains, things both tangible and intangible. Most people who dared climb those slopes simply vanished; a few returned safely, usually with tales of narrow escapes and horrendous nightmares. A handful came back dazed or insane, either babbling wildly or unable to speak, and of these, about half eventually returned to their senses.

All of them, if they could speak at all, talked about dreams.

Arlian did not fear dreams. As for monsters and ghosts and magic, he had his sword, and magical things were said to fear cold iron; he had silver, and the dead were said to fear silver.

He stared at the southern horizon, thinking.

Hathet had said that Arithei was a land of magicians, that the people there *had* to use magic simply to survive in that land.

Magic was precious and rare in the Lands of Man, as Arlian had overheard Sandal say. If he wanted to trade his swords and daggers for something that would be valuable back in Manfort, he could scarcely do better than to go to Arithei and buy magic with them.

He didn't know enough about magic to guess what form that magic might take, but there would be time for that in Arithei—if he got there.

Magic would bring him wealth and power back in Manfort. It would help even the balance between Lord Dragon and himself. It might even provide a means to strike at the dragons themselves; after all, while the dragons had kept the wild southern magic out of the Lands of Man, the wild southern magic seemed to have kept the dragons out of Arithei, as well.

And Hathet—if he had told the truth, then his family was somewhere in Arithei, unaware of what had befallen him.

Arlian still had the bag of amethysts—one hundred and sixty-eight of them. If Hathet had told the truth, and they had some protective magic, those might be worth more in Arithei than the swords were!

Arlian had doubted that Arithei existed; it did. He had doubted that there was any Aritheian ambassador to the Lands of Man, but Lady Thassa and Lord Drens had met one. He had doubted that the southern lands were as magical as Hathet said, but he could see the magic in the southern skies for himself. Perhaps *everything* Hathet had said was true, no matter how absurd it had sounded.

Arlian owed that old man a debt, and he wanted to pay it. Here was an opportunity to do that. If Hathet had told the truth about his origins, then Arlian could go to Arithei and tell Hathet's family what had become of him, and give them the amethysts. The stones were theirs, by right, as Hathet's own blood, and not his.

Lady Thassa was heading in the right direction, but would not cross the Dreaming Mountains. Arlian could not stand the idea of coming so very close, and then turning back. He owed it to Hathet at least to *try* to reach Arithei.

The road had been closed for years, too dangerous for passage—everyone agreed on that. But had they *tried* it?

Arlian resolved to head for Arithei—on his own, if he had to. Aside from his debt to Hathet, he wanted to sell his weapons where they would not fall into bandits' hands.

"Only a madman would attempt it without a guide and magicians and guards," Lady Thassa told him when he asked her to reconsider.

"I'm going, whether with you or alone," Arlian said.

She shrugged. "Then you're mad, and I'll have no part of it. But you're free to do as you choose."

When she had gone Arlian sat thoughtfully for some time, considering the situation.

Thassa wouldn't attempt the Dreaming Mountains without a full complement of guards, but Arlian thought he would do better traveling alone; he might be able to hide from the worst dangers, and what good would guards be against magic?

He talked to Quickhand about his plans, as the two of them inspected his wagon for any damage that might need attention.

The guardsman looked troubled. "I don't want to go to Arithei," he said. "I've no business there."

"I'm not asking you to accompany me if you don't want to," Arlian said. "I can drive and tend oxen well enough now."

"The masters pay me to guard the caravan, my lord; if you leave the caravan, you leave me."

"Fair enough," Arlian said.

Quickhand hesitated, then said, "I think you're making a mistake, Lord Ari."

"I'm sure you do," Arlian said. "And maybe I am—but I have business in Arithei." Hathet had made his early years in the mines bearable, had taught him so much—the best he could do toward repaying the old man was to go to Arithei.

And the possibility that he might turn his wagonload of weapons into a fortune did nothing to discourage him.

"I wish you'd talk to Black before you go."

"He's ill," Arlian said. "I won't trouble him."

More accurately, he feared that if anyone could talk him out of going, it would be Black, and he didn't want to risk it. Instead he devoted himself to preparing for the journey.

He had only three oxen left to draw his wagon, which left too small a margin of error; he hastily used a part of his share from the six dead merchants to buy a fourth.

The following day at dawn, as the three masters sorted out the wagons, Arlian set his four oxen, new and old together, on the road south. He rode alone; Quickhand was traveling with Lord Sandal.

The journey was uneventful at first, but Arlian knew, four days later, that he had crossed the border and left the Lands of Man behind; the wind, which had been blowing hard from the west for more than a day, no longer howled but laughed. The sky above was streaked with orange even at midday. He glimpsed things from the corner of his eye, but when he turned to look at them they were gone.

It was strange and unsettling, but he saw no real danger in any of it, and pressed on.

The worst part, at that point, was the tedium of traveling alone. The oxen moved so slowly that the scenery did not change quickly enough to be interesting, and he had no one to speak to. He met travelers on the road occasionally, and for the first few days he often passed farms and villages, but he made camp alone each night, sleeping in the wagon, rather than finding lodging; he did not trust these people.

When he did speak to someone—at wells or village markets, when he stopped for provisions—the conversations were hardly satisfying; the southerners spoke with strange accents that made it hard to follow their words, and seemed wary of him.

That was hardly surprising; they were brown-skinned and dressed in loose multicolored robes, while his skin, even after his travels, remained relatively pale, and he wore a white shirt, tight blue breeches, and a broad-brimmed black hat.

They gave him directions when asked, though, and assured him that he was still on the right road. Since he had seen no other routes he had been fairly sure of this, but confirmation was welcome.

The road was overgrown in places, clearly used little, if at all, in recent years, but he was able to follow it well enough.

A week after he crossed the border, one foggy evening when he was onto the lower slopes of the central ridge of the Dreaming Mountains and had not seen another human face for two days, the first attack came. He was making camp for the night when something black and shapeless leaped at him out of the darkness.

He saw it coming from the corner of his eye, and dodged, diving to one side. He drew his sword as it wheeled and came at him again; he never saw it clearly in the mist and gathering gloom, but had a vague impression of great smothering arms, gleaming fangs, and a black, furry chest. He thrust, plunging his blade into it.

It burst and melted away at the touch of steel, leaving nothing but a wet smell and a damp smear on the ground.

Arlian stared into the night, astonished at the ease with which he had defeated the thing.

"That can't be the sort of monster that everyone's scared of," he said aloud.

The wind laughed derisively overhead, and he looked around uncomfortably. The monster had been absurdly easy to destroy—*if* it was really destroyed—but he had been awake, with his sword on his belt. What if another attacked while he slept? He had no one to stand guard; the best he could hope for would be that the oxen would be disturbed and awaken him with their bellowing.

He didn't have much choice at this point, though.

He slept in the wagon with his sword by his hand, and was awakened from uneasy dreams once that night—not by the oxen, but by a slithering sound close by. He slashed at it, but didn't hit anything so far as he could tell.

For the rest of his journey he never had a good night's sleep. The nightmares he had anticipated never came; his dreams were never worse than vaguely disturbing. Strange sounds and sudden attacks became commonplace, though, and not all monsters were as readily defeated as that first one. Cold steel did indeed repel some, or destroy them by its mere touch, but others had to be fought and butchered as if they were common beasts, rather than magical horrors.

That they *were* magical horrors Arlian had little doubt, given that many changed shape or vanished when slain. The worst in that regard was the poisonous spider-creature that became a girl of twelve or thirteen when he beheaded it; Arlian was ill after that, and wept intermittently for the next few days whenever her dead face returned to his thoughts.

The hardest to kill were the venomous black rat-things, simply because of their size and numbers; they left only glowing bones that dissolved when the sun rose.

He considered turning back—but he had already come so far! He decided to keep going.

The condition of the road continued to deteriorate; now and then he had to stop and hack down a sapling that had sprung up between the two faint ruts, and the oxen grew accustomed to simply trampling anything smaller.

On the eighteenth night after leaving Sweetwater something got one of the oxen. Arlian never saw it, nor heard it, nor knew what it was, but when he arose the next morning he found nothing but the ox's empty skin wrapped around dry bones; the flesh and blood had been sucked out through half a dozen gashes.

The three remaining oxen were terrified but unharmed, and Arlian pressed on; he was now descending the southern slopes of the Dreaming Mountains, far past the point where turning back would make any sense.

That was the last serious threat, however; the following two nights were troubled only by sounds, fleeting apparitions, and something large that moved invisibly but audibly through his camp, extinguishing the fire and tarnishing the brass wagon fittings as it passed. The quality of the road seemed to be improving again, as well—he no longer had occasion to stop and poke through the underbrush to find the faded traces when the way was unclear, but could simply follow the obvious path.

Two days later his wagon rolled through black iron gates into the first Aritheian village, where the natives greeted his arrival with astonishment and delight. Children ran shrieking and pointing alongside; adults gaped openly as he passed.

He had developed a very definite set of priorities in his travels; he ignored the attention until he had stopped at the trough in the village square and watered his surviving oxen. The villagers kept a respectful distance as they stood and stared at him, whispering to one another.

Once the oxen were drinking, Arlian turned to look at his new hosts.

They were dressed strangely, all of them, men, women, and children in short, loose gowns dyed in bright colors—not the flowing pale robes of the Borderlands, but abbreviated garments in much more intense hues. Their legs were bare, their feet sandaled. He realized that his white blouse, blue breeches, and broad-brimmed black hat must look as peculiar to them as their garb did to him; no wonder they stared! Had someone walked into Obsidian robed in scarlet, yellow, and parrot green when he was a boy, he would have stared just as rudely—and in fact, except for staring, these people were being quite polite. No one had shouted at him or tried to touch him, his wagon, or his oxen.

That was promising.

He could not make out a word anyone said, however, which was not quite so encouraging. "Excuse me," he called. "Does anyone speak my language?"

No one replied. A few of the villagers exchanged unintelligible words among themselves; two or three men slipped away, presumably tiring of the spectacle.

He shrugged, and returned to tending his oxen.

Half an hour later the interpreter arrived.

Chapter Twenty-Five

Arithei

Meriei, the interpreter, was a young man—older than Arlian himself, by at least a year or two, but far less sure of himself. Although he appeared to speak Arlian's native tongue fluently it took some time before Arlian was able to make his intentions clear.

"I have come to Arithei to find the family of a man named Hathet," Arlian repeated, as the two of them stood by the trough where Arlian's oxen were placidly drinking.

"I know of no one named Hathet in the House of Slihar," the interpreter said.

That was an improvement over his first two replies, but still not very satisfactory. Did that mean that Hathet had been lying after all, and had not come from Arithei? Or did it mean that this interpreter was too young to remember the old man? Or did it merely mean that there was still some sort of confusion about what Arlian wanted?

Arlian sighed and looked around at the crowd surrounding them, wishing somebody else here could speak Man's Tongue. Evidently no one else did, and he had to make do with what he had. "What is the House of Slihar?" he asked. "Is that the name of this town?"

"No, no," the interpreter said. "This town is Ilusali. Slihar is a *House*. A ... a family of families."

"And there are other Houses?"

"Yes, yes. Eleven Houses. Slihar and ten more." The interpreter tapped his orange-robed chest. "I am Meriei, of the House of Slihar."

"Then perhaps Hathet belonged to one of the other Houses," Arlian suggested. "Or to no House at all—does everyone belong to a House?"

"Everyone belongs to a House," the interpreter agreed. "It is the House of Slihar that traded with the lands beyond the mountains. This is why I know your tongue."

"And no other House has ever sent anyone to Manfort?"

Meriei was clearly struggling with the unfamiliar language—he knew it, but Arlian suspected he had had little use for it until now. "It is the House of Slihar that traded with the lands beyond the mountains," the interpreter repeated.

"Hathet was not a trader," Arlian said.

The interpreter merely looked more confused than ever.

Arlian could stand it no longer. "Take me to someone from another House," he said. "I've come to find Hathet's family, whether it's Slihar or not."

"It is the House of Slihar that trades with people from beyond the mountains!" Meriei insisted.

"I am not trading!" Arlian shouted. "I'm looking for Hathet's family!" Meriei looked at the wagon. He said nothing, but his expression was plain enough.

"Trade *later*," Arlian said. "After I find Hathet's family, and not until then!"

"You do not trade with Hathet?"

Arlian started to explain that Hathet was dead, but then bit the sentence off before the first word was out of his mouth. "I do not trade with Hathet," he agreed. "I seek Hathet's family, but not to trade."

"When you are done, you trade with the House of Slihar?"

"Maybe," Arlian said.

The interpreter hesitated, then shrugged. "We must go to Theyani to find all eleven Houses," he said. "Only six Houses are in Ilusali."

Arlian frowned—why not start with those six? "What is Theyani?" he asked.

"It is…" The interpreter struggled, obviously looking for the right word. "It is the chief city. The center of Arithei."

"Ah!" That sounded promising; after all, if Hathet had been sent as an ambassador for all of Arithei, he had presumably come from the capital. "Yes," Arlian said. "Take me to Theyani."

The interpreter looked at the sky; the sun was brushing the mountaintops to the west. "Tomorrow?" he asked.

"Tomorrow," Arlian agreed.

The interpreter smiled. "Can we both ride?" he asked, pointing at Arlian's wagon.

"Of course."

"And tonight…"

"Tonight I'll stay right here," Arlian said.

The interpreter bowed deeply in acknowledgment. "I will see you in the morning," he said.

Arlian bowed in response, and the interpreter turned away.

Dragon Weather

Arlian clambered back into his wagon, and settled himself comfortably. The village of Ilusali might well have an inn, but if it did he had not recognized it, and attempting to deal with an innkeeper without speaking his language was more than Arlian cared to handle—he was exhausted from his journey over the mountains and his awkward conversation with Meriei. Sleeping in his familiar wagon would be fine.

At least here he wouldn't need to worry about magical monsters. The worst he would expect here would be human thieves, and even those seemed unlikely. He looked out at the villagers who stood on all sides, staring.

If they stayed there he wouldn't need to worry about thieves at all, since he'd have half a hundred witnesses to any attempted depredations. He sighed, and leaned back against one side of the wagon, thinking and planning.

Some of the villagers were still gawking when, hours later, he blew out his lamp and retired for the night.

The village square was deserted when he awoke the next morning—apparently even the most determined gawkers had eventually grown bored— but it filled quickly as the sun climbed the eastern sky, and he and Meriei had an audience of dozens when the wagon finally rolled southward, out another iron gate onto the road to Theyani.

The entire length of that road was lined with iron posts—not an actual fence, but isolated posts, one every hundred feet or so, each one the height of a man and as thick as Arlian's forearm. Each shaft was plain, but the top of each post was wrought into fantastical shapes—bizarre faces, wings, talons, or blossoms, seemingly at random. Arlian pointed one out to Meriei and asked, "What are those?"

"Ditiae," Meriei replied. "They keep away evil magic."

Arlian looked around at the surrounding countryside. The air overhead rippled with strange colors; to either side of the highway shadows moved in impossible ways. Orange trees bent and twisted in various directions, as if they were struggling beasts. He could hear whisperings and rustlings that did not sound like wind blowing through leaves or grass, no matter how much he wished they would, and strange smells, like hot metal one moment and heavy perfume the next, reached his nose. This land wasn't as fierce or wild as what he had seen in the mountains, but it was still a hostile, unnatural place.

Keeping away magic seemed like a very good idea, and the iron posts seemed to work. The bare yellow dirt of the road stayed in place, retained its natural color, and produced no sounds except the occasional crunch of hooves or wheels on pebbles.

He tried to converse with Meriei after that, to pass the time and to distract them both from their eerie surroundings, but every attempt to discuss anything more complex than the weather quickly broke down in confusion. Eventually Arlian gave up, and they rode in silence.

At each human habitation they passed people stopped what they were doing and stared at the strange wagon and its foreign driver. It was quite obvious that regardless of what the House of Slihar might claim, *no one* had traded with the north for some time—or at least, Arlian corrected himself, no foreigners had come to Arithei; Aritheians might have ventured into the outside world.

Arlian had expected the journey from Ilusali to Theyani to take several days; accustomed to his vastly more spacious homeland, he had badly misjudged the size of the crowded little land of Arithei. They arrived at the ornately worked gates of the capital while the sun was still high in the west.

These gates were iron, of course, and part of a black iron wall surrounding the city. At a shout from Meriei the gates swung open, and Arlian's oxen plodded unhindered onto the pavement beyond.

The city was tiny compared to Manfort, but still larger than any other town Arlian had seen, with several large, fine buildings, most of them constructed of white or yellow stone with black iron fittings—iron gutters, iron shutters, and so on. Long streaks of rust stained most of the walls. The streets were of brown brick, but so covered in yellow dust as to almost appear unpaved. The entire place smelled of heat and dust.

Arlian had no idea where to go once they were inside the walls, and looked to Meriei for guidance.

"That way," the interpreter directed, pointing across a broad plaza to a white stone building.

A few moments later, while the oxen waited placidly outside, Arlian found himself standing more or less ignored in a large, elegant room while a dozen Aritheians argued with Meriei and each other. Every so often another person would enter the room, take one long, surprised look at Arlian, and then plunge into the ongoing discussion.

Arlian admired the room—it was largely open on two sides, with broad blue awnings providing shade while admitting every breeze, and the rich scent of a garden wafted in from somewhere. The furnishings were suitable for a dining hall or conference chamber, built all of thick dark wood, simple but not in the least primitive. The brown tile floor had half a dozen small, brightly colored rugs scattered across it, giving it a festive touch to counter the heavy appearance of the massive wooden table and chairs. The whole place was unlike anything Arlian had ever seen before, but it seemed practical and comfortable.

Every so often as he stood there looking about Arlian heard the name "Hathet" spoken by one of the Aritheians. Other than that he could understand nothing at all of what was said, and could do nothing but wait.

Finally one tall old man stepped out of the crowd, and the others fell silent.

"I am Hirofa, of the House of Slihar," the old man said in flawless, almost unaccented speech far better than Meriei's command of Arlian's tongue. "Whom do I have the honor of addressing?"

"I am Lord Ari of Manfort," Arlian said, bowing.

Hirofa bowed in acknowledgment. "And why have you come to Arithei?"

"I have come to pay a debt to a man named Hathet, who befriended me when I was a child," Arlian replied.

"Hathet is a name from the House of Deri," Hirofa said. "The House of Deri does not trade with Manfort. How did you come to meet this man?"

Arlian hesitated. He had had some time to think, and had remembered that Hathet had claimed his enslavement was the work of his political enemies.

The House of Slihar might well be those enemies. To tell the whole truth might be unwise.

"I nursed him when he was dying of fever," Arlian said. "He wanted his family to know that he would not return. He was too ill to tell me their names, or how he came to be in Deep Delving, where I met him, but I promised to find them, and to tell them how he died."

"He told you no names?"

"None," Arlian said.

Actually, Hathet might have named names, but if so, none of the other miners had paid any attention, and Arlian didn't remember them.

Hirofa turned away and conferred briefly with the others, then turned back to Arlian.

"To refuse a deathbed promise would dishonor our House," he said. "I will tell Hathet's family of his death."

Arlian frowned. "I promised I would tell them myself," he said.

"You do not speak Aritheian."

"I will need an interpreter," Arlian agreed, "but I want to see them with

211

my own eyes, and hold their hands to share their grief."

"Very well," Hirofa said. "I will take you to the House of Deri."

Several of the others protested—apparently others besides Meriei and Hirofa knew Man's Tongue. Hirofa turned and spoke a single sharp sentence, and the protests stopped. Then he beckoned to Arlian.

"Come," he said.

Arlian obeyed, and the two men made their way back out onto the plaza. Hirofa started to lead the way down a nearby street, but Arlian stopped by his wagon.

"You can leave that where it is," Hirofa said.

Arlian shook his head. "No," he said. "I am a stranger here, and you must forgive me my customs. I will bring my wagon with me."

Hirofa obviously didn't like the decision, but made no further objection as Arlian led the oxen alongside.

By the time they reached the rust-streaked golden palace Hirofa indicated as the House of Deri a crowd of curiosity-seekers was following them, staring at every motion Arlian and his oxen made.

Hirofa led Arlian up to a central archway and turned a handle set in the red-and-gold-enameled door; somewhere inside a bell rang, barely audible.

A moment later the doors swung open, and an Aritheian in an all-red gown stepped out. He and Hirofa exchanged a few words—but Arlian did not hear the name "Hathet."

"I'm here about Hathet," he called.

The man in red glanced at him, startled.

"Hathet," Arlian repeated.

Hirofa turned and glowered at him briefly, but said nothing.

The man in red glanced back and forth between Arlian and Hirofa, then at the crowd of onlookers. He said something, beckoning to Arlian—Arlian didn't understand the words, but the message was clear enough.

Arlian pointed at his wagon. "Can someone guard this?"

The man in red understood the question, even if he didn't recognize the words; he held up a hand to indicate that Arlian should wait, then turned and shouted, to someone inside.

A moment later three men emerged, clad not in the customary short robes of ordinary Aritheians, but in brown leather with strips of black iron across their chests—armor, of a sort. They had no swords, but carried wooden staves, each almost six feet long. They took up positions around the wagon and oxen.

Satisfied, Arlian turned and looked questioningly at the man in red, who beckoned him inside.

He followed.

Hirofa also started to follow, and the red-clad steward, if that was what he was, looked questioningly at Arlian.

Arlian shrugged, and the steward held up a hand to prevent Hirofa's entrance.

Hirofa protested, and the two men argued loudly for several minutes before Hirofa turned away in disgust.

With that settled, Arlian followed the steward through an elegant antechamber, down a long stone passage, and into a lushly appointed room.

There a woman in a blue-and-green robe was sprawled comfortably on a rattan settee. She looked up at Arlian's arrival and sat up straight.

The steward spoke to her for a moment, while Arlian waited; then the woman rose and addressed the foreigner directly, in his own tongue. Her speech was clear, if not as free of accent as Hirofa's.

"You are from the Lands of Man?" she asked.

"Yes," Arlian said.

"You have news of Hathet?"

"Yes."

"Then you must see Grandmother. I am to prepare you."

"Good," Arlian said.

Chapter Twenty-Six

The House of Deri

A dais at one end of the reception chamber held three chairs, all of them occupied; a handful of other people, all of them well fed and handsome, stood to either side.

This room was larger than the one where he had met Hirofa, and only open on one side, but similar in design. The awnings were green instead of blue, and the chairs were all pushed back against one wall, but the floor tiles were the same shade of brown, and the furniture made in the same style. Presumably this was the norm for Arithei—or at least for the headquarters of the great Houses.

As instructed, when he had crossed the room Arlian knelt before the three people on the dais—two women, one young and one old, and an old man—and made the gesture of respect the interpreter had taught him—hands pressed together palm-to-palm before his face, head tilted back.

The old man spoke, in Aritheian.

"They welcome you to the House of Deri," the interpreter explained.

"Please tell them that I am Lord Ari of Manfort, and I am honored to be here," Arlian said.

The interpreter relayed the message, heard the reply, and told Arlian, "They ask your business here."

Arlian looked up at the old couple. He asked, "You are the family of Hathet, who was sent as ambassador to Manfort many years ago?"

His interpreter quickly translated the question into Aritheian, and the tall, white-haired woman replied with a few brief words.

"They acknowledge the relationship," the interpreter said. She gestured at the tall woman. "Grandmother Iriol was Hathet's sister."

"Then I regret to say I bring sad news," Arlian said. "Lady Iriol, your brother Hathet is dead. I was present when he died, and held him in my arms."

The interpreter relayed this, and received another question from the tall woman in response while the half dozen others in the room whispered excitedly to one another.

"How did he die?" she asked.

"Of a fever," Arlian said. "I tended him in his illness, and did all I could for him—he had been kind to me."

When the interpreter had translated this several of the Aritheians spoke at once, though the tall woman remained thoughtfully silent; the interpreter looked lost as she tried to decide whom to listen to.

"What are they saying?" Arlian asked her.

"They want to know where it happened, whether you are a northern physician or perhaps a sorcerer, when this happened ... everything."

Arlian waved for the family's attention, then began his story, pausing after each sentence so that the interpreter could do her job.

"As a boy, I was captured by slavers," he said. "I was sold and sent to a mine in Deep Delving, and I met Hathet there. He befriended me, protected me and taught me. He said that he had been sent from Arithei as your ambassador, but no one believed him, not even I. He said he had been waylaid by bandits on the journey north—he had made it safely into the Lands of Man, but was taken captive in the Desolation, the wasteland between the Borderlands and Manfort. He believed this capture was the doing of his political enemies, because he was not held for ransom, as he expected, but was instead sold as a slave and taken to the mine where I met him."

Several people muttered as this was translated. Arlian hesitated, then admitted, "We did not believe this story—we had never heard of Arithei, and we could not see why bandits would neither kill nor ransom him. At any rate, he lived out the rest of his days working in the mine; he caught the fever there, weakened, and in time died." He reached into the waistband of his breeches and pulled out the crude little pouch he had carried for so long. "He had collected these in the mine— in the Lands of Man they're worthless, nothing but pretty stones, but he said they were precious here. When he died I took them to remember him by, not knowing I would ever find Arithei, but now that I am here I believe you should have them." He opened the pouch, still kneeling, then poured the purple stones out onto the dais.

A sudden hush fell; the whispering that had gone on while he spoke ceased completely, and it seemed the Aritheians had even stopped breathing as they stared.

"Amethystoi," someone said at last.

"Amethysts," Arlian agreed, looking around at the stunned observers. Obviously, Hathet had not exaggerated the value of his prizes.

The interpreter had been staring at the jewels as intently as anyone; now she looked up at Arlian. "I begin to understand how you got here," she said.

Arlian made no attempt to hide his puzzlement. "What?"

"The dreams have been strong lately, and the wizards careless; no one had dared cross the Dreaming Mountains for years, not even those of the House of Slihar, until you arrived. When we saw you we all wondered how you managed to reach Arithei alive—some of us suspected you were a wizard, or a demon, or a homunculus, rather than a true human." She gestured at the dais. "Now I see."

"See what?"

"The amethysts—don't you know why they're precious?"

"No," Arlian said. "Hathet said they could be used for some sort of protective magic, and I thought they were prized for their rarity and beauty, but that's all I know."

The interpreter made a curious jerk of the head that Arlian was beginning to realize indicated denial in Arithei. "They are not merely used in magic," she said. "They *are* magic, in themselves. An amethyst placed in a cup and a simple spoken word will cure drunkenness. They resist madness of any kind, and they keep bad dreams away." She gestured toward the direction whence Arlian had come. "In the mountains, bad dreams can kill. These kept you safe."

"Those, and my own sword, perhaps," Arlian said. "I encountered certain difficulties on the way."

"Yes, your sword," the interpreter agreed. "Cold iron. We use iron for protection here." She looked at the hilt on Arlian's belt and added, "And silver?"

Arlian looked down at the silver filigree of his sword's pommel. "Silver and steel, yes," he said.

"The creatures of darkness fear silver," the interpreter said. "The creatures of air cannot abide cold iron. And the creatures of dream cannot pass near amethyst. You are protected as few ever are."

Arlian thought back to the things he had seen and fought on the road across the mountains, to what had remained of his fourth ox, and shuddered—if that was what it was like when he carried magical protection, what would have happened had he been without such defenses?

Obviously, he would have died. No wonder so little traffic passed between Arithei and the Lands of Man! And no wonder the Aritheians had placed iron fences around every town, and those strange posts along their roads.

And he had just given away all his amethysts; the journey back north might well be his last. He could scarcely reclaim them *now,* though …

The tall woman spoke.

"She's asking if this is all Hathet gave you," the interpreter reported.

"Yes," Arlian said. "That's all."

The tall woman then stooped and chose the largest of the purple stones, one as large as the top joint of Arlian's thumb. "Then keep this," she said, speaking slowly in Arlian's own tongue. "For nursing my brother in his illness."

Arlian hesitated, trying to decide whether he should argue or not, but the memory of those things in the mountains decided him. "Thank you," he said, accepting the stone.

"Wear it around your throat," she said. "More effective that way."

Arlian bowed in acknowledgment of this advice.

The tall woman then addressed the interpreter in Aritheian.

The interpreter listened carefully and asked questions before finally turning back to Arlian.

"She says you have the protection of the House of Deri any time you may need it, and she wishes to know whether Hathet ever mentioned any names, anyone he thought might have been involved in the plotting against him."

"No," Arlian said. "He never mentioned any names."

"Then she wishes me to tell you that nonetheless, from events after Hathet's departure, and the events surrounding your arrival, she has a fairly strong suspicion of who was involved, and how. Your arrival has brought not merely news, but wealth…" She gestured at the gem-strewn dais. "… and the prospect of vengeance and a restoration of the former prominence of the House of Deri. You managed to bring this to *us,* to Hathet's House, despite the interference of those you first encountered. You came here even though you had met others who surely did not wish you to. For this, the House is greatly in your debt."

Arlian noticed that the interpreter did not mention the House of Slihar by name, but he did not doubt that she was referring to them. Although he knew almost nothing of Aritheian society, it was easy enough to guess that the House of Slihar and the House of Deri had competed for control of trade with the Lands of Man, that the Slihar had been responsible for Hathet's abduction, and that his disappearance had allowed them to dominate—for a time.

"I merely did what seemed right," Arlian said. "Hathet was kind to me when I needed kindness."

The tall woman said something without waiting for the translation—obviously, while she preferred to use the interpreter, she knew something of Arlian's language.

"Yet you came to Arithei to bring us this," the interpreter said, gesturing at the amethysts.

"I also came to Arithei to sell swords," Arlian said. "And to buy goods to sell in the north. I have silver to pay."

The interpreter and the tall woman stared at him.

"Swords?" Hathet's sister said.

"Silver?" the interpreter said.

"That's right," Arlian said.

"Silver cannot pass Tirikindaro," the interpreter said.

"No one stopped me," Arlian said. "Tirikindaro was quiet when I passed."

"But..." The interpreter groped for words, then began again, speaking slowly. "Our ancestors fled from the dragons long ago and came to Arithei," she said, "but later they found that they were trapped here by the magic that surrounds this place. We have remained here ever since. We live confined by the dreams, the wizards, the creatures that live in the mountains, unable to leave this one safe valley because we lack protections from the magic in the hills. We found iron, all the iron we needed, to build our ward-fences, but none of us had the knowledge of making steel for swords, and iron alone is not sufficient against the creatures in the mountains. We have found no silver anywhere, though we have looked. We had a few amethysts our ancestors had brought from the north; these were carried by our traders and ambassadors, but they have gradually been lost over time as their bearers fell to the other hazards around us—Hathet carried the last stone our House possessed, and no doubt some bandit gave it to his children to play with. The House of Slihar had three or four more stones that allowed them to send *their* ambassador, and their traders, for a few years after Hathet disappeared, but those, too, have now been lost. We were confined here, without hope."

She sighed, then said, "The people of the lands beyond the mountains did nothing to help us, but we do not fault them for this. We dared not tell them the secret of using amethysts to cross the Dreaming Mountains for fear of invasion, and they knew we had a secret we would not share. Mistrusting us in return, they would not sell us steel or silver." She made a gesture of dismissal. "We do not blame them; we gave them no reason to trust us."

Arlian started to protest, then thought better of it. The interpreter continued, "For centuries we have resigned ourselves to living in isolation here, behind our iron walls, and of late we have even resigned ourselves to having no contact with the outside at all—and now you come here, unbidden, with all these precious things, and offer us the world!"

The effusive gratitude that concluded the explanation made Arlian uncomfortable. "I owed Hathet a debt," he said.

Hathet's sister reached out and put a hand on Arlian's shoulder.

"My friend," she said slowly, "your words, and these stones, paid that debt many times over. If you have brought us silver and steel as well, you will be *very* rich."

Chapter Twenty-Seven

The Trade Delegation

Black looked at his empty mug, debating whether to order another cup of wine. They watered it here, of course—these southerners always did—but even when he knew he was paying for as much water as wine, it was still far cheaper than decent beer in Sweetwater.

He was tired of watered wine. He was tired of constant sunlight. He was tired of Sweetwater. He had been stranded here for months, and he was quite thoroughly tired of everything about it and eager to be moving again. He was completely recovered, his wounds healed and the infection long gone, but two of the caravans weren't yet returned, and Lord Drens wasn't about to head north until they were back.

He could hardly cross the Desolation by himself, but he very much wished that those other two caravans would hurry up and arrive.

The door of the inn opened, and Black turned at the sound—any interruption at all of the usual dull routine would be welcome.

A figure was standing in the doorway, silhouetted by the afternoon sun—a tall man in a broad-brimmed hat. He stepped in, and Black recognized him.

"Ari!" he said.

"Hello, Black," Arlian said, smiling broadly. "Lord Drens said I'd find you here."

"Ari, it's you!" Black repeated, as he got to his feet and started toward the new arrival.

"I may not want to use that name anymore," Arlian said. "I haven't decided, but I think something more elegant may be appropriate." Then he fell silent for a moment as the two men embraced. He clapped Black on the back as they separated.

"They told me you'd headed across the Dreaming Mountains, bound for Arithei," Black said.

"I did," Arlian said.

"Alone, they said," Black said.

"That's right." Arlian grinned at him.

Black grinned back. "You do realize the contradiction between this and your current presence here, still alive, don't you?"

Arlian smiled. "I made it to Arithei alone," he said. "There's no contradiction; I had protection you didn't know about." The smile twisted awry. "For that matter, I didn't know about it, either."

"I see," Black said. "And this mysterious protection also saw you safely back to Sweetwater? Or am I to understand otherwise from your phrasing?"

"Oh, I had other protection on the way back," Arlian said. He gestured toward the door.

Black peered out into the sunlight and saw a dozen men and women, all dressed in strange, bright costumes, all wearing broad leather sword belts that looked out of place on the garish robes, and with glittering silver medallions on chains about their necks.

"The Aritheian trade mission," Arlian explained. "They escorted me back."

Black was well aware that there had been no trade with Arithei in a decade or so, but he had no reason to doubt Arlian. He had never seen an Aritheian, but he had no reason to think these strangers were anything else.

"Of course," he said. He stepped up to the door and looked out.

Arlian's familiar, battered wagon stood in the town square, just behind the Aritheians, but four more exotic wagons stood beyond it, each open-sided and roofed with red-dyed canvas stretched over a wooden frame, each drawn by a pair of fine horses. Another horse, a big black gelding, stood nearby, tied to a palm tree.

All five wagons seemed somehow indistinct, and a trifle brighter and more colorful than they should be. Black had been in the Borderlands long enough to know what that meant.

"Magic," he said.

"Quite a bit of it, yes," Arlian said. "It's what the Aritheians do best, and I think they were quite generous with me."

Black nodded. "You found a market for your weapons, then. Good for you, my lord."

"And a market for the silver, too. I brought the metal that made those pendants."

Black studied the nearest Aritheian's necklace. A purple stone was set in it, he noticed. "Excellent."

Arlian glanced at the wagons. "Let me introduce you," he said.

"If you like," Black said, as he followed Arlian out into the sun.

The Aritheian names were strange, and Black doubted he would remember them all. The head of the Aritheian delegation was a thin, eagle-eyed man called Thirif, but a plump, smiling woman named Hlur was to serve as the new ambassador to Manfort.

"I wasn't aware a new ambassador was needed," Black remarked.

"Sahasin is…" Arlian began. He hesitated, then said, "Well, let us just say that I think a new ambassador *will* be needed."

Black did not ask for further explanation; he continued with the introductions. It became clear that only about half the Aritheians had even a smattering of Man's Tongue, but all of them smiled and nodded and seemed pleased to be in the Lands of Man, and pleased to meet Black.

The wagons were so full of magic that even standing near them made Black's skin prickle; he could not resist looking in the open side of one at the bundles and boxes.

Arlian noticed his glance.

"That's all prepared enchantments," he said. "Thousands of them. Powders and potions and gems, decoctions of herbs and dreams in iron cages—all of them things unknown in the Lands of Man. I'll have something to sell at every town on the road north, from Stonebreak to Benth-in-Tara, and should still have most of it left when we reach Manfort."

"Indeed," Black said in a noncommittal tone.

"The Aritheians tell me that even the greatest magician can't make magic from nothing in Manfort," Arlian said. "There's something lacking in the air or earth. But they can bring these prepared magicks there to sell."

"Sorcerers seem to manage," Black pointed out.

Arlian waved that away. "The Aritheians don't seem to consider our sorcery to be true magic," he said. "They tell me that these are all spells that sorcerers can't make."

"What sort of spells?"

"Oh, any number of different ones," Arlian said, as the two man strolled around the wagon, looking in at its contents. "Poisons and protections and aphrodisiacs, love philtres and enthrallments, illusions and glamours—I don't know all of them myself. The House of Deri had been stockpiling them for twenty years against the day they found a way to reopen trade."

"And are all these yours to sell, then?"

"Most of them," Arlian admitted. "My old wagon and two of the others are mine; the other two belong to the House of Deri. Allies of mine."

"And these Aritheians who came with you?"

"Well, Shibiel and Isein and Qulu work for me," Arlian said. "The others are merely traveling with us. Thirif and Hlur and one or two of the others plan to join the caravan and accompany us to Manfort—after all, an ambassador would hardly be any use anywhere else. The rest have already had enough of adventure in getting this far, and prefer not to cross the Desolation—I can scarcely blame them for that! They'll be staying here in the Borderlands, trading for the things Arithei lacks."

Black nodded. "Those first three you mentioned are your slaves, then? You bought them?"

Arlian stopped dead, shocked. He turned to stare at Black.

"No," he said. "I would never own slaves. I have *been* a slave, and lived among slaves—I won't hold another in bondage. These are free people in my employ."

"Employees?" Black said. "Then you are truly a lord now, and not merely playing the part."

"Yes," Arlian agreed. "I am a lord. And I think," he said, "that at last I'm ready."

Black looked at him inquiringly.

"I'm a grown man now," Arlian said. "I'm strong and whole, and have, you say, the heart of the dragon. I've learned the manners of a lord, and found the money to establish my claim to the title beyond question. You've taught me the basics of swordsmanship, and on the roads I've killed a man and a dozen monsters. The Aritheians have provided me with more magic than almost anyone else in Manfort could possess. I believe that in wits, courage, and capabilities I'm a match for most men." He took a deep breath, and let it out slowly.

"The time has come," he continued, "to return to Manfort and find Lord Dragon and his looters, and punish them for their wrongs. No more delays. The time has come to find Sweet and free her, and any of the other women who aided me who may yet survive, and to punish all the owners of the House of Carnal Society for *their* wrongs. And when that is all done it will be time to seek out the dragons in their caverns beneath the earth, the beasts who slew my family, and destroy them."

"Oh, is *that* all," Black said. "Overthrow a dozen lords and wipe out the dragons—child's play!"

Arlian grinned at him.

Black glowered back.

For a moment the two of them stood silently by the wagon; Black turned to look over the boxes and bundles once more.

He knew that even a simple love philtre was worth a dozen times its weight in gold, and here Arlian had three wagonloads of magic. The boy was not merely a lord, but a very wealthy lord indeed.

His thoughts were interrupted by a polite cough. He turned back to his friend.

"Have you ever considered giving up your career in the caravan trade?" Arlian asked.

"Why?" Black asked warily.

"Because a proper lord must have a household, of course, and I'll need a bodyguard and steward. I value your counsel and your friendship, Black—I'd be pleased if you'd take the job."

Black stared at him silently for a moment.

"You must think I'm a fool," he said at last.

"I'll pay time and a fifth your present contract," Arlian said.

"You will?"

"Yes."

"In gold?"

"Of course."

"In that case, my lord," Black said with a bow, "I *am* a fool. The moment my current contract is completed, I will be entirely at your service."

Book 3:

Lord Obsidian

Chapter Twenty-Eight

Rumors

Coin looked up as the door flew open and the spring rain blew in. The man in the doorway was of moderate height, dark-haired, and clad in black leather.

She closed the ledger and asked, "May I be of service?"

"I understand you manage certain properties in the upper city," the man in black said.

"I do," Coin acknowledged.

"I represent Lord Obsidian," the stranger said. "He has sent me ahead while he tends to certain other business in Westguard. He seeks suitable accommodations for an extended stay in Manfort."

"I might have a suite of rooms…" Coin began.

The man in black smiled crookedly. "No, no," he said. "Suitable accommodations for *Lord Obsidian*. We require a house and garden, at the very least."

"And at the most?"

The man's smile broadened. "I doubt very much that anything you have could be more than we can use. Or more than Lord Obsidian can afford."

Coin snorted. "As it happens, I have charge of the old ducal palace—the one abandoned by the grandfather of the present Duke of Manfort when the Citadel was completed. I scarcely think…"

"That would suit us perfectly," the man in black interrupted. "If I might see it? Immediately?"

Coin stared at him for a moment, trying to decide whether the man was a fool, or deranged, or joking, or simply unaware of what such an establishment would cost. She had never heard of any Lord Obsidian, so far as she could recall, and surely she would have heard of anyone who could afford the Old Palace.

But then, "Obsidian" might be an alias—perhaps for Lord Enziet, or another of the city's elite, who had grown bored with more modest accommodations. She rose.

"I'll get the keys," she said.

* * *

The watchman thought the stranger staring at the New Inn looked familiar, but could not place him. His yellow silk shirt and lush wool coat, the sharply trimmed hair laid bare when he doffed his plumed hat, the fine sword on his belt, and a dozen other details marked him as a wealthy man, but his black boots were scuffed and showing wear, the hair just slightly wrong for the current fashion.

Curious, the watchman ambled over. It was a quiet day, and he had nothing in particular he should be doing other than simply remaining visible on the street, so no one could object if he offered the young man a bit of advice, and maybe asked a few questions.

The stranger did not look around as the watchman approached; instead he continued to study the New Inn, as if trying to identify the individual stone blocks of the façade. His coat flapped in the chill wind, and the hat under his arm struggled to escape.

"They've not chosen a name yet, or put up their sign, but it's an inn, my lord, if you're seeking lodging," the watchman offered.

The young man turned. "An inn?" he asked. "Just an inn?"

"That's right."

"I had been told that a rather different establishment might be found here."

"Ah," the watchman said. Matters were becoming clearer. "Well, there was one, until about two years ago—the House of the Six Lords, some of us called it. It's gone, burned down."

"Oh? Burned? How did that happen?"

"One of the six lords had it done."

The stranger frowned. "Really? That's hardly usual, is it, to deliberately burn down a building in the middle of town?"

"Not usual at all, my lord," the watchman agreed. "And we might have protested, but he had come with a letter from the Duke of Manfort, granting him full authority to do as he pleased, and ordering all of us in the guard to obey him."

"Indeed! Now, *that's* not usual either, is it?"

"No, my lord."

"Could it have been a forgery, do you suppose?"

"He had the Duke's seal on it, and one of the Duke's own guards with him, my lord."

"Who was this man, then, that had so much of the Duke's favor?" The question was perhaps a trifle more eagerly asked than might have been expected.

"I don't know, my lord; he gave no name."

Arlian tried to hide his disappointment. "Oh, but surely someone must have recognized him!"

"Not to my knowledge, my lord."

"Was he masked, then?"

"No, he was not—but really, my lord, who here in Westguard would know all the lords of Manfort by sight?"

"Are you telling me you didn't know who *any* of these six lords were?"

"Not a one of them, my lord. After all, the tradesmen and housewives of Westguard are hardly likely to attend the palace balls in Manfort. I couldn't put a name to more than a dozen lords—why, I'd scarcely know the Duke himself if he were to walk by! For example, you've a familiar air about you, but I can't pin it down…"

Arlian smiled. "I'm no one you'd know," he said.

He turned and walked away, clapping his hat back on his head and holding it against the wind.

The watchman hesitated, but did not pursue. Prying into the affairs of the wealthy was no part of what was expected of him—on the contrary, it could be very unwise.

And really, the handsome young lord was probably just reluctant to have it known that he had come seeking an infamous brothel.

* * *

Word of the mysterious Lord Obsidian's impending arrival spread quickly through Manfort. The city's tradesmen watched as men and wagons arrived, both local and foreign, and the work of restoring the Old Palace to habitable condition began. Several of these tradesmen found their way to the postern to inquire whether the household might need their services.

The steward, a formidable man who called himself Black, was cautious in making his choices; grocers, butchers, chandlers, stablemen, and the like were questioned about their terms, and then about who they might recommend in trades other than their own, and were then sent away with polite but noncommittal replies.

The one exception was a slave trader who came to the postern. He introduced himself, then began, "Naturally, while I don't know Lord Obsidian's particular desires, we can provide almost anything he might require—all ages, both sexes…"

"Lord Obsidian does not hold slaves," the steward replied disdainfully. "All our staff will be free."

"Ah, but surely there are certain roles…" the slaver wheedled.

The steward did not allow him to complete the sentence. "Lord Obsidian does not hold slaves," he repeated.

The slaver frowned and suggested, "Then perhaps you might be interested yourself…"

"No."

"Lord Obsidian need not know."

"I said no."

"If I might have a word…"

"That's enough," the steward barked, his hand falling to the hilt of his sword—a nobleman's sword, the slave master noticed, hardly appropriate for a steward. "Get out!"

The slaver hesitated, but then shrugged and left without further protest.

Later he mentioned the incident to a few friends. Word spread, and others, curious, began to ask discreet questions of the steward.

"Lord Obsidian does not hold slaves," Black told them. "Nor do I. That's all. It is his choice, and mine."

Interest in Lord Obsidian, widespread ever since Coin first reported that she had found a buyer for the Old Palace, heightened as this odd quirk became known. Obviously, Obsidian was not one of the established elite of the city, since none of them had ever had any compunctions about slavery—he was a stranger, an outsider.

Some inhabitants of Manfort joined Obsidian's staff, and the rumors grew.

Obsidian himself had reportedly not yet arrived at the palace, but in addition to the steward and the people hired locally there were half a dozen foreigners in residence—people not merely from outside the city walls, but from somewhere beyond the Lands of Man entirely, four men and two women. They spoke among themselves in some unknown tongue, and spoke Man's Tongue haltingly or not at all, and often dressed in bizarre, outlandish robes.

The wagons that brought supplies to the palace were heavily guarded, and some of them carried freight that was promptly hidden away in locked storerooms.

The steward was said to be asking questions about more than where he might find the best suppliers of fresh produce or clean lamp oil; he was rumored to be interested in sorcery, and in volcanic glass—presumably Lord Obsidian's choice of name had something to do with that. He reportedly inquired after those knowledgeable about dragons, as well, and about all the lords of Manfort.

But all this was hearsay. All that reached the streets was rumor and gossip, no hard facts, and the people of Manfort waited for Lord Obsidian's arrival with great anticipation.

Black could hardly be unaware of this, and one evening, as he stood gazing out the window in one of the upper rooms, he remarked, "The whole city is curious about you."

Arlian answered, "That was the idea."

Arlian was seated comfortably in a velvet-upholstered chair, a glass of good red wine on the table at his side. He had arrived a few days ago, along with those of the Aritheians who had chosen to come to Manfort. Arlian had driven his own wagon, and now wore the garb of a coachman, rather than a lord—anonymity had its uses, and a coachman's broad-brimmed black hat kept his face shaded, so that later, when Lord Obsidian had made his grand appearance, the facial similarity would not be *too* obvious. Ari the teamster would get a very different reaction than Lord Obsidian among the shopkeepers of Manfort, and Arlian thought both might be useful.

"I'm still not convinced it's a *good* idea," Black replied.

"Well, what else am I supposed to do?" Arlian asked. "Search the city street by street in hopes of spotting Lord Dragon or one of his henchmen? In Westguard I couldn't find anyone who would admit to knowing anything about him. I heard a few rumors, got some support for my suspicions as to the names of the others among the six lords, but nothing more about Lord Dragon—and I can't be *sure* of any of those names. Rose told me one of them, but he could have lied to her. No, if I'm to find those I seek, I've got to make *them* come to *me*."

"So you're asking about dragons," Black said. "What if your Lord Dragon never used that name again? Suppose he took it entirely at random, just that once, or if not at random, simply because he was intent on looting a dragon-ravaged village? Then who would come to you with word of him?"

"No one," Arlian replied, "but as you said yourself, I have time. If this doesn't work, I'll try something else. I've *already* tried something else, and I'll try more. Several somethings, in fact."

Black glanced at his employer. "Like the obsidian."

"Yes."

"It's been almost ten years since the obsidian was stolen, Ari, and so far we haven't seen a single piece you could say for certain came from your village—do you really think *any* of it can be traced back to the looters?"

"Why not? We've hardly tried yet. Once we start buying pieces, and asking where they came from, why would anyone fail to tell us?"

"Perhaps because he doesn't know. A piece could have changed hands a dozen times by now."

"How often does a physician's knife or a piece of frippery change hands?" Arlian asked.

"How long does a physician remember where he bought each of his tools?" Black countered.

"How often does a woman forget where she obtained each of her baubles?"

"So you learn that Lady Whatever bought her pendant from a particular shop in the Street of the Jewelers—what if the shop is five years gone, or six?"

"What if it is? I'll keep searching."

Black sighed, and changed tack. "And this gala you're planning—I assume you'll leave the old Aritheian ambassador to the Aritheians, but suppose Lord Dragon *does* attend, and he recognizes you? Might he not decide to kill you before you can confront him? Might he not flee?"

"How would he recognize me?" Arlian laughed bitterly. "I was a boy of eleven when we first met, and he probably thinks I'm still hacking away at stone walls in Deep Delving. I doubt he even saw me in Westguard two years ago, nor would he know me to be anything more than a gawking passerby if he did."

"You're assuming he's an ordinary man."

Arlian took his time in answering, "No. How could an ordinary man have known that dragons would destroy Obsidian, and leave it open for looting? And in Westguard he had the Duke of Manfort's grant of unlimited authority, apparently legitimately. I have no doubt that Lord Dragon, whoever he may actually be, has access to knowledge beyond the commonplace. He may well be a sorcerer. But he's still a man, not a god, nor even a dragon; I do not think him infallible, and the Aritheians have taught me that sorcery has limits, and rather narrow ones. I assume Lord Dragon, whoever and whatever he is, has as much curiosity as anyone. I think he'll attend the festivities, and I do not think he'll know me." He shrugged. "If I'm wrong—well, then Fate is unkind, and I'm wrong."

"And if you're wrong you may well wind up dead."

"True enough. And while it's kind of you to be concerned, that's really *my* business, isn't it? Why are you so determined to talk me out of risking it?"

"Partly just my natural perversity, but also because I think you're being a fool, throwing away a wonderful life. You're young, handsome, rich—yes, you were wronged as a child, you were sold as a slave, but you're free *now,* and you have so much. Why risk everything in pursuit of some abstract justice? It seems foolish to me. When a man has wronged me, I don't seek him out; I *avoid* him, and go on about my business."

"I can't do that," Arlian said. "You and I are different in that, Black. I can't ignore what was done to me."

"Not even for a year or two, until you know the city better?"

"Black, every day I think about Lord Dragon and his gang, and about the dragons. Every day I'm alive I remember that dragon's face. I can't wait a year."

"So you're going to get yourself killed."

"Perhaps."

"I can't say I like the idea. If *you* wind up dead, I won't get paid."

"Assuming you don't wind up dead beside me."

"Exactly. Not that I intend to allow anything of the sort to happen."

Arlian smiled crookedly. "I have no heir, Black; if I die, and you live, all I have here is yours."

Black blinked at that.

"Oh," he said.

Arlian's grin broadened. "And now I suppose I need to watch my back around you."

Black snorted. "Hardly. As long as you pay me enough, I'll be content to play steward—given the popularity of dueling and assassination I suspect stewards usually live longer than lords around here. And furthermore, I don't think I would care to be hanged as a murderer."

"I'll keep that in mind." Arlian sipped wine. "And how are the preparations going?"

Black sighed, and began an accounting of everything that was being done to ready the once-elegant Old Palace for the planned debut of Lord Obsidian in Manfort's high society.

Arlian listened carefully.

He was aware that Black's criticisms of his plan might have some truth in them, but he could think of no better way to locate those members of Manfort's elite whom he intended to destroy—as well as Lord Dragon, there were the other five lords who had owned the brothel. He only knew one name, that of Lord Kuruvan; he knew that Lords Inthior, Drisheen, Salisna, and Jerial had been patrons, and might have been owners, and he intended to get a good look at each of them. He also wanted to know about any others who had been involved in the creation and destruction of the House of Carnal Society. That might well be a significant portion of the city's elite.

An unrelated member of the elite who Arian thought deserved attention, as Black had mentioned, was Sahasin of the House of Slihar, the Aritheian ambassador whose faction had almost certainly been responsible for Hathet's enslavement. Locating the ambassador and dealing with him was no problem—the Aritheians who had accompanied Arlian and Black to Manfort would tend to him, and there was no reason for any natives of the Lands of Man to involve themselves.

Black, at Arlian's order, had sent a direct invitation to Sahasin, urging him to attend the upcoming festivities. He doubted the man would refuse.

The rest were not so simple. If Arlian attempted to hunt those six lords who had owned the brothel down individually, to find and free Sweet and the rest of those poor crippled whores and to avenge their four dead comrades, he could scarcely expect to deal with more than one or two of the lords before the others realized what was happening and fled or joined forces against him. They might use the women as hostages against him, or hire assassins to deal with him, once they knew he was in pursuit. That would, at the very least, endanger the women and make his vengeance more difficult.

What better way to gather them together, so that he could confront *all* of them, than to throw a party they could not resist? With any luck he would be able to identify them simply by asking a few questions, and once that was done he could meet them, speak with them, judge their weaknesses, all on his own ground, on his own terms, and then take action swiftly and appropriately.

And as for the six looters who had worked with Lord Dragon—Shamble, Hide, Stonehand, Cover, Dagger, and Tooth—how else could he find them, other than by tracing the goods they had stolen?

If he had simply tried to track those people down by name, by inquiring after their present whereabouts, word would surely have gotten back to them. They might hide, or flee, when they knew someone was looking for them.

Besides, Arlian suspected that half the would-be assassins in the city called themselves Dagger. Even though most of them would be male, where he was after a female, that would not make matters any simpler.

Sooner or later, though, Arlian promised himself, he would find them all. He would locate each of the looters, each of the six lords who had owned a share in the House, and he would see that each of them received what he or she deserved. He would rescue as many of the dozen women as he could. He would let Hathet's own clan deal with the usurper ambassador, but the others were his.

And if he lived long enough, and the opportunity arose, there were other old enemies he might want to find. Lampspiller might deserve some attention eventually, and the Old Man, too—using slaves to work a mine was no crime by the standards of the Lands of Man, but the Old Man was a little too careless in how he acquired his workers—neither Arlian nor Hathet should have been there—and Lampspiller was far more brutal than necessary.

And when all that was done, he would seek out the dragons in their deep caverns—and probably throw away his life in doing so, but still, he felt that he had to do it.

He had asked the Aritheians if they knew of any way to kill a dragon, of any magic that would work against the great beasts, but they knew no more of dragons than he did—perhaps less. He would be on his own in finding the caverns and destroying their occupants, but he could not rest until he had done so.

And after that …

Well, there probably wouldn't be any "after that." If there were, he would worry about it when it arrived.

Chapter Twenty-Nine

Stammer

Black opened the door only a few inches, trying to keep the rain and the wind outside. Spring was well advanced, but the weather was still unseasonably cool and raw. "Yes?" he asked.

The woman huddled on the postern doorstep looked up at him. "Your ... your pardon, my lord," she stammered.

"I'm not your lord," Black said, as he glanced around in the wet gloom of gathering twilight. The woman was far too ragged to be pursuing any honest trade, and he saw no cart or companion; she might be a beggar, or she might be bait.

He saw no one lurking in the shadows, ready to pounce when the door was opened—but an attacker might just be well hidden. And even if the woman were not part of a gang of thieves intent on looting the palace, a would-be burglar might happen along at any moment and seize the opportunity if Black stood there with the door open on such a miserable, dark day as this.

"I'm so...I'm sorry," she said, ducking her head and spilling water from the hood of her cloak onto Black's boot.

"Get in here," he said, grabbing her by the shoulder and yanking her inside.

He slammed and barred the door, then turned to her, half expecting to see a drawn blade in her hand.

Instead she had fallen to her knees and was cowering on the stone floor of the entryway, clutching her cloak about her.

Black frowned.

Beggars were rare in Manfort—*very* rare. Just about anyone who slept unguarded in the streets or missed enough rent payments, no matter how decrepit, was likely to be taken by the slavers and sold. Still, this woman probably *was* a beggar, he decided, one the slavers hadn't caught yet, drawn to the Old Palace by the local gossip, looking for somewhere to get out of the

238

rain and get a bite to eat. Anything else was just his morbid imagination, driven by the miserable weather and the uncertainties of his present situation. The announced date of Lord Obsidian's "arrival" and reception was approaching rapidly, and it was getting on his nerves.

The woman was almost certainly harmless. Her obvious terror was probably because she expected him to sell her into slavery, despite the rumors, not the result of nervousness about her involvement in some dire scheme.

"Get up," he said.

She hesitated. He reached down and snatched away her cowl, revealing short-cut hair and a bony, half-starved face that might have been attractive if better fed. It was hard to judge, given her condition, but he guessed she was perhaps thirty, no more than forty.

She cringed.

"Get *up,* I said." He grabbed her arm and hauled her upright.

She stood unsteadily, looking up at him.

"Now, what did you want?" he asked. "Food? A drink?"

She shook her head, and fumbled with the inside of her cloak. "I heard..." she began. "I heard that you...that Lord Ob... Obsidian would pay..."

And her hand emerged from a hidden pocket clutching something. She held it out, and opened her hand.

It was a brooch, an oval of carved and polished obsidian set in elaborately worked gold, all of archaic design. A black velvet backing that would keep it from chafing appeared to have been added later.

It was almost certainly stolen, Black thought—the woman's cloak was ancient, stained and ragged, and what he could see of the dress beneath was no better. This woman could hardly have come by so fine an item honestly. It was probably a family heirloom she had snatched from an unguarded room somewhere.

Still, it was obsidian, and perhaps she could be convinced to say where she had stolen it. He and Arlian had looked at two dozen pieces already, brought to the door by jewelers, merchants, and people of less obvious employment, and had noted down half a dozen names for further investigation; one more would do no harm, and chasing the poor creature back out into the rain seemed unnecessarily cruel.

"Come on," he said. "Let me get you something to eat, and you can sit by the fire while I see if Lord Obsidian's jeweler is available."

He settled her on a stool beside the kitchen hearth, with a heel of bread and a cup of tea to dunk it in—he hadn't gotten a look at her teeth, but they were probably in bad shape.

If she opened the door before he got back and let in a horde of thieves, it would serve him right for being too soft-hearted, Black thought as he hastened up the stairs to fetch Arlian. If the palace had had a full-time staff in place he would have put a guard on her, but so far only he, Arlian, and the six Aritheians who had made the long journey to Manfort slept there; for now the locally hired servants all worked days, and returned to their homes at night. That made it easier to maintain the fiction that Lord Obsidian had not yet arrived.

Black looked forward to the day after the grand gala—once that was over and done with he could hire a proper household staff.

A few minutes later, when Black and Arlian returned to the kitchen, the woman was still there, huddled on her stool, her cloak steaming in the warmth of the fire. Black hurried past her to check on the postern, and found the door still securely barred.

"Let me see the brooch," Arlian said, holding out his hand. He wore coachman's livery in black piped with white—the colors he had chosen for himself, representing the black of obsidian and the white of justice. He doubted this woman would recognize his attire as inappropriate for a jeweler.

She set down her empty teacup and fished out the brooch. "I…It's all we have left," the woman said as she held it out. "It was my betrothal gift."

Black was just reentering the kitchen when Arlian accepted the brooch and got his first good look at it. Black saw the young lord's jaw drop, his eyes snap wide open; he saw Arlian's body tense, his back arching as if he had been struck.

"Sorcery!" Black said, his sword in his hand; suddenly he was at the woman's side, the blade at her throat.

"No!" Arlian said, holding up a hand. "No—no, I'm fine." His voice was rough; he blinked away tears.

"Then what…"

"The brooch," Arlian said, holding it up. The gold sparkled redly in the firelight.

Black did not lower his sword, but kept it at the woman's throat, his left hand on the back of her neck. He could feel that she was rigid with terror. "What about it?" he demanded.

"It's my mother's," Arlian said.

240

The woman gasped, then let out a low, sobbing moan.

Black was not yet entirely convinced there was no sorcery involved; his hands did not move. "You're certain of that?" he asked.

"See for yourself," Arlian said, turning the bauble over and peeling away the velvet backing.

"Don't...!" the woman said, starting to snatch at the brooch—but Black's sword held her in place.

Arlian held up the golden surface thus revealed and pointed at an inscription. "It's hard to read, with the glue on it," he said, "so look for yourself, and tell me whether it says, 'To Sharbeth, with all my love.'" He looked at the woman. "Sharbeth was my mother."

"He st...but..."

Black released his hold on the woman's neck and accepted the brooch. He had to squint to make out any of the inscription, as it was clogged not just with glue but with dirt and ash and bits of black velvet, but the lengths of the words were right, and the longest word did look like "Sharbeth."

"So it's your mother's brooch," Black said. "It would seem I may have been overly pessimistic regarding your plans—but now what?"

"Where did you get it?" Arlian demanded, staring the woman in the eye.

She turned an imploring gaze on Black. "The...the sword," she said.

"Sheathe it," Arlian said.

Black frowned, but obeyed. It would seem no sorcery was involved after all, and in that case two strong men should be able to handle one beggar woman. He slid the blade into its sheath, but kept his hand on the hilt.

"Now," Arlian said, stepping forward and stooping to look the woman in the eye, "where did you get that brooch?"

"My husband," she said. "It was my betrothal gift. We...we didn't know it was stolen, I swear! The velvet was...it was there..."

"Who is your husband?" Arlian demanded. "*Where* is he? Still alive?"

"He...he's sick. Very sick. That's why I needed money. He didn't want...all these years..." She stared at the brooch in Arlian's hand.

"What's your husband's name?" Arlian demanded. "Where is he?"

"His name is Yorvalin, but everyone calls him Cover," she said. "He's in our room on Broom Street."

"Cover?" Arlian straightened, and he and Black stared at each other over the woman's head.

"It can't be that easy," Black said.

"I wouldn't have thought so," Arlian agreed, "but sometimes Fate is kind, as I know better than almost anyone."

"What are you talking about?" the woman asked, looking from one man to the other. "What is easy?"

"What's *your* name?" Arlian asked.

"I'm...I'm called Stammer," she said, flushing.

"Of course," Arlian said, with audible distaste. Sometimes he didn't think much of the cognomens people bestowed upon one another. "Well, Stammer," he said, looking down at her, "I want to talk to your husband."

She hesitated, clearly wishing she hadn't said as much as she already had. "You won't hurt him?"

Arlian sighed. "I can't promise that," he said.

"I won't...then I won't take you."

Black raised his sword hilt an inch or two from the scabbard, but Arlian gestured for him to put it back.

"Stammer," he said, kneeling and looking up into her eyes, "do you know just how bad your position is? You've come here uninvited and tried to sell me stolen merchandise. From the look of you it's obvious you have no money, no family, no patron—and here you are in Lord Obsidian's home, arguing with his staff. Black could kill you, and claim he caught you stealing from us, and no one would ever doubt it. We could call a slaver in and sell you—and you're still young and pretty enough that there's no telling where you'd wind up as a slave. Now, we don't want to do anything like that—we don't want to harm you at all—but we *do* want to find your husband. You've already said he's in your room on Broom Street—we'll find him eventually, no matter what you do. You can save us the trouble of searching. And it's your home—if we released you we would follow you, and sooner or later, wouldn't you go back to your husband?" He fished in his pocket and pulled out a gold ducat. "I'll pay you for your trouble, if you like—or not, if you think that would be too much like selling him."

She stared down at the coin. "I...I'll sell you the brooch," she said.

"The brooch is mine by right," Arlian said coldly. "It's not yours to sell. Your services as a guide, though, are your own."

She looked from Arlian to Black, but found no support there—Black's expression showed only detached interest, Arlian's intense determination.

"Give me the money," she said, snatching the gleaming coin.

Arlian let her take it.

"Now take us to Cover," he said.

Stammer nodded. She got to her feet, and Arlian straightened up to follow.

Black raised a hand to halt him. "It's raining," he said. "Perhaps you should change your clothes, or at least put on a hat."

Arlian looked down at himself, and agreed.

An hour later Arlian saw the first of the intended targets of his revenge, stretched out before him in the wretched dwelling he now inhabited, close up under the roof of a crumbling, narrow tenement.

There was no bed; Cover lay on a pile of rags on the bare planks that served as a floor. The entire room had clearly been improvised—the planks lay loose across the tie beams, creating a little wooden island seven feet above the attic's true floor, accessible only by a rickety ladder. There were no windows or other means of ventilation, and the air was chokingly thick, stifling hot, and horribly still, full of the scents of wood and mildew and sweat. Light came from a single candle on a table below, and from the lantern Black held.

Most of the family that lived in the attic proper watched silently as Arlian, now clad in nondescript traveling garb rather than his coachman's livery, climbed up to Cover's niche, his hat in one hand; Black, in his customary leather and carrying a drawn sword in his right hand with the lantern in his left, stood guard at the foot of the ladder. Stammer watched nervously from one side.

The mother of the attic family sat in one corner with her youngest at her breast, ignoring the entire affair, and two of the other children were too busy squabbling to pay attention, but Arlian still had half a dozen pairs of eyes focused on him. In consequence he moved more slowly, and with greater caution, than he might otherwise have. He was eager, very eager, to see whether this was in fact the Cover he had met all those years ago in the ruins, the man who had lifted him up out of the cellar where Arlian's grandfather had lain dead.

The man on the rag pile did not look at Arlian as he rose into view—or at anything else. He lay on his back, his eyes closed, his breath rasping feebly. His skin was mottled with patches of unhealthy red, plainly visible even in the dim, uneven light.

Arlian swung himself off the ladder, stooping under the rafters, and stepped across the platform so that he leaned over the sick man.

"Cover," Arlian said.

The man licked his lips, but otherwise did not move.

"Look at me, Cover," Arlian demanded.

The sunken eyes opened, and the head turned, and Arlian knew that this was, indeed, the same man. He had lost weight, a great deal of weight—his flesh was stretched tight over his bones, and Arlian could count his ribs through the filthy, frayed shirt that covered his chest—but it was Cover.

Despite the heat of the stuffy attic, Arlian shivered. For years he had intended to punish this man for his crimes, for robbing the innocent dead of the village on the Smoking Mountain and for allowing Lord Dragon to sell Arlian into slavery—but what could he do to punish this pitiful creature who lay before him?

"How did you come to this?" Arlian asked. "When last I saw you you were well and strong, working for Lord Dragon."

Cover stared at him for a long moment, then spoke. "It's you?" he asked, his voice faint and breathy. "The boy from the cellar?"

"You recognize me?" Arlian asked, startled.

"Dreamed of you," Cover said. "I'm so sorry."

Arlian stared at him silently. He had not expected contrition. And the dreams…were they simply reflections of Cover's own concerns, or did the man have the gift of prophecy? After his experiences in Arithei Arlian no longer doubted that some dreams were more than just the sleeping mind at play.

Had someone *sent* the dreams?

Had Cover really dreamed of him at all? Perhaps the man was delirious.

"How did you find me?" Cover asked after a moment, when Arlian still had not spoken.

"Your wife tried to sell me my mother's brooch," Arlian replied, forgetting about the dreams.

"Her brooch? She shouldn't have done that. I told her she must never sell it. I gave it to her…" He coughed, cutting off his speech.

"She had nothing else left to sell," Arlian said.

"But it wasn't ours, not really. I never told her, but I knew you'd come for it someday. I gave it to her for our betrothal so she would never part with it."

"How could you know I would come?" Arlian demanded, suddenly angry. "Why didn't you *tell* her it was stolen?"

"I couldn't," Cover said. "I'm a coward. Couldn't stop thinking of you, and your village. I wouldn't work for Lord Dragon after that—that was my first job, and I couldn't stand it. Saw your face everywhere after that—I knew sooner or later justice would catch up with me, that I'd be punished for what we did."

That explained why Cover remembered Arlian so clearly—if he had never again joined in looting or raiding, the one event would stand out.

"What *did* you do, then?"

"I looked for other work—but I didn't know a trade. And I couldn't get work from any of the lords after that, once I had told Lord Dragon no—the Dragon Society cast me out, marked me as unclean."

"The Dragon Society?"

"Lord Dragon's friends. The other lords. They wouldn't help anyone he frowned upon."

"You didn't beg for forgiveness? You never went back to work for him again?"

"Couldn't *find* him. And I didn't want to." Tears began to well up in Cover's sunken eyes. "I married Stammer, and did what work I could find, but it was never much. We stayed one step ahead of the slavers—and then last year I got sick."

"And you never tried to find *me,* in all those years, to make amends?" Arlian asked. "You never came to the mine to buy me free? You never tried to return the brooch or any of the rest of it?"

"No," Cover said weakly. "I didn't dare. And I needed my share of the money to live on." He held out a trembling hand. "I'm sorry."

Arlian stepped back toward the ladder and did not reach for the hand.

"So am I," he said. He gripped the hilt of his sword—but he hesitated, and did not draw the blade.

He could not punish this man—Cover had already punished himself far more effectively than Arlian could. Killing him would be no worse than letting him live.

Arlian was wealthy; if he chose he could take Cover in, feed him, give him a home—the illness might well be caused as much by malnutrition as anything else. Furthermore, the Aritheians knew a great deal of magic, and while they said magic could not heal everything, some diseases could be treated with their herbs and amulets. Perhaps they could cure the wasting disease that was eating Cover alive...

But why should Arlian help? Cover had never done anything to atone for his crimes. He had never sought out Arlian; by his own admission he had never even tried.

No, Arlian owed Cover nothing—neither vengeance nor succor.

But that didn't mean he had no further business here.

"Are you going to kill me?" Cover asked, interrupting his thoughts.

"No," Arlian said. "I am going to leave you here, unharmed—and unaided. I am going to take my mother's brooch, which is rightfully mine, but there may be something else you can sell me—if not for your own benefit, for your wife's."

"What is it?"

"I want to find the rest of your party of looters," Arlian said. "Shamble, and Dagger, and Hide, and Tooth, and Stonehand. And I want to know everything you can tell me about Lord Dragon—is that how he's generally known?"

"I can't... I..."

"I will pay one ducat for each of your former comrades I locate through your information," Arlian interrupted. "And I will pay *five* ducats for Lord Dragon's true name."

"I don't *know* his true name!" Cover gasped desperately. "I don't know where they all are anymore—I haven't seen any of them in years."

"Tell me what you can, then," Arlian said. "Tell me what you can, and it may be enough."

Dragon Weather

Chapter Thirty

Cover

Cover had been an eager, if foolish, young man when he hired on with Lord Dragon. The younger son of a farmer of no great wealth, he had sold his birthright to his elder brother and come to Manfort seeking his fortune.

He had, instead, found taverns and gaming and bad companions—and one good one, the girl Stammer, whom he had befriended when others mocked her.

But then the money had run low, and his friend and drinking companion Hide had offered him employment with Lord Dragon. He took the job gladly, and he and the others had followed Lord Dragon out of Manfort to the south and west, and up the slopes of the Smoking Mountain.

The sight of the burned-out ruins and the scattered bodies had changed Cover. The horror of it had settled into his heart. He had looked upon the devastation the dragons had left behind, and at the other looters, and he had realized that his companions were blind to the evil he saw there; they saw only unguarded valuables waiting to be taken.

When he and the others had pulled Arlian from the cellar, Cover had seen it at first as a sign that they were not simply thieves desecrating the dead—they had saved a boy, they had done something good, something to redeem themselves and to balance what they stole.

And then Lord Dragon had sold the boy as a slave, and Cover's hopes of redemption were dashed.

Later, when they were almost back to Manfort, Lord Dragon had told them he had another job for them, in the east—and Cover had refused. He had demanded his share of the profits and returned to his old haunts in the city.

At first everything had been fine—but then the others had completed whatever task they had had in the east and come back to Manfort, and word had begun to spread. Cover never learned just what was said, but he found that his credit had been cut off at the taverns, the odd jobs he had done for spending money were no longer offered, and he was not welcome among people who had been his friends. One of those former friends mentioned that Shamble had spoken a few words of warning; others would not give even that much reason.

Stammer had stayed with him, though. Throughout it all she had remained loyal and true. He had married her, giving her his only remaining thing of value—Sharbeth's brooch—as a betrothal gift.

"Why did you stay in Manfort, if you could find no work here?" Arlian asked.

"Where else would I go?" Cover replied.

Arlian had seen enough of the world that he could easily have listed a dozen places, but he did not bother. "Go on," he said.

That was really all there was to it. Cover and Stammer had survived as best they could, finding whatever work was available. They had had a daughter, their only child, who had died of a fever when she was three.

And then Cover had begun to sicken, and the last of their money had run out.

The last Cover had heard of Shamble had been four years ago; Shamble had continued to work for Lord Dragon or his wealthy friends, doing whatever unpleasant tasks might need doing.

Stonehand had joined the Duke's personal guard some six years past, and for all Cover knew was still there.

Tooth had disappeared long ago; there had been rumors about involvement with a sorcerer.

Dagger had killed a well-connected man two years after the destruction of Obsidian, and had fled from Manfort; Cover had heard nothing of her since.

And Hide...Hide had saved up proceeds from his work for Lord Dragon, and had opened a fashionable little shop in the Upper City, dealing in baubles and curiosities. Cover and Stammer had never spent much time in the Upper City, and ragged and ill-fed as they were they had not dared venture there in years, but Cover believed the shop was still there.

"And Lord Dragon?" Arlian asked.

"You want his real name," Cover whispered. "I don't know it."

"Do you know where I can find him?"

Cover shook his head, which triggered a coughing fit; when he had recovered and taken his hand from his mouth Arlian saw bright blood smeared across the fingers.

"No," Cover said. "I only knew of him through Hide. I know he goes by several names, and that he's important, very rich—he has the Duke's ear, I think, and knows something of sorcery. It's said he's a master in one of the secret societies—maybe there really *is* a Dragon Society. I meant it as just a turn of phrase, to describe those around him, but perhaps it's the truth."

Arlian frowned. He had known, from his stop in Westguard, that Lord Dragon had more than casual contact with the Duke of Manfort; this confirmed it. As for the rest...

"Secret societies?"

Cover waved a hand helplessly. "Rumors. There are said to be secret societies throughout the Lands of Man but most particularly here in Manfort. Societies of lords, societies of sorcerers..." He began coughing again.

"A society of whores," Arlian muttered under his breath. He suddenly understood that the name of the House of Carnal Society might be a joke of sorts, a cruel parody of these supposed secret societies. "And in which society did Lord Dragon claim membership?"

Cover, still coughing, shook his head helplessly.

He didn't know. All he could provide was rumors; Arlian saw that now. "I will pay for Stonehand and Hide," he said. "Two ducats. The others—we'll see."

Cover managed to speak again through a foam of bloody spittle. "Thank you," he said. "Forgive me."

"Perhaps in time I will," Arlian said. "For now I will merely withhold judgment."

He turned and climbed carefully down the ladder.

At the bottom he tucked his hat under one arm as he opened his purse and drew out two ducats, which he handed to Stammer.

"You earned the first that I gave you before," he said. "Your husband earned these others."

She stammered, and he held up his hand.

"Go to him," Arlian said. "He's very ill; I don't think he has much longer."

She gasped, and hurried to the ladder.

Arlian did not watch her climb; instead he beckoned to Black, and the two men started down the stairs.

"He's dying?" Black asked as they descended. He walked a pace behind, holding the lantern high; the stairwell had no other light.

"He's coughing up blood," Arlian said. "I never saw a man do that for long and live. Oh, a few drops from a scratched throat, perhaps, but this blood was bright and red…" He shook his head.

"I take it you feel no need to hasten his end, under the circumstances."

"None whatsoever," Arlian agreed.

They had reached the third floor landing; they wheeled onto the next flight down, and continued in silence. They had just started down from the second floor to the first when Black spoke again.

"I take it you feel no need to make any attempts at healing him, either."

Arlian did not answer immediately; in fact, they were on the front stoop, just a step from the street, when he replied.

"I thought about it," he said, clapping his hat on his head and tugging his collar up to keep out the drizzling rain. "I'm still thinking about it."

Black grimaced. "And if you did heal him, would you then slay him?"

"No," Arlian said immediately. "I'm not so vindictive as that. He robbed the dead of my village, but he's been punished for it ever since, by his own conscience, and he has not otherwise wronged me—nor anyone, to my knowledge." He stepped out into the street and turned toward the Upper City.

"Ah—he's repented?"

"Maybe. He may know what's in his heart; I don't."

Black looked at the younger man's face. "And do you know what's in *yours,* my lord? You seem troubled—isn't it an easing of your burden to know that you've found this man, and he has suffered for the wrongs he committed? While you toiled away in the mine and drove your wagon across the Desolation and fought through the Dreaming Mountains to Arithei, he was *not* making merry with his ill-gotten gains, but was instead suffering as well. And now, when you are free and rich and able to do as you please, he lies dying on a heap of rags in a Manfort attic. This would seem to me to be a fine display of justice, of Fate working out matters as we would choose, rather than in the perverse and unfair fashion it so often prefers."

"I suppose," Arlian agreed unhappily, as they ambled up the sloping street toward the Old Palace. A scavenging dog hurried out of their way, unnoticed.

"Then why do I see you with a face more suited to a merchant assessing losses than one counting profits?"

Arlian stopped walking and turned to look at his companion.

"I don't know," he said. "Perhaps I *am* assessing losses."

"Is revenge so sweet, then, that you regret the missed opportunity?"

"No," Arlian said, resuming his pace. "No, that's not it. I am thinking, rather, of Stammer's loss—*she* had no part in any wrongdoing that I know of."

"And she's free to leave Cover, should she choose to," Black pointed out.

"But she loves him. I'm almost tempted to try to help him, just for her sake—but I swore vengeance…"

"A family is a risk, my lord; we all suffer when those we love suffer, whether through their own fault or not, and the entanglements of concern and affection weave everywhere. There's no scheme of justice in all the world so complex that it might untangle *all* the strands that bind the innocent to the guilty, the wronged to the blessed."

"There should be," Arlian said.

"But there isn't—unless Fate and the gods are subtler than we know. I've learned to live with that; you should, too."

Arlian shook his head. "It's all so complicated," he said. "I could show mercy, have the Aritheians look at Cover—perhaps they could heal him, or perhaps not. But what would come of it?"

Black shrugged. "We never *know* what's to come, my lord; we can only make our best guess."

"And that's often wrong. When I saved Bloody Hand's life, it brought me hatred—and my freedom. I still haven't decided whether I was right or wrong, or whether *he* was right or wrong." He sighed. "I had thought my vengeance would be simpler. Looting Obsidian in the dragons' wake was an evil thing—I don't think any could question that. Selling me as a slave, rather than letting me make my own way as best I could, was wrong. I had thought that the people who did those things, when I found them, would be evil, that by killing them I would be ridding the world of a continuing threat to the well-being of innocents—and instead I find Cover a sick, harmless beggar who seems to have hurt no one in years, who is clearly loved by his wife. What if the others are the same?"

"What if they are?" Black responded. "Does that wipe out the wrongs they did?"

"I don't know," Arlian said quietly.

"Ah," Black said. For half a dozen paces neither man spoke; then Black suggested, "Perhaps, if you're still determined upon your vengeance, you should concentrate on those six lords, then. The mutilation of sixteen young women, and the murder of four, is surely harder to forgive than a mere

252

looting and enslavement."

"Five women murdered, not four," Arlian said. "Lord Dragon slew Madam Ril with his own hand."

"Ah, indeed, five it is—though she was herself a party to crimes against the others, was she not?"

"Yes," Arlian said. "And if *I* had killed her, for those crimes…but Lord Dragon cut her throat for failing him, not for abusing her charges." He bit his lower lip. "She would be just as dead in either case; does it really matter who killed her, or why?"

"Not to me," Black said. "You are, of course, free to form your own opinion, but I say that dead is dead. And whether she deserved to die or not, there were still the other four."

"It's so very tangled," Arlian muttered.

"Indeed," Black agreed. "Life generally is."

They walked the rest of the way in silence, Arlian's shoulders hunched against the rain.

Chapter Thirty-One

Lord Obsidian's Debut

Arlian made no attempt to locate Hide or Stonehand over the course of the next few days; instead he threw himself into the preparations for the feast and dance that he was to host, as Lord Obsidian, to celebrate his arrival in Manfort.

He put some effort into his own appearance, even considering asking his Aritheian employees to throw a glamour on him, though in the end he settled for the more natural methods he had learned during his stay in Westguard.

He did, however, teach the Aritheians an elaborate code of signals that he would use, should he have any need of their services during the gala. He taught Black the same cues.

"Do you think," Black asked, after a final review, "that perhaps you've taken rather too much upon yourself?"

Arlian frowned. "How do you mean that?"

"I mean that you are one man—a strong and clever man, with the heart of the dragon, but a single man—yet you're determined to take on at least seven enemies."

"I'm not alone," Arlian protested. "I have you, and Thirif and Qulu and Shibiel and Isein."

"And the lords will undoubtedly have their own hirelings and allies."

Arlian shrugged. "The six lords and Ambassador Sahasin and the looters and the mine's overseers may or may not be too much for me; we'll see. But they're just the start."

"You speak of the dragons."

Arlian nodded. "The world is not safe for anyone so long as those monsters still live."

"You stand no chance against any dragon, Arlian," Black said resignedly. He had told Arlian this before, many times. "No man has *ever* slain a dragon. It's not even known whether they *can* die."

"I know," Arlian said. "So I'll probably die horribly in some cave somewhere." He waved it aside. "We all die sometime, and if no one ever *tries*, we'll never know whether there *is* a way to kill dragons."

"You're mad, you realize."

Arlian grimaced. "Quite possibly. Seeing one's family slaughtered, spending much of one's life as a mine slave, crossing the Dreaming Mountains, drinking human blood and dragon venom—I'd suppose that to be enough to drive a man mad."

"You didn't see them killed, save your grandfather," Black corrected.

Arlian smiled wryly. "Literalist. It was close enough." He clapped Black on the shoulder. "Come on, let's get on with it—I want this party to be perfect."

The first coach arrived at midday. A handful of early arrivals, people who had come on foot but who had been milling about the gates, reluctant to be first to enter, took this as their cue.

Black greeted the arrivals at the great front door, ushering them through the entry hall into a long mirrored gallery some hundred feet long and two stories in height. The servants were waiting with wine and sweetmeats amid a vast display of fine tapestries, elaborate drapery, and artful arrangements of flowers. Perfume had been added to the water in the vases, to enhance the flowers' own scents, and a lutenist played unobtrusively on a central balcony.

Arlian stood out of sight behind the draperies of another balcony, listening to his guests; he intended to withhold his grand entrance for some time yet. From this post he caught only snatches of conversation, but he found them informative.

"...place cleaned up nicely..."

"...finally have a chance to meet the mysterious..."

"...from the south somewhere. I understand his people have been selling..."

"...probably hasn't been in here since his father..."

"Eccentric, definitely. I wonder how long he'll last in Manfort?"

"Dead or fleeing in a month, I would..."

"I don't remember that picture on the ceiling—was it there before?"

"I would assume, from the name, that he's dark..."

"You know your mother would never..."

Arlian noted that at least some of his guests had been in the Old Palace before—that was hardly surprising. Speculation about their host was also to be expected. He had hoped for more gossip about the other guests, and remained in place, listening. Perhaps when they had had a bit more time to exhaust the most obvious subjects he would hear more.

He knew more coaches were arriving; the crowd below was growing steadily.

Then there was a stir, and normal conversation died away in a rush of whispering. Arlian risked leaning out for a quick glimpse.

A white-haired man attired in a fine blue coat and white shirt was entering, attended by half a dozen guards in white livery. The crowd backed away, making room for this new arrival.

From the response and the whispers he caught, Arlian realized that this was the Duke of Manfort himself—the hereditary warlord, the only lord whose position bore no relationship to his wealth or business, the person nominally in charge only of the city's defenses but in practice the closest thing to a ruler the Lands of Man possessed.

The Duke waved to the other guests and looked around.

"And where is our host?" he asked.

Arlian backed away from the draperies, tugged his sleeves straight, then turned and hurried for the stairs. He had not expected the Duke to appear—certainly not so early! It would be very bad form to keep the warlord waiting any longer than absolutely necessary.

On the way across the landing he signaled to a waiting servant, and as he descended the stairs he signed to Isein, the Aritheian woman who was waiting near the bottom. Both hurried away to prepare his entrance.

A moment later Arlian stood ready at the corner just beyond the end of the long gallery. The lutenist ended his piece with a flourish, and four trumpeters stepped out on the other balconies and began a brief fanfare.

The skin at the back of Arlian's neck tingled, and he knew the Aritheians were invoking the spells he had asked them to ready. He stepped forward, striding into the gallery.

Sure enough, images of brightly colored birds were dancing in great swirling patterns overhead; Arlian had seen such birds in the Dreaming Mountains and knew the species really existed, but to anyone who had never ventured south of the Desolation he guessed they would appear the exotic creation of fevered dreams, with their vivid green and red and yellow feathers and their long, curling tails.

Tiny lights, like fireflies, flickered from nowhere in the air above the heads of his guests. The scent of roses filled the hall. The fanfare ended in an arpeggio of crystalline tones that Arlian was quite sure never came from any mere piece of brass.

And then the birds and lights froze, the music stopped, and silence fell. Arlian paused in the archway entrance to the gallery, raised his hands, and bowed elaborately. "My friends, new and old," he called, "I am Lord Obsidian. Welcome to my home!"

Someone laughed nervously, and somewhere the delicate clap of a woman's hands sounded. Speech returned in a rush amid scattered applause, and men and women in multicolored finery pressed forward to meet their host. The lutenist strummed a chord and began a new air.

Arlian accepted a woman's hand and kissed her fingers, then said, "Your pardon, my lady, but I believe I must attend another." He gestured.

The crowd's eyes followed his wave and saw the Duke of Manfort approaching at a brisk pace, three guards on either side; the throng parted swiftly for him. Overhead the "fireflies" faded away and the bight birds vanished.

"Lord Obsidian!" the Duke called, as he approached. "A pleasure to meet you at last!"

Arlian bowed. "The pleasure is all mine, Your Grace."

The Duke let out a bark of laughter. "I'm sure! Well, let us enjoy ourselves, then—tell me about yourself." He held out a hand for Arlian to clasp. "Where *did* you get the disappearing birds?"

Arlian took the Duke's hand and looked at him.

He had had a wild notion that perhaps the Duke of Manfort himself was Lord Dragon, but any such thought was plainly absurd. This man was shorter than Lord Dragon—shorter than Arlian himself—with short-cut white hair and a square, smooth face paler than Lord Dragon's could ever be. His cheek was unscarred, and his watery blue eyes nothing like Lord Dragon's dark ones. His hand was soft and damp, his smile broad and slightly foolish.

The possibility of an illusion had occurred to Arlian, and he glanced up at Thirif, the Aritheian who now stood on one of the balconies.

Thirif gave the hand sign for "no magic in use."

"In Arithei, Your Grace," Arlian said.

"You've been to Arithei? *Yourself?* By the dead gods, my boy, how very remarkable!"

"My business is trading in magicks and sorcery, Your Grace; Arithei is the very foundation of my fortune."

The Duke looked disconcerted. "Indeed," he said.

Arlian hid a smile. It was not done, to speak openly of magic or sorcery in Manfort.

"Arithei is not so distant or strange as all that, Your Grace," Arlian said, as if misunderstanding the Duke's reaction. "I understand that the Aritheians sent an ambassador to Manfort some years back."

"Yes, of course! Sahasin—a fine fellow! I think I saw him as I entered." He gestured vaguely at the crowd behind him. "But I don't believe he's been home to Arithei in a decade or more. It's not a safe journey."

"Indeed, Your Grace, for most it is not," Arlian agreed. "I have been very fortunate."

"Ha! Indeed, you *must* have been, to be able to afford this old pile! You know, one reason my grandfather moved into the Citadel was that it was simply a nuisance, trying to keep this place from falling down around his ears, and yet you've made it look quite splendid."

"Your Grace is too generous." Arlian bowed again, with a flourish.

The Duke stared at Arlian for a moment, then waved in dismissal. "Well, it *has* been a pleasure, my lord, but you have your other guests to attend to—I mustn't monopolize your time!" He turned away, immediately turning his attentions to a buxom young lady in lavender velvet.

Arlian bowed one last time, and when his head came up again found himself looking at the back of the Duke's close-cropped head and blue silk collar. He kept his face expressionless as he turned to his other guests.

How, he wondered, did that insipid twit manage to keep order in Manfort? Was he really the fool he appeared to be, or was it a carefully cultivated act?

That someone had managed to get a letter out of the old fool giving him freedom to do anything he pleased in Westguard no longer seemed quite so surprising. Instead it seemed surprising that the entire city of Manfort had not devolved into anarchy.

But the Duke had advisers, of course, and presumably they were the ones who actually maintained order. Arlian had heard a few of their names during his stay in Manfort—Lord Enziet, Lady Rime, Lord Drisheen.

Arlian had almost met Drisheen on occasion in Westguard, two years before; certainly he had smelled the man's perfume. Rime and Enziet were unknown to him beyond their names and association with the Duke, however. He wondered whether any of those advisers were present.

Well, there was one person he wanted to meet who almost certainly was present; it was just a matter of finding him. Arlian noticed a worried-looking young man, roughly his own age and dressed in gaudy red-and-gold velvets, whose attention seemed to be focused on the Duke. He tapped this man on the shoulder, then bowed—a restrained little bow, not the grand production he had performed for the Duke. "Excuse me, my lord," Arlian said. "I am Lord Obsidian; I don't believe I've had the pleasure of your acquaintance."

"Ah," the young man said. "Of course. I'm Lord Rademi, and I'm delighted to meet you, Lord Obsidian." He bowed sketchily, but was clearly still trying to get the Duke's attention.

"The Duke mentioned the Aritheian ambassador," Arlian said. "Sahasin, I believe the name was?"

"Yes, what about him?" Rademi replied.

"Why, having visited his homeland, I'd like to meet him," Arlian explained. "Could you point him out to me? I don't see anyone in Aritheian attire…"

"No, he's dressed like anyone else," Rademi said. He pointed. "Over there."

"Thank you," Arlian said. Now that his attention was directed properly he could see that the indicated individual did indeed have the darker complexion and rounded features of an Aritheian.

He had deliberately chosen the distracted youth to avoid being drawn into a long conversation, and Rademi was ready enough to let him go, but not everyone was so cooperative; as he made his way across the gallery to the man Rademi had pointed out Arlian found himself accosted by various lords and ladies eager to make his acquaintance.

One woman introduced herself and her husband as Lady Joy and Lord Jerial; Arlian immediately recognized the latter name and took a closer look at the fellow.

Yes, this was indeed the man who had abused Sweet while Arlian watched from the closet. Arlian suddenly contrived to sneeze, thereby avoiding the customary handclasp as his right hand was instead employed in dabbing his nose with a lace handkerchief.

"Your pardon, Lord Jerial," he said, as he returned the handkerchief to his pocket. "Lady Joy, a pleasure to meet you."

Lady Joy was a plump little woman who could no longer honestly be called young, and who had probably never been beautiful; she appeared to be a little older than her husband, and Arlian wondered why Jerial had married her.

For money, probably. His activities in Westguard had made it plain that he was not particularly devoted to her; perhaps he restricted his violent tendencies to other women so as not to antagonize a source of funds.

259

"I have heard so much about you," Arlian continued, addressing Lady Joy. He lifted one of her hands in his own. "I really do hope we can become better acquainted—perhaps we might dine together one night?"

Joy blushed with pleasure. "I would be delighted," she said. "We really must make some arrangement at the first opportunity!"

"The pleasure will be all mine," Arlian said, touching her fingers to his lips. "If you'll forgive me, though, I have other guests I must attend to just now. I do hope we'll have a chance to speak again soon." He released her hand and swept on.

And finally, he reached the man who had been pointed out as the Aritheian ambassador. He was a gray-haired man of sixty or more, of medium height, running to fat.

"Lord Sahasin?" Arlian inquired.

"Just Sahasin," the other corrected him, as he turned to face his host. "I own no enterprises, make no investments."

"Oh, but surely, as the representative of your homeland, you are entitled to be addressed honorably!" Arlian protested.

"If my lord pleases," Sahasin said with a smile. "You know me?"

"I have heard of you," Arlian replied.

"And how have you heard of me, then? The rumors say that you dabble in sorcery and the buying and selling of magicks—are you from the Borderlands, perhaps?"

Arlian said, "Rather, I trade with Arithei."

The ambassador's smile faded somewhat. "Oh?"

"Indeed. I was there just last year."

The smile vanished completely. "But the road has been closed…"

"It is closed no longer," Arlian interrupted.

"Are you sure? Why have I received no word?"

"I am quite certain—and I have brought word with me." He raised his left hand, fingers spread in one of his prearranged signals.

The ambassador looked up at Arlian's hand, then past it, at one of the balconies—where an Aritheian was just disappearing through the draperies. He paled.

"What sort of word?" Sahasin asked. "Who are you?"

"I am a friend of Hathet," Arlian said. "As for what word, his family and the House of Deri would like to discuss that with you."

"What…is this a threat?"

Arlian shook his head. "I make no threats," he said. "However, there are six representatives of the House of Deri, six of Hathet's kinsmen, who wish to speak to you regarding certain suspicions they hold regarding the House of Slihar—*your* House. If you satisfy them, then I am satisfied. If you do not, well…they will have the opportunity to deal with you first. If that does not end the matter—are you familiar with our custom of dueling?"

"This is ridiculous," Sahasin said. "Hathet was killed by bandits in the Desolation! I had nothing to do with it!"

"Your house profited from it, or you would not be here," Arlian pointed out.

"Yes, of course," Sahasin said, "but there's no crime in that! Someone had to take his place, and I was available, and my House had the means to send me, as the Deri did not!"

"And if that's all there was to it, then you have nothing to fear," Arlian told him. "You need merely convince six Deri magicians that you are telling the truth."

Sahasin looked up at him, terror-stricken, then turned, saying, "I won't have it! I'm innocent!" and began making his way toward the door.

Arlian made no move to stop him; at least four of the six Aritheians would be waiting for him at the entrance, and as Arlian had said, as Hathet's family their claim to vengeance took precedence over his own.

And it might well be that Sahasin was telling the truth after all, that he *was* merely an innocent beneficiary, in which case the others would do him no real harm. They had brought the necessary magic to interrogate him quite thoroughly.

Several people had overheard all or part of this conversation; others noticed Sahasin's indecorous flight. For a moment a pall of silence fell over the crowd; then a renewed chatter burst out.

That was one matter dealt with, Arlian thought. First Cover, now the ambassador—he was making progress.

He wished he could find Lord Dragon, though. He looked out at the crowd but could see no one who might be the tall, scarred lord.

Well, there were still others to deal with.

"Your pardon, my lady," he said to a nearby woman. "By any chance would you know whether Lord Kuruvan is here?"

Chapter Thirty-Two

The Festivities Continue

Lord Kuruvan was there—a tall, thin man with thick black hair and a nervous smile, elegantly clad in maroon and buff and smelling ever so faintly of musk. As with Jerial, Arlian managed to avoid shaking his hand or making the usual polite proclamations of pleasure while still establishing friendly relations and insisting that they must meet again.

"I believe I heard your name mentioned in Westguard," Arlian said. "Something about a building you owned there having burned down?"

"I don't know what that would be about," Kuruvan said, but his expression, while remaining nervous, ceased to be a smile. "I own an inn outside the city walls, but it isn't in Westguard."

"Oh, this wasn't an inn, and was definitely in Westguard," Arlian said. "Perhaps you only owned a share in it?"

Kuruvan turned up his hands. "I've invested in a good many ventures," he said.

"Ah! Well, perhaps we might compare notes one day," Arlian said. "I might know of a few enterprises where another partner would be welcome—if not yourself, then perhaps one of your friends."

"Perhaps," Kuruvan said uneasily. "I can't speak for them."

"Of course," Arlian agreed. He studied the man's face, trying not to be obvious about it.

Lord Kuruvan was by no means the vapid fool the Duke appeared to be, but he scarcely seemed a mastermind, either. He had been clever enough to buy that inn, clever enough to put aside a keg of gold coins against some future emergency—and careless or stupid enough to tell a slave who hated him where that money was hidden. Surely, there was some way to get the names of the other five owners of the House of Carnal Society out of him.

Not here, though, amid the crowd and the festivities.

Arlian leaned close. "Seriously, my lord," he said, "there is a matter I would discuss with you in private, a matter concerning a mutual acquaintance and a large sum of money. Might I perhaps call on you at your home—soon?"

Kuruvan frowned. "How soon?"

"Tomorrow?"

He shook his head. "Impossible—and surely, you'll scarcely want to conduct business the day after hosting such an affair as this!"

Arlian laughed. "A very good point, my lord. When would you be available, then?"

Kuruvan studied Arlian's face just as Arlian had studied his, then shrugged. "Not tomorrow, but the day after I will be home—in the afternoon, of course, not the morning."

"Then I will do my best to see you then," Arlian said. "Ah ... but I am new to Manfort, and as yet unfamiliar with the Upper City; could you perhaps see that my steward knows where your home is to be found?" He beckoned to Black, who had been standing unobtrusively nearby.

Kuruvan glanced at Black and his drab black livery with distaste. "My coachman is outside," he said. "He wears maroon and gold."

Black bowed, and hurried away.

"You are kindness itself, my lord," Arlian said. "I look forward to spending more time with you."

Kuruvan frowned again. "I hope you do not mistake me, Lord Obsidian," he said. "I am an ordinary man."

"Oh, surely more than merely ordinary! But perhaps you mean rather that whatever your virtues, you do not stray too far from the natural pursuits of mankind? Wine, women, and the clink of gold coins?"

"Exactly," Kuruvan said, visibly relieved, and Arlian realized that the references to the brothel and other secrets had worried the man. Perhaps he had thought Arlian intended to blackmail him by accusing him of perversion—or that Arlian was himself a pervert, seeking a partner in vice.

And perhaps Kuruvan *was* a pervert, though Rose had not mentioned any actions on his part that were out of the ordinary for her clients. That might explain his caution.

Arlian had no very clear idea just what the debauched lords of Manfort might consider a perversion, though. He snatched a wineglass from a nearby tray and handed it to Kuruvan. "I can provide you with wine readily enough," he said, "and we'll speak of gold another day, but I'm afraid that you'll have to find your own women." He gestured at the crowd. "There are certainly beauties here—is there any that takes your fancy? Are you married?"

"I'm not," Kuruvan replied. "I've never found a woman who suited me for long. And yourself? You must realize that half of Manfort is wondering about you."

Arlian's teeth clenched—no, Rose hadn't suited him for long, and he had left her lying there with her throat cut. At least when he killed Kuruvan he would not leave behind a grieving widow.

And if Kuruvan was, as Arlian believed, one of the erstwhile owners of the House of Carnal Society, what had become of the two women he had carried off when that establishment was destroyed? He hadn't married either of them, obviously—were they still alive?

Arlian forced a smile. "No, I have not yet found a wife," he said. "I'm still young, and I have generally devoted myself to business to the exclusion of all else."

The business of survival and revenge, he added silently.

"Then perhaps I might introduce you to someone," Kuruvan said. He turned and indicated one of the handful of people who had gathered around him as he and Arlian spoke. "This is Lady Fiala..."

"Fan-Fan," the woman—scarcely more than a girl really—said eagerly, stepping forward and offering her hand. "Call me Fan-Fan. Everyone does."

Arlian bowed and kissed the girl's fingers. She smiled delightedly and curtseyed in return, then said, "I understand you are a great traveler, my lord."

"I have traveled," Arlian admitted.

"Oh! I have scarcely been outside the city gates. Tell me where you've been."

A moment later Arlian found himself describing Arithei to a growing and appreciative audience—an audience that did not include Lord Kuruvan. After that he fell into a discussion of the Desolation, and the best routes and methods for crossing it, with a Lady Irmir.

The presence of beautiful women eager to know him better was distracting, but Arlian had had to learn to resist such distractions in order to survive his stay in the House of Carnal Society. He reminded himself that he was not here to enjoy himself, but to pursue his revenge against those who had wronged innocents—the memory of Sweet's face as he had last seen it from a distance, as she sat terrified in Lord Dragon's coach, insulated him from the charms of these other faces. In time he tore himself away from the little knot of listeners and made his way through the throng, meeting more of the city's nobility, and always looking for some sign of Lord Dragon.

A buffet supper was served in the two dining halls—there were too many guests for a seated meal—and the party spilled from the gallery into those rooms. Thence it spread to the ballroom, where pipes, drums, a virginal, and a shawm provided music for dancing. Wine flowed freely. Whenever spirits showed signs of sagging Arlian signaled to one of the remaining Aritheian magicians, and some new display would be forthcoming—a rain of flowers, a forest growing up the walls and then vanishing, rainbows playing across the room. Each was greeted with applause and laughter.

The final display, launched at midnight, was one that Black had counseled him to drop, but Arlian had insisted—the image of a great black dragon appeared in the air above the heads of the crowd, flew the length of the gallery, then vanished.

There was no laughter that time, and only halfhearted applause. Arlian knew that Black had been right—the image of a dragon was in poor taste. He had hoped, though, that it might stir a reaction from someone, that something in the crowd's response might give him a hint about Lord Dragon.

His hopes were dashed; no one seemed to associate the image with anything but mankind's traditional enemy and ancient overlords, the dragons themselves.

After that the party began to break up; in ones and two the revelers drifted away, out to waiting carriages or the city streets. When the Duke of Manfort took his leave the trickle became a flood, and within an hour Arlian and Black were standing alone in the gallery.

Arlian had been introduced to dozens, perhaps hundreds, of the city's elite, including several tall scarred men—but he had seen no sign of Lord Dragon. He had not identified anyone else associated with the House of Carnal Society except Kuruvan and Jerial. Lords Inthior, Drisheen, and Salisna had not made their presence known, if they had been there at all, nor had Arlian learned whether any of them had in truth owned shares in the House of the Six Lords.

He had made a date with Lord Kuruvan, though, and Sahasin, the Slihar ambassador, had been dealt with.

He stood for a moment, thinking over the evening, then asked Black, "Is the Duke as great a fool as he appears?"

Black hesitated, considering, then said, "He has been accused of wisdom to his face, but behind his back? Never."

"Then why is he still seen as the master of Manfort? Why has no one usurped his position?"

"Who says no one has?" Black asked. "The Duke remains the Duke because he makes a useful figurehead, but I've no doubt the real power lies elsewhere."

"Where?" Arlian asked. "Who was here tonight who wields real power?"

Black shrugged. "I don't know," he said. "There are the secret societies—I suspect they do more to determine what actually gets done than the Duke. And of course, the Duke has his advisers—fool or not, he's smart enough to take their advice. If he did not he might wake up one morning with his throat cut, or find some interesting toxin in his wineglass."

"Who are his advisers, then?"

"My lord, what does this have to do with your revenge?"

"I don't know," Arlian admitted. "But I'm convinced that Lord Dragon must be a very powerful man, one close to the Duke—who better than one of his advisers?"

Black sighed. "I don't know who all his advisers are. I've heard a few names mentioned, just as I'm sure you have—Lord Hardior, Lord Enziet, Lady Rime—but whether those are all of them, or what their positions really are, I couldn't say."

"I met Lord Hardior tonight," Arlian said thoughtfully. "I hadn't known he was one of the Duke's advisers. I didn't meet anyone called Enziet or Rime—I did know those names, and I would have remembered."

"I don't know whether they were here at all, but if they were you might have met Rime under her true name, or Enziet under some other cognomen," Black said.

Arlian stroked his beard. "I might have, at that." He tried to remember how many men he had met who had not given their true names. One would hardly give a false name at an affair of this sort, but plenty of people had been introduced only by nickname.

Manfort was very fond of nicknames, more so than almost anywhere else Arlian had visited—a relic of the long struggle against the dragons, when the human resistance to draconic authority dared not give true names for fear of reprisals. Ordinarily this was a pleasant and harmless habit, one Arlian had taken advantage of himself, but there were times when it could be confusing or inconvenient.

Arlian began pacing the length of the gallery—but then Black's outstretched arm caught him across the chest. He looked up, startled.

"Ari, it's late," Black said. "Rest. Sleep. You can look for Lord Dragon in the morning."

Arlian stared at him blankly for a moment, then glanced out the gallery's

266

tall windows at the night sky. Thick clouds hid the stars; a thin crescent of moon shone dimly through the overcast.

"You're right," he said at last. "You're quite right. To bed. We'll start fresh in the morning."

Black smiled at him.

Chapter Thirty-Three

Lord Wither

Arlian, unsurprisingly, slept late. By the time he arose and broke his fast the sun was approaching its zenith.

When he had eaten he ambled down the great gallery, noting the debris that the servants had not yet cleared away and the sour smell of spilled wine that still lingered, and spotted Thirif in one of the side-chambers. He paused, and then, momentarily overcome with curiosity, he asked, "What did you do with Sahasin?"

The Aritheian looked up. "You do not want to know," Thirif replied.

Arlian hesitated, and decided that Thirif was right—at least for now he did not want to know. It was enough that the House of Deri, Hathet's family, was satisfied.

He still had plenty of others to concern himself with. He would see Lord Kuruvan tomorrow, and that would be his chance to get the names of the other lords—including Lord Dragon! And once he had dealt with the six of them, once Sweet was free and Rose avenged, he could track down Stonehand and Hide and the rest.

He started to turn away, but Thirif called after him. "Your pardon, my lord," he said. "A man was here this morning with a question that may interest you."

Arlian turned back. "Oh?"

"He spoke to me, as he came to buy magic and the others were not yet available," Thirif said. "He wanted to buy dragon venom."

Arlian smiled. "Did he, indeed?" There were any number of reasons a person might want dragon venom—as a poison, or as a drug, or as an elixir of life. This inquiry might mean nothing—or it might lead back to Lord Dragon. Kuruvan would probably give him all the names he needed, but it would do no harm to have a second path to the information he sought—and even if this failed to provide any such link, it might well teach him more about dragons, and give him information that would be useful when he sought out the monsters in their caverns. "Who was he?"

"A servant. He wore homespun, not livery, and would not name his employer."

"What did you tell him?"

"That I could not sell dragon venom without consulting you, and that you would undoubtedly prefer to deal with his master. He is to return later today."

"Excellent! When he comes, I want to speak with him."

Thirif bowed. "As you say. Thank you, my lord."

Arlian walked on, feeling cheered. Things were starting to happen. He had put events into motion. At long last he was pursuing his vengeance. There might still be distractions and side paths along the way, but he was headed the right direction. The day when Lord Dragon would pay for his crimes and Sweet would be free was drawing nearer.

Either that, or the day Arlian would die at the hands of one of his foes was approaching. The chances of punishing *all* his enemies, human and draconic, and surviving it all, were still slim.

Odd, Arlian thought, that even knowing he might be on the way to his death failed to counteract the pleasure he felt in knowing he was closer to his goal.

Death or justice—he was nearing one, but he had no way of knowing which.

He spent the next few hours on housekeeping and business—his agents, Aritheian and otherwise, were continuing to invest his assets, both financial and thaumaturgical, and Black and his subordinates were finally employing a proper full-time staff for the Old Palace.

Those little magicks he had brought from Arithei and used so freely at the previous night's festivities brought fantastic prices, Arlian knew, but just how fantastic still surprised him. He was seated in his study, totting up his profits in frank amazement, when a servant knocked at the door.

"A caller, my lord."

Arlian looked up and smiled to himself. This would be the person seeking dragon venom. Arlian and the Aritheians had no dragon venom to sell, of course—the magic they sold all came from Arithei, where no dragon had ever breathed. There was no need to admit this, though.

"Show him in," he said. He turned to face the door, but did not rise; as a lord he had no need to stand when greeting a messenger.

When the door opened, however, Arlian got to his feet, startled. The man who stood there was clearly no mere messenger.

Lord Obsidian's guest was slightly below average height, and somewhat stooped. His face was thin and wrinkled, and seemed shrunken, almost buried beneath a great mop of gray hair that was pulled loosely back into a thick ponytail—neither the traditional workman's braid nor the nobility's usual custom of unbound and stylishly cut hair. His physical appearance, while hardly impressive, was not that of a messenger.

His attire *was* impressive; he was dressed in green silk embroidered in spun gold, trimmed at throat and cuffs with lace and pearls. A belt of black leather set with emeralds supported a beaded scabbard; his sword hilt, hung for a left-handed draw, was chased with silver and adorned with pearl and diamond. This was clearly a nobleman's sword.

Gorgeous as the visitor's clothing was, Arlian hardly gave it a glance; instead he found himself caught by his guest's green eyes, deep-set but unnaturally bright, staring at him with an intensity Arlian had rarely seen.

"Lord Wither," the footman holding the door announced.

Arlian had been so focused on the stranger that he had forgotten the servant was there. Thus reminded, he started to wave for the man to go, then paused.

Lord Wither should not be wearing his sword in another lord's home—not when Arlian's own sword was elsewhere. He should have surrendered it, and the servants should have kept it by the door, to be returned when Wither departed.

On the other hand, meeting those eyes, Arlian suspected that it would take a brave man to demand anything of Lord Wither that Lord Wither did not care to give. Arlian was not paying footmen for their courage.

He waved, and the footman left.

"Welcome, Lord Wither," Arlian said, holding out a hand.

"Lord Obsidian," Wither said, in a deeper voice than seemed appropriate to his size. He ignored the hand, and for the first time Arlian realized that the man's right arm was crooked, misshapen and shorter than it should be; the loose silk sleeves and drooping lace cuffs hid this deficiency well, and had presumably been designed to do so.

That explained the name, the left-handed sword, and perhaps more—buckling and unbuckling a sword belt one-handed was perhaps more than courtesy could ask, and unsheathing the sword under a host's roof would hardly be suitable.

Arlian lowered his hand and said, "It is a pleasure to meet you, my lord.

270

Did you attend last night's festivities? I do not recall…"

"I wasn't there," Wither said. "I'm too old for that sort of nonsense." He spoke sharply, biting off his words.

"As you say," Arlian said. "Nonetheless, I am pleased to meet you now. How can I be of service to you?"

"You sell magic," Wither said. "Sorcerous baubles, spells, potions."

"Indeed I do," Arlian agreed. He gestured to a chair. "Would you care to sit down?"

"I'll stand. It's simple enough. I want to obtain a small amount of fresh dragon venom—a thimbleful would suffice. Can you oblige me?"

"I would need to know the use you propose for this substance," Arlian said. "Forgive me, my lord, but dragon's venom is a most potent fluid, as I'm sure you know. It's said that a single drop can, if properly administered, enthrall a man, or kill a dozen. It can reportedly shatter locks, corrode the will, intoxicate even the mad."

"It can extend life, as well as end it," Wither replied.

"Ah! You wish to extend your life? Certainly a reasonable…"

"Not mine," Wither interrupted. "My mistress."

Arlian stopped, bemused, as he considered that. Wither was an old man; how old could his mistress be, that he was concerned with her longevity? A man of his obvious wealth could surely have any number of young women at his beck and call; who was the woman he sought to preserve?

Did he think dragon venom could preserve or restore a woman's youth? If so, was he right? Arlian had no idea just what the stuff could do—he had only rumors, legends, and hearsay to rely upon.

"Do you have it or don't you?" Wither demanded.

"I don't have any on hand," Arlian admitted slowly. "I may have a source where I can obtain it. May I ask, perhaps, who the intended recipient is, and how you intend to apply it?"

"She's called Opal; you haven't met her. I intend to mix it with human blood and let her drink it," Wither said impatiently. "That's the only way it works, so far as I know."

Arlian nodded. "And the blood…"

"Anyone's. It doesn't matter. I'll pay someone to donate it. That part's easy."

"And you don't want enough for both of you?"

Wither snorted. "I've had mine, Obsidian. Long ago, probably before your grandfather's grandfather was born. I was one of the *founders* of the

Dragon Society, back when Manfort was all we had and Duke Roioch was still alive. Look into my eyes and tell me you can't see it for yourself."

Arlian started at the mention of the Dragon Society—Cover had spoken of it, but had not known one really existed. Then Arlian caught Wither's eyes, as instructed, and stared.

He knew the name for what he saw there. "The heart of the dragon," he said, more to himself than to Wither.

"Of course. You've got it yourself, don't you?"

Arlian, without thinking, nodded.

"I'd scarcely believe you could have the venom if you didn't," Wither said. "Now, *do* you have any venom, or can you get it?"

Arlian held up a hand and turned away, forcing himself to look away from those fearsome green eyes. "A moment, please," he said. He fixed his gaze on the floor, trying to clear his thoughts.

Those eyes had a power to them, a ferocity—and Wither said that was the dragon's heart that Black had spoken of, that he had it himself.

And he said it came from drinking dragon's venom and human blood. He said it as if he *knew,* beyond question, that it was so.

Was that why Black had agreed to teach Arlian the sword, and become his companion? Was that why Sweet had invited him in and taught him so much? Was that why Bloody Hand had set him free? Had those accomplishments been bought with his grandfather's life?

Arlian could hardly doubt it; looking into Wither's eyes he could hardly deny *anything* the old man said. And that ferocity—was his *own* gaze as fierce as Wither's?

He could not imagine that it was—yet Wither saw the heart of the dragon in him. Perhaps not as strong, as he was so much younger, but that same power lay within him, fallen there in his parents' cellar all those years ago.

And it surely lay within Lord Dragon as well. Even after nine years Arlian could remember the intensity of those dark eyes.

Wither and Cover had both mentioned the Dragon Society, as well—that was another mystery that must be explained.

"My lord," Arlian said, not meeting Wither's glance, "bear with me. I have only recently come to Manfort from Arithei, and while I know much of matters you would consider arcane, I know little of your homeland. Would you be kind enough to answer a few questions from me, before I answer yours?"

"If that's what it takes to get the truth from you," Wither said. "What do you want to know?"

"Several things," Arlian said. "Let me take it one step at a time. Am I to understand that long ago, you chanced to imbibe a mixture of dragon's venom and human blood?"

"Of course I did, you idiot," Wither said. "Didn't I just tell you that? It was in one of the early defenses of Manfort, when the dragons had not yet resolved to abandon the fight for the city. One of them bit into my shoulder, and then made the mistake of flinging me into a pit where it couldn't reach me. I wiped the blood from my wound with my hand, then licked my hand before I lost consciousness, and the deed was done. My arm was withered and my shoulder ruined forever, but I recovered from my fever and lived."

"That was centuries ago."

"Yes, of course. Eight hundred years, more or less."

Arlian nodded, still not meeting Wither's eyes.

"I had heard that this mixture could prolong life, but not that anyone who had actually drunk it still lived."

Wither snorted. "Of course we do! Oh, it's rare that anyone survives a meeting with a dragon, but it does happen, and those of us who have tasted venom and blood don't die. Naturally, then, some of us are still around."

"And you believe that I, too, have drunk this elixir?"

"Of course. I don't know when or how, but I can see it in your face. You have that air of authority, of certainty. I've never seen it in anyone who *hadn't* tasted the venom."

Arlian stroked a finger across his cheek as he thought this over. "And now you ask me to give this same gift to someone else?" he asked.

"Marasa," Wither said. "She calls herself Lady Opal."

"You love her?"

Wither frowned. "I don't want her to die," he said. "I'm tired of watching my women grow old and die. I've had a dozen wives and a score of mistresses, and I don't want to ever see another wither away while I watch."

"I can see that," Arlian said. The image of Rose sprawled across her bed with her throat cut came suddenly to mind. "I can understand that quite well."

"I've tried before," Wither said. "I've tried spells and potions. I tried feeding Vorina my own blood, in hopes it would carry the magic, and instead it poisoned her—she died writhing in agony." He let out a shuddering sigh. "That was unpleasant—*worse* than unpleasant; when she died I felt as if I should now be the one writhing in agony. I had never imagined, in all those centuries, that my own blood could be toxic."

273

Arlian blinked and looked down at his own hand, at the veins faintly visible beneath the skin. Was *his* blood similarly tainted?

"It's been years—decades—since Vorina died," Wither continued. "I had said I would do without the love of women, rather than see another person I cared for die, and resolved to restrict my attentions to the purely physical, but then I met Marasa, and I was lost.

"I won't risk killing her. No more experiments. The only thing I *know* will work safely is the same mixture that worked for me, and for all the others in the Dragon Society. Blood and venom."

"Blood and venom," Arlian said. "The Dragon Society—you mentioned that before. What is it?"

"Just what it sounds like," Wither replied. "Those of us who have drunk the venom aren't hard to recognize, not once you've met a few of us, and long ago we formed a society, a place where we could gather privately with our own kind, and need no longer pretend to be ordinary mortals, need no longer be, willingly or no, the dominant figure in any gathering by virtue of the power in our blood. A place where no one would stare at—or so obviously avoid looking at—our deformities, for of course most of us bear the scars inflicted upon us by our draconic benefactors. You're fortunate, in that your face and hands are unmarked—are there scars elsewhere, perhaps? Or did you in truth find some way to obtain venom without a fight? It was when I heard you carried the dragon's heart yet bore no obvious scars that I thought to seek you out, in hopes of preserving my Marasa."

Arlian remembered Cover's belief that Lord Dragon was the master of the Dragon Society, and that his secret society controlled much of what went on in Manfort. "This society," Arlian asked, "is there a person who calls himself Lord Dragon?"

Wither shrugged. "I have heard several of us use that name, now and again. I do not attach it to any one person. Now, boy, I've answered enough questions—can you help me, or not? Did you find a way to get the venom without facing a dragon's wrath? How did you drink it yet remain unscarred?" His voice shook with eagerness.

Arlian shook his head. "I'm sorry, my lord," he said. "I drank my grandfather's blood as I lay trapped beneath his corpse. I will not deceive you further—I have no venom, nor the means to obtain it, at present." He cleared his throat. "I do have the services of half a dozen Aritheian magicians, and I will set them to seeking what you want, if you like."

Wither stared at him for a moment, then growled, "May the dragons blast you for leading me on!" His left hand fell to the hilt of his sword.

"My apologies, my lord," Arlian said, standing up straight. He recognized, with a sudden thrill of excitement and horror, that he was facing a challenge—his first since attaining sufficient status to be entitled by tradition to duel. "I am unarmed; if you wish to avenge this slight upon my flesh, I pray you let me fetch my blade."

"No," Wither said in disgust, his hand dropping. "The fault is not worthy of such a cost, and further, I might well be violating my oath by slaying you here."

Arlian frowned, relieved to know he was not going to be forced to fight this fearsome old man, but also puzzled. "How is that, my lord? What oath do you speak of?"

"The oath of the Dragon Society, required of each member upon joining, is that none of us shall attempt to slay another member within Manfort's walls," Wither explained. "With more than a score of us gathered in one place for centuries duels would be inevitable, without that restriction—and what a waste to cut off a life that might, for all we know, last millennia! And so few new members ever appear that in time we would destroy ourselves, I'm sure."

"I am not a member, though," Arlian pointed out. He very much wanted to be one, though, now that he knew the Dragon Society really existed, for surely the man he knew as Lord Dragon was a part of it, even if not the master Cover had believed him.

"Oh, you are a member in all but name," Wither said with a wave of his good hand. "I don't concern myself with needless formalities. You can merely present yourself, undergo our little initiation, and swear to the oath, and you'll be as much a member as I. The only difficult requirement is the first, the elixir that renders one suitable, and the mark of your eligibility is plain."

Arlian considered that. "I was going to ask that the price of setting my magicians to searching be your sponsoring my application to join," he said.

Wither shook his head. "You needn't bother. You can join at any time simply by answering the ritual questions and swearing the oath."

"Yet I owe you for the honest answers you've given me," Arlian said. "I will set my magicians their task—though I cannot promise any result."

"A kind gesture, sir," Wither said. "Thank you." He bent his head briefly in acknowledgment.

"Ah, thank *you!*" Arlian replied. "I have but one last request."

"Ask it, then, and I'll be on my way."

"How am I to find this Dragon Society, should I choose to join?"

"Simple enough. Go to the intersection of Citadel Street and the Street of the Black Spire, and walk down the Street of the Black Spire toward the city gates until you come to a black door with a red bar across it. That is the Society's hall; knock, and when the doorkeeper sees your face you'll be admitted, I have no doubt."

"Thank you." Arlian bowed.

A moment later Lord Wither was gone, and Arlian settled into his chair, thinking hard.

This was his chance, surely—this Dragon Society could be the key to everything he sought. Everything was going as well as he could have hoped, as if fate itself was on his side.

Only belatedly did it occur to him that he had not inquired whether Wither had owned a share of the brothel in Westguard, but he shrugged that aside. There would be plenty of time to ask the old man later.

Arlian did see at least one potential problem ahead, however.

If he joined the Dragon Society and swore the oath, and found that Lord Dragon and the others he sought were members, then he could not try to kill them—at least, not within the city walls. Would he ever have a chance to meet Lord Dragon outside Manfort?

There were other questions remaining, as well—questions of timing, of strategy...

And the questions of preparation. Was he truly ready to meet Lord Dragon in combat?

He would know soon enough, he told himself. One way or another, now that he knew of the Dragon Society, he would find Lord Dragon. When he saw that hated face he would know whether or not he was ready to act.

Dragon Weather

Chapter Thirty-Four

Lord Kuruvan

As Arlian climbed into the coach the next afternoon he had still not decided how and when he should approach the Dragon Society. He had spent the previous evening running various plans and schedules through his mind, until at last he had made his way to bed having decided only that the meeting with Lord Kuruvan would come first.

For one thing, the possibility had occurred to him that Kuruvan might be a member of the Society himself, and he wanted to satisfy himself on that account before proceeding further.

He arrived at the gate of Kuruvan's palace without incident and clambered from the coach, throwing Black, his driver, a quick salute. He was greeted by a pair of footmen, and escorted into a salon paneled in unfamiliar reddish wood. He surrendered his hat and sword to a maroon-robed slave girl, silver chains jingling on her wrists as she carried them away.

Before he could take a seat a handsome, gray-haired man in a more elaborate version of Kuruvan's maroon-and-gold livery appeared and bowed. "If you would accompany me, my lord?"

Arlian had assumed the meeting would be in the salon, but he made no protest as the steward showed him down a passageway and into a smaller, more cluttered room where Lord Kuruvan was waiting.

"Lord Obsidian," Kuruvan said, rising from his chair. "A pleasure to see you again!"

Arlian bowed in acknowledgment, forestalling any offered hand. "The pleasure is mine," he said.

Kuruvan gestured toward a chair, and a moment later the two men were seated facing one another. Arlian studied his foe, looking for some sign of the intensity Black and Wither called the dragon's heart, but found none.

"Now, my lord," Kuruvan said, "I believe you said you wished to discuss a private matter?"

"Indeed," Arlian agreed. "Before I explain myself further, however, I really must ask for the names of your five partners in the House of Carnal Society in Westguard. I believe this matter concerns them, as well, though in a lesser degree."

He tried to appear calm, but this was a decisive moment for Arlian. He had Rose's word that Kuruvan had claimed to be one of the six lords who owned the House, but while he trusted Rose, Kuruvan might have lied to her. His reaction now would show Arlian whether or not Rose had been deceived, whether or not he had found one of her killers.

Kuruvan sat back and stared at Arlian; his fingers fidgeted on the arms of the chair. He laughed nervously. "You have me at a disadvantage," he said. "You obviously know something about me, while I am in utter ignorance of your own history and connections. I don't know your true name…"

"I deal in magic," Arlian interrupted. "I dare not give my true name." He did not let his relief show, but Kuruvan's response removed any doubts—this *was* one of the men Arlian had sworn to kill.

Kuruvan nodded an acknowledgment. "Fair enough. Can you tell me *nothing* about yourself, though?"

"I will trade you, fact for fact, if you like," Arlian suggested, trying hard to sound unconcerned. "To begin the exchange, I will tell you that while I was born and raised in the Lands of Man, I never set foot in Manfort until two years ago. Now, tell me the name of one of your partners—by preference, the dark-haired man with the scarred cheek who cut down Madam Ril and carried a letter from the Duke granting him immunity from the consequences of that act."

Kuruvan, his hands now motionless, stared at him. "You know the oddest details," he said. "You know about Ril, and the letter, but you don't know Lord Enziet's name?"

"I do now," Arlian said, his blood pounding. "I had heard the name, but did not know him by sight, and had not made the connection."

Now he had, though, and pieces began to drop into place. Lord Enziet, chief adviser to the Duke of Manfort, was Lord Dragon. He was certainly a member of the Dragon Society, as well, scarred as most of the members of the Dragon Society were scarred, with that dragon's gaze that let him command others as he had commanded the looters so long ago in Obsidian—and that undoubtedly let him command the Duke and many of the other lords of Manfort.

That he had not told the looters his identity, nor revealed his true name in connection with the ownership of a brothel, now made perfect sense—someone so highly placed would naturally want to keep his distance from anything so sordid. And that no one in Westguard had recognized him also became understandable—Lord Enziet was known to be reclusive; he spoke with the Duke and the Duke's other advisers in private and was rarely seen in public.

Killing Lord Enziet would not be easy. He was said to keep largely to himself, staying within his own manse just to the east of the Citadel, behind dozens of guards, but he was no coward, no helpless fop—he just didn't want to be disturbed. He was said to have fought a dozen duels, invariably killing his opponent. He was rumored to be a sorcerer, as well. He was famous for his cold brilliance and ruthless efficiency, both in his advice to the Duke and his own affairs. He had no known family, and few real friends.

This, Arlian thought, would be a worthy challenge. "It is, I would say, your turn to ask a question," he said.

Kuruvan considered him. "And I take it that I am not yet entitled to an explanation of this private matter you came to discuss?"

"Not until I have the other four names," Arlian said. "True names, if possible, not just nicknames."

"I have little patience for these games, O mysterious guest; I'll give you the names, and you'll tell me what this is about, and then you'll owe me three further answers on subjects of my choice."

"Good enough," Arlian said. "Though I have another question of my own I'll want to ask in time. The names?"

"Drisheen, Toribor, Stiam, and Horim."

Arlian was disappointed to realize he knew only one of them by name—Lord Drisheen had visited the House on occasion during Arlian's residence in the attic, and was reputed to be a sorcerer and an adviser to the Duke, though one of the lesser ones. Except for an overindulgence in scents Drisheen had not been extravagantly unpleasant in his treatment of the women in Westguard, nor had he otherwise made the thought of killing him easier to handle—but the six lords were all enslavers and murderers, and Arlian *would* kill them all if he possibly could. He had sworn as much.

"Thank you," he said.

"And the matter you wished to discuss?" Kuruvan demanded impatiently.

"Ah," Arlian said. He considered asking his other important question, but decided he really did need to give something in return before he could expect a reply. "You own an inn called the Blood of the Grape, I believe."

"Yes," Kuruvan agreed. "What of it?"

"You stored a keg of gold there, long ago, against the eventuality that you might someday wish to flee Manfort."

Kuruvan sat bolt upright. "Who told you that?"

"Someone who is now dead," Arlian said. "You need not worry that any of your other secrets might escape."

"You owe me three more answers, Obsidian, and that must be one of them—*who told you that?*"

"Rose," Arlian said. He found himself trembling as he said her name, though he could not say whether he shook with grief or fury or something else entirely. "A crippled whore called Rose."

"*She's* the mutual acquaintance you mentioned?" Kuruvan rose from his chair.

Arlian nodded.

Kuruvan took a step toward Arlian, fists clenched. "What else did she tell you?"

Arlian looked up at him and struggled to remain calm in the face of Kuruvan's rage. "I spent a considerable amount of time in Rose's company, and we spoke a great deal. Could you be more specific?"

"What else did she tell you about *me?*"

"That you were one of the owners of the House of the Six Lords," Arlian said. "That you can't hold your liquor. That you had promised to take her with you if you ever fled Manfort." He shrugged—which took a real effort in his tense condition; his shoulders were more inclined to shake than to rise and fall. "That's all, really. No more secrets."

"And my gold?"

"It's gone," Arlian said. "Taken by the youth who called himself Lord Lanair."

"Him! The one at the inn down the street?" Kuruvan started to turn away, to pace the floor, then stopped. He turned back. "You're Lanair, aren't you? You made yourself rich with *my gold?*"

"I was Lanair," Arlian agreed. "And I invested your gold in a caravan to Arithei, which was one element in how I became wealthy enough to be here, your fellow lord, today."

"Have you come to pay it back, then, as if I'd made you a loan? Or are you here to taunt me for my foolishness in telling that faithless bitch where I hid it?"

Arlian rose and faced Kuruvan from mere inches away, looking up into

Kuruvan's bright brown eyes.

"I am here to avenge her death, Kuruvan," he said. "I needed the names of the other owners, and you've been kind enough to provide that; now, will you tell me where the two women you took from the House are, or will I need to search for them after I've killed you?"

"You mean to kill me?" Kuruvan stared. "Over a whore? A slave?"

"Over a woman you wronged, and for a dozen other crimes."

"You, a thief, call *me* a criminal?"

"And you, who had women enslaved for your pleasure, and mutilated and murdered them at whim, dare deny it?"

"Of *course* I deny it! Those women were bought openly, and what we did with them was entirely within our legal rights!" Both men were shouting now, standing nose to nose, Arlian's head tipped up and Kuruvan's tipped down.

"Within your power, perhaps, but no law can make it right," Arlian replied.

"You think you're above the law, then?"

"I think *you* have abused the very concept of law!"

Kuruvan stepped back, making a visible effort to calm himself. Holding his voice to a normal conversational level he asked, "And you intend to kill me? Have you a knife tucked in your boot, then, or were you planning to use your Borderlands magic?"

Arlian lowered his own voice to match Kuruvan's. "I intend to meet you fairly, sword in hand, at a time and place of your choosing, and convenient to us both."

"A duel?" Kuruvan sneered. "You think yourself a nobleman, and not a mere assassin?"

"I am no assassin," Arlian replied. "I own businesses that are run for me by others—does that not entitle me to the rank I claim?"

"You bought them with stolen money!"

"Nonetheless, I own them. Choose where and when we shall meet, Lord Kuruvan, and I'll take my leave until the appointed time."

"You're an unarmed thief, here in my home—why should I meet you honorably? Why should I not have you slain on the spot?"

Arlian smiled a tight little smile. "I see at least two reasons," he said. "Firstly, if we do meet fairly, I will bring with me a keg of gold equal to what I took from you at Rose's behest—and in return I ask that you bring the two women, the survivor to claim all."

"And...?"

"And secondly, I have friends and retainers awaiting my safe return, including half a dozen of Arithei's most powerful magicians, who do not consider me a thief; do you really want to risk their vengeance?"

Kuruvan stared at him.

"Were I the assassin you think me, you would already be dead," Arlian said. "You may have heard what happened to Sahasin."

Kuruvan considered that before replying slowly. "You intend to fight me fairly? And you think you can kill me?"

"Indeed I do," Arlian said.

"I'm twice your age. I have trained with the sword since I was a beardless child."

"Then perhaps *you* will kill *me,*" Arlian said. "Either way, my need for vengeance will be at an end, either satisfied or destroyed."

"You must be mad," Kuruvan said. "You seek me out, confess to robbing me, then challenge me to fight to the death over a dead slave. You boast of complicity in the assassination of the Aritheian ambassador..."

Arlian interrupted. "On the contrary, I do not even know whether Sahasin is truly dead. Otherwise, yes, you've stated the case accurately—and perhaps I *am* mad. You're not the first to suggest it."

Kuruvan stared at him a moment longer, then said, "Very well, I will face you. Tomorrow, at my own gate at midday."

Arlian smiled broadly and bowed. "I will be there," he promised.

Then he turned and marched out.

Chapter Thirty-Five

A Meeting at Swordpoint

"Remember, you'll have raw speed and strength on your side," Black said, leaning down from the driver's seat of the coach, "but he's far more experienced than you are, as he said. He'll probably react faster simply because he won't need to think about it."

Arlian nodded, then opened the door of the coach. He felt cold and stiff, as if the blood were cooling and thickening in his veins. He had fought before, and he had killed beasts, monsters, and even a man—creatures in the Dreaming Mountains had perished on his sword, and the bandit on the southernmost edge of the Desolation had died at his feet.

But despite all his plans and dreams of vengeance, he had never before deliberately set himself in front of another human being with the intention of killing him in cold blood. It felt different. It felt *wrong.*

He glanced at Thirif, who sat silently in the coach, but the Aritheian said nothing.

"He's taller than you," Black said, as he climbed down. "He'll have a longer reach. Don't let him use it; stay in close or get clear, don't fight at full extension."

"You told me that," Arlian said.

"I know I did—I want you to remember it!" Black retorted. "I want you to live through this."

Arlian didn't answer as he stepped out of the coach. He stretched, straightened his jacket, straightened his sword belt, and faced his enemy's home.

The air was warmer than it had been in days, but still cool and redolent of spring; vines twined up the gateposts, and blue flowers bloomed splendidly on one side, catching the bright light of midday. The gate of Lord Kuruvan's mansion was closed, as it had not been when Arlian arrived the day before; guards wearing the maroon and gold of Kuruvan's household, including gold-trimmed breastplates, stood on either side outside the fence. They held pikes.

There was no sign of Lord Kuruvan, or of the two women he had carried away from the brothel in Westguard. Arlian glanced up; the sun was straight overhead, so far as he could tell.

Had he put too much faith in Kuruvan's honor and respect for tradition? Had the man perhaps fled, rather than face him? After all, Kuruvan had once made preparations to flee Manfort on short notice.

The guards were still there, though. Why would they stay if Kuruvan had fled?

Then the grand front door swung open, and Kuruvan's gray-haired steward emerged. He strode to the gate with smooth assurance, then bowed, his head almost scraping the black iron bars.

"Lord Obsidian," he said.

"Sir," Arlian replied. He stepped forward and stopped a yard from the gate. "I believe I have an appointment with your employer."

"Indeed," the steward said, straightening. "However, Lord Kuruvan has asked me to speak with you briefly first."

"Has he? Why?" Arlian placed a hand on the hilt of his sword, not so much as a threat as simply to indicate his impatience.

"In hopes, my lord, of preventing unnecessary bloodshed. While he has no fear for his own safety, he hesitates to deprive Manfort of a man of your own obvious intelligence and courage, and therefore hopes that this quarrel can be composed by more peaceful means."

"And has he some proposal for atoning for his crimes?"

"Indeed," the steward said. "He proposes to give you the two slaves you sought, in exchange for the gold you took from him. He will lay no claim to any interest or profit upon the stolen funds."

"And what about the four women he helped murder—Rose, and Silk, and the others? What about mutilating a dozen women for the sake of pleasure and profit?"

The steward frowned. "I know nothing of that, nor do my instructions cover it. Lord Kuruvan assures me that he broke no law in the matters you accuse him of."

"The women were slaves—but they were still women, not beasts." Arlian hesitated. He did not want to kill anyone, not really—but Kuruvan was a murderer. Slaves were human beings, and no one, owner or not, had the right to maim and kill them with impunity.

Still, if he could be made to pay some other way…

"I propose a counter-offer," Arlian said. "If Lord Kuruvan frees every

285

slave in his possession, and swears never again to hold a person in bondage, I will consider our quarrel settled and justice done. He cannot give those four women back their lives, nor the others their feet, but if he grants life and freedom to others, perhaps the scales will be balanced."

The steward hesitated. "I must consult with my lord," he said. He bowed and turned.

Arlian watched him go. Black stepped up beside the younger man.

"Thirif says he senses no magic anywhere nearby," Black whispered. "And if I were you, I'd have taken the deal he offered."

Arlian shook his head. "And leave him free to torment and kill others who had the mischance to be taken by slavers? I don't think so."

Black shrugged. "Please yourself."

"Get the gold ready," Arlian told him.

A moment later the door of the mansion opened and Lord Kuruvan stepped out and strode across the small paved yard. He wore a sleeveless tunic of thick oiled leather and a nondescript pair of leather breeches, not at all like the finery Arlian had seen him in before—these were serious fighting clothes, and the sword and swordbreaker on his belt were plainly meant for use, not show. Arlian reached for the clasp of his own cloak.

"Not yet," Black advised. "Give him a moment. He may yield yet."

"And if I give up my right to own slaves," Kuruvan shouted without preamble, well before he reached the gate, "what then? Will you carry this insane crusade of yours on to my friends and associates? Do you mean to stamp out the entire institution of slavery, so that the poor will starve in the gutter while vital work goes untended?"

"I would like to, yes," Arlian called back. "I doubt I shall live long enough, but indeed, an end to slavery would suit me very well."

"If I make peace with you, you'll go on to pursue this mad vengeance of yours? You'll challenge Drisheen and Enziet and the others?"

"Yes, I will," Arlian said.

"You *are* mad, then," Kuruvan said, "and I cannot in good conscience accept your proposal. I can't trust a madman to keep his word, or not to come up with some other wild scheme, some other imaginary crime that must be avenged. You, sir, are a menace to society, and it is my duty to remove you."

"Or die in the attempt," Arlian said, hoping that Kuruvan would back down. His own nerves were raw with anticipation.

"Ha!" Kuruvan signaled to the guards, then drew his sword and swordbreaker as the gate began to swing open.

"Wait!" Arlian said, his voice cracking. "Where are the women?"

Kuruvan called over his shoulder, "Bring them out."

The door of the mansion swung wide, and two footmen appeared, each carrying a naked woman—Hasty and Kitten. They blinked in the bright sunlight.

Kuruvan pointed, and the footmen seated the women side by side on a stone bench beside the arched doorway. They looked about in obvious confusion. Kitten tried to tuck her ankles under the bench, to hide the fact that she had no feet; Hasty made no such effort. Although the outside air was cool, neither seemed troubled by her lack of clothing—though Arlian was. He tried not to stare. He remembered how accustomed he had become to casual nudity during his stay in the House of Carnal Society and tried to recall that indifference—but it had been two years.

The two women had been little altered by the intervening time, though. Both wore their hair differently, and Hasty's belly was somewhat more convex than Arlian remembered, but those were no great changes. Their faces were as lovely as ever.

The sight of them brought back a flood of memories, and Arlian's heart ached. He suddenly wished he were fighting Lord Enziet, rather than Lord Kuruvan, so that he could see Sweet again, rather than these two.

But he was here, and they were here, and Sweet would have to wait just a little longer. This pair seemed almost untouched by the passage of two years; Arlian could only hope that Sweet was likewise unharmed.

Then Hasty spotted Arlian. "Triv?" she said. "Kitten, it's Triv!" She pointed.

Kitten turned and saw Arlian. Her jaw dropped. *"Triv?"*

"It appears they do, in fact, know you," Kuruvan remarked. "Interesting. Now, I believe you have something of mine?"

Arlian signaled to Black, and Black brought out a keg, deliberately made as much like the one in the cellars beneath the Blood of the Grape as Arlian had been able to contrive, even to having the words "sour wine" chalked on it. He set the keg on the ground.

Arlian doffed his cloak and handed it to Black; then he drew his own blades and moved forward.

Kuruvan stepped back. "Come in," he said. "Let us duel like the nobles we are, not brawl in the street like ruffians."

Arlian nodded and stepped warily through the gate onto the paved courtyard, his sword held ready.

The guards backed away; the footmen who had brought out the women vanished. Only the two swordsmen stood in the square of pavement between gate and door.

"Take your first stroke, if you will," Kuruvan said, moving his sword into a guard position.

Arlian was not fooled; he knew better than to charge in directly against a foe with arms and blade longer than his own. He waited, his own sword raised, swordbreaker poised at his waist.

As he stood he found himself wondering if he was being a fool. He was risking his life—he knew he was a good swordsman, but how could he be sure Kuruvan wasn't a better one? Certainly, Kuruvan's leather showed a greater sense of self-preservation than his own black silk. He had dressed for elegance and freedom of movement, and given no thought at all to turning his foe's blade.

And he had been offered a chance to free Hasty and Kitten without bloodshed—what right did he have to turn it down and pursue some abstract concept of justice?

Might he not just as well have simply tried to buy free the dozen surviving women? He glanced at the two of them, sitting naked there on the bench...

And saw the stumps of Hasty's ankles at the same instant that Lord Kuruvan, seeing his opponent distracted, lunged forward.

Arlian dodged, parried, but missed the riposte completely. He staggered slightly as he moved to the right, away from Kuruvan's blade—and then that blade was withdrawn, shifted, thrust again, before Arlian had fully recovered. His parry was awkward, almost slapping away Kuruvan's sword rather than turning it with any grace or skill. Kuruvan smiled thinly and pressed his advantage.

Arlian started to retreat, then realized that the iron fence was less than a yard behind him—he had no room to retreat without being cornered. He ducked and ran to the side instead.

Kuruvan whirled and took a step forward, but not quickly enough to maintain contact; the two men once again stood apart at twice a sword's length, facing each other. No blood had yet been drawn.

"You are a fool, as well as a madman," Kuruvan said. "Not half the swordsman you thought yourself, eh?"

Arlian made no answer, but he was silently cursing himself. He could not afford doubt or hesitation; however it had come about, and whatever the wisdom or foolishness in bringing himself to this, he was fighting for his life.

And for justice. The image of Hasty's ruined legs dangling from the bench was fresh in his mind, reminding him of the injustice to be avenged. The image of Rose, lying naked on her bed beneath a thickening cloud of smoke, throat cut and eyes staring blindly at nothing, returned to him as well.

"There's still time to end this peacefully," Kuruvan said, as the tip of his sword moved threateningly. "I'll still trade those two for the gold, and your oath to trouble me no more. I think you may have learned a lesson here—and let me assure you, Lord Obsidian, or Triv, if that's your name, that I am by no means the best swordsman of the six you've chosen as enemies."

He might have intended to say more, but midway through the word "enemies" Arlian strode forward, ducking, trying to get his blade under Kuruvan's guard.

Kuruvan was not caught off guard that easily; he caught Arlian's blade on his own and turned it aside. His sword-breaker came up, but not in time, as Arlian withdrew.

But he did not withdraw fully; instead he thrust again, this time aiming for Kuruvan's right thigh and stepping in closer.

Again, steel clashed on steel as the swords crossed; Arlian's left hand whipped out, and the tip of his sword-breaker slashed across the leg of Kuruvan's breeches, scarring but not piercing the leather. This time it was Kuruvan who retreated a quick two steps, breaking contact.

Arlian, suspecting a trap, did not pursue immediately; he stepped back as well and began to circle to the left.

As he did, one part of his mind considered Kuruvan's words. In fact, it was quite likely that some of the other lords were better swordsmen than Kuruvan. Enziet, in particular, with his dragon's heart and fearsome reputation, might well be more formidable.

For that matter, some or all of the other four might also be members of the Dragon Society. Whether that would really matter Arlian didn't know. Certainly his own supposed draconic gifts didn't seem to have intimidated Kuruvan.

And he *needed* to intimidate Kuruvan. It was too late now to do anything but kill or be killed, and Arlian had no intention of dying.

Arlian suddenly stopped his leftward circling and charged to the right, lunging, trying to catch Kuruvan unaware, evade his sword and strike at his left side.

Kuruvan's swordbreaker swept up, but Arlian dodged it. His blade slashed across the bare skin of Kuruvan's left arm midway between shoulder and elbow—not the truly damaging blow he had hoped for, but first blood, all the same.

And Kuruvan's own sword was sweeping in from Arlian's own left, high and wide, headed for his ear; Arlian's left hand snapped up, swordbreaker ready, as he ducked his head.

Kuruvan's blade cut through Arlian's hair, and a sudden warmth on his scalp told Arlian that he had been wounded, but then he heard the click of steel as his swordbreaker slid around Kuruvan's weapon.

Arlian smiled, and twisted—and Kuruvan's blade slipped free, apparently undamaged.

And Kuruvan's own swordbreaker was coming up toward Arlian's heart; in his stooped position, escaping the sword, he could see the approaching dagger blade clearly.

Already aslant, Arlian threw himself back and further to the right, right knee bent and left leg straight, and the swordbreaker slashed up across his left shoulder, ruining fine black silk but drawing no blood. Arlian's sword swept up, behind Kuruvan's swordbreaker, aimed at Kuruvan's throat.

Kuruvan flung himself backward, and the two men staggered apart.

Kuruvan's left arm was bleeding steadily, Arlian saw, and while his sword was not broken, it *was* very slightly bent.

Arlian's own weapons were undamaged, but his left shoulder felt bruised and the cut-open shirt was sliding down onto his left arm in a most distracting fashion. He knew he was bleeding from his scalp, as well, but that was well back on the left, too far back for the blood to get in his face and interfere with his vision, so he ignored it.

Arlian thought that all things considered, he had gotten the better of that exchange. He wondered if Kuruvan knew his sword was bent; swordsmen were trained to watch their *opponents'* swords, not their own. If he hadn't noticed, Arlian might be able to use that.

But he would only be able to use it *once* before Kuruvan discovered it, and the sooner the better. Arlian launched into a direct attack, turning his body to present a smaller target as he thrust his blade forward.

This was the sort of attack that Black had warned him against, the sort where Kuruvan's greater reach was an advantage, and sure enough Kuruvan's sword met his own in what should have been a deadly parry and riposte—but slid harmlessly aside, across Arlian's chest, as Kuruvan misjudged where his bent blade would go. Arlian stepped forward, inside Kuruvan's guard, his own sword arm pulling back for a lethal thrust—but Kuruvan's swordbreaker came up, catching the tip of Arlian's sword.

Arlian twisted, swinging his sword free, and stepped forward again. Now Kuruvan's right arm was outstretched across Arlian's chest, and his left pinned by Arlian's right; there was nothing to stop Arlian's left arm as he rammed the point of his swordbreaker through oiled leather into Kuruvan's belly.

Arlian had thought that was a killing blow, and that the duel was over; he expected Kuruvan to gasp and crumple, as that bandit in the Desolation had.

But Kuruvan pulled away, still upright, still fighting, and slashed with his sword, drawing a bloody line across Arlian's left arm and chest, slicing through black silk into flesh.

Arlian stabbed again with his swordbreaker, but this time the two were angled differently and not quite so close, and the thick leather turned the blow. Kuruvan's swordbreaker cut across Arlian's right arm as the two men pulled apart.

And then Arlian's shorter arms worked in his favor; as they drew back, his sword came free, and he was able to thrust it forward and down into Kuruvan's side. It was not a deep cut, but it was another telling blow.

Kuruvan gasped and staggered, but broke free and brought his sword up to guard.

"Stop it!" someone shrieked—Hasty, Arlian realized. "Stop it, both of you!"

Neither man paid any attention. They were intent on one another.

Kuruvan was apparently no longer interested in speaking, or in attacking; he appeared to be having difficulty breathing, though his weapons did not sag nor his movements falter. He was bleeding several places, and his face was unnaturally pale.

Arlian was bleeding as well, but was convinced his own wounds were all superficial, while at least two of Kuruvan's were not. That meant time was on Arlian's side; Kuruvan would weaken with every passing moment, every drop of blood he lost.

The two men stood facing each other, neither one ready to attack, for what felt like hours; then Kuruvan's eyes rolled back in his head, his weapons fell from his hands, and he collapsed upon the pavement.

Arlian started to move forward, to attack; he had been awaiting an opportunity so long that it took him a few seconds to realize that any other action was possible. Then he caught himself and stopped, his sword almost at Kuruvan's throat.

There was no honor in killing an unconscious man; in fact, to strike now would be murder under the dueling laws. Arlian stepped back, and realized he was panting and trembling.

Footmen in maroon and gold were hurrying forward to attend to their master; Arlian stepped back again, giving them room. He glanced down at himself, at his own bloody chest and arms; he tugged at the tatters of his silk blouse with his thumb, then noticed the blood on his sword. He blinked.

Dazed. He was dazed, he realized. The duel had only lasted a few minutes, and hadn't really been so very strenuous, but still, he knew he was not thinking clearly anymore.

"Black!" he called, starting to tremble uncontrollably.

And then his steward, his friend, was there, handing him a cloth. Arlian dropped his swordbreaker to accept it, then wiped his sword carefully, struggling to keep his hands steady enough for the task. He sheathed the sword, then retrieved the swordbreaker and cleaned and sheathed that, as well.

Then he stood, still shaking, his mind momentarily a blank.

"I'm glad to see you have your priorities straight," Black said, putting one arm around Arlian, "but we'll need to get you cleaned up, too."

Arlian nodded. His thoughts were beginning to clear. "The women," he said. "Get them in the coach. And the gold."

"And you," Black said. "Come on, now."

Arlian allowed himself to be led away.

As he sat in the coach, still trembling, waiting for Hasty and Kitten to be carried over from the bench, he saw Kuruvan being carried inside. The gray-haired steward gave Arlian one last hate-filled look; then the mansion door slammed shut.

Arlian stared at that closed door, trying to think whether he hoped Kuruvan would live or die, and utterly unable to decide.

Dragon Weather

Chapter Thirty-Six

Tending to Wounds

Despite his battered condition, Arlian later remembered every detail of the ride home—the two naked women staring at him, Thirif sitting silently beside him, the worry in Black's voice as he called to the horses, the stinging when a cut on one arm brushed against the upholstery. He had wanted to speak to the women, to reassure them, but the shifting expressions on Hasty's face deterred him—she seemed angry as much as frightened, and as scared of him as of anything else. He couldn't find the words to speak to her over the creaking of the coach, the rattle of harness, the beating of the horses' hooves, and his own weary confusion.

Kitten's expression was closed and unreadable.

Arlian had never known Kitten well to begin with, but Hasty had been his friend, and her antagonism worried him.

The ride was a short one, in any case, and when they pulled up at the door of the Old Palace Arlian had still not said a thing.

He opened the coach door and climbed out before Black could dismount, then turned, with the idea of carrying one woman inside while Black fetched the other.

Thirif looked meaningfully at his chest, and pointed at the blood on his arms, and Arlian thought better of carrying anyone. Instead he stood aside as Thirif and Black brought Hasty and Kitten into the small salon.

"Where are we?" Kitten asked, craning her neck to look at the gilding, tapestries, and fretwork.

"Home," Arlian said. "Welcome home!"

Hasty stared at him. "Triv, are you insane?"

Arlian, very much aware of his injuries, was in no mood to argue with anyone. He frowned at her. "Why do people keep asking me that?"

"Because you're *acting* like a madman!" Hasty squeaked. "What's going to happen to us when the owner of this place comes back?"

"I *am* the owner of this place," Arlian said patiently. He gestured at

Black and Thirif. "Ask them."

"If he's mad, it's nothing as obvious as that," Black said. "He's the true Lord Obsidian, all right, and he does own this palace."

"But he's just Triv!" Hasty protested. "He's an…he's nobody!"

"Not anymore," Black told her. He glanced at Arlian. "Someday you'll have to tell me why they call you Triv."

Arlian shrugged. "It's not important." He smiled to himself at this answer.

"I'll agree with that," Black said. "What's important is cleaning and dressing those wounds before any of them turn poisonous."

Arlian glanced down at himself.

"Black speaks wisely," Thirif said.

Arlian yielded. "Get these two some clothes," he told Thirif. "And food. Whatever they want."

The Aritheian nodded, and Arlian allowed himself to be led away.

An hour later, heavily bandaged and attired in fresh new clothes, Arlian returned to the salon.

Hasty and Kitten were seated on two settees; Kitten wore a black silk tunic that reached just below her knees, while Hasty was wrapped in a velvet robe.

"We have no women's clothing on hand, my lord," a footman explained before Arlian could remark on this garb.

"That's fine," Arlian said. He crossed the room and stooped to kiss Hasty on the forehead. The scent of her hair filled his nostrils, and he smiled broadly. "It's good to see you again!" he said.

"It's good to see you, too, Triv," Hasty said, looking up at him, "but why did you do it?"

"Do what?" Arlian asked.

"Fight that horrible duel! You could have been killed! You might have killed Vanni!"

Arlian stared at her, a puzzled frown upon his face. "He was holding you prisoner," he said.

"Vanni? Oh, he was sweet," Hasty protested. "He's a poor silly boy!"

"Lord Kuruvan, you mean," Arlian said, baffled.

"Yes, Lord Kuruvan. Vanni."

"Lord Kuruvan is a poor silly boy? He must be forty years old."

Hasty shrugged. "He's still a boy," she said.

"He was holding you in bondage," Arlian pointed out.

"Well, but he wasn't *hurting* us!" Hasty replied.

"He was one of the owners of the House of Carnal Society," Arlian said. "He was one of the six men who put you there and had your feet cut off."

"But the House is gone!" Hasty protested. "That's all over!"

"It is *now*," Arlian said grimly. "For you two, at any rate."

"But it was over *years* ago! For two years we haven't had to please anyone but poor Vanni. And he was hardly ever rough, and when he was he'd feel bad afterward and give us candy and wine to apologize."

Arlian stared silently at her for a moment. Hasty had always been prone to confusion and thoughtlessness—that was where her name had come from, after all—but this seemed more than Arlian could deal with.

"Hasty," he said, "he ordered your feet chopped off! He agreed to have Rose and Silk murdered! He had to be punished for those crimes."

Now it was Hasty's turn to stare in incomprehension.

"Murdered?" Kitten said. "Rose and Silk are dead?"

"When the House was closed," Arlian told her. "Each of the six lords took two women, and then the guards cut the throats of the other four and burned down the house."

Hasty's confusion turned to shock. For a moment she and Kitten sat motionless, staring at Arlian.

"We didn't know," Kitten said. "And Kuruvan didn't abuse us. We... it wasn't a bad life there, really."

"You were slaves," Arlian said.

"Well, of course," Kitten replied. "We always have been. We still are."

"No, you aren't," Arlian said. "Lord Kuruvan wagered your freedom on that duel. You're free."

Hasty's eyes were suddenly full of tears. "But we *can't* be!" she wailed. "What will I do if I'm free? I'm a cripple, with no feet! I may be carrying Vanni's child, and I'm not married! I need to be a slave. I've *never* been free, I never *asked* to be free! I don't know how!" She flung herself forward, wrapping her arms around Arlian's waist and burying her face against his belly.

Arlian tried to comfort her, and looked at the other woman for guidance.

Kitten's expression was somber. "I'm glad to be free, Triv," she said, "but Hasty has a good point. What will become of us? Neither of us knows a trade, and who would marry a cripple?"

"You're welcome to stay here for as long as you please," Arlian said, as he patted Hasty comfortingly. "I made my fortune with money Rose gave me, money she said should have belonged to the women in that brothel—to me, that means that one-twelfth of my wealth is at your disposal, each of you. I took that money to avenge the injustices you and the others suffered."

"So we'll be parasites instead of slaves?" Kitten asked.

The day's accumulated stresses finally broke Arlian's calm. "Would you rather be dog food when your Lord Kuruvan tired of you?" he demanded. "You earned that money! You paid for it be giving up the ability to walk! And if you don't think so, then go ahead and learn a trade—a seamstress doesn't need to walk, does she?"

Hasty snuffled miserably.

"You're right, Triv," Kitten said. "I'm sorry. This was so unexpected! We had settled into our lives with Kuruvan, and we were comfortable there—though you're right that it probably wouldn't have lasted long. You meant well."

Arlian stared at her for a moment.

Meant well?

He had risked his life to see that justice was done for these women. He had fought down his fears and misgivings and had crossed blades with an experienced swordsman, he had shed his own blood, and still faced the very real possibility of wound fever. The duel with Kuruvan had been no elegant display of skill, but an ugly, awkward, messy brawl that ended not in a clean death for one that left the other unscathed, but in numerous wounds and great pain on both sides. Arlian had gone through all that not for himself, but to have justice for these women, and he had carried away Hasty and Kitten, not to keep them, but to give them their freedom.

He had thought they would be grateful.

He hadn't fought for their gratitude; he had fought because it was the right thing to do, because it would serve the cause of justice. Still, Hasty and Kitten were the immediate beneficiaries, and he had thought they *would* be grateful.

He hadn't expected to be told he had *meant* well.

He should have known better, he told himself. He remembered Bloody Hand, back in the mine, shouting at him for having dared to save him from the falling ore.

He had done what was right. He had saved Bloody Hand's life—and he had tried to take Kuruvan's. He had tried to make a little justice in the world.

He frowned as he stroked Hasty's hair. Why was it right to save Bloody Hand, and to kill Kuruvan?

Because it *was*. Bloody Hand had killed Dinian, yes, but by accident. He had not been a sadist like Lampspiller. He had been trying to survive as best he could, to do the job he had been given.

Kuruvan had maimed and killed women because he *wanted* to, because it was convenient and profitable.

That was wrong. No matter how pleasant he had been to Kitten and Hasty afterward, it was wrong, and Kuruvan had done nothing to make amends.

Perhaps now he would—assuming he survived his wounds. Arlian resolved to check on Lord Kuruvan, if he recovered, to see whether he still considered himself free to kill slaves.

But first, there were five more lords to deal with—Stiam, Horim, Toribor, Drisheen...

And Lord Dragon. Lord Enziet. The man who had looted Arlian's home and sold Arlian into slavery, the man who had killed Madam Ril and ordered the House of Carnal Society burned, the man who had carried Sweet and Dove away with him.

Arlian would deal with them all, including Lord Dragon, and would rescue Sweet and the other women—and from now on he would not expect gratitude.

He disentangled himself from Hasty and set her back on the settee. "I'll have someone show you your rooms," he said. "If you want anything, my servants will get it for you."

Then he turned and headed for his own chambers, to rest—and to plan. He knew now who all his enemies were—the six lords, the looters, the dragons. He had wounded Kuruvan, forgiven Cover ...

He paused on the stairs. Was he finished with Kuruvan, then? Should he go back and finish him off?

And that offer he had made, to let Kuruvan go unscathed if he forswore all future connection with slavery—where had that come from? Was that truly what he sought? Did he think that the institution of slavery was something that must be abolished? That was not any task he had consciously set himself. He had been seeking justice; was slavery then inherently unjust? Was it any more unjust than the rest of the world?

Would Hasty be happier free than she had been as Kuruvan's slave? Certainly *he* was happier free. And Rose would still be alive had she been free.

He was not ready to say that slavery was always wrong. He *was* convinced that it was abused, that Lord Dragon—Lord Enziet!—had been wrong to sell him to the mine, that the six lords had been wrong to maim their whores and kill four of them.

They had demonstrated that they could not be trusted with slaves—*that* was why he had made his offer to Lord Kuruvan. The question of whether *anyone* could be trusted with slaves he would leave open for now.

That decided, he continued up the steps.

As for whether Kuruvan had paid sufficiently for the evil he had done—well, perhaps he should leave that to Fate. If Kuruvan recovered from his wounds, and committed no more atrocities, then Arlian would let him live.

After all, he had the others to deal with.

Lord Enziet would be next, of course. He was the one Arlian was most determined to see punished, now that he knew who Lord Dragon was; the others could wait. Enziet was also the one who held Sweet. Arlian dared not risk getting himself killed fighting one of the others, leaving Lord Dragon untouched and Sweet still in his possession.

He would have Black visit Enziet's mansion and arrange a meeting, and when he was sufficiently recovered from his own injuries he would pay Lord Dragon a visit.

And he wouldn't leave Enziet alive, as he had Kuruvan.

He would question him about his knowledge of dragons, how he had known that Obsidian would be available for looting—and for that matter, why the village had been worth looting in person, for surely a man of Enziet's prominence could have sent an employee to attend to it.

He would learn everything Lord Dragon could tell him, he would finally know why his family and childhood had been snatched away, why his life had been twisted into an obsessive quest for revenge—and then he would kill him.

That settled, Arlian tumbled onto his bed, exhausted—but elated, as well.

He was making progress. Cover and Kuruvan were done, and Lord Dragon was next! At last, after all these years, Lord Dragon was next!

Chapter Thirty-Seven

Approaches to Lord Dragon

Black marched in the doorway of Arlian's study and crossed to the writing table where Arlian sat. "He won't see you," he said without preamble.

Arlian put down his quill and blinked up at his steward. "What do you mean, he won't see me?"

"I mean he won't see you," Black repeated. "I delivered your message, and I recited it myself, just to be sure, as well as handing over the written copy—'Lord Obsidian wishes to call upon Lord Enziet at Lord Enziet's convenience about a matter of some importance to them both, and would appreciate a word as to when that might be possible.' They told me to wait at the gate, and a footman brought me back the reply—that Lord Enziet has no intention of seeing Lord Obsidian at any time, and that henceforth I am not to inflict my presence further upon any member of his household, at any time."

"You protested?"

"Of course I protested. Loudly. And I was told to wait again, and someone fetched this." He handed Arlian a folded sheet of paper.

Arlian accepted it and opened it, and read, "Lord Enziet busies himself with the Duke's business and his own concerns, and has no time to waste on social niceties. Let Lord Obsidian amuse himself elsewhere."

"This verges on deliberate insult," Arlian said, looking up from the little square of paper.

"I'd say so," Black agreed.

"Do you think Enziet knows why I want to see him?" Arlian asked.

"It's entirely possible," Black said. "After all, Lord Kuruvan had time to talk at some length before the fever set in."

Arlian frowned at the reminder.

That Kuruvan's wounds had festered and brought on a fever was hardly surprising, but Arlian was not happy about it. His own injuries had healed well, but they had been far more superficial. Kuruvan had been stabbed in the belly, and while to Arlian's surprise the wound itself had not been fatal, it had turned foul; the reports that had reached the Old Palace said that Kuruvan was now bedridden and delirious, burning up with fever, his abdomen as swollen and red as an overripe peach. He was not expected to live much longer.

It was a slow, nasty way to die. Arlian had wanted Kuruvan dead, but would have preferred a quick death—he wasn't interested in inflicting suffering upon the guilty so much as in removing a menace from the world.

But that was in regard to Kuruvan; Arlian would be pleased to see Lord Dragon suffer. He had hoped to bring that suffering about.

Instead, Enziet was insulting him, defying him.

And of course, why shouldn't he? Lord Obsidian was nobody—rich, yes, but with no serious commercial ties in Manfort, no known family, no powerful friends.

That still did not entitle Lord Enziet to be openly rude to a fellow nobleman, and perhaps that was all the excuse Arlian needed. He opened a desk drawer and found a sheet of paper. He took up his quill, dipped it, and wrote, "I find the tone of your message inappropriate, and must ask that you apologize. It is essential that I speak with you."

He signed it "Obsidian," with a flourish, then blotted it, folded it, and handed it to Black.

Black had read it over his shoulder. "It may not do any better," he said.

"You're welcome to make suggestions."

"You're the lord here," Black said with a shrug. "Anything else?"

"Check on Kuruvan," Arlian said. "See if you can find out, without being obvious, whether he did communicate with Enziet." A thought struck him. "And check on Cover, too. Perhaps he knows something useful—where did he meet Lord Dragon, all those years ago? Did he have any way to send Lord Dragon or any of the others a message?

Black nodded and tucked the note inside his tunic.

Arlian watched him go.

It seemed clear what had happened. The duel with Lord Kuruvan had hardly been secret—duels couldn't very well be kept secret. The reason for the duel would surely have become known, as well—Kuruvan would have had no reason not to speak of it. That meant that the other proprietors of the House of the Six Lords all knew that Lord Obsidian meant them ill.

Furthermore, the fact that Kuruvan, a very respectable swordsman, had *lost* his duel meant that they would probably not be eager to face Arlian openly. He would be unlikely to catch any of them off guard, and luring each of them into a duel might well be impossible.

But perhaps he could still bully them into fighting. Demanding that Lord Enziet apologize was a first step in that direction; by the code of honor the lords of Manfort observed, if Enziet refused to apologize Arlian could escalate the conflict until Enziet had no choice but to fight.

And if he *did* apologize, well, Arlian could insist the apology be made in person, and matters could proceed from there. He was not yet stymied.

He might be in danger himself, though. Lord Dragon had had no hesitation about killing Madam Ril when she displeased him. While Ril had been a mere employee, not a fellow lord, might he not attempt to kill Arlian by some method less open than dueling? Assassination was not legal, but it happened. Arlian had no idea how one went about hiring an assassin, but he was sure Enziet did.

And that didn't even consider the fact that Enziet was reputed to know something of sorcery. Arlian frowned and rose from his desk; he left the study and trotted down the stairs to the office where Thirif conducted his business.

The Aritheian was seated cross-legged on a mat in one corner, meditating. He looked up as Arlian entered.

Arlian quickly explained the situation—that he had intended to visit Lord Enziet and challenge him to a duel, but that his polite request for an audience had been met with an insulting refusal.

"I believe my enemies may be aware of my intentions," he concluded. "I also suspect they may attempt to take action against me by dishonorable means."

Thirif asked, "Do you mean assassins?"

"Or sorcery," Arlian said.

Thirif nodded. "Do you want me to place wards?"

"I'm not sure," Arlian said. "I've heard the word, but could you explain what you mean?"

"A ward is…" Thirif frowned. "I know no other word for it in your tongue. It is a device or magic that surrounds a place and turns aside malign influences. The iron fences in Arithei serve as wards against wild magic, but would not stop any mortal, nor a properly made spell; for that we have magical wards. Any who try to enter a magically warded place while wishing the inhabitants harm will feel a compulsion to turn aside—a strong will may resist this compulsion, though. Hostile magic cannot enter a warded place unless it is stronger than the ward. If an enemy enters despite the ward, the magician who placed the ward will feel it and know what has happened. If the ward is broken by stronger magic, that, too, will be felt."

"That sounds ideal," Arlian said. "Can you do that here?"

"Of course. We brought many wardings with us, and they have not sold well—your northern sorcerers can create wards of their own. It is one of the few things that sorcery can do well—had we known that, we would not have brought them."

"But you did bring them?"

"Yes."

"Then by all means, place wards around the palace immediately. Strong ones."

"As you wish." Thirif unfolded his legs and rose from his mat.

"Thank you," Arlian said.

Thirif bowed an acknowledgment, then departed.

Arlian stood gazing thoughtfully after the Aritheian for a moment. There was so much he didn't know about magic! Wards were clearly a basic spell, yet he had needed an explanation.

And there was so much he still didn't know about Manfort, and about the city's lords.

And so much he didn't know about dragons, about Lord Dragon, about the connections between Enziet and the dragons. Maybe Lord Enziet had not been told anything by Lord Kuruvan, but had known Arlian meant him harm by other means. How had Lord Dragon known that the dragons would destroy Obsidian, and that he could loot it?

Enziet was a mystery. Was Sweet safe in his hands? Lord Dragon had taken her—what had he done with her, and with Dove? Were Sweet and Dove still alive? Hasty and Kitten were safe and well, but Lord Dragon was not Lord Kuruvan.

At that, Arlian's thoughts turned to his two houseguests. Kitten seemed to be settling in reasonably well—she had not yet taken up learning any sort of skills, but she professed to be thinking about it, and she had discovered the library. Arlian had not had time to use it himself, but the Old Palace had a library, and it had been furnished with a modest collection of books when he bought the place. These were presumably the books not considered worth the trouble of moving to the Citadel, but Kitten apparently found them interesting enough. She spent much of her time there.

Hasty, on the other hand, had no interest in books—Arlian was not sure she knew how to read. Instead, during the several days Arlian had spent recovering from his wounds, she seemed to have devoted herself to harassing Arlian's servants, demanding to be carried hither and yon for no reason, deliberately seducing and then abandoning one young man after another.

He supposed she would get over it—especially if she was correct in suspecting that she was pregnant with Kuruvan's child.

As for himself, he had kept busy through his convalescence with his household and business. He had now sold off, through his agents, a significant fraction of the magical artifacts he had brought north from Arithei, and his income from those was augmented by investments he had made with the money thus generated. Keeping track of those hundreds of thousands of ducats was a considerable task, and working at it kept his mind off his plans for revenge, plans that could only circle endlessly and pointlessly in his head until he was again fit to fight.

Now, while Thirif set wards and Arlian waited for Black's return from the errands Arlian had assigned him, Arlian returned to his study to go over the latest business records once again. Until he had more information there was little else he could do.

He had closed the account books and eaten supper, and was sitting in the salon, glass in hand, when Black returned. Arlian looked up from his wine expectantly as the steward stood over him.

"Cover is dead," Black said. "Five days ago."

That was not really a surprise—if anything, he had lived somewhat longer than Arlian had expected. "And Stammer?"

Black shrugged.

"If she can find nothing better, offer her a job here," Arlian said.

Black sighed. "As you say," he said.

"And Enziet?"

Black hesitated.

"Lord Enziet," he said, "spoke to me at some length. To be specific, at sword's length."

"What?" Arlian put down his glass.

Black sighed again.

"Sit down," Arlian said, "and tell me all about it." He gestured at the decanter and an empty glass.

Black sat and poured himself a drink. He downed it in a gulp, then poured another.

"I was kept waiting for some time after I gave your note to a footman," Black said, "but at last Lord Enziet himself came to speak to me." He grimaced. "Not alone; he had half a dozen guards with him, and his own sword ready in his hand."

"What did he say?"

"I remember his very words," Black said. "He told me, 'Your master has nerve, demanding an apology from a man he intends to murder.'"

"Oh," Arlian said.

"He went on at some length, as I told you," Black said. "He is aware that you consider yourself wronged by the proprietors of the House of Carnal Society; he has no interest in the truth of such accusations, or for that matter in any sort of justice, fairness, or revenge. Instead he wants me to warn you that if you harass or harm him or any of his surviving partners further, or attempt to enter his home, he will kill you—and not in anything so formal as a duel. If I return, he will kill *me*. If you send any other messenger, he will kill the messenger. He is not concerned with rules or custom, and is confident that his hold over the Duke is more than enough to ensure he won't suffer any legal consequences for any of these deaths should he choose to bring them about. He strongly advises you to leave Manfort and go back wherever you came from. That he hasn't *already* killed you, he says, is only because he does not care to antagonize your Aritheian allies—but having now warned you, that won't stop him if you persist. He assumes that once you're dead the Aritheians can be made to see reason. Furthermore, if by some chance you *do* kill him, he has made arrangements to ensure that you will be killed in return."

Arlian swallowed.

"He also says to tell you that the wards won't stop him. I don't know what that means, but I assume you do."

"Yes," Arlian said.

"Ari," Black said, "I had never met Lord Enziet before. Remember not long after we met, I told you you had the heart of the dragon in you? Well, Enziet has the heart, soul, liver, and lights of the dragon. I don't doubt for a minute that he means exactly what he says, and can do it."

"I don't doubt it, either," Arlian agreed. He picked up his glass and swallowed the rest of his wine. The heart of the dragon, he thought. Credentials for membership in the Dragon Society. Lord Enziet was undoubtedly a member.

"He may decide to go ahead and kill you even if you *don't* harass anyone," Black said. "I think maybe you *should* go home. Or back to the Borderlands."

"No!" Arlian flung his glass away; it shattered against the wall as Arlian got to his feet. "*This* is my home! Dragons destroyed my first home; Lord Dragon burned the next; *this* is my home now, and they won't take it away from me!" He grabbed Black by his shirt. "I will kill that bastard somehow! If he won't let me do it openly and honorably in a duel, I will find another way!"

"If he doesn't kill you first," Black said, locking his hands around Arlian's wrists. "It would seem to me that you ought to concern yourself with staying alive before you worry about killing someone else. I'd point out that even if you *do* somehow get Enziet, that leaves at least four others who'll want you dead—not even counting the Duke, once he's deprived of the man who tells him what to do."

Arlian released Black's shirt and stepped back. He looked thoughtfully at his friend. Staying alive was indeed a prerequisite for any planned revenge, and Lord Enziet was clearly a powerful man—Arlian remembered the casual way Lord Dragon had slashed Madam Ril's throat with a single sweep of his sword, how he had paid no attention to the bright blood that had spurted from the wound, how no one had dared to step forward and oppose him or hinder him in any way.

A man who could kill like that, a man who had all Manfort's resources at his disposal… Arlian knew that if Lord Dragon were to decide Arlian must die, then Arlian would die, unless he took drastic measures to protect himself.

Bodyguards, soldiers—he could afford them, but could he trust them? Did he want to live surrounded by them?

He could flee the city, as Enziet suggested, but that would be defeat; it would mean giving up any chance at vengeance, and on a much less exalted level it would mean losing a significant portion of his fortune, since he could not hope to sell the Old Palace readily. He had paid far more than he should have to buy it and restore it, in the interests of impressing and intriguing the city's nobility and advancing his planned revenge.

And it would mean leaving Sweet and Dove in Lord Dragon's clutches.

What other means of protection could he find, then? Enziet had already discovered the wards Thirif had placed and dismissed them as inadequate, and Arlian did not think he was boasting. From what he had seen and heard, Lord Dragon had never struck him as boastful. Was there other, stronger magic he could employ?

He could think of none. He was no magician. He would talk to Thirif, but he doubted that salvation lay in that direction. Both the Aritheians and his own people had told him that magic was deceitful and untrustworthy stuff, as likely to destroy you as preserve you.

The best solution would be somehow to change Enziet's mind, to convince him that killing Arlian would be a bad idea—and there might, Arlian realized, be a way to do that.

"You spoke with him," Arlian said. "Do you think he's a man of honor?"

"No," Black said promptly. "But he may *think* he is."

"Would he break an oath?"

"Probably. It would depend on the consequences."

The obvious next question, not spoken aloud, was whether he, Arlian, Lord Obsidian, would break an oath, given sufficient incentive.

He wasn't sure of the answer.

Perhaps he wouldn't need to. Perhaps he could find a way around it.

But regardless of the oath, the time had come to walk down the Street of the Black Spire to a black door with a red bar. It was too late now, but come morning, he would go there.

That was where he could find Lord Dragon and confront him without need for any invitation into anyone's home. And that was where he could at least make it expensive for Lord Dragon to kill him, make him an outcast and oath breaker if he carried out his threats. If Arlian joined the Dragon Society, Lord Dragon would be sworn not to kill him within Manfort's walls.

That Arlian would be required to swear in return not to kill Lord Dragon was a matter he would deal with later.

Chapter Thirty-Eight

Behind the Black Door

"Wait here," he told Black.

The other man nodded and leaned back comfortably against a gray sun-warmed stone wall.

Arlian stepped up to the black door. It was riveted iron, blackened, unpainted save for a broad red stripe across it. The handle was cast in the shape of a beast of some sort, but so worn that Arlian could not be sure just what it was meant to represent. It might have been a dragon.

The building around it was gray stone, like so much of Manfort, but larger than most. There were few windows, and those there were were tall and narrow and horizontally barred with black iron.

He reached out and touched the metal door; it was cold and slightly damp, rough with a thin layer of rust, and felt very solid. He pressed a palm against it, then made a fist and rapped.

The resulting sound was so faint he was sure it couldn't be heard inside the building. He looked around for a bell pull or knocker, but found none; he tried the latch, but it did not yield. Seeing no alternative, he shrugged, then pounded on the iron door with his fist.

This time it rang, a deep, dull sound.

Arlian waited, and a moment later the latch rattled and the door swung open, revealing a small, dim antechamber. A heavily built man dressed in dark green finery stepped around the door and looked Arlian in the eye.

"Yes?"

Arlian bowed. "I am Lord Obsidian," he said. "Lord Wither tells me that I might be welcome here."

The man in green stared at him, studying Arlian's face in a way that would ordinarily have been objectionably rude; Arlian stared back. For a moment the two men stood, eye to eye.

"You're *very* young for this place," the man in green said at last, "but the mark does seem to be there."

Arlian snorted. "Lord Wither had no doubt of it, and he didn't have to count my eyelashes."

And for that matter, Arlian had not needed to stare as long as he had to recognize the dragon's mark on the man in green—the doorkeeper was presumably a member, not merely a servant or slave. That explained his attire, which was far richer than any servant would wear.

"Lord Wither is an exceptional man," the doorkeeper said. "I don't have a tenth his experience. And I must be sure before I let you pass the inner door."

"Are you sure, then?"

"I believe I am. You wish to join the Dragon Society, then?"

Arlian took a deep breath. "I do," he said.

"If you enter, you *must* join," the man in green warned him. "Once inside you cannot change your mind; you join or you die."

Arlian hesitated. He had not expected that. Lord Wither had said it was easy, though, for one with the heart of the dragon.

"It's not too late to turn back," the doorkeeper said, in reassuring tones.

"No," Arlian said. "I've come this far. I'll join."

"You're certain?"

"Certain enough."

"Enter, then." The man stepped back, ushering Arlian inside.

"I have my steward…" Arlian began.

"No," the man in green said firmly. "Only members and applicants pass through this door."

Arlian shrugged; he waved a farewell to Black, then stepped inside. The doorkeeper closed the heavy iron door behind him, shutting out the sunlight.

For a moment he was in utter darkness and near-total silence, broken only by the scuffling of the doorkeeper, and he feared that his enemies had arranged a trap, that Lord Enziet had foreseen an attempt to join the Dragon Society and arranged to prevent it; then the inner door opened.

The room beyond was vast, rich and strange, and brightly lit—not by sunlight, though it was a cheerful cloudless morning outside, but by dozens of assorted candles, perched on tables and shelves or mounted in wall sconces and candelabra. Thick carpets covered the floor, and where not hidden by shelves or cabinetry the walls were polished wood panels; the high ceiling was coffered and gilded. Chairs, sofas, and tables, all heavy and elaborately carved, were so numerous as to make the chamber seem cluttered and mazelike, despite its size; perhaps a dozen of the chairs were occupied. Most of those occupants were busy with their own concerns and did not look up at the new arrival. The air smelled of dust and candle smoke.

The room's truly strange features were neither the people nor the furnishings nor the unnatural lighting, but the knick-knacks and curiosities that filled the cabinets and shelves and stood on several of the tables. Most of them seemed to have been collected and arranged without rhyme or reason. A row of human skulls adorned one ornate cabinet; a mummified hand lay upon a nearby table, ignored by the woman who sat at that table, reading an old leather-bound book. The complete skeleton of what appeared to be a large lizard, held together with bits of silver wire, stood on a shelf. Odd and unfamiliar devices of wood, wire, and glass glittered from various niches.

The majority of the trinkets, however, were carvings or sculptures—wood, stone, metal, and glass, crude or sophisticated, all scattered about with no order that Arlian could see. A rough-hewn wooden phallus lay beside a golden eagle; a nude woman in white marble stood with her back to a jade monster; a glass dragon loomed over an architect's model of a palace.

And dragons, not usually depicted in the Lands of Man, were the most common subject for the carvings and other illustrations—paintings here and there, a small tapestry, embroidered upholstery, etchings, bas relief, and more. The dragons varied from stylized symbols to statuettes so detailed and realistic that Arlian felt uneasy merely looking at them. He was not entirely free of the common superstition that representations of dragons were bad luck, and this place was full of them.

The doorkeeper picked up a brass bell from a shelf by the door and rang it. The people in the room looked up, startled.

"We have an applicant for membership in this august body," the man in green announced.

"Who is it, Door?" a dark-haired woman asked.

"Lord Obsidian," the doorkeeper replied.

One man, a thin white-bearded fellow, smothered an oath; another, a barrel-chested bald man in an eyepatch, leaped to his feet, knocking over his chair. He drew his sword and stood at guard, facing Arlian.

"Is Obsidian his true name, then?" another, older woman asked.

"Who cares what his true name is?" the man with the sword demanded. "He's the one who wants to kill me!"

"And *your* name, my lord?" Arlian called, his hand on the hilt of his own sword.

"Toribor," the swordsman said. "That's what Kuruvan told you, isn't it?"

"Then yes, I'm sworn to kill you," Arlian acknowledged. "Would you care to attend to it immediately?"

"Oh, stop it," the first woman said, obviously disgusted. "Belly, if he joins, he *can't* kill you—and you can't kill him. And if he *doesn't* join, well, he's already dead. Put your sword away."

Toribor frowned; his sword lowered, but he hesitated.

"A moment," Arlian said. "As I understand it, if I join your Society as I intend, I must indeed swear to make no attempt to kill any of my fellow members *inside Manfort's walls*—am I not correct in believing that nothing is said about what might happen *outside* those walls?"

"Oh, I like this," the second woman said. "You're sworn to kill Belly—that is, Toribor? But you're willing to swear not to harm him in the city?"

"Exactly," Arlian confirmed.

The woman laughed, and for a moment no one spoke.

"That's insane," someone muttered at last.

"Delightfully so," the woman agreed. "I think I may enjoy this. Yes, Door, by all means, let's have him join!"

Toribor's sword wavered.

"I came here intending to join this Society," Arlian said, "and that is still my intention. If Lord Toribor would prefer to fight me to settle the matter between us before I continue, I have no objection."

"If you won, you'd still need to join," a man said.

"Yes, of course," Arlian agreed.

"And if you lost, you'd die—even if Belly did not kill you cleanly," the man continued. "You can't leave this room alive unless you join, and you could not join were you too injured to continue a fight, nor would we provide medical attention. We would instead finish you off."

Toribor looked around. "You're all standing about discussing this as if it were nothing!" He focused on the thin white-haired man. "Nail, aren't *you* going to say anything?"

For a second or two the others, including the man addressed as Nail, simply stared at Toribor; then the older woman said, "You'd need to fight right here, you know—young Lord Obsidian can't leave this room except as a full member of the Dragon Society."

Arlian said nothing, but he couldn't help glancing around at the maze of furniture and the clutter everywhere. A duel in here would be absurd; he and Toribor would be stumbling over everything.

"Well, *I'm* not cleaning up the mess if they fight here," someone said.

"The survivor would clean it up," the woman replied.

"There'd be breakage," another woman said.

"Something valuable might be smashed," a man remarked.

"Oh, may the gods rot you all," Toribor said in disgust, sheathing his sword. "I won't fight him here. Can't we just kill him as an intruder?"

"He's eligible for membership," Door said.

"And *I* want him to join," the older woman said. "He amuses me."

"He deserves the same rights as any other newcomer," a man said.

"He *has* stated his intention of killing five of us," the man called Nail said in a whispery, unhealthy voice.

"What of it?" the woman demanded. "That's what the oath is for."

Toribor looked around and found no support for his suggestion. He growled, then said, "Fine, then. Go ahead and initiate him. If he swears the oath, that makes my life that much easier. But don't expect me to shake his hand and laugh with him over the wine." He turned away. "Nail? I'm going—are you going to stay and watch this travesty?"

"I believe I am," Nail replied.

"Then may the dead gods spit on you, too," Toribor said. He pushed past his neighbors' chairs and stamped out; Arlian stepped warily aside to let him past.

Toribor glowered at him but said nothing more, and did not touch him nor draw a weapon. A moment later he was gone, and Arlian turned back to face the others.

"Now," Door said, "welcome, Lord Obsidian, to the Dragon Society. You have come here as a stranger, but after today you will be a stranger to us no more—you will be one of us, or one of the dead. Which of those options we choose will be determined by how you answer questions put to you. You must answer truthfully and completely, to the best of your ability. Do you understand?"

"I think so," Arlian replied. "Am I permitted to ask questions, as well?"

"You are permitted to ask, but we are not required to answer," the older woman said.

"And many of your questions will probably be answered in the initiation process, in any case," a man said.

"Come in and take a seat," Door said. "This may take some time." He gestured for Arlian to step forward.

Arlian moved warily into the room and found an unoccupied chair. He seated himself, being careful to keep his sword and swordbreaker from becoming entangled in the legs of the furniture.

No one had asked him to remove them, nor had Toribor removed his; what's more, looking around, Arlian saw that most of the men in the room wore swords. Even one woman had a knife on her belt long enough that it might generously be considered a sword.

As he watched, the members of the Society came and seated themselves in a semicircle facing him, and Arlian looked them over.

He counted fourteen—eight men and six women. All were significantly older than he was, but only Nail was white-haired. All wore expensive clothes, supple leathers or fine fabrics, but not all wore them well—several garments were visibly frayed, faded, or wrinkled.

Many of the members were maimed or visibly damaged in some way—no fewer than three, counting the departed Toribor, wore patches over ruined eyes; one man lacked a right hand, and one older woman's left leg from the knee down had been replaced with a wooden peg, while several merely had masses of scar tissue one place or another.

All of them, despite their disfigurements, had strong faces and piercing eyes, and being the focus of their attention was unsettling. Arlian found himself remembering that long-ago moment in his parents' pantry when he had looked into the face of a dragon; these faces might be human, yet the resemblance was plain.

The experience was far less intense, though. "The heart of the dragon" was not a wholly inappropriate name, but these faces did not show the heart so much as a faint, pale reflection of a dragon's eyes.

"Who wants to begin?" Door asked, as he took a place for himself to Arlian's right.

"I will," the older woman said. She had taken a place at the center of the semicircle, directly in front of Arlian. Her hair was black streaked with gray, pulled back tightly into a long ponytail; her skin was rough and brown, but her face unscarred. Her eyes were dark and intense, but she was smiling. As she leaned forward over an oaken table she held an elaborately carved ebony cane in one hand, and a polished white bone in the other.

The cane made a connection for Arlian, and he realized that this woman was the one missing half a leg.

Door bowed. "Lady Rime," he said. "You may begin, then."

Chapter Thirty-Nine

Initiation Rites

The woman nodded an acknowledgment to Door, then met Arlian's gaze across the table. "You have been permitted in this room," she said, "because we believe you possess the trait we all share, the trait that sets us apart from the rest of humanity. Do you know what that trait is?"

"I assume you refer to what my steward calls 'the heart of the dragon,'" Arlian said.

"And can you tell us how you acquired this trait?"

"Not with certainty," Arlian said. "My steward believed some people are simply born with it. On the other hand, Lord Wither said that it came from drinking human blood mixed with dragon's venom."

"And have you drunk human blood mixed with dragon's venom?"

"I have."

"Tell us how that happened."

Arlian hesitated. He was not eager to share those memories with these strangers—and with Nail, in particular, who was presumably either one of the six lords himself or a close friend to some of them, and who might find a way to use any information about Arlian's origins against him.

But he had promised to answer fully. He drew a deep breath and began.

"Dragons destroyed my home village," he said. "At least three of them. They came nine years ago, during a long spell of dragon weather. I was in the family cellar, taking inventory to see how much we needed to add before winter, when they attacked. My grandfather was killed by a blast of venom that failed to ignite, and he fell down the cellar ladder onto me as he died; his blood, and the venom, spilled into my mouth as I lay stunned beneath his corpse."

Rime asked, "Have you any witnesses?"

"Of course not," Arlian said. "I was the only survivor."

"Have you any scars left by the experience?"

"Only on my heart, from my family's death," Arlian said. "The dragon's venom itself did not touch me."

"Then can you provide any proof, any evidence at all, that you are telling us the truth?"

"I will give you my word," Arlian said. "Beyond that, how can I? Lord Wither said he could see it in my face; if that isn't enough, what more can I do?"

Rime nodded. "Good enough. Those are my questions, as required; now let me give you the first instruction. The Dragon Society takes its name from our origins, of course—all of us have drunk blood and venom, and received the dragon's heart thereby—but also from its purpose. We are not questioning you merely for our amusement, but because the Society exists in part to study the ways of dragons, to learn everything about them that we can, so that someday, if we choose, we might destroy them, and free the world forever from their vile presence. It is because of this that we may ask you, over and over, to tell us every detail of your encounter with those dragons you say destroyed your village." That said, Rime used the bone in her right hand to prod the man next to her. "I've had my turn, then—you're next, Shatter."

The left side of Shatter's head was a hairless, shapeless ruin, a mass of scar tissue, but he still had both his eyes, and he stared intently at Arlian.

"What's your true name?" he asked.

"Arlian," Arlian said.

"And your village, that you say was destroyed?"

"Obsidian, on the Smoking Mountain." A few heads nodded at that; they had heard of the incident.

"You call yourself Obsidian—why?"

"After my home village."

"Have you used other names?"

"Yes."

"What were they?"

"I can't be sure I remember them all," Arlian warned. "I called myself Lanair a few times, I traveled with a caravan under the name Lord Ari, and there were several people who called me Triv for a time."

"Why did you use those other names?"

Arlian shrugged. "It was convenient to do so."

"Had you a reason to refrain from using your true name?"

Arlian frowned. "Yes. Need I explain it?"

"Does it concern dragons?"

"No."

"Then you need not." Shatter leaned back in his chair. "My true name is Illis," he said. "The custom of using false names is an old one, and most people don't remember its origins, but some of us here were among those who first instituted it, in the ancient days when the dragons ruled over us. This is your second instruction—that we gave false names to one another so that if we were caught by the dragon's human servants we could not reveal the true identities of our companions in the struggle for our freedom. Those servants are gone now, long dead, and so we all reveal our true names here, so that we know we can trust one another—but the dragons still live, beneath the earth, and we keep the custom alive in case they ever return, and we must once again organize ourselves to oppose them." He gestured to the next man in the circle.

Nail.

"Do you know who I am?" the old man asked, in that thin, harsh voice.

"No," Arlian said warily. "I heard you addressed as Nail."

"My name is Stiam; I believe you have announced your intention of killing me."

"I haven't exactly announced it," Arlian corrected him. "I revealed it to Lord Kuruvan."

"Whom you mortally wounded."

"I beat him in an honorable duel. I do not know whether his wound was mortal."

"And there were others you listed as your foes?"

"Yes. Lord Enziet…"

He paused as two or three of the members gasped at the name, but then collected himself and continued, "… Lord Toribor, Lord Drisheen, Lord Horim, and yourself."

Nail leaned forward across the table. "Are you aware that all of us save Kuruvan are members of the Dragon Society?"

"Uh… no. I knew some of you were, and particularly Lord Enziet; I was not aware all of you were."

"Then you did not join the Society to find us?"

"Not exactly."

"Why *are* you here, then?" Nail stared at him intently.

Arlian looked around the circle, partly to escape that basilisk stare and partly to judge the mood of the others, then sighed. He did not dare try to lie to these people. "I recently tried to arrange a meeting with Lord Enziet—I admit I did so to further my plans to destroy him, but I merely asked to meet with him. He not only refused this reasonable request, but threatened to kill me if I ever troubled him again. I have seen him kill a woman for failing in a commission he gave her, and I know he killed four others merely for being

317

inconvenient; I did not doubt that he meant what he said. I also believed, from a conversation with Lord Wither, that he is a member of this Society, and that no member of the Society may kill another within the city's walls, and furthermore that I, too, am eligible for membership. I therefore came to join to protect myself from Lord Enziet—while he is a ruthless man, I believe even he would hesitate to break your oath."

"Then you're abandoning your grudge against us, whatever it was?"

"Oh, by no means!" Arlian said. "I have every intention of eventually meeting each of you outside the city walls, when I can do so on even terms."

Nail stared at him for a moment longer, then blinked, straightened up, and said, "I'm not sure whether you're a coward or a fool or something else entirely. You come here fleeing Lord Enziet, yet you fought Kuruvan and offered to fight Toribor. You openly admit to my face that you still intend to kill me if you can."

"I do not believe I'm a coward," Arlian said. "Is not Enziet a powerful and dangerous man who does not hesitate to act as much from expedience as honor? Is he incapable of hiring assassins, or using dire sorcery? To defy him openly seems not courage, but foolhardiness. I will be glad to meet him, or any of the six of you, openly and fairly; I do not care to be waylaid on the street by Enziet's guards, and left dying in an alley somewhere."

"You accuse him of such treachery?" Nail leaned forward again.

"I certainly believe him capable of it. His warning to me did nothing to convince me otherwise."

"And you don't hesitate to say so?"

"I am required to answer all the questions put to me here honestly and completely, am I not?"

"You *are* a fool, then," Nail said, slumping back into his chair. "Or at any rate, a very young man who has not yet learned when to hide the truth in sarcasm, or pretty words, or circumlocutions. I think Belly—Lord Toribor—was hasty, and having you here in the Dragon Society may be a good thing after all—the day may come when we meet outside the walls, but I'm in no hurry, and the longer we have to study each other, the more entertaining that day may eventually be." He stared at Arlian for a moment, then sat up.

"My instruction," Nail said, "is this: The Dragon Society's purpose is in part as Rime stated it, to study our draconic foes; however, the original impetus was simply loneliness. You're still very young, and you haven't yet learned this, but we truly are a people apart from the rest of humanity. We are

318

all tainted, we are all marked, we are all blessed and cursed. We have the power to influence others to some extent, to bend them to our will—but that sets us apart; the shepherd, however beloved by his sheep, is not a part of the flock. We live long lives, and are free of disease; we can walk unscathed through streets heaped with plague-ridden corpses—and this means that those around us age and sicken and die as we watch, and we can do nothing to prevent it. When Wither and I first met, centuries ago, and recognized one another as kindred beings, it meant an end to decades of loneliness, for we now had each other as companions—no matter what his failings, a fellow shepherd must surely be better company than the finest of sheep. And when Enziet found us, and Rehirian, and Sharrae, we gathered them to us gladly, and the Dragon Society was begun. We created the oath, and had this place built for us, and bethought ourselves as to what goals we might set the Society. Others have found us over the centuries, and joined for their own reasons, just as you have—but in time, each one has come to see that whatever other purposes we may have, the simple need for the companionship of our peers is reason enough for the Society's existence. In time you, too, will come to prize all of us, and if we have indeed wronged you, you may find it in you to forgive us. When this initiation is done, let us speak, you and I, and see if we can work this out amicably, shall we?"

Arlian hesitated. "Maybe," he said.

Nail nodded. "I can wait—and so can you, child." He turned to the woman beside him. "Ask your questions, Flute."

Flute was tall and thin, with a long nose and a scar across the right side of her jaw; even unmarked, her face would have been far from beautiful.

"What do you know of sorcery?" she asked, in a cool, distant voice.

"Almost nothing," Arlian said. "I have crossed the Dreaming Mountains to Arithei and back, so I have seen magic in many forms, and I have spent a great deal of time with Aritheian magicians, but I have not studied the arts myself. I deal in magical devices, potions, and other such things, but I am only the merchant, not the manufacturer, and besides, I do not believe this magic is properly considered sorcery—I brought my goods and my magicians from Arithei, and they dismiss our northern sorcery as a different and lesser sort of magic than their own. Like the rest of you, I am a nobleman—I own a business, I do not dirty my own hands with the labor of running it. I am therefore familiar with what Aritheian magic can do, and what the wild magic beyond the Borderlands looks like, but that's all."

"You learned nothing from your village elders or the local sorcerer as a child?"

"Nothing at all. We had a sorcerer in Obsidian, but he and I rarely spoke, and even more rarely of his specialty. My grandfather told me a few tales, but nothing more."

"Do you know what I mean by sorcery, as opposed to mere magic?"

"No."

Flute sighed.

"Then my instruction, Obsidian, must be very rudimentary, for you haven't the knowledge for more, and it may sound like mere nonsense. Long ago, *very* long ago, the legends tell us, the dragons dwelt amid chaos and were displeased by it. They drove the chaos back and imposed order; they drove it southward, for the most part, out of the lands they had chosen for themselves. Or another version has it that the gods accomplished this, and the dragons later usurped their place, but the point is unchanged: Chaos is at the very root of magic—instability, change, and deception, these are the core of magic, and the dragons dispelled them from the Lands of Man.

"It may be that the dragons are themselves creatures of magic, and did not want competition. It may be that the dragons are somehow the *opposite* of magic. We don't know. We do know that in the lands where the dragons once ruled, the lands that are now the Lands of Man, magic is a dry well, while south of the Borderlands it's a flood. Perhaps the dragons drank the magic; perhaps they swept it away; perhaps they *are* this land's magic. Whatever the reasons, beyond the Lands of Man magic runs rampant, and anyone with a little skill can learn to manipulate it—but no one can truly *control* it, for it's too powerful, too wild.

"And here, in Manfort, magic is so weak, so feeble, that it must either be brought in from outside, as you are doing, in which case it's strong and easy but flawed and fades over time, or it must be coaxed and teased out in tiny threads, and the skills to do this are so arcane, so difficult, that it takes a lifetime to master them.

"These skills, the ability to use the thin traces of magic native to this land, are sorcery; what the Aritheians do is not, but is mere crude thaumaturgy. Sorcery is subtle and strong and lasting; thaumaturgy is bright and impressive, but unstable and untrustworthy.

"And because sorcery takes so long to master—well, who do you suppose is best suited to study it?" She waved at the gathering around her. "*We* are, we who can devote centuries to the task. Members of the Dragon Society are expected to learn at least the rudiments of sorcery—though there's no need to hurry. You'll have all the time you need."

"If Enziet doesn't kill you," a woman further around the circle muttered.

"My lady, are you implying that our own Enziet might break his oath?" Door asked.

"No," the woman replied, "I'm suggesting that someday young Arlian may set foot outside Manfort's gate."

Door could hardly argue with that, and it was not his time to speak; he subsided, and the man to Flute's right asked, "Is it my turn? I don't recall anything else essential, so I'll ask what I'm sure we're all wondering—why in the world are you determined to kill Enziet and the others in the first place?"

Arlian had expected this. "He kidnapped me and sold me into slavery when I was a child," he said. "And he and the others killed four women I cared for."

"*Did* he! Well, then, you must tell us *all* about it!"

Arlian sighed. He collected his wits for a moment, then began, "I was in the cellars with my grandfather when we heard screaming…"

Chapter Forty

Contemplating Eternity

The iron door swung open and Arlian stepped out into the street. He was not surprised to find it dark; after all, he had just come from a candlelit chamber where he had lost all track of time.

He *was* somewhat surprised to find Black still waiting for him, and said so.

"This street's as good a place as any to wait," Black replied. "I had a chance to chat with Lord Toribor, for example."

"Did he say anything of interest?"

"He thinks you're completely mad; is that of interest?"

Arlian grimaced. "It seems to be the consensus." He clapped Black on the shoulder. "Come on; let's go home."

The two men set out toward the Old Palace, making their way through the badly-lit cobblestone streets; the moonlight was sufficient to see them through those areas where no torches, lanterns, or illuminated windows served.

"If you'd brought a lantern…" Arlian began as he stubbed his toe on an uneven cobble.

"If I'd brought a lantern I'd have been demonstrating a truly remarkable prescience," Black retorted. "We came here at midmorning, remember? I hadn't expected to stay all day. Had you not emerged soon I might well have given up and gone home."

"As I thought you would have," Arlian replied penitently. "Thank you for waiting, and forgive my unreasonableness."

Black waved that away.

They walked on for a moment longer, and Arlian glanced sideways at his companion.

Why *had* Black stayed? What had Arlian done to inspire such loyalty? He wasn't paying Black for this sort of attention.

But Black was his friend—whether because of the dragon's heart Arlian possessed, or because of some more natural human magic. That was a gift Arlian appreciated, but sometimes, he thought, not enough.

He thought over what he had heard in the Dragon Society's hall. The

323

questioning and instruction had dragged on and on; new members, beyond the original fourteen, had wandered in now and then, and had joined in, sometimes repeating things that had already been said—Arlian had not kept count, but thought he had met and spoken to perhaps a score in all. He was, he had been told, the forty-third living member whose current whereabouts were known.

The eight skulls on that one shelf were some of the deceased members, all eight of whom had died violently at various points over the past seven centuries, in duels, accidents, assassinations, or other mishaps; a few others had died in such fashion that their bones were not recovered. The whereabouts of some members were not known, nor whether they were living or dead.

There was no requirement that every member speak to him; only that those present at the time each question him, and each offer some instruction in exchange. They had done that.

Arlian had told them every detail he could remember of the destruction of Obsidian on the Smoking Mountain; he had admitted to being an escaped slave, and had described something of his stay in Deep Delving. That had not caught anyone's fancy very strongly, though; the passage through the Dreaming Mountains, and his visit to Arithei, had gotten much more attention. He had also admitted his residence in Westguard.

And in exchange he had heard a great deal of the Dragon Society's history, how it had been part of the resistance against the dragons in the final days of their rule, how its members had been among Manfort's rulers, how the traditions of secret societies, false names, and noble privilege had been established or preserved by the Dragon Society for the benefit of its members, the better to hide their strangeness from ordinary mortals.

He knew now that the governance of Manfort was manipulated by the Society as a whole, most directly by Lord Enziet and the other advisers such as Rime and Drisheen but also by other means, for their own ends. The Duke of Manfort was not a member, might not even be aware the group existed, but most of his advisers belonged to the Society and were as interested in its welfare as that of the city as a whole.

Chief among those advisers was Lord Enziet, of course—the man Arlian had known for years as Lord Dragon. Arlian had learned a little about Enziet, but not much; he had made no attempt to press, since the others were clearly reluctant to gossip about one of their senior members.

Lady Rime had been present, but had said nothing of her own work with the Duke, and Arlian had no special interest in her. Lord Drisheen, another adviser who was also on the list of six lords Arlian meant to destroy, had not appeared, and Arlian had learned no more about him than about Enziet.

Arlian had heard a great deal about what the blood-and-venom elixir actually did, though. He knew now that he would probably never sire children—no member of the Dragon Society had ever produced offspring after joining, although a few had descendants from before their draconic encounters, and it was assumed that this lack was due to induced sterility, since there had been no shortage of opportunities for procreation.

He knew that he need never fear disease or infection—that he had had even a mild case of fever in the mines startled the others, and he was assured that that could only have happened in his very earliest years after drinking the elixir. He had been assured that he could expect every wound that did not actually kill him to heal quickly and cleanly—only the injuries inflicted by dragons left scars.

And he knew that he could expect to live for centuries—but probably not forever. The very oldest of those who had drunk the elixir were gone, and presumed dead—although each had left Manfort willingly, under his or her own power, they had never returned. Wither, Nail, and Enziet were the three oldest survivors, each approaching a thousand years of age.

Wither had turned up briefly at one point, and had questioned Arlian viciously about whether he really knew where venom might be obtained.

Enziet had not come, which was probably just as well—but it was also disappointing. It would have been satisfying for Arlian finally to see him face to face again, after all these years, and to see his reaction upon learning who Obsidian was, and to knowing for certain that he was bound by the same oath Arlian had sworn.

"By whatever gods may hear, be they living or dead," he had recited when the questioning was done, "I swear that I shall abide by the covenant of this society, to share whatever knowledge I may have of our common foes, the dragons. I swear to make no attempt to do mortal harm to any other member while we are within the walls of this city, nor to aid or abet another in any effort to do such harm to any member."

That oath might prove inconvenient—but at the same time, it had given Arlian an opportunity to speak freely with Nail, and that had been worthwhile.

Nail claimed that he had taken a share in the House of Carnal Society at Enziet's urging, not on his own impulse; further, he was willing to set Lily and Musk free in Arlian's care. "I tired of them long since," he had said. "They've been working in my kitchens."

He had taken an interest in Arlian's own humanitarian impulses and views on justice, but he hardly subscribed to them. "You'll outgrow that, I fear," he had said.

Nail had seemed quite certain that Arlian would outgrow a great many things, that in time he would become more like Nail himself, more like most of the others—cool, cynical, unconcerned with the lives of people he would outlive anyway.

Arlian hoped he was wrong, and noted Toribor's anger and Wither's devotion to his mistress Marasa as signs that neither great age nor dragon venom need quench *all* passions.

But a general detachment from the rest of humanity seemed to have affected all the members, and Arlian wondered whether in time he too would grow cold.

He studied Black as they walked.

Would he eventually come to think of Black as his inferior, rather than his equal? As a thing to be used, rather than an adviser and companion?

He could not easily imagine it—but then he remembered Lord Dragon's face and voice telling him that he was nothing but plunder to be sold, remembered Lord Dragon's sword cutting Madam Ril's throat. A natural man could not be so cold.

He hoped that he would never become a creature like that. He thought he would almost prefer to die in one of the duels he intended to fight outside the city walls.

But no one in the Dragon Society had seemed the least bit surprised or dismayed by his explanation of why he had sworn vengeance against Lord Dragon; they had all accepted Enziet's actions as normal, if unpleasant.

"He didn't know you'd drunk the venom," Nail had said.

"And if he had, would it have made any difference?" Rime had asked, and the consensus was no, not for Enziet; he'd have done the same in any case.

So Enziet was probably the worst, but all of them had something of the same cold detachment and ruthlessness. And presumably, in time, so would Arlian—if he didn't already. He remembered how he had insisted on fighting Kuruvan…

But he also remembered how he had felt when the duel was almost upon him, how he'd felt sick and scared and doubting; that had not been anything

326

he would expect from a member of the Society.

Maybe he was different. Maybe he would always be different. And maybe, if he *did* start to turn cold, he would notice the change and do something about it.

But Black would probably be long dead by then.

Black would be dead, and he would be living on, untouched by age. Maybe *that* was what turned the Society's members cold—not the venom, but watching their friends and family age and fade and die.

Then a thought struck him, and he smiled to himself.

He was being absurd. He wasn't going to live long enough to turn cold. He had sworn an oath, after all; once he had disposed of Lord Enziet and the others he would hunt down the dragons themselves, and try to kill them.

He wouldn't need to commit suicide to keep from turning heartless; the dragons would undoubtedly kill him if Lord Enziet didn't.

He needed to find some way to get Enziet and the others outside the city, and away from their friends and guards, where he could meet them on even terms.

With that, his thoughts began to slip back into older, more familiar paths, and concerns about his own nature faded away.

He still had his vengeance to carry out. He had not yet met Lord Enziet, Lord Drisheen, or Lord Horim at the Dragon Society hall; Lord Nail was an old man who didn't seem to be inclined to cause trouble, and Lord Toribor was a hothead who could probably be lured out easily.

But there was no need to hurry, was there? He would have centuries in which to realize his plans.

Centuries. That was a hard concept to accept.

He was back to those new ideas, the new information about the Dragon Society and his own strange circumstances.

There were still things he didn't know, though. No one had explained how Lord Enziet had known that a village on the Smoking Mountain was going to be destroyed, or why a man as rich and powerful as Enziet would bother looting a ruined village or investing in a brothel. He had told them all what had happened to Obsidian, but no one had said anything about that.

At some point he would have to ask someone about those points. They might be important. He would go back to the Society's hall tomorrow or the day after and see if anyone there could tell him.

They were at the gate of the Old Palace now, and there were more immediate matters to attend to.

"Have you eaten anything?" he asked Black.

"No. Have you?"

"Not really. So we'll go to the kitchens—it's too late for a proper meal."

Black nodded, and the mention of the kitchens reminded Arlian of something.

"By the way," he said, "we'll want to have some rooms prepared—Lord Nail...that is, Lord Stiam will be turning two more women, Musk and Lily, over to our care."

Black glanced at him, startled. "That's good," he said. "How did you manage that?"

Arlian thought for a minute, then said, "I'm not entirely sure."

Then the doorkeeper opened the great front door, and they stepped into the familiar foyer of the Old Palace.

* * *

The following day found Arlian and Nail chatting again, as they had after Arlian's initiation, but this time in the Old Palace rather than the Society Hall.

"Why did the six of you establish the House of Carnal Society in the first place?" Arlian asked, as he poured wine. Musk and Lily were getting comfortably settled in their new home, none the worse for their two-year stay in Nail's mansion; Nail had overseen their delivery personally, and at Arlian's invitation had stayed for a drink. The two men were comfortably settled on the blue silk couches in the small salon, sharing a bottle of good red wine from Kan Parakor, in the western hills. "Surely you could have found better investments."

Lord Nail pursed his lips thoughtfully. "I don't know that we could have," he said. "Oh, financially, perhaps—though in fact it was quite profitable—but there were other uses."

Arlian's own lips tightened. "You took your own pleasures there, I suppose?"

Nail snorted. "I? No, I did not. Kuruvan did, certainly, and I believe Drisheen as well, and perhaps Toribor or Horim on occasion, but not I, nor Enziet."

"Then what uses do you refer to?"

"Political uses, my boy," Nail explained. "There are those in Manfort we find it expedient to control, one way or another, and inviting them to

Westguard, as one hot-blooded nobleman to another, provided a means to accomplish that."

"Ah…" Arlian hesitated, but then asked his question bluntly—despite calling Arlian a young fool for his honesty, Nail did not seem to believe in wasting time with euphemism or indirection himself. "Bribery or blackmail?"

"Both," Nail said. "Sometimes at the same time, men being the odd creatures they are. Intimidation, as well. And other things—some men, after such an experience, find themselves saying things they would not ordinarily reveal."

Arlian could hardly doubt that, given what Rose had told him about Lord Kuruvan—whose death had been reported that morning; his wounds had indeed been mortal.

And Arlian had killed him—an idea that was uncomfortable, frightening and satisfying at the same time. He wasn't the first man Arlian had killed; that had been that bandit on the southern slopes of the Desolation. Kuruvan, however, was the first Arlian had deliberately hunted down, fought, and slain.

He had surely deserved it, despite what Hasty said; the image of Rose lying dead was always lurking in the back of Arlian's thoughts, troubling his dreams. Still, it was odd to know that he was a killer himself, even a justified one.

It was also odd to be sitting here calmly drinking wine with another of the men responsible for Rose's death, both of them knowing that Arlian had not forgiven the crime and still meant to someday avenge it.

"We put the House in Westguard for several reasons," Nail said. "One was so that our guests would not be seen by their neighbors or family; another was so that there would be time, on the ride back to Manfort, for loosened lips to spill secrets." He sighed. "And of course, that's why it had to be destroyed," he said. "We had too many people who could not tolerate the thought that they might be spied on there, or might have *been* spied on there. When we found out you'd been hiding there… well, it was safest to destroy it."

"Was it necessary to kill four of the women, though?"

"No, I suppose not," Nail said. "One gets out of the habit of thinking of slaves as human, though—or at least, I have. And their lives are so short and pointless anyway that…well, it doesn't seem to matter if they die."

"It matters to *them,*" Arlian said. "Because they have so little, you feel free to take what they have? There's no justice in that."

"No, there isn't, is there?" Nail gazed into Arlian's eyes. "You *do* have the dragon's heart, but you haven't yet lost your own. I'm not sure I can say the same anymore."

Arlian shifted uncomfortably.

"You still want to kill me, to punish me for what I did to those girls, don't you?" Nail asked quietly.

"You saw them, being carried in here," Arlian said angrily. "None of them will ever walk again. And I don't suppose you saw the others lying dead in the smoke, but I did—lying there with their throats cut as the flames spread…" He shuddered. "You did that. It's only right that you pay for it."

"I suppose it is," Nail mused, his face turning aside for a moment. He sipped his wine thoughtfully. "I suppose it is, at that." He looked at Arlian again. "You'll understand, though, that I'm in no hurry to do so. I've lived well over nine hundred years now, and while I do grow weary, I am not eager to end it. I've seen little justice in all those years; the good perish and the evil thrive—sometimes, at any rate. Other times the evil die and the good live, and throughout it all most people are neither good nor evil, but merely human." He put down his glass. "I'll tell you what, Lord Obsidian—I will meet you outside the gate, on even terms, my sword against yours, for a fair fight to the death, once you have dealt with my four surviving partners. I sincerely feel that my fault in this is less than theirs, for I was brought in out of friendship for Enziet, Drisheen, and Horim, not because I had any great interest in the benefits that might accrue. I have all the wealth I need, and little interest in power, but I do try to oblige my friends. You've seen I didn't harm the two women I took; I doubt my partners can all say the same. And though I can't prove it, I voted against the destruction of the brothel and the murder of those four. So I will meet you, but only when you have first met the others."

"And if I die fighting one of them, then you'll go unpunished," Arlian said.

Nail smiled and shrugged. "You understand me too well," he said. He picked up his glass again. "Life is not fair, my young friend, and justice is not always done." Then he raised the glass in salute and finished the wine in a gulp.

He stirred, evidently about to rise; he had clearly meant that as his parting shot. Arlian, however, had more to say.

"And will you help me coax the others out of the city?" he asked.

Nail hesitated. Then he shook his head.

"No," he said. "I will not. Whatever love I may have for justice, I have more for my friends and myself. I do not deny we did wrong, but I find myself able to forgive and pardon our crimes. That you do not is certainly understandable, but I trust this is one failing on my part you will find equally understandable."

"Of course," Arlian said. He stood as Nail stood, and watched as the old man departed. Then he turned to find Black standing in the other doorway, observing him.

"You're getting to like the old bastard, aren't you?" Black asked.

"After a fashion," Arlian said.

"But you still plan to kill him?"

"I don't know," Arlian admitted. "I think so."

"Those two women, Musk and Lily, have nothing against him," Black said. "After the first month they barely saw him."

Arlian shrugged. "That's not the point," he said.

"Oh? You're not in this for the sake of rescuing pretty women from horrible fates?"

"Not really," Arlian said. "I certainly don't want any innocents to suffer horrible fates, but that's not what I'm after. I'm trying to see that evil does not go unpunished, so that the world might be that much better to live in."

"And a man like Lord Nail does such evil that you're sure the world would be a better place without him?"

Arlian hesitated.

"I don't know," he said. "I'm not a god, able to see past and future and look into people's hearts. I only know that Lord Nail and the others did do wrong. They committed a hideous crime, and that crime calls out for vengeance, and I am the only one who might avenge it." He shrugged. "Perhaps the gods who still live, if there truly are any and they see us at all, will intervene, and make sure that justice prevails; perhaps they'll show me a vision, or see that I learn something that will make me forgive my enemies. Perhaps the workings of Fate will ensure that I never touch a hair on Nail's head. Left to my own devices, though, I intend to continue as I have. It's not as if I'm murdering any of them in their beds, as they murdered Rose and Silk; we fought an honest duel, and Kuruvan might have killed me as readily as I killed him."

"You have the dragon's heart, as Kuruvan did not."

"And who else among my foes is so bereft?"

"A good point," Black acknowledged. "So you'll trust to Fate, then, to see that you aren't butchered like a hog when you do coax Horim or Toribor outside the walls? These men have far more experience than you, after all."

"As you say," Arlian said. "I'll trust in Fate, the gods, your training, and my own skills."

"I don't particularly like that idea," Black said. "I've never found the gods to be much use."

Arlian shrugged.

He was unsure whether there were gods guiding his destiny, or whether he was part of some fate working itself out free of divine meddling, or whether the only agents working upon him were natural and mortal, but he could not help but see, in his escape from the destruction of his village, his escape from the mines of Deep Delving, the vast fortune that had fallen into his possession, and his admission to the society of near-immortals, signs that his life had a purpose beyond mere survival. It was plain to him that he was meant to pursue justice and revenge, that he had been spared and given power so that he might right the wrongs done to those around him. If he died in that pursuit, then at the very least he had lived longer than the rest of his townspeople, had tasted freedom before he died, had set an example in Lord Obsidian's refusal to traffic in slaves, and had achieved at least a partial vengeance for Rose and Silk and the others.

He would much *prefer* to live, of course, and to enjoy what Fate had given him, but if it meant simply accepting the evils done around him—no, he could not do that.

"I don't suppose you would be willing to ambush or assassinate the rest of them," Black said.

Arlian shook his head. "I won't stoop to that," he said.

"The odds are that you'll die before you've dealt with all of them," Black pointed out.

Arlian shrugged again.

"I don't want to inherit anything from you," Black said.

Arlian looked at him thoughtfully. Just yesterday he had been contemplating what had seemed the near certainty that he would outlive Black by centuries, yet here he was, facing the prospect of throwing away all those years.

"I do intend to fight them all, and kill them all," he said slowly, "but there's no great hurry." He remembered the duel with Kuruvan, how he had trembled at the outset, how the swordplay had degenerated into clumsy hacking and stabbing. "Would it comfort you if I asked you to continue my training with the blade, and put off any attempt to lure my opponents out of the city in the next few days?"

"It certainly wouldn't distress me," Black said.

"Well, then," Arlian said, "let it be so."

Chapter Forty-One

Challenges Made

Arlian was seated comfortably in a corner of the Dragon Society's main hall, in a velvet-upholstered chair with each arm carved into a dragon's head, his feet under a round oaken table. Diagonally across from him sat Lady Rime, and the two of them chatted amiably.

"Are any of the members married?" Arlian asked. "I haven't heard anyone but Lord Wither mention spouses."

"Lord Spider and Lady Shard are married," Rime replied, leaning back in her chair, "though I don't know how much longer it will last. They've been together more than a hundred years, and few marriages survive beyond that."

Arlian had met Lady Shard, but had heard no previous mention of Lord Spider. He had met most of the members now—his own initiation had taken place some four days ago, and he had come here every evening, when Black declared the fading light inadequate for further swordplay.

He still had not encountered Lord Horim, Lord Drisheen, or Lord Enziet, however, save for one brief meeting with Lord Drisheen, a chance encounter on the Street of the Black Spire just outside the Society's door as Drisheen left and Arlian arrived. Arlian had recognized Drisheen's perfume first, and then his face, but by then Drisheen was around the corner, and Arlian had thought better of pursuit.

"Lord Spider's true name isn't Horim, is it? Or Enziet, or Drisheen?" Arlian asked. He did not like the idea of killing a married man.

Rime shook her head. "No, no. Horim calls himself Lord Iron, and Enziet and Drisheen we simply call Enziet and Drisheen. Enziet has used a dozen other names over the years and we can't be bothered to remember them, while Drisheen has never used any name but his own. Our Lord Spider's true name is Dvios, and Lady Shard's is Alahi."

"Is Lord Iron married, then?"

"No. Nor is Enziet. Nor Drisheen, nor Nail, nor Belly. You needn't worry about leaving any grieving widows."

"That's just as well," Arlian said. Then he noticed the curious half smile on Rime's face, and the way she was watching him as she toyed with the bone she always carried. "Do I amuse you?" he asked.

"In fact, you do, dear Obsidian," Rime said. "You can't seem to make up your mind whether you're a warmhearted fool or a cold-blooded killer."

"I would prefer to be neither a fool nor cold-blooded," Arlian said.

"A warmhearted killer is something of an oddity, though, wouldn't you say?"

"And are we not all oddities here?" Arlian asked, taking in the entirety of the hall with a sweep of his hand. "For example, you say that none of the men I'm sworn to kill are married—surely, that's rather odd, that *none* of a group of five men would have a wife?"

"For ordinary men it might be odd," Rime agreed, "but you're speaking of five dragonhearts, and furthermore, five who once owned a brothel. Would a man with a wife at home invest in such an enterprise?"

"Why not?" Arlian asked. "Do you think it would offend a wife's sensibilities?"

"It very well might."

"Did it offend yours?"

"In fact, it did."

"Yet you did nothing to stop it."

"What could I do? They broke no laws, defied no ducal edict."

"Yet you thought it wrong?"

Rime sighed. "No. I thought it, at worst, inappropriate. It was none of my business, and unlike yourself, I do not generally choose to meddle dangerously in matters that do not concern me."

Arlian frowned and leaned back, unsatisfied; for a moment the two sat silently, Arlian motionless, Rime holding her bone in one hand and running the fingers of the other along its polished length.

"You call them dragonhearts?" Arlian asked after a moment.

"It's a useful term," Rime said. "And I call us all dragonhearts, my lord—you and myself as well as the rest."

Arlian nodded. "Of course," he said. "And are Spider and Shard the only married dragonhearts, then?"

"Oh, I believe three or four have mortal partners," Rime said. "I couldn't say which; I don't keep track."

"Because they die," Arlian said. He didn't need to make it a question.

"Yes, because they die. I have lived four hundred years, Obsidian; I can't be bothered to remember details that may not last a score of years."

"And have you never married?"

Rime's fingers stopped their stroking, and the smooth white bone dropped to her lap.

"I was married," she said. "I had a husband and four children when the miners from our village disturbed a dragon's rest. I fell into our well, bleeding and aflame, as I fled from its anger, and the water put out the fire and hid me. My husband was not as clumsy as I."

"I'm sorry," Arlian said, ashamed that his question had caused her pain.

"The well was poisoned after that," she said. "Venom, or the dragon's foul breath, had tainted the water. I tasted it, and knew it was unfit to drink, so when I grew thirsty I sucked the blood from a gash on my hand." She held out her left hand, and Arlian saw a faint white scar across the palm. "I'd cut myself on the stone as I fell in, you see, and venom must have gotten into it somehow, though I didn't know that for certain until years after."

"And your leg—was that from the bad water?"

"That?" She glanced down at the wooden peg below her left knee, then lifted the bone in her hand and studied it for a second. Arlian, who had heretofore considered the bone merely a minor eccentricity, like Black's insistence on wearing black, suddenly realized that what she held was a human shinbone.

And he had little doubt as to whose.

"No, no," she said, lowering the bone. "That happened years later, when I was snowbound in the Sawtooth Mountains. I was more or less intact when I climbed from the well and found what was left of my family."

"I'm sorry for your loss," Arlian said.

Rime shrugged. "It was a long time ago."

"And you've never remarried?"

"Why bother?" she asked bitterly. "I can't have any more children; what do I need with a husband? I've built a fortune simply by living long enough to save and invest, so I don't need a man's money. Companionship?" She snorted. "Look around; do you see any of these men who would make a decent husband, knowing that we'll both live for centuries? Oh, an affair or two, certainly, but a marriage? And as for anyone *other* than our fellow dragonhearts, I don't have any interest in growing to love a man, and then watching him age and die while I can do nothing to prevent it."

"Oh," Arlian said.

"And that's why so few of us are married, Obsidian, because the dragons have made us cold-hearted, self-obsessed, and sterile."

"But are you all? You still speak with passion," he protested. "Wither seems devoted to his Marasa, and Nail seems eager to befriend others."

337

"They're struggling against the inevitable," Rime said. "As I am. The longer we live, the colder we become—like Enziet, who is, I believe, oldest of us all. Wither and Nail are old, too, but it may be that they've lasted as long as they have because of their passions—and Nail, at least, seems to me to be acting more from wistful memory than genuine warmth."

"But why? Is it just from weariness, from seeing so much suffering and death over the years?"

She shook her head. "I don't believe it's long life alone that's responsible," she said. "Remember, though, how we became as we are. We have all tasted blood and drunk venom, and whether it pleases us to admit it or not—and most often, it does not—each of us has a bit of dragon in her heart. The human part of us cannot live forever; while our bodies survive, our hearts, with time, grow more like dragons, cold and hard and ruthless, taking as much pleasure from others' pain as from any more natural delights."

Arlian frowned. "Do you think, then, that the venom has such an effect?"

Rime laughed at that. "My dear foolish boy, *look* at us! We cannot bear children—or sire them, in your case. We age at only the tiniest fraction of the normal rate. Our very blood is poisonous—surely Wither told you that? Now, does that sound more like men and women, or like dragons?"

"Like…" Arlian began, but before he could speak a second word he was interrupted by a bellow.

"You!" a deep voice shouted, a horribly familiar voice. "Arlian! Get up!"

Startled, Arlian turned to see three men standing by the door, all still wearing hats and cloaks—and all with their cloaks flung back and their hands on the hilts of their swords. On the left was a short, stocky man he didn't recognize, clad in brown, with a curious brass sheath on one arm; on the right was Lord Toribor, clad in green and silver—even his eye patch was green; and in the center was Lord Dragon, resplendent in black and gold. His feather-trimmed hat appeared to be the same one Arlian had seen him wear atop the Smoking Mountain, so long ago, and his thin, scarred face was likewise unchanged.

Arlian pushed away from the table and rose. He felt himself starting to tremble at finding himself thus facing his elusive adversary, and fought it down. He looked at that grim face and remembered the smoking ruins of Obsidian, the bright blood spilling from Madam Ril's throat, Rose's dead eyes as she lay across her bed amid the flames.

"Lord Enziet," he said, his voice steady. "We meet again."

"Indeed," Enziet replied. "And I am not pleased about it. Why are you here?"

"I am a member in good standing of this society," Arlian replied.

"Why are you in *Manfort?*" Enziet demanded.

"Why would I not be? My business is here; my friends are here; and my sworn enemies are here."

"I advised you to leave," Lord Dragon said. "I am not accustomed to having my advice ignored."

"I am not the Duke, nor any other of the fools you bully," Arlian retorted. "I do as I see fit."

"You are an annoyance," Enziet replied, "and I do not intend to tolerate your presence here."

"You are sworn to do me no mortal harm, I believe," Arlian said. "How, then, do you intend to remove me?"

"You spoke of your friends and your business," Enziet said. "I am not sworn to leave *them* alive. I believe I have lives in my own possession you would prefer not to see snuffed out."

Arlian had managed to keep himself under control up to this point, but now his veneer of control cracked. "You would make these base threats against innocents?"

"There *are* no innocents," Enziet said. "We are all creatures of filth and disgrace, foul and stinking, festering in our cramped little lives and pretending we have some value. I am not deceived, though you may be; we are no more than beasts, and those who have not drunk the blood and venom are even less. Removing a few short-lived nuisances a decade or two before their inevitable demise would occur in any case does not trouble my conscience in the least, and if it will rid me of *you,* then yes, I will do it."

Sincerely shocked, Arlian asked, "Have you no honor?"

"I abide by my vows," Enziet replied. "I recognize no other obligations."

"And if I heed these threats, what are you asking of me?"

"That you leave this city forthwith. You may take your time in removing your household, but I want *you* outside the walls by sunset."

"And if I refuse?"

"One of your precious 'innocents' will die for each night you linger."

"You would not balk at such murders? You fear no retribution?"

"You forget who I am, Arlian."

"No," Arlian replied, "I will never forget that. You are a monster in human form, an aberration that must be removed from the face of the earth."

"I am chief adviser to the Duke of Manfort, and the eldest of the Dragon

Society. I do as I please, and none dares defy me."

"*I* dare," Arlian retorted. "And if you harm those I care for, I will return the favor—starting with the Duke himself."

He heard audible gasps at that, and even Lord Dragon seemed taken aback.

He had answered without really thinking, simply making the first counter-threat that occurred to him. Having said it he could hardly back down, but he had to struggle to hide his own doubts. The Duke was a harmless old fool; killing him would be wrong. His greatest evil probably lay simply in listening to Enziet, and that was mere weakness, hardly inexcusable in a mortal confronted with the dragon's heart.

And the Duke would certainly have guards on all sides—but there were ways.

If his threat was to do any good at all, Enziet had to believe it.

"I have magic at my command," Arlian continued. "Not your fine northern sorcery, but wild southern magic from Arithei and the Dreaming Mountains. I have other weapons as well. Be assured, I can destroy the Duke if I choose. And while you might well ingratiate yourself with his heir, do you really want the inconvenience of doing so? And how would you explain that you cannot order my execution for the crime?"

"You would kill both the Duke and myself in your pursuit of this chimerical justice of yours?" Enziet asked.

"I would," Arlian replied instantly.

"You would throw all the Lands of Man into confusion simply to satisfy your own lust for vengeance?"

"I would," Arlian repeated.

Lord Dragon smiled bitterly. "So you care no more for order and authority than I do for innocence and honor."

"Precisely."

"There's a legend that if the Duke's line dies out, the dragons will return," Enziet remarked.

"There are many legends," Arlian said. "I hope that one is untrue, but true or not, it doesn't matter."

"You would risk overthrowing humanity's freedom, then?"

"I have no intention of killing the Duke unless *you* carry out your own vile threats," Arlian retorted. "If this legend is genuine, then whatever comes of it will be as much your responsibility as my own."

"Charming," Enziet said through clenched teeth. "So you propose to continue our stalemate, then?"

"By no means," Arlian said. "I would be pleased to meet you outside the walls in a duel, fought fairly and to the death. I would need your word that there will be no treachery, that none of your hirelings will strike me down from hiding..."

"*I'll* fight you," the man in brown interrupted. "An even match, as you say. Better that than listening to you rave!"

"Iron, remember," Toribor said. "He killed Kuruvan."

"Kuruvan was a mortal," the man in brown answered, his eyes locked on Arlian. "He's a dragonheart—but just a boy, for all that."

Toribor glanced at Enziet, who stroked his chin thoughtfully.

"That might well solve the entire problem," Enziet said. "If you want to, Iron, I am not inclined to object."

"Lord Iron, are you?" Arlian asked. "Also known as Horim?"

"I am," Horim replied. "Do you dare face me, child?"

Arlian smiled.

"I would be delighted," he said.

Chapter Forty-Two

Swords Beyond the Gate

T he city gates stood open, and Arlian marched steadily down the cobbles toward them. Horim walked in parallel several yards to Arlian's left. The normal street traffic parted before them, and their assorted companions trailed behind.

Black broke from the little crowd, trotted up behind Arlian, and whispered, "You know this is a trap, don't you?"

Arlian glanced over his shoulder at Lord Enziet and the rest of the party, coming along to observe.

"No, not them," Black said. "It's Lord Iron. How do you think he got that name? He's killed at least a score of men, and probably a few women as well. He's one of the deadliest swordsmen in the Lands of Man. I suspect Lord Enziet set this whole thing up to get rid of you."

Arlian glanced at Enziet again, then at Horim. He saw no sign of fear or even nervousness on either face.

"You're probably right," he said. His mouth tightened into a frown, and his stomach knotted at the realization that he was striding boldly to near-certain death. "Then it seems I'm to die with my revenge incomplete," he said, struggling to keep his voice steady. "I trust you to tend to my business and household, and see the women and the Aritheians to safety."

"You could still turn back," Black suggested.

Arlian smiled sadly. "No," he said. "I couldn't."

"Idiot," Black said.

"Maybe I am," Arlian said. "I'm trusting in Fate, I suppose. I couldn't live with myself if I turned back now."

"Ah!" Black threw up his hands in disgust. "Fine. Have it your way." He turned aside, and Arlian marched alone through the city gates.

He was scarcely past the outer edge of the wall when the sound of a sword leaving its scabbard warned him; he spun to find that Horim, also now just past the gates, had already drawn his blades and was charging across the cobbles toward him.

Women screamed and the travelers and tradesmen in the gateyard scattered.

The sword was in Horim's left hand, swordbreaker in his right—Arlian had less experience against left-handed foes. He noted that detail even as he dodged sideways and unsheathed his own sword, barely in time to parry the attack. He recovered quickly; by Lord Iron's second lunge Arlian had his own swordbreaker out as well.

Oddly, he was not surprised or unsettled by the attack; in fact, he was relieved. He was committed now. Perhaps Black's warning was responsible for his calm acceptance. He felt none of the sick uncertainty he had felt in the duel with Kuruvan; Horim had challenged him and was seriously trying to kill him, whereas Kuruvan had been bullied and goaded into fighting.

Horim's left-handedness was an inconvenience; using the swordbreaker for anything other than parrying Horim's became problematic. Arlian had practiced this sort of asymmetric swordplay, but not as much as he now wished he had—he had known Lord Dragon was right-handed, and had not anticipated finding himself in his present position.

Horim knew that, of course, and was trying to take advantage of it, making circular attacks that would have been stupid against a fellow left-hander, but which got handily around Arlian's guard. Arlian dodged, but felt the sword blade tug at his velvet jacket.

One of the watchers gasped. Arlian was only vaguely aware of the wide ring of people that surrounded the two of them; his attention was entirely on his foe.

He remembered one ruse Black had shown him—parry and lock blades, but unevenly, so that his opponent would have an opportunity to use his swordbreaker in the way that gave it its name. Except while he was doing that, Arlian would be able to plunge his own swordbreaker into Horim's side or belly, more or less as he had struck Kuruvan.

It was a risky maneuver, but he was at a disadvantage here—he had the greater size and reach, but Horim was strong and quick, with far more experience at cross-handed combat. He made the attempt, deliberately parrying too far along his blade...

Horim laughed aloud; he dropped his swordbreaker to guard even before Arlian moved to strike, and used the deliberately faulty position of Arlian's sword to force the blade aside and launch an attack of his own. Arlian had to turn and bring his swordbreaker up across his chest to deflect Horim's sword.

That left him in an awkward, half-twisted position, his swordbreaker locked with Horim's sword, his own sword turned uselessly off to the right, and Horim's right hand and swordbreaker free. Lord Iron tried to take

344

advantage of this, plunging the swordbreaker toward Arlian's side, but Arlian rammed his left elbow down and knocked the blade away, ducking under Horim's sword. That left his shoulder open to a slash, but that would not kill him, where the point of either the sword or swordbreaker might.

And it gave him a chance to bring his own sword back into position.

That put the two men back on even terms, and too close together to fight effectively; both stepped back, almost simultaneously.

Arlian saw that Horim was grinning; he was obviously enjoying himself. Arlian was not.

Horim feinted, and Arlian parried. Horim slashed, and Arlian dodged.

He needed a plan, Arlian thought. He needed to do something more than react to Horim's attacks. His own stunt hadn't worked at all; Horim seemed to have expected it. He was obviously familiar with the usual tricks used to counter a left-hander's advantage.

Arlian tried to think through the situation without distracting himself from the fight. He was younger, maybe faster, taller, with a longer reach; Horim was stronger and more skilled.

Horim also wore that peculiar brass tube around his right arm. That puzzled Arlian; if it were meant as armor, shouldn't it be on his *left* arm? And why did a man called "Iron" wear brass?

Attack, parry, riposte, counter, feint, parry, in a lightning exchange.

Horim was vastly older than Arlian, and it might be possible to tire him out, wear him down—but he was a dragonheart, so it might not be.

Feint, lunge, parry.

What *was* that thing on his arm? Arlian could see that it was made in two pieces, hinged together on one side and overlapping in a sort of latch on the other.

The two men circled each other, there on the pavement, in an open area roughly fifteen yards across encircled by the men and women watching the duel.

That damnable brass gadget fascinated Arlian; it gleamed in the sunlight and he almost missed a parry. Angrily, he reversed his grip on his swordbreaker.

Horim's wolfish smile faded at that, and he looked puzzled. A swordbreaker held point-down was of no use in any normal fight.

Then he shrugged and went into a high attack. Arlian parried it readily enough, but instead of a riposte or disengagement he charged in closer, locking the swords together so that they crossed at face-level.

Horim's right hand came up to block an attack with the swordbreaker, but Arlian's short blade was pointing *down,* not at Horim's throat or chest, so the block missed, and Arlian was able to ram the point down toward Horim's arm and into that latch.

He pried, and the brass tube snapped open and fell away with a tearing sound.

Horim's right hand spasmed, and his swordbreaker dropped from twitching fingers; he screamed, then retreated, tearing away as quickly as he could, giving Arlian a chance to slash the tip of his sword lightly across Horim's chest as they separated.

Arlian did not pursue immediately; instead he took a good long look at his foe.

Horim had gone pale; he was obviously in pain, unable to control the fingers of his right hand. His right forearm was a thin, sickly-white thing, nothing like the strong, tanned left; it was misshapen, gnarled and twisted.

And Arlian saw why. Half of it was missing, and what was left was largely scar tissue, bearing the badly healed marks of gigantic teeth. Like so many members of the Dragon Society, Horim still bore the signs the dragons had left upon him. He had braced his ruined arm with metal—but that had probably weakened it further in some ways, as the flesh received no air or sunlight and the muscles could not move freely, could not exercise properly, did not support their own weight. With the brace in place he could use it—his grip was probably as strong as ever when his wrist wasn't spasming—but without the supporting metal he was crippled.

No sensible opponent would ever have bothered to attack the one place Horim was armored, as Arlian had; it had been a mad curiosity, rather than any conscious reason, that had prompted Arlian's action. Still, it had worked very much to his advantage.

Arlian kicked Horim's dropped swordbreaker away and advanced.

Horim still fought, but now he was on the defensive, and he was obviously unaccustomed to fighting without a swordbreaker. His right arm twitched and his empty hand flopped up whenever Arlian attacked on that side.

His sword hand was still strong, though, and his skill had not deserted him; he parried attack after attack, retreating across the pavement. The audience retreated as well, pulling away as Horim approached.

Arlian was careful to keep Horim moving *away* from the gates; he was not about to lose this opportunity for vengeance to his Society oath.

The duel dragged on for what seemed like hours, and both men began to weary. Swords flashed back and forth, darting at throat and chest but always turned aside. Arlian pressed forward on his left, Horim's right, more than would have been wise ordinarily—but this was no longer an ordinary match, and Horim responded by twitching away.

And then finally Arlian lunged in with his swordbreaker, and Horim brought his sword over to counter, and Arlian's sword punched up under Horim's jaw, through the soft flesh beneath his beard and up into his brain.

Horim made an appalling gurgling noise; his eyes flew wide and blood spat from his open mouth, blood that seemed to shine unnaturally in the summer sun. Then he slumped to his knees, his head falling back, and as Arlian withdrew his reddened blade Horim crumpled lifelessly to the ground. Blood ran from his mouth and throat, pooling on the paving stones and shimmering as if blown by a faint breeze.

Arlian felt no breeze; he thought that trace of movement must be from Horim's fading pulse. He stepped back and waited, arms tingling with fatigue, as Lord Toribor dashed forward into the circle to attend to the fallen Lord Iron.

Arlian could not imagine how even a dragonheart could have survived that thrust, but he did not leave, nor clean and sheathe his blades, until he heard what Toribor found.

For that matter, he could scarcely trust Toribor not to carry on the fight himself so long as they were both outside the gates; he stood with steel still bare in each hand, waiting.

"He's dead," Toribor said, kneeling over the body, his hand behind Lord Iron's ear feeling for a nonexistent pulse. "He's cooling already; he must have been dead as soon as he hit the ground."

Arlian let out his breath in a long, wavering sigh. Then he turned and marched toward the city gates, his weapons sagging but unsheathed.

As he did he listened carefully for any hint that Toribor was coming after him, and he scanned the crowd for Lord Dragon. He would not have been at all surprised to find one or both of them attempting to finish off the job Horim had failed at.

No one moved to stop him, and no attack came. When he set foot on the threshold of the gates Arlian let out another sigh and slowed his pace. He sheathed his sword-breaker and groped for a handkerchief as he walked on into the city.

Then Black was there beside him. "Not bad," he said.

Arlian let his breath out with a shudder and mopped his face with one end of his handkerchief. He sat himself heavily down upon the edge of a stone horse trough, then set to wiping his sword clean with the side of the cloth that was not already moist with sweat.

Black stood beside him, watching the crowd warily. No one came near them; apparently no one wanted to congratulate the victor. Toribor and three others were hauling Horim's corpse across the plaza and into the city, and the crowd was beginning to disperse; Lord Dragon was nowhere to be seen.

"The women," Arlian said. "Horim had two of the women. Who are his heirs? We'll want to buy the women free."

Black didn't reply; instead he remarked, "We have company."

Arlian looked up to see Lady Rime hobbling toward him, cane and peg leg thumping and wobbling on the cobbles. He stood and sheathed his sword.

"My lady," he said.

"Lord Obsidian," she said. "My congratulations on your victory. An impressive performance—did you know about Iron's arm, or was that luck?"

"A guess," Arlian admitted. "Or an experiment." He hesitated, then said, "Lord Horim had possession of two of the women from the House of Carnal Society—I want them freed. Who are Horim's heirs?"

"I doubt he has any," Rime said, with a crooked smile. "Have you forgotten everything I told you?"

"You don't marry," Arlian said. "And dragonhearts sire no children."

Rime nodded. "The custom, in fact," she said, "is for us to leave our worldly goods to the Dragon Society itself. That would make you part owner of those slaves already, and I'm sure the rest of us will be reasonable in selling them to you, or simply freeing them."

Arlian, exhausted as he was, managed to smile at that. "Good," he said. Then a thought struck him, and the smile vanished. "I can think of two or three members who may not be reasonable," he said.

Rime glanced up the street at Toribor and his companions, carrying the body to Horim's home. "Enziet," she said. "And Belly, and Nail, and Drisheen?"

"I think Nail will be reasonable," Arlian said. "But the others, yes."

"Enziet might surprise you," Rime said, as she settled herself carefully onto the rim of the trough. "He's as cold-blooded as any of us, usually, and if he decides it's easier to cooperate with you in some minor matter, he'll do it."

Arlian looked doubtful as he sat beside her.

"Why is he so determined to be rid of you, Arlian?" Rime asked. "What secrets have you not told us?" She glanced up at Black, who suddenly took an intense interest in watching the crowd, rather than listening to the two nobles. Rime's tone turned chiding. "You're not supposed to keep secrets from the Society," she said.

"I'm not keeping secrets," Arlian protested. "I told you, I've sworn to kill him for what he did to Rose and Sweet and Dove and the others, and what he did to *me* when I was just a boy."

"That's why *you* want to kill *him*," Rime agreed. "But why does *he* want to be rid of *you?*"

He blinked at her, puzzled. "I'm sworn to kill him," he said. "Isn't that enough?"

"No," Rime said flatly, shaking her head. "Not for Enziet. I've known him for two hundred years—closer to three—and no, it's not enough at all. You swore not to kill him as long as you were both in Manfort; that removes you as an immediate threat. Enziet is a patient man—or at least, he always has been before. He could easily have waited ten years, or twenty, until you set foot outside the walls on your own, and then ambushed and slain you; that he did not, that he risked Lord Iron's life to dispose of you sooner, means that there's something more involved, something urgent, something that meant he needed to be rid of you *now.*"

Arlian stared at her. "But what could it be?" he asked.

"I don't know, child," Rime said wryly. "That's why I asked you."

"I don't know either," Arlian said, still staring. "I told you everything at the initiation, I swear it."

Rime rocked back and slapped her thighs, then reached for her cane. "Well, then," she said, "that's something to think about, isn't it?"

"Yes," Arlian agreed, not moving from where he sat. "Yes, it is."

Chapter Forty-Three

Conversations and Questions

Horim's steward sneered openly at them as Rime and Arlian stood on the tessellated marble floor of the dead man's palace foyer. He made no pretense of welcome, or even courtesy, and did not invite them into another room, nor offer them seats, despite Rime's obvious infirmity. "There are no women here," he said, crossing his arms over his chest.

"None?" Rime asked mildly. "In all the household, not a scullery maid nor laundress?"

"None," the steward asserted. "My lord did not choose to keep women around. Certainly no female cripples."

"He took this pair from Westguard two years ago, in the spring," Arlian said, resting his left hand on the hilt of his sword—at least partly to keep himself from drawing it with his right. "I saw it myself. If he didn't bring them here, what happened to them?"

"Two years ago?" the steward said, startled. He raised a hand. "Ah! Now I understand. *Those* two."

"Yes, those two," Arlian said, annoyed and resisting the temptation to grab the man by the throat. "Where are they? Did he sell them?"

"No, he killed them," the steward said. "Long ago. I think the second one might have lasted as long as a month."

Arlian's hand tightened on the hilt of his sword. *"Why?"* he demanded. "In the name of the dead gods, why would he kill them?"

"Because he had no use for them," the steward replied. "Why waste money feeding a slave you don't want?"

"He could have *sold* them!" Arlian shouted. "Or set them free!"

The steward shrugged. "They knew something my lord did not want known, I believe."

"So he simply killed them?" Arlian asked in disbelief.

"Yes."

Arlian's right hand balled into a fist, while his left gripped his sword so tightly his knuckles went white. He clenched his teeth and forced himself to turn away—striking the steward would not accomplish anything useful.

"Do you know their names?" Rime asked the steward. "Did they have any family, and were their families informed?"

"I have no idea," the steward replied.

Without turning back, Arlian said, "Sparkle. Amber. Cricket. Daub. Ferret. Brook. Velvet. Sandalwood. Are any of those names familiar?"

The steward frowned. "Daub might be," he said. "I'm not sure, though, and I don't believe I ever heard a name for the other one."

Arlian's jaw tightened again. Poor little Daub, dead? Merely because Lord Horim had had no use for her? That bastard probably hadn't even known she could paint, or that she was expert with cosmetics and had a sly sense of humor. Horim had probably seen her as nothing but a crippled whore, not human at all.

And the steward didn't think he had ever even heard the other woman's name! It could have been any of the others. Arlian knew that Sweet and Dove had gone with Lord Dragon, but which of the others still lived, and where, remained a mystery.

"Can you describe her?" Arlian asked through gritted teeth.

"After two years?"

"Did you assist in so many murders that these two don't stand out?" Arlian growled.

"I took no interest in them," the steward said defensively. "I did nothing to them."

Arlian made a wordless noise of disgust. "You said one lived here, in your home, for almost a month!"

"And I saw her only rarely," the steward insisted. "She was not my concern. Lord Iron kept her locked away, out of my sight."

"And you didn't care."

"Why should I?"

"Lord Obsidian," Rime said, interrupting before Arlian could say any more, "perhaps it's time we went elsewhere."

Arlian stared at her for a moment, then glanced at the steward.

"Yes," he said. The steward was a hateful, uncaring wretch, in Arlian's opinion, but the world was full of such people. He couldn't change them all. He had to concentrate on the most important, most dangerous men—such as Lord Enziet.

"Yes," he repeated, "let's go."

Together they were escorted to the door of the late Lord Iron's manor, and a moment later they were again on the cobbled streets of Manfort.

There they hesitated; then Arlian suggested, "Come home with me, and we'll talk."

Rime nodded, and together they made their way toward the Old Palace. For the most part they walked silently, each lost in his or her own thoughts, but at one point Arlian said, "He killed them."

"Apparently," Rime agreed. "Unless they're hidden away somewhere—but I can't imagine why that would be so, and I don't want to give you any false hopes."

"We should have asked what became of the bodies," Arlian suggested.

Rime shook her head. "If I judged Lord Iron's character correctly, I think perhaps we'd be better off not knowing. He was a dragonheart, and no sentimentalist."

Arlian, remembering what Rose had said so long ago about what became of old whores, did not reply. Instead he said, "If I had come to Manfort at once, instead of going south with the caravan, I might have saved them."

"Might you?" Rime asked sharply. "How?"

Arlian reluctantly admitted, "I couldn't have. I had no money then, and no magic, and no sword, and I didn't know how to use a blade if I'd had one."

"Then don't trouble yourself about it," she said. "Think rather about what you *can* do. You've saved four women, have you not? That's better than what you'd have accomplished by getting yourself killed two years ago."

Arlian made no reply, but his teeth ground together in frustration.

At the Old Palace Black welcomed them in from the cold, and the three of them settled themselves in the small salon with wine and a plate of fruit.

When Black had been informed of the results of their visit to Horim's estate, Arlian turned to Rime and said, "You said that you thought Enziet must have some other motive for wanting to be rid of me."

"Of course he does," Rime replied. "He's certainly had enough other brave young men wish him dead over the years, even if they weren't dragonhearts, and I've never before seen him involved in a scene like that one at the Society's hall, nor has he ever before sent one of his friends to fight a duel on his behalf."

"Horim fought on his own behalf," Arlian pointed out. "I was sworn to kill him, as well as Enziet and the others."

"Lord Iron did as Enziet asked, never doubt it," Rime said. "He would never have challenged you if Enziet had not advised him to."

"You're certain of that?"

"I knew both men for two hundred years, Lord Obsidian. Yes, I'm sure.

In the past Enziet has taken his time, waited for the right moment, let his opponents make mistakes that he could capitalize on; he hasn't sent them threatening messages or let his companions fight them openly. He urgently wanted you removed, as he never did his previous antagonists. The question is, why? What is there about you that makes you a threat to him?"

Arlian frowned. "I'm not keeping secrets," he said. "I'm no more than I appear—a man seeking to right the wrongs I've seen done to those I care about."

Rime smiled. "Oh, I doubt that," she said. "I suspect there's a great deal to you that isn't obvious—perhaps there's more to you than even *you* know."

"Well, the same could be said of any man," Arlian protested. "I see nothing that would make me different from anyone else who sought revenge upon Lord Enziet—save perhaps that I am, as you say, a dragonheart."

"Did Enziet even know that?" Black asked. "Had he met you, and seen the signs?"

"He hadn't seen my face since I was a boy, there in the ruins of the Smoking Mountain."

"Someone might have brought him word," Rime suggested.

"There's a question," Black said, "of just *when* he became determined to remove you. When I spoke to him as your messenger, after you fought Kuruvan, he was not inclined to oblige you, but he did not simply have you murdered, either. He warned you away."

"That's true," Arlian said. "That was why I joined the Dragon Society."

"Perhaps he had not known you possessed the dragon's heart until you joined," Black suggested.

"He could have killed you easily at any time before you joined," Rime agreed. "That he did not would indicate that the reason to remove you did not yet exist, or at any rate was not urgent, prior to your initiation."

"Then is it *because* I joined the Society?"

Rime shook her head. "He has had enemies among us before," she said. "He still does, though no others who have sworn to kill him. You probably noticed that he was never there when you visited the hall—there's a reason for that."

"But what, then?"

Rime thoughtfully tapped her shinbone on the arm of her chair. "Consider the timing," she said. "He knew you for his enemy when you killed Kuruvan, but he merely warned you to leave him alone. That's as he has always acted in the past. But then, at some time after your initiation,

354

something changed—he came to the hall in the company of his friends, Belly and Iron, to confront you, to give you a chance to submit your will to his, or to leave the city, or to die. What had changed?"

"I don't know," Arlian said. "I swore an oath *not* to kill him while in Manfort—would that not make it *less* urgent?"

"Of course it would," Rime agreed. "In fact, I would have expected that to settle the matter as far as he was concerned—he would have simply ignored you until business drew him out of the city, which might not be for years yet, and would have then arranged to kill you when you pursued him. There would be no need for a duel, no need to risk Lord Iron's life—though I'm sure he thought it only a small risk, and indeed, it's a wonder that it's you who lived, and he who died."

"Then something else changed, besides the oath," Black said. "But what?"

"Something became a *threat*," Rime said. "Now, what else had changed?"

"I was forced to bide my time, as you say he does," Arlian said.

"And you came to the hall fairly often as you did it," Rime pointed out. "You spoke with me, and with Nail, and with others there."

"Did he fear I would learn some weakness he possesses, that you might know of?"

Rime snorted derisively. "He has no weaknesses I know of," she said, "and if we knew of any, he would have found ways to remove that danger long ago. I told you he has other enemies among the Society's membership."

"Then perhaps he feared that *they* would learn something from *him*," Black suggested. "From Lord Obsidian, I mean."

"That fits," Rime said thoughtfully. "He would have learned of this threat, whatever it might be, only when he heard the accounts of your initiation; if he did not know until then that you possess…well, whatever it is you possess…" Her voice trailed off as the bone in her hand tapped rhythmically against the polished wood of her chair.

"What could this threat be, though?" Arlian asked. "You were there; you heard all I said. Did I speak of anything that could pose a greater threat to Lord Enziet's life than my own sword?"

Rime stopped tapping. "His life?" she asked. "I don't think we're speaking of a threat to his life. I doubt that Enziet fears death after all these centuries."

Puzzled, Arlian asked, "What, then? What else could I threaten?"

"What else does he value?" Black asked. "That's always the trick in handling an enemy—know what he cares about and what he doesn't."

Rime nodded. "That's very true," she said.

"But what does Enziet care about?" Arlian asked. "You say he doesn't fear death, so it's not his life he values; what, then? His honor? His family?"

"He has no family," Rime said. "He never has, so far as I've seen or heard."

"And he has no honor, from what *I've* seen," Arlian said.

"It's certainly not something he prizes greatly," Rime agreed, "though I've always heard that he keeps his oaths. If he did not, the Dragon Society would probably have long ago come apart in a rain of blood."

"He's chief adviser to the Duke of Manfort," Black said. "Does he care about *that?*"

"In a way," Rime said. "I think he values power."

"But what could threaten his power?" Arlian asked. "The Duke himself is a harmless old fool—a man like Lord Enziet can't possibly fear him."

"Of course not," Rime said. "The Dukes have been the Dragon Society's puppets for centuries, probably since before the dragons themselves departed."

Black cleared his throat. "I don't think I heard that," he said. "Please don't repeat it."

"The dragons," Arlian said slowly. "Does Enziet fear the dragons?"

"I don't know," Rime said. "Certainly many of us fear them. And more of us hate them, as I do, and as I think you do."

"I do," Arlian agreed, "but does Enziet?"

"What if he does?" Rime demanded. "Where would that get us? You're hardly in a position to bring the dragons up out of their caverns to overthrow Manfort."

"Could that be possible?" Arlian asked. "The Dragon Society has been studying the dragons for centuries, hasn't it? You must know a great deal about them."

"Nowhere near enough," Rime replied, tapping her bone again. "And I'd have said that Enziet knows more about them than any of us. If there's a way to wake them, he would know it—and he would know that the Society would not want to use it. If you *did* know a way, that would be no threat to Enziet—he need merely tell us you proposed something so insane, and we would *all* want you dead."

"You're right," Arlian said. "Not the dragons, then—but what else could threaten his power?"

Black cleared his throat again. "You understand I don't know anything about any secret societies," he said, "or anyone who might have had undue influence on the governance of Manfort or the Lands of Man, but if there *were* such a secret society, working behind the scenes, couldn't that society pose a threat to Lord Enziet?"

"But he's a *member* of the Dragon Society!" Rime said. "The senior member, in fact, and the one most concerned with politics."

"Does he think there's some way I could turn the rest of the Society against him?" Arlian asked.

Rime froze, the shinbone suspended at the top of its arc. She stared at Arlian.

"*Do* you know something that could turn us all against him?" she asked. "Because I can't think of a more probable threat you could pose."

Arlian stared back.

"I don't know," he said.

"It would need to be something mentioned at your initiation," Rime said. "Something we didn't notice at the time, but which Enziet spotted."

"But what?" Arlian asked, baffled.

"I don't know," Rime said, turning her chair to face Arlian more directly, "but I intend to learn. Tell me, then, Arlian of the Smoking Mountain, everything you said at your initiation."

Arlian gathered his thoughts and began speaking.

He reviewed his discovery of the Dragon Society's existence and his early childhood, and described the long spell of dragon weather that followed his eleventh birthday, culminating in the dragons' attack on Obsidian. He went through every detail he could recall of the attack, his fall, his grandfather's death, and how the vile mixture of blood and venom had dripped into his mouth.

He went over waking up, and being rescued from the cellar by Lord Dragon's men, and his meeting with Lord Dragon.

Every so often Rime interrupted his narrative with questions, trying to elicit more facts, details Arlian had forgotten or seen no significance in. These sometimes jumped back and forth in the story, and in fact Arlian had begun on the unhappy journey down the Smoking Mountain toward Deep Delving when she frowned and asked, "How long were you unconscious, there in the cellar? Several days, I suppose?"

"Oh, I don't think so," Arlian said wearily. He grimaced at the memory.

"My grandfather's body had not yet begun to stink when I awoke, and I was thirsty, but not seriously dehydrated. The ruins were no longer aflame, but still smelled strongly of woodsmoke. The weather had broken and turned cool, but that could happen quickly up on the mountain. I would say that I slept at least several hours, but probably no more than a single day, or two at the most."

Rime frowned. "But then how could the looters have gotten there? Isn't the Smoking Mountain at least five days' ride from Manfort?"

"Oh, more than that," Arlian said. "Eight or nine, I'd say. I've wondered for years how Lord Dragon happened to be there so soon, and have assumed that he somehow knew the attack was coming. I understand he's an accomplished sorcerer, so I suppose…"

"Sorcery can't do that," Rime snapped, cutting him off.

"Maybe he was in the area and saw the attack from a distance, and seized the opportunity," Black suggested. "After all, why would someone like Lord Enziet bother looting a village?"

"But Cover said that he was hired specifically to loot the village," Arlian said. "So he *must* have known it would happen, and he did nothing to stop it. That's all the more reason to seek revenge for his actions there."

"Why *would* he bother looting it?" Rime asked.

Arlian shrugged. "He wanted the obsidian," he said. "He asked me repeatedly where the workshops were."

"This is Lord Enziet we speak of," Rime said. "He could have *bought* the obsidian, all of it. He could have bought the *entire village*."

"Why would he want obsidian, anyway?" Black asked.

"It's used in sorcery," Rime said. "It has power against fire and darkness. But it's not so precious as that!"

Arlian nodded. "We had a sorcerer in the village who worked in it," he said.

"It doesn't seem to have protected the village against the dragons," Black said, "and if they aren't fire and darkness…"

"They're a good bit more than fire and darkness," Rime said, "and sorcery is limited in what it can do."

"Then why would Enziet bother with this obsidian?" Black asked.

"It's better than nothing," Rime said, shrugging. "And I suppose he didn't buy it because he didn't really need it, but when he found the village destroyed he decided he might as well take it."

"But he didn't simply *find* the village destroyed," Arlian protested. "He *knew* it would be destroyed, before it happened. It wasn't anything he did, of course—the dragons did it—but he *knew* it was coming, or he couldn't have been there so soon."

"But he *couldn't* know," Rime insisted. "I was assuming that he came there with his hirelings to get the obsidian—to steal it, since he wouldn't need the others to buy it—and that he found the village destroyed."

"I've always thought he knew the dragons were coming," Arlian said. "I assumed it was sorcery."

"Sorcery can't foresee the future," Rime said. "If he *had* known the attack was coming, then going to the village would make sense—he might have sought dragon venom or other traces of their presence, or simply more information about dragon behavior. That's well within what might be expected of any member of the Dragon Society."

"But did anyone else go to the village, then?" Arlian asked. "The destruction of Obsidian was no secret."

"Oh, much later, some of us went for a look, yes," Rime said. "I wasn't one of them—I don't travel easily, with this leg of mine. They didn't learn much; venom and some of the other traces fade quickly." She frowned. "Enziet didn't say he'd been there. No one mentioned that."

"He was there," Arlian said.

"Do you think that's what he's afraid you'll learn?" Black asked.

"I don't know," Rime said slowly. "It could be. Or maybe it's something we haven't gotten to yet—something in the mine at Deep Delving, or the brothel in Westguard. Let's go back to your story."

Arlian obliged, resuming his narrative with an explanation of how Hide had pulled him from the cellars. Rime had him provide detailed descriptions of each of the looters who had accompanied Lord Dragon, but nothing in his account caught her attention.

They broke for supper after that, and then returned to the small salon and resumed with an account of Arlian's years in the mines. He told her everything he knew of Hathet, of Bloody Hand and Lampspiller, and of all his fellow miners. She questioned him at length about the amethysts, and about the possibility that the mine's tunnels were approaching the caverns where the dragons slept, but none of them could connect these questions to Lord Enziet.

He described his escape, his flight cross-country, and his arrival in Westguard. He described each of the sixteen whores in the House of Carnal Society, as well as the guards and the dreaded Mistress, Madam Ril.

Rime took a special interest in his description of Rose, and coaxed out half-remembered details. Her expression hardened as he spoke.

"Who actually killed her?" Rime asked.

"Who held the knife?" Arlian asked. "I don't know. She was killed at Lord Dragon's order, though, I'm certain."

Rime frowned, her mouth drawn tight. "Go on," she said.

Arlian continued his tale.

By the time he was done the candles were burned down to stubs, all the servants but Black were long since abed, and every drop was gone from the decanter of wine they had brought.

"We may be missing some key detail," Rime said thoughtfully. "If we are not, I see two possible areas of concern for Enziet. One is a personal matter, and would mean both that he knows a secret I thought well guarded, and that he deliberately sought to harm me; I doubt that's the case, and will assume it was mere mischance at work. The other is the mystery of how he came to loot the village on the Smoking Mountain so soon after the dragons struck—and that *is* a mystery." She glanced at Arlian. "That best fits what we know. When you were merely Lord Obsidian, or Lanair, seeking vengeance upon the Six Lords, he did not seem overly concerned; when he learned you were Arlian, from the Smoking Mountain, you became an immediate threat. He wouldn't know what befell you in Deep Delving after he sold you, but he would know what you saw in Obsidian. I'd say that must be what troubles him."

"But why?" Arlian asked.

"That is, as I said, a mystery," Rime replied. "And I think it's one that deserves investigation."

Arlian, muddled with wine and fatigue, stared blankly at her.

"Go to bed," she said, reaching for her cane. "Think it over." She rose, then hesitated.

"Please, Lady Rime," Arlian said, leaping to his own feet despite his weariness, "be my guest for what remains of the night—I won't forgive myself if you venture out on the streets at this hour!"

"Thank you," she said.

Black took his cue. "I'll show you to your room," he said, taking Rime's arm.

The two of them departed, Rime leaning heavily on Black as she hobbled, leaving Arlian standing alone in the dim salon. One of the candles had guttered out, and others were fading.

He looked around, reluctant to retire while so many questions remained unanswered, but he could see nothing more he could do in the salon. He sighed, and set his feet toward the stairs. His thoughts were far from clear as he made his way slowly to his own bed, but he was already planning further investigation.

Chapter Forty-Four

Hide and Seek

The following day Arlian put his plans into effect. If it was true that Lord Enziet desperately wanted to conceal something about his visit to the Smoking Mountain, then obviously Enziet himself wouldn't say anything about it, and Arlian couldn't see what it would be himself—but the two of them were not the only people who had been there on that day. There had been six others present.

Cover was dead. The whereabouts of Dagger and Tooth were a mystery, and one or both of them might be dead, as well. Shamble was probably still working for Lord Dragon, and would almost certainly be impossible to approach without alerting Enziet. Stonehand had joined the Duke's guard, and was therefore also still, at least indirectly, under Lord Dragon's thumb.

Hide, though, was reputedly a dealer in gemstones and curiosities on the Street of the Jewelers, just a few hundred yards away from Arlian's front gate. What could be more natural than that Lord Obsidian, known to be a collector of obsidian trinkets, should pay Hide's establishment a visit?

Accordingly, Arlian put on his best satin blouse, wrapped a fine velvet cloak about himself, clapped on a dashing feather-trimmed hat, and set out for a brisk walk to the Street of the Jewelers. Once there, however, he encountered a delay he had not foreseen, one so obvious that he cursed himself for not expecting it.

He didn't know which shop it was.

There were signboards, of course, and even names painted on window glass, but he would hardly expect a jeweler to use the name Hide. Jewelry was meant for display, not concealment.

He ambled down the street, glancing in windows, looking for some indication and trying to conjure up Hide's image in his mind's eye.

It was still there—that moment when Hide had beckoned to him and said, "Come on, lad. We'll get you out of here," was burned into his memory—but it was not as clear as he might have liked. And of course, that was nine years ago—Hide would undoubtedly have changed considerably.

Most of the shops, he noticed, did not make ostentatious display of their contents—but then, what jeweler could afford to keep enough stock on hand to make a grand presentation, and to risk showing it where a bold thief might break in and grab it? The displays Arlian saw were modest—one goldsmith had a single pair of ornate gilt candlesticks in his window, while a nearby jeweler made do with simply the tools of his trade.

A silversmith by the name of Gorian, on the other hand, had an impressive decanter and matching goblets surrounded by lesser works—buckles, brooches, even a silver-trimmed leather slave collar—in his window, behind heavy iron bars.

And just beyond, Arlian saw, was an even gaudier display—crystal, mother-of-pearl, rare woods, onyx and jade, made into boxes and candelabra and statuettes. Arlian stopped and studied this assortment, hoping to catch a sight of the shop's proprietor.

A plump young woman emerged from the shadowy interior and called through the open door, "Is there something you'd like to see better, my lord?"

"No, thank you," Arlian said, tipping his hat. He turned away. She might be Hide's wife, or sister, or even daughter, but she was certainly not Hide…

But she might know where Hide could be found. Arlian turned back.

"Excuse me," he said. "Perhaps you could help me after all. Someone mentioned that an old acquaintance of mine who went by the name of Hide now has a shop on this street, but I'm afraid I've forgotten the details of how to find it. Might you know? He was a well-built fellow when I knew him, and had a sleeveless leather jacket he was fond of, but I can't think of his true name at all."

She smiled charmingly at him. "He doesn't use his true name," she said. "And in truth, my lord, I think you'd know his new name when you saw it, even though it's not Hide."

"Oh?" Arlian smiled back. "What is it, then?"

"Seek," she replied.

"Oh," Arlian said, grinning foolishly.

"He specializes in finding unusual items," she explained. "He and I have done business on occasion—when I've come across something so strange that he'd have an easier time selling it, or when he's acquired a fine piece that isn't sufficiently out of the ordinary for his customers." She pointed down the street. "I don't think you'll have any trouble finding him."

"Thank you, madam," Arlian said, with an elaborate bow and flourish. "I am in your debt."

"Then perhaps you'll pay that debt by sending me some trade, eh?"

"I will, indeed," Arlian said. "For now, though, I really *must* find

Hide—or rather, Seek." He made a second, smaller bow, then turned to go.

"It's on the right!" the woman called after him, and he waved his hat in acknowledgment.

A moment later he reached his goal, and recognized it immediately.

Seek's shop was small but elegant; the signboard read simply *SEEK, CURIOSITIES*, and the window held nothing but a blue velvet cloth and a white card reading, "The Finest Exotica in Manfort." The door was equipped with a glass bell that tinkled brightly as Arlian stepped in.

He found himself in a small room furnished with two velvet-upholstered chairs and a counter faced with an unfamiliar wood. The walls were paneled with the same material, and polished to a silky gleam. Whatever the wood was, it had a grain that curled and twisted like nothing Arlian had ever seen before.

There were three small shelves on the right-hand wall, providing the only display of merchandise to be seen. One held a set of four goblets made from inverted human skulls set on claw-shaped silver stems; the next bore a display of gemstones carved into detailed likenesses of various insects and spiders; and on the last sat an elaborate construction of gold wire, crystal rods, and orbs of multicolored glass that Arlian could make no sense of whatsoever.

Arlian was looking at this last, trying to puzzle it out, when the blue velvet drapery behind the counter parted and Seek stepped out.

Arlian turned and studied him.

It was a man of roughly the same size as Hide, and the right build, and the face was familiar, but Arlian was not absolutely sure it was the same man. This person was visibly older, visibly softer and plumper, and far better dressed than the Hide Arlian remembered—the shopkeeper's hair and beard were trimmed and oiled and flawlessly arranged, his cream-and-gold vest was embroidered silk rather than leather, and his entire appearance generally that of a wealthy, sophisticated man.

"May I help you, my lord?" Seek asked, resting his palms on the counter.

"I hope so," Arlian said.

"If what you desire can be found, my lord, rest assured, we can find it for you," Seek said. "It may take a significant amount of time and money, of course."

"I don't think much time or money will be needed in my case," Arlian said. "It may be that all I want will be certain information I suspect you may already possess."

"Oh? *May* be?"

"That's right; I haven't yet decided whether there might be more I want of you." He looked Seek in the eye, seeking some sign of recognition, some indication of what sort of man this was, that it was indeed the same Hide he had come looking for.

Seek stared back, unperturbed. "And what would this information be?" he asked.

Arlian hesitated for a second; Seek waited patiently. Finally, Arlian asked, "Nine years ago, when you were still called Hide, why did you go to the village of Obsidian, on the Smoking Mountain?"

Seek's eyes widened, but he showed no other sign of surprise or distress. "I was paid to go," he replied calmly. "Five ducats, all expenses, and my share of the loot. At the time that was more than sufficient to entice me." He leaned forward across the counter. "I take it that you are Lord Obsidian? The one who disposed of Sahasin, Lord Kuruvan, and Lord Iron?"

"I am known by that name, yes," Arlian admitted.

"And have you come here to kill me, too, to avenge the looting of that village?"

"Should I?" Arlian challenged him.

Seek smiled for the first time since he had come through the curtain, a crooked, sardonic smile. "I am, of course, biased," he said. "But no, I think killing me would be disproportionately harsh. After all, who was harmed by the looting of ruins? Any heirs those villagers might have had would probably be no more than distant cousins, and stealing property they had not earned and might never have thought to claim at all simply doesn't strike me as an offense deserving death." He turned his palms up and shrugged. "Of course, your own view may differ, since you seem to have appointed yourself the gods' avatar of vengeance for various wrongs. As I said, I am biased in my favor."

"And what of selling into slavery a free-born boy who had just been orphaned?"

The smile vanished.

"That was unfortunate, at the very least," Seek agreed. "If you wish to make the punishment fit the crime, though, I would still not consider it deserving of death. Death is so very final. Wouldn't enslavement be more fitting?" Before Arlian could respond, he added, "I compliment you on your sources of information."

"No compliments are called for," Arlian replied. "Then you believe yourself deserving of enslavement?"

Seek frowned.

"That depends," he said. "I concede that on the most basic level of an eye for an eye, a life for a life, and so on, it would seem just that I serve a term of years as a slave in the mines of Deep Delving. I take it, though, that the boy did eventually regain his freedom, and that you know him? He's alive and well?"

Arlian nodded.

"Then you see that death would be inappropriate—and enslavement would never quite match up properly, since he must have emerged from the mines still a young man with his life ahead of him, while I could not count on anything of the sort. And furthermore, am I really the foolish young man who helped loot that village? I've changed since then, my lord—not merely in appearance, but in any number of ways. I would not stand idly by now, as I did then; I would at the very least speak a few words of protest. Is it just to punish the man you see before you, the honest businessman, trusted by his clients and, I flatter myself, respected by his fellows, for crimes committed by a man desperate to find a place for himself, willing to do almost anything to make enough money to ensure he would not find himself in a slaver's net? Had you apprehended me back then, why yes, enslavement would have been a fitting penalty for my crimes—but now? I am not so certain. Consider also what that boy might have become had we *not* allowed Lord Dragon to sell him—his family was dead, his home destroyed. We did not know whether he had kinsmen living elsewhere, or whether any such would take him in. Had we left him as we found him, might he not have starved to death? Or might he not have found himself in the clutches of other slavers?"

"He might," Arlian conceded, "but had he—had *I* no right to take that risk, if I chose?"

"A child's fate is never his own," Seek said with a sweeping gesture. "He is always at the mercy of those around him, whether his parents or other adults, as we are all at the mercy of gods, dragons, and Fate."

"We will never know what might have become of me had you not found me," Arlian said. "I don't think, therefore, that that should be weighed in the balance. Airy suppositions cannot be made to support anything."

"True enough." Seek tipped his head and eyed Arlian. "So you were that boy? I'd never have recognized you."

"Oh? Cover did," Arlian said.

"Did he? Well, his memory must be better than mine. What's become of

Cover?"

"Dead of a fever. He was dying when I found him."

"He saved you the trouble of punishing him, then."

"Maybe," Arlian admitted.

Seek studied him. "And you're still considering killing me?"

"Maybe," Arlian repeated.

Seek smiled his crooked, humorless smile again. "As I said, we are all at the mercy of Fate, and clearly Fate has brought you here, out of Deep Delving. Yet we are free to act or not, as we please; we can refuse the opportunities Fate thrusts upon us."

"You're suggesting I should let you go unpunished?"

"Well, naturally, I would prefer it," Seek said with a shrug. "I would offer to pay compensation, but from what I understand, you have become wealthy enough that any payment I could make would be insignificant. I stood by and let Lord Dragon wrong you, and I concede that you are justified in thinking ill of me, but I question whether any penalty you might impose at this late date would be appropriate. If the purpose of punishment is to ensure I never repeat my crime, why, then you need do nothing—I would never again do anything of the sort. I'm content with my lot here in Manfort, and have no intention of gallivanting about with a band of brigands, looting ruins, ever again. If the purpose is to discourage others, consider the possibility that you might merely convince the next man in my situation to kill any potential witnesses outright, lest they come back to haunt him, as you have manifested yourself here. And if the purpose is to ease your own mind and satisfy your own anger, then judge your own emotions carefully."

"And what if I seek to please the gods by seeing that justice is done?"

Seek shook his head. "Surely whatever gods may yet survive know what justice is better than we mere mortals, and can take care of their own needs in that regard."

Arlian smiled wryly. "You speak convincingly," he said.

"I make my living by convincing people they need what I have to sell," Seek said, with a wave of his hand. "Knowing that my life is at risk here impels me to do my best."

"By your own admission, though, you wronged me—does that put you in my debt?"

"I will agree that it does," Seek said. "Indeed, a chance to repay you would be welcome, if the payment is not exorbitant. Was there something I have that you wanted?"

"Information," Arlian said. "As you say, I have all the wealth I need—but not all the knowledge I need."

Seek bowed as low as he could while behind the counter. "I am at your service, my lord."

"Then tell me," Arlian said, "every detail you remember of your expedition to the Smoking Mountain. How did Lord Dragon recruit you? Did you know his true name? Do you know it now? Did he tell you where you were bound, and what you would find there?"

Seek took a deep breath. "Well," he said. "Let me see…" He scratched his head thoughtfully.

He had been a boy when he started running errands for a man known as Parcel; the story Hide had heard was that he was called that because he was like several men bundled into a single package, and he had paid Hide a ducat to carry a message. Hide had then asked for more work, and Parcel, amused, had provided it.

It hadn't all been as harmless as carrying messages; he had thrown a rock through a lord's window, stolen a lady's dagger, spilled oil on pavement where a duel was to be fought, all at Parcel's direction. As he had grown he had been trusted with other jobs, and one day Parcel had told him, "Follow me," and he had followed, and he had met Lord Dragon, Parcel's master, for the first time, in a rented room on the Street of the Roses.

"An impressive man," Seek said. "Even now, and to the lad I was then…well, I was proud just to be there."

"I can understand that," Arlian said, remembering how impressive Lord Dragon could be.

"I met Tooth and Shamble that first time," Seek continued. "They were already in Lord Dragon's employ. Dagger came later, and I recruited Stonehand myself, to replace Parcel. And I suggested Cover, but he only joined us on that one errand—he seemed a likely candidate, but did not work out." He grimaced. "I regret that."

He sounded sincere—but Arlian reserved judgment; as Seek himself had said, he made his living convincing people. "What happened to Parcel," Arlian asked, "that you were called upon to replace him?"

Seek shrugged. "I don't know," he said. "One day he wasn't there, and Lord Dragon told me he was dead. I asked how, and Dragon said it was none of my concern, and I didn't dare press the matter further. He wasn't the only one to disappear—Tooth vanished later, though in that case Lord Dragon never said whether she was dead or alive, merely that she was gone and I was not to worry myself about it. Nor were those I've named so far the only ones I worked with in Lord Dragon's service; others came and went as the occasion arose."

Arlian nodded. "Go on," he said.

Lord Dragon had found plenty of work for Hide and the others, in Manfort and elsewhere. He rarely told them just what was going on, or why they were doing the tasks he had assigned them. Sometimes they were sent as a group, other times alone or in twos or threes; sometimes Lord Dragon would accompany them, and other times he would simply instruct them and leave it to them to carry out those instructions. Often months would pass in which Hide would not see Lord Dragon himself, but would only receive letters.

"Did you know who he was?" Arlian asked.

Seek shook his head. "Not then," he said. "And he never told us. But I had my suspicions soon enough."

"Why?"

"It wasn't so very difficult to see who benefited politically from a particular rock through a specific window, or a note passed to a given lady. When I began working for Lord Dragon the Duke was said to be bored with Lord Enziet, and displeased with the counsel he had received of late; not long after that Enziet's position was stronger than ever, and his rivals exiled, dead, or out of favor. And the descriptions matched—the rumor that Lord Enziet never appeared in public because his face was scarred certainly fit."

"Tell me about the journey to the Smoking Mountain," Arlian said.

It was one muggy afternoon late in a long, appallingly hot summer that Lord Dragon had summoned his employees and told them to be ready to travel at dawn the following day. Hide had not bothered to ask where they were going; Dagger, however, had wanted to know, saying she needed to know what provisions to pack, and Lord Dragon had told them they were bound for the Smoking Mountain, and that tools for digging would be appropriate.

"Weapons?" Stonehand had asked.

"I don't expect to find anyone alive," Lord Dragon had said, "but please yourself. I suppose there might be hazards on the road."

Hide had had that in mind later that evening, when he spoke with Cover in a tavern on Gate Street. He hadn't thought Cover would be much use in a fight, or for anything tricky or dangerous, but he seemed fit for digging—not that Hide had any idea what they would be digging for, or where. Cover had been complaining about his inability to find work, and Hide had suggested he join them at dawn, and see if Lord Dragon would take him on.

Lord Dragon had, and the party had set out for the Smoking Mountain.

The weather had been utterly miserable for most of that summer, and Dagger had complained about it on the road. Seek remembered hearing Lord Dragon's reply.

"Dragon weather," he had said. And he had smiled as he spoke, a smile Hide hadn't liked at all.

Arlian shivered at the words, at the memories they evoked of his grandfather standing on the mountainside and staring at the sky.

When they were within sight of the Smoking Mountain, Seek remembered, they had actually seen dragons in the sky, far in the distance, and then, not long after, they had seen pillars of smoke pouring up from flames on the mountain. Dagger and Cover had wanted to turn back—Dagger had thought the mountain was erupting. "We can't dig through hot lava!" she had protested.

"You won't need to," Lord Dragon had told her.

"I don't remember his exact words after that," Seek said, "but he made it clear that we were seeing a burning village, not the mountain's own flame, and that we would be looting the ruins. 'And it will be cooler then,' he said, 'so the digging won't be too arduous.'"

Arlian stared. "He *knew* that?"

"Yes," Seek said. "He knew."

For a moment neither man spoke; then Arlian said "Go on."

The remainder of the tale held no surprises; the weather had broken that night, and in the morning Lord Dragon had led his crew up the mountain, where they had systematically looted the smoldering wreckage of the village, gathering up the meager valuables the townspeople had owned, the cache of obsidian, the sorcerer's talismans and devices—his papers had burned, which had irked Lord Dragon greatly.

And they had found Arlian, of course, and carried him away.

"He knew," Arlian said. "He *knew* the dragons were coming. And he knew about the *weather*—but how could he?"

Seek shrugged. "Sorcery, I would assume. Lord Enziet is known to dabble in the hermetic arts."

Arlian started to reply, then stopped. "Of course," he said.

"And have I earned my life and freedom, my lord?" Seek asked.

"Conditionally," Arlian said. "I may require that you repeat this tale, under oath, to certain acquaintances of mine."

"I would have no difficulty in accommodating such a requirement," Seek said.

"Are you aware that in telling me this, you may have endangered your life anew?" Arlian asked.

Seek cocked his had. "How is that?"

"I suspect you have just told me certain things that Lord Dragon very much wished to remain unrevealed."

"I have said nothing I undertook to keep secret," Seek protested. "I swore no oaths, made no promises."

"I would suppose that Lord Dragon did not feel such artificial restraints to be necessary. Surely, it was understood that certain things were not to be spoken of?"

"Of course! But..." Seek frowned. "I had not thought any of this to be of great significance to Lord Enziet, but perhaps you know more than I of his concerns."

"Perhaps I do," Arlian said. "Indeed, I think so."

"Then I may have forfeited to him what I gained from you?"

"I hope not," Arlian said. "I sincerely hope not."

"Fate is fond of these little jokes."

"Indeed."

And with that, Arlian took his leave and set out for the hall of the Dragon Society.

Chapter Forty-Five

The Truth in Flames

Arlian found Rime and Wither in conversation in one corner of the Society's candlelit main hall and joined them there, taking a seat at the table beside Rime, across from Wither, under the gaze of a small stuffed crocodile.

It was a moment before they deigned to notice his presence; Arlian did not rush matters. He did not want to be seen as an overeager youngster, hurrying his elders, so he restrained his impatience.

Eventually Rime turned and greeted him, and he was included in the conversation. Then it took only a few minutes to bring the discussion around to Arlian's investigations, and after some prefatory comments Arlian said, "I have now learned, beyond doubt, that Lord Enziet knew beforehand that dragons would destroy my village."

Wither stared at him, frowning. "How could he have known?" he asked.

"I don't know," Arlian said, "but I have a witness who is willing to swear to the truth of it—one of the people who aided Lord Dragon in looting the ruins."

Rime and Wither exchanged glances.

"It's not possible to predict the future," Wither said.

"Not reliably," Rime agreed. "Knowledge of the future gives one the power to change it. That puts it outside the realm of sorcery."

"I've heard of prophetic dreams," Arlian objected. "In Arithei they seemed to be fairly common."

"But that's wild magic," Rime said. "The Aritheians don't *control* these dreams, do they?"

"No," Arlian said. "They just happen, when the winds carry magic down from the Dreaming Mountains."

"Sorcery's different," Wither said.

"Besides, are these dreams always accurate?" Rime asked.

"No," Arlian admitted. "They're...well, they're unpredictable. Sometimes they're true, sometimes they're not, and even when they are, they're sometimes too vague or obscure to be of any use."

"So even if Enziet had somehow had such a dream, which is scarcely possible in Manfort to begin with, could he rely on it sufficiently to launch his expedition to the Smoking Mountain?" Rime asked.

"Um…not if it were like the Aritheian dreams, no. But couldn't he have found some sorcerous method to produce reliable prophecies?"

Rime and Wither looked at one another.

"It shouldn't be possible," Rime said, "but if anyone could make it work, it would be Enziet."

"If he has," Wither said, "then he's honor-bound to share it with the rest of us."

"He's had nine years to do so, and he hasn't said a word of this," Rime said.

"Maybe that's why he wants me dead," Arlian suggested. "So you won't find out that he's kept it secret. It could be very useful in controlling the Duke and the rest of Manfort, couldn't it?"

"It certainly could," Wither growled.

"But if that's what he's up to, then wouldn't he have seen that you were a danger to him much sooner, through these very prophecies you think him capable of, and killed you long ago?" Rime asked.

Arlian shrugged. "Maybe it's not *that* reliable."

Rime grabbed her cane and pushed back her chair. "I want to meet this witness of yours," she said.

"As do I," Wither agreed, rising.

"Gladly," Arlian said, getting to his feet. "He calls himself Seek now, and has a shop on the Street of the Jewelers."

"Lead the way, boy," Wither said.

Arlian led the way—but even before they turned the corner onto the Street of the Jewelers he began to fear that something had gone wrong; he smelled smoke more strongly than usual. This was not merely Manfort's perpetual background odor, but something sharp and fresh. He broke into a trot; Wither accompanied him, but Rime, hobbling along, could not.

"You go ahead," she called, with a wave of her cane.

Arlian broke into a run when he saw the billowing smoke lit orange from beneath, and heard the crackle of flame. A crowd had gathered, blocking the street, and buckets were being passed, so that he had to stop and could only stare helplessly as Seek's shop burned.

"Did Seek escape?" he asked a man in the crowd.

The man turned and glanced up at Arlian.

"No," he said. "He's dead on the floor in there. Someone said his heart gave out, and he knocked over a lamp when he fell.”

Arlian stared helplessly at the flames. The buckets of water being flung upon the blaze were having an effect; Arlian could hear the hissing as the fire was fought back. Through the smoke and the shattered remains of the storefront he could make out a dark lump on the floor.

That was undoubtedly Seek; the fire might soon be under control, but it would be too late for him.

Wither came up beside Arlian and asked, “That’s your witness?”

“I’m afraid so,” Arlian admitted.

“Quite a coincidence, his death.”

“It’s no coincidence,” Arlian said. “Lord Enziet killed him, I’m sure of it. He must have overheard somehow—more sorcery…”

“More likely, if it’s as you say, he had men spying on *you,* boy, and saw you talking to this merchant. Wouldn’t need sorcery for that.”

“Oh,” Arlian said, swallowing.

In a way, then, he had himself killed Hide after all, even after deciding not to.

He should have thought of the possibility that he was being spied upon, Arlian told himself. He bit his lower lip in angry frustration as he watched the flames. He had failed Seek and himself.

His eyes began to tear—from the smoke, Arlian told himself.

“That’s assuming, of course, that you’re telling the truth,” Wither said, interrupting Arlian’s thoughts. “And that you didn’t kill him yourself before you came to fetch us. It wouldn’t have been much of a trick to spill a lamp and set a candle in the puddle as a fuse.”

“What?” Arlian whirled to stare at Wither.

“Well, you said yourself that this was one of the looters you wanted revenge on,” Wither said conversationally. “And we have nothing but your word, now, that Lord Enziet’s done anything out of line, and we all know you want vengeance on *him.* So why should we take your word that it’s he, and not yourself, behind it all?”

“But…but why would I kill my witness?”

“Why, because he *wasn’t* your witness,” Wither said. “Supposing that it’s you, and not Enziet, who’s plotting and planning here, then this man Seek might have called you the liar you are, and thrown your whole scheme awry. Now you needn’t worry about that; a dead witness can’t change his tale. And if we believe you, then we condemn Lord Enziet as a murderer trying to cover his tracks, and cast him out of the Society when he won’t reveal the secret of sorcerous prophecy—a secret that, assuming this is all the true situation, has never existed. Then you've broken his power and freed yourself of your oath not to kill him, and can pursue your revenge further."

"But that's not what happened!" Arlian protested, as Rime hobbled up to join them.

"What's not what happened?" she asked.

"I was just pointing out to the boy," Wither said, "that with his witness dead, there's no proof of his story. It might be Lord Enziet covering up treachery, or it might be Lord Obsidian casting blame on Lord Enziet where none should be."

"His man's dead, then?" Rime asked.

"Apparently," Wither said.

"That's bad," Rime said. She looked at Arlian. "Did you kill him?"

"No!" Arlian said. "Enziet did, I'm sure of it!"

"It couldn't have been an accident?"

Arlian, feeling very beset, was suddenly uncertain. "Maybe it could have been," he said.

That would relieve him of any guilt in Seek's death—but it would also be an amazingly cruel trick for Fate to have played upon him. It was far easier to believe that Enziet or his underlings had murdered Seek and set the shop ablaze.

"It might be best all around if we find out just what *did* happen," Rime suggested.

"And be careful about your accusations, boy," Wither said. "I've known Enziet since the dragons ruled, and I've known you since last week. Enziet's a cold bastard, I'll give you that, but if I had to trust one of you, I think I'd take his side all the same."

"But…!" Arlian began.

Rime cut him off with a raised hand. "For what it's worth, I'd probably choose you over Enziet," she said, "but I can understand Wither's position. You're a stranger here, and you're trying to tell us that a man we've known for centuries, the most powerful man in Manfort, has been deceiving to us, lying to us, all these years. We're going to need something more than your word; are there any *other* witnesses? Ones that you might bring to us while they're still alive?"

"I can't bring them to the hall," Arlian protested. "Outsiders aren't permitted."

"Then there *are* other witnesses?" Wither asked.

"Four of them," Arlian said. "If they're still alive, and if I can find them."

"Then you find them, and take them to the Old Palace, and keep them there, well guarded, and send a messenger," Rime said. "Don't come yourself; don't leave them with anyone else."

Arlian frowned. "Lord Enziet could kill the messenger," he said.

Rime's mouth twisted into a wry half smile. "I suppose he could," she said. "You'll just have to be careful." She reached up and patted Arlian's cheek. Wither snorted.

"If you're telling the truth," Wither said, "you find another witness. And be more careful than you were with this one!" He turned and stamped away.

Rime smiled encouragingly, then she, too, turned away.

Arlian watched them go, then turned back to face the fire again.

Cover and Hide were dead, which left four witnesses, as he had said—but Dagger and Tooth had both vanished years ago. That meant there were really only two he had any hope of locating. Stonehand was in the Duke's guards; somehow Arlian did not think he would be quite so cooperative as Seek had been, and threatening a guardsman to force a confession would be dangerous, perhaps suicidal.

Shamble, though, had still worked for Lord Dragon at last report. Arlian remembered him as big and stupid and vicious, and in his experiences in Deep Delving and with the caravan those traits often went along with cowardice; perhaps Shamble could be intimidated into testifying to Lord Dragon's perfidy.

And as someone who still worked for Lord Enziet Shamble might know other useful secrets, as well. And he might know Sweet's present circumstances—Arlian was constantly haunted by the knowledge that she was still in Enziet's possession, and ever since learning what Horim had done to Daub and her anonymous companion he had feared that Sweet and Dove might be long dead.

But then, Enziet had made threats about the lives of innocents that Arlian had assumed were directed at Sweet and Dove. Enziet might have lied, but Arlian hoped the implications were true.

There were many things he wanted to know about Enziet. He could hardly expect Enziet to tell him anything, but Shamble would be an ideal informant, if Arlian could get him to cooperate.

The first part of dealing with Shamble would be to find him and capture him; getting him to cooperate, once captured, would probably be relatively easy. After all, Arlian was a lord, with the heart of the dragon, and Shamble was to all appearances a mere brute.

But Arlian would need to get inside Lord Enziet's estate to have any chance at capturing him.

Well, then, he told himself, he would have to get inside Lord Enziet's estate. Now, how could he do that?

Lord Enziet was rich, powerful, and well versed in sorcery.

He was, from all Rime and Wither had said of him, a cautious, patient man, not given to taking careless risks. His home would undoubtedly be well guarded, and kidnapping someone out of it would require something special.

It would call for magic, Arlian was certain—Aritheian magic. He had more of that than anyone else in all the Lands of Man, and this was the time to use it.

He turned away from the dying flames and set out at a trot for the Old Palace.

Chapter Forty-Six

Into the Lion's Den

Arlian walked past the ruins of Seek's shop on a dank, misty morning in early autumn, and paused for a moment to study the remains.

The place had been stripped of everything of value even before the fire was completely extinguished, he knew; the members of the bucket brigade had taken Seek's treasures as payment for their services. Arlian had sent Black to the Street of the Jewelers after the fire to make sure that the body was given a proper burial, and had attended the brief graveside ceremony himself. Seek was undeniably dead and gone, and all that remained of the shop now was stone and wood and water-stained bits of cloth.

Eventually someone would claim the site and build anew, but as yet no one had. The wreckage still lay untouched.

All the same, that was past and done, Arlian told himself. He had no time to grieve over Seek—and after all, Hide had been a scoundrel, a looter, a thief. His crimes had caught up with him, after a fashion.

That fashion had not been what Arlian intended, of course; it had been one more of Lord Enziet's crimes.

And Arlian was determined to see that Lord Enziet's crimes were also paid for.

At that moment, Arlian knew, Lord Enziet was on his way to meet with the Duke of Manfort for a detailed review of various matters of state. After numerous delays Lord Obsidian had finally met with the Duke himself two days earlier for an informal luncheon—purely a social call, of course, as Obsidian was not one of the Duke's advisers, nor did he seek to be. He had, however, talked with the Duke about various subjects, including the workings of the city's governance, and he had managed to learn the date and time of the next policy conference with Lord Enziet.

It had taken much longer than Arlian liked to obtain this meeting, and he had lived in fear that Enziet would act against him—that he would wake up one morning to find an assassin at his bedside, or that a messenger had delivered one of Sweet's fingers as a fresh warning to leave Manfort. He had kept the wards around the Old Palace in place, and so far they had been undisturbed.

Sweet was probably still alive—at any rate, Enziet had not admitted otherwise. The thought of the poor woman in Enziet's hands was a constant nagging pain for Arlian, but there was little he could do about it.

And Enziet had made no further attempt to use Sweet or Dove to blackmail Arlian. He was biding his time, as Rime had said he might. By killing Seek in such a way that made he and Arlian equally plausible murderers Enziet had created a fresh stalemate—anything Arlian could say was suspect now that his supposed witness was dead. With the stalemate in place, Enziet could afford to wait and see what developed.

But that couldn't last forever; sooner or later one of them would find a way to gainsay the other, and Arlian intended to do it by capturing Shamble. When he had finally been able to arrange the luncheon at the Citadel he had jumped at the chance. That fool of a Duke had thought he was merely making idle conversation, answering Obsidian's casual curiosity about how the Duke conducted his business.

The curiosity he had satisfied, which was far from casual, had been about Lord Enziet's schedule. If he was at the Citadel, then Enziet would not be at home, and if he was, as Arlian believed, the only sorcerer resident in his mansion, that meant the sorcerous wards that protected his estate could not readily be renewed if they were once broken. Replacing them could only be done once Enziet returned home.

Thirif had felt those wards and informed Arlian of their existence; now he had instructions to break them by any means possible, so that Arlian could enter the house while Enziet was busy at the Citadel.

Even Enziet could not simply walk out on a council with the Duke of Manfort when he felt the wards broken; Arlian would have some time. Not much, perhaps, but some.

Shibiel, one of the other Aritheians, had provided Arlian with a glamour—not the sort that simply made a person more attractive and harder to refuse, but a magical disguise. To outward appearances he was no longer Lord Obsidian at all, but a thinner, darker man with a long nose and narrow jaw. If he were seen while trespassing no witnesses would recognize him, and while Enziet would certainly suspect the truth he would have no proof.

Arlian need merely allow Thirif enough time to work, and Lord Enziet enough time to become irretrievably caught up in affairs of state, and he could then slip into Enziet's home in search of Shamble.

Of course, he would still need to get past whatever walls and guards there might be, but he thought he could handle that.

At the end of the Street of the Jewelers he turned right and marched up the slope, toward the modest mansion behind the Citadel.

The thought of simply walking in the front gate occurred to him, but there were guards posted, and he had no desire to harm them; instead he made his way around to the back.

Enziet's home was small and old by the standards of Manfort's elite, but taller than the norm. It stood three stories high, built of smoke-blackened stone, with slit windows in a style that had not been fashionable for at least a century. The house itself was surrounded by a narrow paved yard, which was in turn surrounded by a high stone wall; Enziet did not bother with such niceties as a garden, statuary, ornamental ironwork, or terraces.

Arlian made his way to the alley behind the house, ignoring the locked and barred postern, and strolled slowly along the wall, studying the approaches.

The wall was about eight feet tall, of rough-cut blocks of granite, with no openings of any kind save the two gates; it occurred to Arlian that this would mean the view from any room on the ground floor would be rather drab and limited. The faint lingering morning mist made it hard to distinguish any details, so he gave up any idea of choosing one climbing spot over another on the basis of finding a good hold; instead he found the section he judged to be least likely to be observed by Enziet's servants, as far away from the stables, kitchens, gate, and postern as he could manage. He pulled on his heavy leather gloves, took an Aritheian opal from his pocket, and waited, watching casually for anyone who might happen into the alley.

No one did, and after a moment the opal flared white—Thirif's signal. Arlian tucked the stone back in his pocket, gathered himself, then charged at the wall at an angle, leaping at the last moment and flinging his hands over the top.

As he had expected, jagged edges cut into the leather gloves, but not deeply enough to do any real damage; he pulled himself up, and a moment later crouched atop the wall.

Serrated iron blades had been set into the stone, edge-up—just the sort of precaution Arlian had anticipated. And, as he had also anticipated, no one had tended to the blades in decades, and their edges were blunted by rust and wind and rain, sparing him serious injury.

The mist was thickening into drizzle, and he blinked away moisture as he peered across the pavement at the house. He was above the ground-floor windows, and below the second floor, but visible from any level if he stayed where he was, so he moved quickly, turning and lowering himself down the inside of the wall, then letting go and dropping the last foot or so. He landed with a slight splash, one booted foot in a small puddle.

The yard was no more than twenty feet across, a drab expanse of bare stone; directly ahead of him stood the main house, while off to his right, at the far end, were the stables and carriage house. The postern and kitchens were also to his right—he doubted anyone had set foot on this particular stretch of pavement in years, unless Enziet was sufficiently wary that he had the entire yard patrolled.

Which, of course, might well be the case, and with that in mind Arlian hurried across to the house and began looking for a means of entrance.

The slit windows were not wide enough for him to squeeze through, even if he knocked out the lead frames as well as the glass—which was probably the whole intent behind their design. All the doors into the house would almost certainly be guarded. He frowned.

If he couldn't go through the walls, he had to go either over or under them, and he didn't have time to tunnel. Even a house this size would presumably still have a courtyard, or at least an atrium, and while the slit windows were too narrow to enter through, they provided fine footholds.

Most of them were dark; he avoided any that showed the slightest bit of light, even if it seemed to come from a candle at least a room or two away, and chose his route to the roof. Then he ran forward and leaped upward.

As he climbed it occurred to him that he had done this once before, almost three years ago, when he first arrived at the House of the Six Lords. That time he had been on his way to Sweet's arms, where this time he intended to find Shamble—but the possibility of seeing Sweet was there this time, too. Lord Enziet had taken Sweet and Dove away in his coach, and either or both of them might be inside this house—or, he reminded himself, they might be on one of Lord Enziet's estates outside the city, or they might be dead; he mustn't get his hopes up.

Of course, Shamble might also be elsewhere, or dead, he thought as he stood with one foot wedged into a second-floor window and stretched his hand upward, scrabbling for purchase on the third floor.

This was hardly the time to think of that, though, and he might well find some other damning evidence here—if not a witness, then a diary or journal of some sort…

The rough, damp stone was cold against his cheek as his fingers finally curled over the edge of a third-floor sill; he braced his free foot against the side of a window-slit and pushed upward, and got his hand solidly into position.

The edge of the roof was not as far above the third-floor windows as those windows were above the ones on the second floor, but the foot or so of overhang made the reach much trickier; Arlian could not keep himself pressed against the wall as he stretched upward, but instead had to twist halfway around and lean out.

He was able to reach the underside of the overhang, and crawl his fingers outward before making a final lunge and grab. If he missed, he would fall thirty feet onto stone pavement…

But he didn't miss; instead he dangled from the overhang, both hands gripping the outermost tiles. He swung his leg up, trying to hook his foot onto the roof; his sword rattled in its scabbard. His foot missed, but the shifting weight let him throw one elbow up on the wet tiles.

Another swing, and the toe of his boot lodged between tiles, and he was able to pull himself up.

He paused for a moment to catch his breath and survey the situation.

He was crouched upon the tile roof, safe for the moment—but he had a spectacular view of the Upper City, from the Citadel to the Black Spire; he could peer into the windows of a dozen palaces.

And that meant he was visible to anyone who happened to look *out* any of those windows. He wasted no further time in clambering up the slope, looking for an opening.

When he reached the ridgepole and peered over he saw that there was indeed a courtyard, and the windows looking into it were no mere slits; he hurried over the top and half crawled, half slid down the other side. Ten minutes after starting his climb he dropped onto a third-floor balcony and tried the door there.

It was locked—but the broad casement beside it was not; he pried it open and clambered quickly inside.

He was in a lavishly appointed bedchamber, but one that had an unused air about it. He ran a finger across the bowl of the washbasin by the bed, and the tip came away gray with dust—no one had slept here in days, he was sure.

He relaxed slightly—for the first time since he reached the alley behind the house he faced no immediate risk of discovery. On the other hand, he was trespassing, and at best Lord Enziet would know the moment he set foot through his gate that his sorceries had been broken. He might know even sooner; he might already have sensed their disruption. That depended on what his wards had been, and how successful Thirif had been in matching his skills against Enziet's—Thirif was a powerful magician, but Enziet had centuries of experience and Thirif was working in an unfamiliar climate with limited tools.

Enziet might well be on his way home right now, to seek out the intruder. And while he was sworn to do Arlian no mortal harm, he could not be expected to tell his servants not to kill a burglar. Arlian had no time to waste. He opened the door to the passageway cautiously, and looked up and down the corridor. He saw no signs of life.

He slipped out into the hall and closed the door behind him, noting its location. Then he tried another door, and found another empty bedchamber. The next door was locked; the one beyond that was a storeroom full of linens.

That brought him to a corner stair, but he passed it by, moving on into the next passage.

A door at the far end was barred; curious, Arlian passed by the rooms along either side and crept up to this barrier.

Whatever lay beyond, Lord Enziet obviously didn't want it to get out; the oaken bar was as thick as Arlian's arm, and held by immense brackets of black iron. Arlian put his ear to the heavy wooden door.

He could hear nothing—or at least, not with any certainty; he was unsure whether there had been some faint sound.

This could scarcely be Shamble's room, but Arlian found himself irresistibly curious about what Lord Enziet felt obliged to confine this way. He stepped back, drew his sword in case the room's occupant was dangerous, then stepped forward and lifted the bar—it pivoted upward and fell against a waiting support. He tried the latch.

The door was locked.

Arlian frowned. He knew he should probably leave well enough alone; he might have very little time, and Shamble would not be here. Still, he wanted to know what was behind that lock. He ran his free hand along the top of the door frame and scanned the surrounding wall, but found no key; he wished the light were better, but the only illumination came from a single slit over the stairs at the far end of the corridor, and the day outside was still gray and overcast.

He fished his own keys from his pocket and tried a few, and to his pleased surprise the third one, its one tooth a simple T designed to pass a single ward, worked.

384

But then after all, he asked himself, why would anyone bother with an elaborate lock here? He was probably going to find nothing but dust and old boxes beyond; the door had probably been barred from habit.

As the lock opened, though, he thought he heard a sob, but he was unsure where it came from; he raised his sword, lifted the latch, and pulled the massive door open.

The smell hit him first—the smell of human waste, blood, and sweat, a thick, earthy smell. Then he saw her.

Sweet sat cross-legged on a straw-tick mattress in the center of a bare stone floor, staring at him. She was naked; yellow and purple bruises covered her arms and belly. Her thick black hair was a tangled, filthy, ropy mess; her face was smeared with dirt and tears.

Still, it was Sweet. Arlian's heart leaped, and he smiled broadly, while at the same time tears filled his own eyes. It was all he could do to keep from shouting.

She stared up at him with no sign of recognition or joy. Her face showed only despair and resignation. Arlian's smile vanished. He stepped into the room cautiously; he held a finger to his lips, signaling for silence.

She sat, waiting.

He hesitated, but decided against closing the door—that bar on the other side would be a serious obstacle, and he had no desire to join poor Sweet as a prisoner.

"Are you all right?" he whispered.

She looked puzzled. "I don't understand," she said.

Arlian glanced uneasily at the open door, then looked around the room.

The room was large and mostly bare. The mattress was almost the only thing resembling normal furniture; a heavy table of rough wood splotched with dark stains stood to one side. Iron bolts were set in one of the stone walls, chains dangling from them, and two large padlocked chests were pushed up against another. Two wooden boxes stood atop one of the chests. A cracked chamberpot sat in one corner. The plank floor was bare, and stained in several places with various things; a fireplace occupied much of one end, but held only embers and ash.

It was obvious that Enziet had not pampered his captives as Kuruvan had.

"Are you seriously injured?" Arlian asked. "I know you can't walk—can you move?"

"I can move," Sweet replied, clearly confused by the question. She uncrossed her legs, showing the stumps of her ankles. "What did you want me to do?"

Arlian stared at her, unsure how to answer. What he wanted her to do was to be safe and warm and happy, back at the Old Palace and away from this cold, harsh, malodorous place, away from Enziet and his ilk—but she didn't even recognize him!

Then he remembered the glamour he wore.

"Sweet, it's me," he said. "Triv."

"What?" She looked up at him, more baffled than ever.

"It's a disguise," he explained. "It's really me. Don't you know my voice?"

She blinked at him. "Triv?" Arlian thought he heard a note of comprehension—but he still heard no hope.

"I've come to rescue you," he said.

He hadn't, of course; he had come looking for Shamble. Rescuing Sweet would be stupid and reckless—but he couldn't leave her here after seeing her like this.

"I don't understand," she said again.

What had Enziet *done* to her? Arlian felt his chest tighten. "I've broken in here to rescue you," Arlian said. "I have a safe place for you—Hasty and Kitten and Lily and Musk are already there. Do you know where Dove is?"

"There," she said, pointing at the larger wooden box atop the chest.

Now it was Arlian's turn to be baffled. He looked at the box.

Coaxing an explanation out of Sweet in her present condition might be difficult; instead he crossed the room and tugged at the box's lid.

It was locked; he drew his swordbreaker, slid the point into the crack, and pried. The lock snapped and the lid flew up.

The box was full of bones—a human skull, half a dozen curving ribs, a broken chunk that might have been a human pelvis, and a litter of smaller bones. A brown something was stuffed down among them, and Arlian pulled it out.

It was a woman's dried scalp, covered with brittle brown hair—hair the exact color of Dove's hair.

"By the dead gods," Arlian whispered.

"That's Dove," Sweet said. "Or most of what's left of her."

Arlian glanced at Sweet, at the flat, calm expression on her face, then opened the smaller box—it was unlocked.

It contained two rolls of oddly textured parchment, a cake of soap, and a jar half full of something yellowish orange—grease or tallow…

"That's the rest," Sweet said.

Arlian slammed down the lid.

"I have to get you *out* of here!" he said. "Now!"

Chapter Forty-Seven

A Belated Rescue

Arlian had not come prepared to carry a naked woman through the streets of Manfort. He had expected to march Shamble out at swordpoint, if all went well, but not to carry anyone.

Still, he had to get Sweet away. His search for Shamble suddenly seemed unimportant by comparison. He swept her up in his arms.

"Do you have anything here you care about?" he demanded.

She stared at him blankly.

"Forget it," he said. "Hold on." He slung her over one shoulder and trotted to the door.

The hallway was empty. He hurried for the stairs without thinking.

He made it down the first flight safely, but halfway down the second he heard footsteps below; he backed up a few steps.

He felt Sweet's body tense, and he whirled, thinking she had seen someone behind them. Turning so fast on the stairs, with Sweet's weight on his shoulder—not that she was heavy; she was pitifully light—threw him off balance; he held Sweet with one arm across her thighs as he stumbled, and caught himself with the other hand, the fist holding his sword whacking the wall. The blade slapped against the stone with a metallic clang.

The footsteps below paused briefly, then proceeded, fading away down the corridor.

Naturally, in a house protected by sorcery, the occupants would not seriously worry about intruders. Whoever had been down there must have assumed the sound was the doing of one of the other servants, and none of his business.

But Sweet was squirming now; he lowered her to the step and looked up the stairs, but still saw nothing.

"What is it?" he whispered, looking at her.

Her face was different now, more alive—not the old, playful Sweet he remembered, but not the listless thing he had spoken with in that ghastly room on the third floor. She stared up at him. "You're *really* Triv? You're really rescuing me?" she asked.

"Yes, of course!" he said. "I'm only sorry it took so long, and that I couldn't be here in time to save Dove."

"But you can't! He'll kill you!"

"Lord Enziet has sworn, before witnesses, to do me no mortal harm within the walls of this city."

"But I…but you can't!"

"I can't leave you *here!*"

Sweet looked back up the stairs, and seemed to collapse inward, back into the beaten creature he had first seen on the mattress upstairs. "You're right," she said. "*Anything* is better than that."

"Do you know a way out of here?" he asked, suddenly hopeful. "A way we won't be seen?"

"No." She shook her head, the tangled hair falling unheeded across her face. "I haven't been outside that room in…in I don't know how long. Since I was brought here."

"Bleeding gods and goddesses," Arlian growled. He looked around warily, but still saw no one. "I can't take you over the roof, can I? And the front gate's impossible, which leaves the postern…"

"Why can't you take me over the roof?" Sweet asked. "Is that how you came in?"

"Well, because…" He stopped. Why *couldn't* he take her over the roof? After all, it wasn't as if she could walk, and it couldn't be any more difficult than fighting his way out the postern gate while carrying her. The postern was locked and barred; he had seen that from outside. At least the roof was open.

She couldn't climb—she simply wasn't tall enough to stretch the necessary distances—but he could wrap her up, lower her to the ground…

He lifted her back to his shoulder and marched back up the stairs, toward the unused bedchambers.

She watched from the bare bed of the room with the balcony as he stripped sheets and curtains and knotted them together into makeshift ropes.

He was not sure just what he would need for the job; he had not been planning on anything like this when he came in. He had expected to use Shamble as a tool or hostage to exit by one of the gates, so he hadn't bothered to take note of exact distances, or the location of useful chimneys or other protrusions he might tie things to. He therefore intended to bring as much of his "rope" as he could.

He had gathered fabric into a heap bigger than the miserable mattress Sweet had slept on for the past two years and was trying to estimate what he might need on the roof when Sweet suddenly said, "I love you, Triv."

"What?" He looked at her, startled.

"I love you," she repeated. "You came for me."

He let out a short, bitter laugh. "It took me more than *two years*," he said. "I should have come for you long ago, guards or no guards. I had no idea he would treat you as he did—but I *should* have guessed. Especially when I found out that Lord Horim had killed the two he took."

"Who?"

"Lord Horim—Lord Iron, he was called. He took two of you, and killed them both. Daub was one; I don't even know who the other was. I failed them both, just as I did Dove. And only gods and dragons might know what's happened to the two Lord Drisheen claimed."

"But Triv, you did come for us eventually. You came for *me*. That's more than I ever expected."

"You probably saved my life back in Westguard," Arlian said. "I had to save you!"

"And I love you for it."

He stared at her, baffled, for a few seconds, then turned back to the pile of fabric. "I think this should do," he said. "I've made it all one big, long rope; I can cut it apart if I need to." He hefted a loop of cloth, then looked at Sweet. "How strong are you?"

"Not very," she said. "I haven't eaten well here. I can't climb that thing, if that's what you're asking."

"I didn't think you could," he said truthfully. "But if I sit you in a loop of it, a sling, and then haul it up, can you hang on?"

"I think so," she said.

"Good." He crossed to the balcony and peered out.

The courtyard was still empty, and most of the windows dark; after all, the cold, damp weather was hardly inviting. Most people who had a choice would be curled up in a warm bed, or huddled in front of a kitchen fire, in weather like this.

That reminded him that Sweet was naked. Cursing himself for not thinking of this sooner, he grabbed a coverlet that had been too thick to make a secure knot, and handed it to her.

"Wrap yourself in this," he said. "It's chilly."

"Thank you," she said as she obeyed. She looked up at him again and forced a tentative smile, the first he had seen on her face since he had fled the brothel. "I do love you. Is…is that face permanent?"

"What? No, it's just a spell. It'll break as soon as I'm safely home again."

"Oh, good. I like the old one better. I'm eager to see it again."

Arlian looked her in the eye, and saw afresh just how thin and pale and weak she appeared. A thought struck him.

"How often did they feed you here?"

"Once a day," she said. "Every morning. They had…" She hesitated. "Every morning," she finished weakly.

Arlian nodded and smiled. "Good. You wait right here, then." He turned and hurried out of the room, down the corridor, and around the corner.

The door of Sweet's prison still stood open; he trotted down the passage, closed it, and dropped the bar into place.

With any luck, they wouldn't even notice her absence until morning.

That done, he hastened back to the balcony.

He couldn't reach the overhanging roof without assistance, but pulling a chair out to the balcony was simple enough. He got that far, then paused, and hauled a second chair out, as well. He sat Sweet on this second chair, wrapped snugly in her comforter; then he tucked one end of his makeshift "rope" through his swordbelt, climbed atop the vacant chair, and jumped for the edge.

A moment later he had pulled himself up on the roof and was hauling his "rope" up behind him.

"Triv?" Sweet called, a note of panic in her voice.

"Shhh!" he hissed, leaning over the edge. "Hush! What is it?"

"I just wanted to be sure you were still there," she said. "That you hadn't left without me."

"Didn't you see the rope moving? Just hold on; I won't go without you, I promise."

She nodded unhappily, and he pulled himself back onto the roof and continued hauling "rope"—woolen counterpane, linen sheet, velvet drape, linen sheet, the cloth slid through his hands and piled up on the tiles.

When the last of it came swaying wildly upward he looked around for an anchor point, and spotted a stone chimney that looked suitable. He crawled over to it on hands and knees, looped a few yards of his "rope" around it, and tied it tight.

Then he measured out a generous loop in the other end, keeping both ends in his hands, and lowered the loop over the edge.

"Grab it!" he called. "Sit on it, then hold on with both hands!"

He felt the jerk as the sling was caught; he felt tugging and shifting. He leaned over to see what was happening.

Sweet had obeyed; she sat in the loop of "rope," looking up at him.

"Hold on tight!" he said. Then he pushed himself back up the roof, sat up, and began hauling.

He heard a tiny smothered noise, a suppressed whimper, as Sweet found herself pulled up out of her chair.

He had her more than halfway when he realized this wasn't going to work. The higher she rose, the worse his leverage; he simply could not pull her all the way up over the overhang onto the roof.

"Can you reach the edge?" he called.

"I don't...you told me to hold on!" she said.

"All right, hold on," he said. "Look, I'm going to stick my leg out where you can see it; when I do, you hold on with one hand, and grab my leg with the other. Understand?"

She didn't reply, but he let himself slide down the roof as he hauled at the sling. He wrapped a length of "rope" around his chest, pulling it tight, so that he couldn't slide too far from the chimney the other end was secured to—but he was uncomfortably aware that because of the angles involved, if he lost his grip on the roof completely he might well find himself dangling several feet below the edge, a dozen yards to the right of the balcony.

That was still better than plummeting to the ground, of course.

He worked his way down closer to the edge until at last he was able to extend his booted foot over the edge.

Almost immediately, Sweet's hand reached up and grabbed at him; instinctively, he jerked away, and she wailed in terror.

"Hush!" he called. "I'm sorry! *Now* grab it!" He thrust his foot out again.

Her hand hooked over his ankle, and he leaned forward, letting the rope around his chest support much of his weight, and grabbed her wrist.

"Now the other hand!" he called.

The other hand appeared, and he grabbed that wrist, as well, and lifted.

Her face scraped against the edge of the tiles as it came up above the roof, and he winced. "Gods, I'm sorry," he said.

"Don't be," she whispered, as she twisted herself away from further injury.

He shifted his grip, pulling her further, and step by step, inch by inch, he managed to haul her up onto the roof.

Her comforter had fallen away, though, leaving her shivering and naked on the tile. Arlian quickly hauled his entire rope up, and slashed a linen sheet from the end. "Here," he said.

She accepted it, but said, "I can't crawl while I'm holding this."

"Oh, blood and death," Arlian muttered. "Give it back, then." She obeyed, and he tucked the sheet into his belt. "Let's get you across here before you freeze, and you can put it on once we're on the ground. Come on!"

On hands and knees they clambered up the slope, across the ridgecap, and down the other side; Sweet was more practiced at this than Arlian and kept up easily, despite her weak and battered condition. The "rope" trailed behind, still tied around Arlian's chest.

At the outer edge Arlian untied himself, wrapped the end of the line around Sweet's chest, then directed her to lower herself over the brink. He sat up, braced himself against the tiles as well as he could, and held the "rope," letting it out hand over hand as she descended.

Once she was safely below the eaves, he began to lower much more quickly, until at last, after what seemed like an eternity, the tension eased—she had reached the pavement below.

That done, he slid himself and the line over until he was directly below the chimney, then threw the rest of the "rope" over the edge and began lowering himself hand over hand.

The knots held until he was almost past the second floor; he landed hard, but evenly and the right way up. He was momentarily dazed, but no worse—no bones were broken, his head had not hit the flagstones, and he was down, safe and sound.

And Sweet was down, as well—she was crawling across the pavement toward him even before his head cleared.

The rope had snapped right at the edge of the roof—the sharp tiles had cut into it, weakening it and allowing the knot just below the edge to unravel. Most of it had tumbled down around Arlian; now, as he got to his feet and brushed himself off, he looked at it and smiled.

If they could just get out of this yard safely, and take that rope away with them, it might be hours, or even days, before anyone had any clue what had happened.

Just then a commotion broke out somewhere off to their left; Arlian took one glance in that direction, then ran to Sweet and scooped her up.

The end of the rope was still securely tied around her chest, so it would come with them if he carried her; he threw her over his shoulder and ran for the far end of the house, away from the postern gate and the stables and the carriage house.

Because he heard hooves, the rattle of harness, voices shouting—Lord Enziet's coach had returned, and presumably Lord Enziet with it, and he would know, if he did not already, that his wards had been broken.

When they were safely around the corner Arlian untied Sweet, wrapped her in the sheet, and began reeling in his line. He balled up one end, then threw it over the outer wall, so that they could pull it out after themselves; then he boosted Sweet up until she could pull herself up onto the top of the wall, with the "rope" and her wrap providing minimal protection against the iron blades.

"It's sharp," she said.

"I know," he whispered. "I'm sorry." Then he took a running leap and pulled himself up beside her.

A moment later he trotted down the mist-damp alley with an immense bundle of fabric on his back. Only the most observant would have noticed the bright pair of eyes peering out through a tiny opening in the tangled cloth.

Chapter Forty-Eight

Sweet's Tale

The small salon was pleasantly warm, heated by a roaring fire; steam rose from the heaped fabrics on the floor. Sweet lay sprawled on a blue silk couch, wrapped in a robe a servant had brought, with an elegantly garbed Musk kneeling beside her while Black and Arlian stood nearby.

"It's not what I had planned," Arlian remarked, "but she might know something."

Musk, who had been bent over a semiconscious Sweet gently wiping her face with warm compresses, looked up. "You aren't planning to *interrogate* the poor thing, are you?"

"Nothing strenuous, I promise," Arlian said. "I don't want to hurt her any more than you do."

Musk looked warily at Black, standing behind Arlian. "What about him?"

"He won't hurt her, either, any more than he's hurt you."

Black snorted.

"Well, she's in no shape to answer questions right now, anyway," Musk said, returning to her nursing.

"That woman with the wooden leg, Lady Rime, might be interested in talking to her," Black suggested. "Maybe she should be here, too."

"A fine suggestion," Arlian agreed. "She said to send a messenger for her if I found another witness."

"Is this a witness?"

"She's the closest thing I have right now, Black. Send someone to fetch Lady Rime."

Black shrugged. "I'll go myself." He turned and left the room, not running, but wasting no time.

Arlian remained where he was, watching Musk tend to Sweet. Then he knelt on the floor beside her and asked tenderly, "How are you feeling?"

Sweet opened her eyes and looked up at him. One of her cheeks was gashed, a broad, shallow gouge where she had scraped against the roof tiles; Musk had dabbed away most of the blood. Her other injuries were all older, but still visible.

She smiled at Arlian. "You have your own face back!" she said happily.

That was true; as arranged beforehand, the spell had broken the moment Arlian crossed his own threshold again.

"Yes, I know," he said. "But how are *you?*"

"I'll be fine," she said. "It's so lovely to be warm again, and to just lie here! And Musk!" She looked up at her old friend, whose healthy face was such a contrast to her own. "Triv *said* you were alive, but I didn't believe it. Is anyone else still alive?"

"Lily and Kitten and Hasty," Musk said. "They're all here and safe. I don't know about the others."

"Rose and Silk and Daub are dead, and three others, but we don't know which," Arlian said. "The others—well, there's still hope."

"Rose?" Sweet's voice cracked. "I saw them kill her. And Velvet. I didn't know about Silk or Daub."

"You saw?" Arlian asked.

She nodded. "And Dove, of course. He made me watch that."

"He *made* you?" Arlian asked. "Why?"

Sweet stared at him in surprise. "For *fun,* of course," she said. "He enjoys watching people suffer. At least, he must enjoy it, because that was what he always wanted to do, but he mostly looked angry while he did it."

Arlian stared at her in silent horror, his fists opening and closing in frustration.

"I *will* kill him," he said at last. "Somehow, someday, I'll kill him."

Sweet closed her eyes. "I don't think anyone can kill him," she said. "He's a sorcerer, you know. He talks to the dragons as if he were a dragon himself. I don't think he can die, any more than they can—maybe he *is* a dragon, in human form. Maybe it's a disguise, like the one you wore."

Arlian continued to stare at her, but his hands were still as frustration gave way to confusion.

"He talks to the dragons?" he said.

"I think that's why he calls himself Lord Dragon," Sweet murmured, her eyes closing. "He *is* a dragon."

Arlian looked around the room, as if for guidance—was Sweet speaking the literal truth, or was this simply the deranged imagining of a woman who had been subjected to two long years of torture and abuse?

It was at that moment that a servant entered with a heavily laden tray of food and drink, providing a welcome distraction. "Set it there," he said, pointing to a low table. Turning to Sweet, he asked, "Can you sit up to eat?"

She started. "Is it morning already?"

"No, of course not—you're *here,* and can eat when you please," Musk explained. "Come on, let me help you."

Together, Musk and Arlian got the exhausted Sweet sitting upright, and a glass of wine to her lips.

She spluttered, then drank, draining the glass eagerly.

A honeycake followed, then raisins, then more wine and a slab of cheese. She ate voraciously for several minutes as Arlian and Musk watched.

Then abruptly she stopped, doubled over, and vomited onto the carpet.

"Too much rich food, too fast," Musk muttered. "She's half starved, the poor thing!" She turned to the servant, still waiting in the corner, and said, "Fetch some broth—something fit for a sick child."

The servant bowed and started toward the door.

"And send someone to clean this up," Arlian added.

The servant bowed again, and left.

When Rime arrived, half an hour later, Arlian and Sweet and Musk were settled in another room, a drawing room where Sweet was curled up in a velvet-upholstered armchair, wrapped in her robe and a blanket, sipping a mug of beef broth. Hasty had joined them, and been repeatedly shushed for arguing with Sweet—Hasty insisted that Enziet simply could not have been that much worse than Kuruvan. Hasty was now visibly pregnant with Kuruvan's child, and determined to think well of the baby's father and all his friends.

Arlian stood when Rime hobbled into the room, and bowed respectfully; the three women could not rise, of course, but Musk attempted a partial bow. Rime waved her cane at them in acknowledgment.

"So is this one of your four witnesses, or just another whore you've rescued?" Rime asked Arlian without preamble. "Black didn't seem very certain on that point."

Wither had accompanied her, and now stepped into the room behind her; Arlian bowed again. Black, who had opened the door for the two guests, now hesitated.

"Come in, all of you," Arlian said, beckoning. "This is Sweet—and yes, she's another of the women I sought to rescue, but she may be a witness to Lord Enziet's treachery, as well."

"Treachery?" Sweet looked up, startled.

"You said he spoke to dragons," Arlian said gently. "What did you mean?"

399

She looked up at Arlian, puzzled. "I meant he talks to dragons. He uses his sorcery and a bowl of water—I saw him do it once. I didn't hear anything, but I saw the dragon in the water, and he told me what it said." She shuddered.

Wither leaned forward and studied Sweet intently; Rime leaned on her cane and stared.

"You're serious?" Rime said.

"Of course I am!" Sweet said, pulling the blankets closer around her.

"What color was the dragon?" Rime demanded.

Sweet hesitated, and glanced at Arlian. "Black," she said. "But maybe that was the magic, because I thought dragons were green."

"They're black," Arlian said.

"Some of them," Rime agreed. "The biggest ones."

"Why did he show you this?" Wither asked.

"And when?" Rime added.

"He was...he was tormenting me," Sweet said. "He was taunting me, saying I would spend the rest of my life as a plaything. I said that no, sooner or later I'd die, just as Dove did, when he got bored and killed me, and he said no, he would keep me alive until I was old and gray and even more helpless than I was then." She swallowed. "I was...I was braver back then—it was, I don't know, a long time ago, in the summer I think, but a long time after he brought me to Manfort. A hot day, I remember. Anyway, I said that he was older than I was, and would be dead before my hair turned gray, and he laughed and said he was a sorcerer and would live forever. And I didn't believe him, so he took the bowl of water he used to wash off the blood, and showed me that he talked to the dragons." She glanced at Arlian, and added, "I think he might *be* a dragon, in human form, but he never said that, I'm just guessing."

"He's no dragon," Wither said.

"Not yet, anyway," Rime added. "He seems more like one every year, though."

Wither looked at Rime. "Do you think it was an illusion?"

"Probably," Rime said.

"But it would explain how he knew my village would be destroyed!" Arlian said. "The dragons *told* him what they were going to do!"

"It would, at that," Rime agreed thoughtfully. She asked Wither, "Could *you* make a dragon's image appear in a bowl of water?"

"Not just like that," Wither said. "Blood in the water … no, that wouldn't help." He looked at Sweet. "Did he use anything else? Any powders or devices?"

"I don't know," Sweet said. "I didn't see any."

"If he just wanted to make an illusion to prove he's a sorcerer," Arlian asked, "why would he choose the image of a dragon?"

"Suppose he *can* talk to the dragons," Wither said. "Why wouldn't he *tell* us?"

"He's keeping it to himself so he'll have resources we don't," Rime said. "But what could he *do* with it?"

"Well, he knew when he could loot the Smoking Mountain," Arlian pointed out.

Wither waved it away. "How often would *that* be of any use?"

"And even if he can speak to them, why would the dragons tell him that?" Rime asked.

"Perhaps he can *compel* them to speak?" Black suggested. Rime and Wither turned, startled, as if both had forgotten that Black was still present.

"Compel a *dragon* to do anything?" Wither countered.

Black shrugged. "Well, you'd know more than I about that," he said, "but didn't someone, or several someones, compel them to leave humanity to its own devices, while they slunk off to their caves?"

"It wasn't…" Wither began. Then he stopped and frowned.

"We don't *know* why the dragons gave up and left," Rime said. She glanced at Wither. "Do we?"

Wither didn't reply, and after a few seconds of uneasy silence, Arlian suggested, "Maybe Enziet *does* know."

"Maybe Enziet knows a great deal he hasn't told us," Wither growled. Abruptly he turned and stamped out.

The others stared after him, caught flat-footed by this sudden exit. "Wait a minute," Rime called. She began to hobble after him, but gave up after a few steps—Wither might be old, and his arm a useless ruin, but there was nothing wrong with his legs, a claim Rime could not make.

"Should I go after him?" Black asked Arlian.

"And do what?" Arlian asked. "Drag him back here by force?" He shook his head. "I don't think so. I don't know where he's going, but wherever it is, what harm can he do us? Enziet's sworn not to kill him, or myself, or Lady Rime, and we have Sweet safe here with us, and the Aritheians to protect us all from Enziet's sorceries. Let him go. If he tells Enziet what we've learned, what of it?"

Rime had heard this as she gave up the pursuit and hobbled back. "You may be making a mistake," she said. "Wither's angry now, but he and Enziet have been friends for centuries."

They heard a distant door slam.

"Well, it's done now," Arlian said. He looked at Sweet. "That's why Enziet didn't want me to visit him, I suppose," he said. "He was afraid I might find Sweet and hear what she had to say."

"Oh, he probably just didn't want to be bothered with you," Rime said. "But letting this girl see what she did, and live—that was a mistake. And there's the tale of your home's destruction—it's unusually careless of Enziet to make two such slips in a single decade, and unfortunate for him that they should involve people who know one another." She shook her head. "He's been getting stranger and stranger of late."

Sweet shuddered. "He's a horrible creature," she said. "What he did to me, and to Dove…"

"What *did* he do to you?" Rime asked curiously.

Sweet looked up at her, and then around at the others—Hasty and Musk, Arlian and Black.

"You don't want to hear this," she said.

"If you want to tell us, we want to hear it," Arlian said. "But if you don't want to talk about it, that's fine, too. Whatever you want."

Sweet hesitated, then said, "I need to tell someone. And I need to tell it soon. When I had a particularly bad customer I used to tell Rose about it, and it made it easier to bear. And she would tell me. But Rose is dead." She suddenly burst into tears, and Arlian hurried to comfort her.

When she had calmed, she began to speak.

"At first I thought it wouldn't be any worse than the brothel," she said in a dull monotone. "I thought it would be the same sort of thing, but with Enziet and his guests, rather than whoever paid Mistress. Dove and I told each other that in the coach, and the first night at the house it seemed we were right—he put us on a bed in an unused room. But then the next day he had the *other* room prepared, the room where you found me, Triv…"

She spoke on and on; she had not even begun on Dove's death by slow torture when Hasty could stand no more and asked to be taken away. Black obliged her.

Musk wept frequently, and covered her ears during some parts of the recitation.

Black returned after carrying Hasty to her room, but had to leave shortly thereafter, after the account of the disposition of Dove's body, to empty his stomach.

Arlian felt ill several times, cried once or twice, but stuck it out.

Rime seated herself at the beginning of the narrative, and simply sat and listened, not visibly moved, until Sweet had finished.

She had begun not long after midday; by the time she finished the sun was down and candles lit. There had been a few brief interruptions, for food and other necessities, but she had spoken almost constantly for several hours. Her voice had grown faint and hoarse.

"…I didn't know him at first," she said, reaching up to stroke Arlian's hair. "He said who he was, but I couldn't believe it. I thought it was a new trick, a new way Lord Dragon had thought up to try to drive me mad. But it truly was Triv, and he carried me out and pulled me up over the roof and lowered me down outside the house and carried me here on his back. And I'll love him for that as long as I live." She pulled him down for a kiss.

"Well," Rime said, reaching for her cane, "I think that's a good way to end the tale, and I'd better be going." She pointed her stick at Arlian. "Tomorrow, midmorning, I expect to see you on the Street of the Black Spire. I believe there are a few things we'll want to talk about there."

"Of course," Arlian said, as he disentangled himself from Sweet's grasp. "Midmorning tomorrow."

"Don't bring her," Rime said. "Keep her safe here, and maybe we'll all come talk to her."

Arlian bowed an acknowledgment.

"And I'd suggest," Rime said, as she hobbled toward the door, "that *all* of you get some rest. I'm sure you're going to need it."

Chapter Forty-Nine

The Calling of the Hearing

The morning was foggy, but the sun's light could be dimly seen overhead, and Arlian was fairly sure the mist would burn off in time—and of course, the outside world always seemed irrelevant once he was inside the Hall of the Dragon Society.

He arrived at midmorning, as instructed, and found several members present, including Rime. He recognized Flute, and Shatter, and several others, and of course Door was guarding the entrance.

Wither was not there, nor was Enziet, nor Drisheen, nor Toribor, nor Nail. Arlian frowned at that. The absence of all four of his surviving foes among the dragonhearts worried him; what if they were conspiring to kill Sweet, to destroy the evidence of their perfidy?

Of course, that assumed that all of them had known of Enziet's unique ability—whether it was prophecy or communing with dragons—and that might not be the case.

"There you are," Rime said, looking up. She was seated at a table near the center of the main room. "Come and sit, and let me explain a few things I couldn't say openly outside these walls."

Arlian took a chair beside her and leaned over to listen.

"The Dragon Society does not have very many rules," Rime told him, "but it does have some, as you know. One of those is that knowledge of the dragons must be shared—that was in the oath you swore. Another, not quite so basic, is that knowledge of any new sorcerous technique must be shared. Enziet has apparently broken at least one of these rules. Nobody here will care that he tortured the girl and killed half a dozen others, but breaking his member's oath—*that* we take very seriously. At least in theory, it means that we must hold a hearing, wherein all interested members shall have the opportunity to interrogate him, as we do at initiations—and just as at an initiation, he must answer truthfully every question put to him. If he fails to do so, we have a choice—expulsion, exile, or death. In the eight hundred years the Dragon Society has existed there has never been such a hearing, so far as I know, but these are the rules as they stand. Given that it's Lord Enziet, I can't imagine we'd vote for his death, but either of the other choices

405

would leave you free to attempt to kill him yourself."

"I suspected as much," Arlian said.

"Of course you did. However, don't raise your hopes too high; Enziet hasn't survived almost a thousand years by being foolish. I assume that he *will* answer the questions truthfully. It may be that he hasn't broken the rules at all, though I can't quite see how that would be so; it may be that he has, but that he will claim there were extenuating circumstances, and will beg the Society's pardon—which will, in all probability, be granted."

Arlian gritted his teeth. "And we'll be back to a standoff."

"Yes, you will. However, let me also bring up some other possibilities not covered by the official rules." She glanced around to see if anyone else was listening, then said, "Enziet was one of the founders of the Dragon Society, with Sharrae, Wither, Nail, and Rehirrian. Wither, Nail, and Rehirrian were all a few years younger; that Enziet *looks* younger than Nail or Wither simply reflects their relative ages when they drank the elixir. Since Sharrae's death three hundred years ago Enziet has been our most senior surviving member, which means he holds the highest rank possible within the Society—all three of the surviving founders are held in high regard, and Enziet is by far the most vigorous of them, the most feared and respected. He is furthermore the chief adviser to the Duke of Manfort, and a sorcerer second only to Lord Drisheen. I am not at all sure that the Society as a whole has the courage to defy him, to expel him, exile him, or kill him. In fact, I think that merely calling a hearing may put an unbearable strain on the Society, and going through with it may shatter the Society—the entire system may break apart into squabbling factions." She paused and looked Arlian in the eye. "Are you willing to risk that?"

Arlian looked back. "Yes," he said.

He said no more aloud, but his thoughts were plain enough—he had no great love for the Dragon Society. He had not been a member long enough to grow dependent upon it; he saw no great virtue in it. He knew that the Society secretly dominated much of the governance of the Lands of Man, and that the members considered themselves a crucial force for stability, but he was by no means convinced of the validity of such a view.

In fact, he suspected that the destruction of the Society might be a very good thing. Could it really be best for humanity to let dragonhearts run the affairs of ordinary mortals? Dragonhearts, cold and detached, without family, unconcerned with age, barely aware of the passage of time—what did they know of the best way to order the everyday world from which they were so estranged?

Rime clearly considered the Society a beneficent institution, but Arlian disagreed.

Rime was still studying his face, as if unsatisfied with his single word of reply, so he elaborated, "If the Society can be so easily broken, can it be worthy of preservation?"

"Ah," Rime said, sitting back. "You're young. Often the most delicate things are those most worth saving."

"Lord Enziet is a criminal by any sane standard, including the rules of this Society he helped create," Arlian said. "He must answer for his crimes."

"Whatever the cost?"

Arlian started to speak, then stopped.

"No," he said at last. "I won't go that far. There are costs that would not be worth paying. The Dragon Society, however, is not one of them."

"Very well then," Rime said, thumping her cane on the floor. She got to her feet, picked up her polished bone, and rapped the table.

"Your attention, my lords and ladies!" she called, in a clear, carrying voice.

The other members present in the room looked up at her with varying degrees of startlement.

"A grave accusation has been made," Rime announced. "A member in good standing accuses Lord Enziet of a betrayal of our trust and a breaking of his oath. Let us summon Lord Enziet to a hearing, that these charges may be made and answered!"

"Enziet? Are you mad?" someone asked.

Rime looked intently at the speaker.

"The accusation has been made," she said, "that Lord Enziet conspires with the dragons themselves."

"That's insane!"

"We have a witness," Arlian interjected.

"Who?"

"She's not a member, and cannot enter here," Rime said. "Three of us heard her story, however, and have reason to believe it to be true."

"If she's not a member, who's making the accusation?"

"I am," Arlian said, rising.

Several voices spoke at once.

"But you've only just joined!"

"Aren't you already sworn to kill Enziet?"

"Why should we believe you?"

Rime raised her hands for silence.

"Lord Obsidian is a member in good standing," she said. "He has the right to call Lord Enziet to a hearing—and if the Society deems the accusation to be frivolous or made solely from personal malice, why, then we can call Obsidian to a hearing in reply."

Arlian looked at her, startled; she hadn't mentioned that possibility.

"I ask that Lord Enziet be summoned before this gathering!" Rime called.

Lord Shatter said, "Door, that's your job, isn't it?"

"If no one else volunteers," Door replied uneasily.

"He shouldn't go alone," Lady Flute called. "Not for *Enziet.*"

"I'll go," Shatter said.

Several voices joined in. Arlian looked at Rime.

"You're the accuser," she said. "You stay here. And by calling the hearing, I've appointed myself overseer of the event, so I stay here, too. If you're worried that they'll help him escape, though, you can ask someone you trust to go."

Arlian looked around, then shook his head. "I don't see anyone I wish to send," he said.

Rime shrugged. "As you please." She turned to see that Door was organizing a party to go collect Enziet from his home, and sat down. "Our part's done for now; now we wait."

Arlian was restless, eager to be active, to be doing something—but there was nothing to be done; he had only to wait until Enziet was brought in. He watched Door's gang of a dozen or so depart, then sat, trying to stay calm—but he couldn't manage it. Almost involuntarily, he got to his feet and looked for something to do, somewhere to go.

"You mustn't leave the room," Rime said. "It's set in the rules. In theory, this restriction is to prevent you from arranging an ambush."

"I could have set one up beforehand, if that was my intent," Arlian pointed out.

"That's true enough," Rime agreed. "I never said the theory was sound."

Arlian stared at her for a moment, then turned away. He thought about sending a message to the Old Palace, to check on Sweet and the others—what if Enziet tried to reclaim his "property"? After all, Arlian had stolen a legally indentured slave.

There were no messengers at hand, though, so instead he moved about the room, looking at the dozens of peculiar artifacts gathered there, asking Rime and the other members questions about some of them.

The minutes dragged by and added up, little by little, until Arlian was certain that hours had passed, if not entire days; then suddenly the door slammed in, and a babble of excited voices drew the attention of everyone present. The party that had gone to fetch Enziet spilled in—but Arlian saw no sign of Enziet, or Toribor, or Drisheen.

Wither was there, though, and Nail.

"He's gone," Door announced as he stepped into the room. "He and several of his guards and servants and hirelings, together with Lords Drisheen and Belly and parts of their households. They gathered at the Enziet's manse at dawn this morning and left the city."

"But we found these two arguing at the gate of Enziet's home," someone added, pointing at Wither and Nail.

"Then question *them,*" someone else called. "I want to know what the truth is here!"

Wither turned and glared at the speaker.

"By what right?" he bellowed.

The chatter of the others stopped instantly.

"By what right do you dare to suggest I be questioned?" Wither continued. "Am I, too, accused of withholding information I am sworn to share? If so, show me my accuser!"

"No one accused you of anything," Door said wearily.

"Then speak not of questioning me, as if I were a peculating servant or a naughty child!" Wither shouted, gesturing. "I am older than you all; I stood on this city's ramparts and fought dragons before you were born!"

Nail cleared his throat. Rime smiled crookedly at that, and whispered to Arlian, "No one's sure which of those two is older."

"My lord," someone called, "we *demand* nothing of you, but we would *ask* that you grant us the favor of telling us what you know of the case at hand—in your own way, and as you will."

A murmur of agreement ran through the gathering.

"Fair enough," Wither said with a nod. "Sit down and be still, and I'll speak."

The various members, Arlian among them, found seats—all in all, more than a score of the Society's members sat listening to Wither's words. Nail sat close by Wither's side; Door took a place behind him, blocking the doorway.

"Yesterday," Wither said, "Lord Obsidian came into possession of a slave who had been in Lord Enziet's house. This slave, who Lord Obsidian knew years ago and believes to be truthful, told Obsidian, Rime, and myself that Lord Enziet had boasted to her of certain sorcerous powers unlike any known to the rest of us, and had demonstrated these powers for her. While Rime and Obsidian saw fit to make this the basis of their accusations against Lord Enziet, I chose instead to go to him yesterday evening, present the facts as I understood them, and demand an explanation." He paused for breath, and looked around at roughly two dozen rapt faces.

"He had no explanation," Wither said. "He told me that there were extenuating circumstances involved, circumstances unknown to me or to any of you, that had prevented him from telling any of us the truth—that an oath sworn prior to the founding of the Dragon Society had prevented him from telling us every little detail of his sorcerous knowledge, and continued to prevent him from revealing what was asked.

"I told him that was insufficient, and he said that all he could do to appease me was to travel to a certain place and ask to be released from his ancient oath—that if I would allow him to do so, he would go, and would return promptly, and would then answer to the Society. I agreed, and he gathered his household, invited certain friends to join him, and early this morning he departed."

"Where is he going?" Flute asked.

"I don't know," Wither said. "I asked, but he would not tell me. He said he would be gone for a considerable time, but would return—by spring, most likely, and certainly within a year."

"But he's left Manfort," a woman called Glass said, looking at Arlian.

"Yes, he has," Wither agreed.

Nail snorted and rose. "It's a trap, of course," he said. "Enziet told me as much, and invited me to join him and the others. Oh, he's off on some mysterious errand to satisfy Wither, that's true enough, and I don't know a thing more about that than Wither's told you, but it's no coincidence that this is a chance for Arlian and *all* his sworn foes but me to meet outside the city walls." He looked directly at Arlian. "You can go after him if you like," he said. "He expects you to—and he'll be waiting."

Arlian stood and asked Wither, "Is this true?"

"I suppose it is," Wither admitted. "And the best thing all around is to get all of you out of here, so you can settle your disagreements once and for all and leave the rest of us undisturbed. Yes, I expect him to kill you, but if you go after him and *you* kill *him,* I won't weep—I'll be surprised, but I won't weep." He stepped closer and lowered his voice. "You've been stirring up trouble ever since you arrived, Obsidian, and I don't like it. One way or the other, I want it settled, so that the Society can go on in harmony as it always has."

"Spoilsport," Rime muttered.

Arlian glanced at her, then turned to Nail. "And why didn't you accept Enziet's invitation? Why didn't you go with him? I've sworn vengeance against you as much as the others."

"I'd prefer that you forsake that oath," Nail replied calmly. "I'd much rather have your forgiveness than your blood; I have apologized for my crimes before, and I will do so again, if you so desire. I have made what amends I can, and will make what further amends may be reasonably required of me. If after that you still insist on slaying me, well, I won't make it easy for you—I'll stay within these walls as long as I can. Enziet may be determined to see you destroyed, and Wither may wish an end to this stalemate, but I would much prefer to continue as we are."

Arlian stared at him for a moment, then at Wither.

"Why did you do it?" he asked. "Why did you warn him, and let him escape?"

The old man leaned over to him and whispered, "Listen, Obsidian—you were right. Enziet speaks with the dragons. He admitted it to me. But don't you see what that means?"

"No," Arlian said angrily. "Other than that he's deceived us all."

"It means he knows where they are!" Wither hissed. "He can go to them, and they won't kill him on sight, and he can fetch out venom!"

Arlian stared at him. "For your woman," he said.

"Yes!" Wither slapped the table. "For Marasa! And for *your* woman, if you have one! For anyone you choose! We can *all* be immortal!"

"And in exchange for his promise to fetch you venom, you let him go free," Arlian said bitterly.

"Yes." Wither sighed. "I didn't want to see this opportunity thrown away. I didn't want to see the Dragon Society destroyed by the feud between the two of you. So yes, I let him go, and when he returns, if he has the venom I intend to support him wholeheartedly."

"*If* he returns," Arlian corrected. "What if I kill him first?"

"That's a risk I'll take," Wither replied.

"Are you going after him?" Rime asked.

"It *is* a trap," Nail said.

"But it's also the opportunity you wanted," Wither said. Three of them, outside the walls."

Arlian looked from one to the other, trying to think.

His enemies were vulnerable, outside the protection of his membership oath—but they were expecting him, prepared and guarded, and he would be grossly outnumbered. Wither had set it up so that he would try, and would die in doing so, ending the conflict within the Society—and getting dragon venom for his mistress as well. Wither admitted as much—he had arranged for Arlian to die trying to carry out his revenge.

And back at the Old Palace, Sweet was waiting for him, still weak from her long ordeal—could he leave her?

There were other matters to consider, as well: Had Drisheen and Toribor taken their captives with them? Were those four women still alive? He would have to investigate that—if he stayed in the city.

But he had sworn to kill those three, and this was his chance.

But Sweet was in the Old Palace, in need of his care.

Perhaps he could wait, and then follow later, and catch Enziet and the others off guard after all—but if he waited, how would he know which way they had gone?

"Are you going?" Rime repeated.

"I don't know," Arlian said, burying his face in his hands. "I don't know!"

Chapter Fifty

A Sweet Parting

A rlian was troubled as he walked up the path to Lord Drisheen's mansion; Sweet was not recovering as quickly as he had expected. In fact, she had looked weaker than ever when he left her to come here.

He glanced at the guards on either side of him. He had arrived at the gate and asked after Drisheen, as if he had not already known the man was out of the city for an extended journey, and the gatekeeper had told him that Lord Drisheen was traveling, but had left detailed instructions of what to do if Lord Obsidian came visiting.

That should have worried him, but he was too concerned with Sweet's condition to think about it much. After all, Drisheen could not have ordered that any mortal harm be inflicted upon him. While the exact wording of the oath might possibly be interpreted to allow it, Drisheen must know that the rest of the Society would not stand for such trickery in this case.

He was being escorted up the front walk, between beds of bright flowers he barely saw, and into the foyer of the main house, a small room with windows of colored glass that streaked the marble floor with blue and yellow light. Here one of the guards who had accompanied him announced to a worried-looking housemaid, "This is Lord Obsidian."

"Oh," the maid said. "The one who…"

She didn't finish the sentence, but looked questioningly at the guard.

He nodded.

This exchange penetrated Arlian's distraction; he looked around, wondering whether Drisheen might have arranged some nonlethal trap.

"This way, then," the maid said, pointing and leading the way.

Arlian followed her down a corridor, around a turn, and finally into a tall library, where a balcony some ten feet above the floor encircled the room, giving access to a second tier of bookshelves.

Two naked bodies dangled from the balcony railing—two bodies with legs that ended in long-healed stumps, two women hanging from nooses around their necks.

"He hanged them last night," the housemaid said. "In a great hurry."

Arlian stared at the two dead women. Recognizing their twisted, congested features was not easy, but he knew them—Sparkle and Ferret.

"He said it was a gift just for you, my lord," the housemaid continued. "A going-away present, one we were to show you as soon as you came."

Arlian's teeth gritted; without a word he turned and marched out.

No one made a move to stop him, which was just as well—his hand was on his sword hilt, and Arlian would have cut down anyone, no matter who it was, who got in his way.

He had known that Enziet thought of other people, those who had not acquired the heart of the dragon, as unimportant, as things to be used or tossed aside as the whim took him; he had not realized that Drisheen shared that attitude.

And two more innocent women were dead because he had not realized they were in danger.

It might already be too late, but there were two more yet unaccounted for. Arlian was running by the time he left Drisheen's land, and wasted no time in proceeding to Toribor's more modest estate, on the southern edge of the Upper City.

"I'm looking for two slaves," he told the gatekeeper without preamble. "Two young women with no feet."

Startled, the gatekeeper stared at him. "Ah—would their names be Cricket and Brook?" the man asked.

"Yes," Arlian replied—by process of elimination, he now finally knew that the other dead women were Sandalwood and Amber; at last, all sixteen were accounted for.

"I thought you must mean them," the gatekeeper said. "They've lived here for years. They're the only ones with their feet cut off."

At least Toribor hadn't killed them long ago, as Enziet had killed Dove and Horim had killed Daub and her unknown companion—but he might have followed Drisheen's hideous example. *"Where are they?"* Arlian demanded.

"Lord Toribor took them with him," the gatekeeper said.

"They're still alive?" Arlian asked, relieved.

"Well, they were when they left," the gatekeeper said, clearly puzzled by the question.

Arlian did not bother to assuage the fellow's curiosity; he turned away without another word and headed home at a trot.

Two more dead—but two still alive! He might yet save them. A smile of relief struggled to be born at the thought, but he fought it down.

Cricket and Brook—he remembered them well. Cricket had been the very smallest of the women in the House of the Six Lords, and had been called upon to play the part of child in some customers' games—a role she hated, so that at other times she tried very hard to act older than her modest years.

And Brook had been named for her habit of humming and babbling quietly when working or when happy.

Those two were yet another argument in favor of leaving the city in pursuit of his foes—but Sweet worried him. She seemed so ill. His stillborn smile vanished completely, and he quickened his pace.

Home at the Old Palace he barely took time to toss his cloak aside before hurrying to Sweet's room. He had given her a chamber in the east wing, with a fine view of the garden—though this time of year that was no great delight, as the flowers were all done for the year and the leaves going brown.

Black met him in the passageway outside her room and said, "She's no better. Ari, this isn't the aftereffects of torture; should I send for a physician? I've asked Thirif if there's anything he or the other magicians can do, and he says there isn't."

"Of course they can't do anything," Arlian said. "Magic is all deceit and destruction. It can't heal. At best it could make her *think* she was well, and that would do more harm than good."

"Then should I summon a physician?"

Arlian shook his head. "Not yet," he said. "Let me talk to her first. She may know more than she's told us."

Black was clearly unhappy with this decision. "As you say," he said. "I've told the servants that there is to be someone in the room at all times, ready to help if anything happens."

"Good," Arlian said, clapping him on the shoulder. "Thank you, Black."

Black hesitated. "My true name is Beron," he said. "I've meant to tell you that for some time now. What of the other women, though?"

"Beron," Arlian acknowledged. He sighed. "Drisheen hanged the two he held—they were called Ferret and Sparkle. Lord Belly took Cricket and Brook with him."

"But they're alive?"

"So far," Arlian said.

"Will you tell her?"

"I'll decide that when the occasion arises."

"Good enough," Black said. With a nod, the men passed one another and Arlian entered Sweet's chamber. He found her lying in bed, talking quietly

415

with Kitten while a servant bustled about, dusting and straightening. Kitten was wearing a long blue gown intended to conceal the fact that she had no feet, and was perched on the edge of the bed, chatting happily.

All three women heard him enter and glanced at the door.

"Triv!" Sweet said, smiling broadly at the sight of him. She beckoned at him. Kitten turned and inched over to make room on the bed.

Arlian took the place offered and leaned over to kiss Sweet's brow. Her skin was clammy and sheened with sweat. When he straightened she raised a hand for him to hold, and he saw that it trembled.

Black was clearly right, as Arlian had already feared—this was more than the aftereffects of her long imprisonment.

"How are you feeling?" he asked.

"Wonderful, now that you're here," she said, beaming.

He smiled back briefly, but then his concern forced the corners of his mouth back down.

"Let me be blunt," he said. "You don't *look* wonderful. You look seriously ill. Should I send for a doctor?"

Her smile wavered. She shook her head. "No, no. I'm fine."

"You're *not* fine," Arlian insisted.

Her smile flickered, then vanished. She looked at Kitten, and at the servant, then up at Arlian.

"Send them away," she said.

"Sweet!" Kitten protested.

Arlian raised a hand to silence her. "I'll be right back," he told Sweet as he rose.

He scooped a protesting Kitten up in his arms, her blue gown tangling around one wrist; she didn't struggle, and threw her arms around his neck, but even as she did she was saying, "Triv, let me stay, please!"

"No," Arlian told her. "I'll bring you back in a moment, I promise." Then he turned to the housemaid, beckoning as best he could while holding Kitten. "Come," he said.

He carried Kitten down the hall to an adjoining chamber and set her in a chair there; the servant followed, and stood by, awaiting instructions.

"Attend her," he said, indicating Kitten. "I'll return soon." Then he hurried out.

A moment later he was again seated on Sweet's bed.

"You know what's happening to you, don't you?" he said. "Tell me what you know."

She smiled weakly at him. "I love you, Triv," she said.

"Then tell me," he insisted

"It's sorcery," she told him. "Lord Dragon's sorcery."

"What sort of sorcery? Has he cast a spell on you?"

"In a fashion," she said. She shuddered. "Every time he came to see me, he forced me to drink his blood."

Arlian stared at her. "But…but his blood is poison," he said.

"You know?" she asked, startled.

Arlian did not know how to answer that; he was not eager to tell this woman he cared for that his *own* blood was likewise polluted and toxic, yet he was demanding secrets from her—did he have the right to keep his own?

He nodded, but said nothing.

"Do you know any more than that?" Sweet asked eagerly. "Perhaps there's hope after all…"

"Tell me what you know," Arlian said, "and perhaps together we'll see what's to be done."

She frowned. "It started not long after he brought me to Manfort," she said. "I would still fight him sometimes back then, and once I bit his hand, hard enough that blood showed on his skin. Angered, after he knocked me away he grabbed me by the hair and said, 'So you like the taste of blood? Then blood you shall have!' And he shoved his hand in my mouth and made a fist, so that the blood oozed up.' She trembled at the memory. "It tasted *foul,* Triv. I've tasted blood before, and this was different. It stank of corruption."

"I can readily believe it," Arlian muttered.

"But then he snatched it away and said, 'No, that's too easy. Spit it out.' And I tried, I spat out all I could, but the next day I woke up sweating and trembling…"

"As you did today," Arlian said.

She nodded. "Yes," she said. "Just as today. And he came and looked at me, and I could see he was thinking. Then he went away for a time, leaving me there, and then came back with a needle. I thought he meant to draw my blood, but instead he jabbed his own hand with it, then forced open my mouth and smeared a drop of his blood on my tongue."

"But why?" Arlian asked, puzzled.

"An experiment, he called it. But it helped—the chills passed away, and I felt well again for a time. After a few days it happened again, and again he fed me a drop of his blood. It became a regular thing, a normal part of my

417

existence in that house. He told me that I was addicted, that my body had been changed forever by the sorcery in his blood, and that if I went without it, if we were ever parted for more than a few days, I would die." She smiled crookedly. "Only a single drop, though—more than that, he assured me, would kill me. After that I sometimes tried to cut or bite him, to draw more blood so that I might end my suffering, but I never managed it. Instead I got the one drop, whenever I needed it." She grimaced. "That went on all the time I was there; I tasted that stinking blood of his a hundred times. I was expecting another visit when you came to rescue me."

"But you believe you'll *die* of this?"

"He said so," Sweet said with a shrug.

"But…by the dead gods, Sweet, why didn't you say something? Why did you let me take you away if you knew you'd die without his blood?"

She smiled up at him. "Because," she said, "I would rather die here with you than live there with him."

Arlian stared silently at her for a moment as his throat tightened and his eyes moistened.

"You won't die," he said. "Not if I can prevent it!"

After all, if she needed the blood of a dragonheart, that was easily come by. He was tempted to draw his sword-breaker then and there, prick his finger, and let her taste a drop of his blood—but that would mean revealing that he was as tainted as Enziet, and he did not want Sweet to see that, not yet.

"I'll be right back," he said. He rose and stepped out into the hallway. There he drew his blade, jabbed the ball of his thumb, and squeezed out a thick drop of dark blood.

He could not let her see that it came from him, though; he smeared it onto the back of his other hand, then sheathed the blade and returned to her bed.

"Here," he said, holding out his bloodied hand. "Lick this."

She stared at the red smudge, then up at his face. "He's *here?*" she squeaked.

"No, of course not," Arlian said. "This came from another sorcerer."

Hesitantly, she lifted her head, closed her eyes, and thrust out her tongue, and Arlian pressed his hand to her lips.

She licked, and then gagged. He snatched his hand away.

"It's *different!*" she said. "It's…it's not the same, not as vile. It's foul, but different."

"It may work, all the same," Arlian said, worried.

"It may," she said, obviously not convinced. She sank back against the pillows and closed her eyes.

Arlian stared down at her. "I'll let you rest," he said.

He checked on her several times that night, and each time was the same—her brow damp with sweat, her hands trembling, her face pale and skin cool.

His blood had not been enough.

He consulted with Wither the next day, at the old man's home—Wither had seen and studied the effects of a dragonheart's blood before, in his attempts to preserve his women.

When Arlian explained the situation Wither's expression turned grave.

"I've never heard of anything like this," he said. "It seems Lord Enziet had *several* secrets he neglected to tell us." After some further discussion he came to the Old Palace, with a bagful of sorcerous equipment, to study Sweet's condition.

She allowed him to examine her, sampling her blood and saliva, only so long as Arlian was present. Arlian stayed with Sweet while Wither took his samples and sorceries away.

When he was done he sent a servant to inform Arlian, and the two men spoke privately in the small salon.

"It's not just the blood that has affected her," Wither explained. "It would appear that Lord Enziet is himself taking drugs, drugs I am not familiar with, and that he has passed on to this poor child in combination with his toxic blood."

"Can you do anything?" Arlian asked. "Can these drugs be duplicated?"

Wither shook his head. "I haven't the slightest idea. There's no way to tell from what little we know."

"Who *would* know?"

"Besides Enziet? I have no idea."

Arlian stared at him for a moment, then turned and called for his cloak and his sword.

Moments later he stood with his blade at the throat of the guardsman unfortunate enough to be at the gate of Enziet's home. Moments after that he was face to face with Enziet's steward.

"He took his medicines *with* him, of course," the steward explained. He was a thin, gray-haired fellow who did not seem particularly distressed by Arlian's forced entry or by the questions put to him; Arlian supposed that he had seen any number of irregular and extraordinary things in Enziet's employ, and had learned to take them in stride.

"What are his medicines?" Arlian demanded. "What does he take?"

"I don't know," the steward calmly replied. "It's secret. Most of the household doesn't even know he *takes* drugs, and none of us know what's in them. He obtains the ingredients himself, makes up the dosage himself—none of us ever interfere. Prying into my lord's affairs is *extremely* unwise."

Arlian stared at the steward angrily—but then released him. It was plain he was telling the truth. He returned home empty-handed.

That night he lay beside Sweet in her bed and told her, "I don't know what to do—should I go after Enziet and try to bring him back alive?"

"No!" she said. "He'll kill you."

"But you may die if he doesn't return."

"I don't mind," she said. "As I told you, it's better to die here than live…" She broke off and gasped suddenly and convulsively, then panted for a moment as Arlian leaped up and looked down at her helplessly.

"I'm sorry," she said, when her breathing had returned to normal. "I couldn't help myself." She laughed weakly. "I never did *that* before!"

Arlian frowned.

She might yet survive; she might fight off the poisons; but he could think of nothing more he could do. He could not imagine any way he could locate and capture Enziet and bring him back in time to help.

All he could do was make her comfortable and hope for the best.

All thought of tracking and killing Enziet had been thrust aside; Sweet's life was more important than his revenge. There would be time enough to deal with Enziet when she was recovered—or dead.

"You shouldn't have let me take you away from him," he murmured as he lay down beside her.

She smiled at him. "Don't be silly," she said.

"I love you," he said.

"That's silly, too," she said. "I'm a footless, drug-addicted whore, and you're Lord Obsidian. You'll be better off when I *do* die."

"No," he said, resting his hand on her heart. "You'll live through this somehow."

They fell asleep there.

Deep in the night, hours past midnight but long before dawn, Arlian awoke suddenly. Something had disturbed him, but at first he did not know what it was. Everything seemed utterly still.

Then he realized that that was it—it was *too* still. The beating of Sweet's heart beneath his hand, the gentle whisper of her labored breath, had stopped.

For a day she lay there as Arlian roamed aimlessly about the palace, weeping at times and silent at others. On the second day she was buried in the garden beneath her window as thin, dry flakes of snow, the first of the season, blew through the city streets.

And on the third day Arlian began preparations for the hunt, the pursuit, the fight that he was determined to win. He swore it over and over again.

Lord Enziet would die.

Book 4:

Lord Lanair

Chapter Fifty-One

In Pursuit

"Still to the south," Thirif said, studying the glowing crystal in his hand.

"Toward the Desolation," Arlian said.

"Yes," Thirif agreed.

Once Arlian had learned that Lord Enziet had headed south he had guessed that his destination lay somewhere in the Desolation, and every subsequent check had confirmed this suspicion.

Arlian reasoned that if Enziet had gone to fetch the venom that Wither demanded, leaving in early autumn, and if the dragons never emerged in cold weather, then he would have to go down into the dragons' caverns. Those caverns were said to be scattered throughout the Lands of Man, but Arlian had given the matter some thought, and concluded that the entrances could only be in deserted places, in wastelands where humans would not see the dragons going to and fro.

That could mean the steeper peaks in the western mountains, or the frozen plains of the far north—if dragons could tolerate such cold even in the summer—or any number of places Arlian had never seen, but Enziet had headed south, and in the rich lands to the south, between Manfort and the magic-haunted Borderlands, it seemed most likely to mean the Desolation.

Besides, Arlian remembered his earlier journey across that wasteland. He had seen signs that might have been left by dragons.

And in the Desolation Arlian expected Enziet to follow the Eastern Road, as it was along the rocky eastern route that caves and sinkholes abounded. The sandy interior seemed an unlikely place to find caverns. On the way to the Borderlands, more than two years earlier, a guard called Stabber had told him that there were caverns to the east of the three caravan routes.

Arlian had not been certain enough of his guesswork to simply head there directly, without further guidance, but the Aritheian magicians, working in concert and basing their spells on what they had learned from Sweet's poisoned blood, had devised a way to track Lord Enziet.

Due to his draconic taint, his great age and power, and the unique mix of drugs he took, Lord Enziet's blood was like nothing else in all the world, and the Aritheians had modified a crystal meant to find lost things so that it would respond only to Enziet. Thirif now held that magical stone in his hand, checking its glow periodically for any sign of change.

Four of the Aritheians had remained behind in Manfort. Hlur had been accepted by the Duke as the new Aritheian ambassador some time ago, and her husband had stayed with her, while Isein and Qulu, despite their poor command of the language, had agreed to stay and run Lord Obsidian's trade in magic.

Thirif and Shibiel had come with him—and would, if circumstances permitted, continue on home to Arithei when either Arlian or Enziet was dead.

Arlian had asked Black to remain behind as well, to look after his affairs and the Aritheians, but Black had refused.

"You'll need a guard," he said, "*Enziet* isn't traveling alone."

Arlian had argued, but in the end Black had prevailed; he now drove the wagon in which Arlian and Thirif and Shibiel—and Lady Rime—rode.

Arlian had more or less expected Black's behavior, but Rime's insistence on accompanying him had been a complete surprise.

"I know Enziet better than you do," she said. "And I have my own reasons for wishing him ill."

"It will be dangerous," Arlian had warned her. "We may very well all be killed by some ambush."

She had laughed bitterly. "I should have died four hundred years ago. I think you need a fellow dragonheart on your side, boy—Arlian's got Belly and Drisheen, and you'll have me. And I won't do anything foolhardy—with this leg of mine I'll hardly be able to. I'll ride in the wagon and keep your magician company, maybe teach him a little sorcery."

"As you wish, then."

And now the five of them were seated around a table in a Sadar inn, while Thirif and Shibiel tested the air for traces of Enziet's passage.

They had left Manfort eight days behind Enziet's party, half expecting to find them waiting in ambush just outside the gates, but while witnesses reported that Enziet had lingered in the area, he had not waited long enough for Arlian to find him. Eventually, days before Arlian set out, Enziet had moved on to the south.

Arlian's party had followed, moving as quickly as an ox-drawn wagon could go. The road was too rough for a coach—those fine springs and elegant spokes would have given out in short order—and while horses could draw a wagon well enough, Arlian considered oxen more reliable.

At Benth-in-Tara they were five days behind Enziet's party, according to the innkeeper, and Arlian had worried that Enziet might have turned aside into the hills.

At Jumpwater they had lost ground—Enziet's lead had widened to six days—but were still on the right trail. Arlian attributed the growing gap to the snowstorm that had struck midway between the two towns.

At Blasted Oak that gap was back to eight days, though no storm had intervened—in fact, the weather had seemed unnaturally warm, though the fields were brown and the trees leafless. Arlian had finally thought to ask the townspeople why Enziet might be moving more quickly, and had learned that Enziet's party was entirely on horseback, rather than riding an ox-drawn wagon—the number of men was estimated at twenty or so, the number of horses at thirty.

That was a great many horses, but Lord Enziet could afford them—as could Lord Obsidian, had he considered it.

"I should have thought of that," Arlian said, when he had told the others. "No wagon at all."

"Can you ride a horse?" Black asked.

"*I* cannot," Shibiel remarked.

"It's too late now, in any case," Rime said. "I wouldn't trust any mount I could find here. And after all, he'll be coming back north eventually."

Arlian had not found that a very satisfactory thought.

Now, in Sadar, they were nine days behind, but Arlian was growing ever less concerned about the possibility of losing the trail. Enziet was clearly following the caravan route to the Desolation. If the weather held, a fortnight would bring Arlian and the others to Cork Tree, and another fortnight would see them past Stonebreak and into the Desolation. Horses would not do any better in that dry waste than oxen.

"I'd say the ambush will be at Cork Tree," Black said. "Probably just north of town, so we'll be tired."

Startled, Arlian turned. "What?"

"The ambush," Black said. "You know, the trap? The attack?"

"What are you talking about?" Arlian demanded. "If they were going to ambush us, wouldn't they have done it long ago?"

Black sighed. "Ari, Enziet is a sorcerer, isn't he? A wily old man, known throughout Manfort for covering every detail?"

"He's right," Rime said. "He'll have been tracking *you,* just as you've tracked him. He'll know we're coming."

"How can he be tracking *me?*" Arlian asked. "He has nothing of mine to work from—no blood or magic." He looked at Thirif.

The Aritheian looked thoughtful. "I understand," he said. "I thought I was mistaken, or seeing old dreams left behind."

"What?"

"He cannot follow you," Thirif said, suddenly businesslike, "but we are passing through places he has been, at a time of year when few travel. He can easily set sorcerous wardings behind him, wards that ordinary people do not disturb but that respond to the presence of our magic."

"He wouldn't know I was bringing you two," Arlian said.

"He wouldn't need to," Rime said. "Remember how we're tracking *him.*"

"The heart of the dragon," Black said. "I still don't know what it is, but it's plain you and the Lady have it. That's what he's using."

"Yes," Thirif said. "I have felt the wards breaking, like an unseen spiderweb, but I did not recognize them for what they were."

"Then he knows we're following him," Arlian said.

"And how far behind we are," Black agreed.

"There's no reason to take Belly or Drisheen up onto the Desolation with him," Rime said. "He could leave them in ambush anywhere he wanted."

"But I say they'll be just north of Cork Tree," Black said, "because they'll want to be based out of a town, where they can sleep in comfort and buy the food they need. Stonebreak is too obvious, and would leave no second chance if we somehow slipped past. They aren't here in Sadar, and the villages in between are too small to hide them well. That leaves Cork Tree." He grimaced. "Sadar would have been better, but maybe he didn't think it through far enough in advance."

"Why didn't you say something sooner?"

Black looked exasperated. "Because," he said, "I thought you'd be bright enough to figure it out for yourself. After all, everyone's said all along that you knew this was a trap. And up until we reached Sadar, I hadn't thought out *where* the ambush would be."

"But I hadn't thought they'd split up, and Enziet's still far ahead of us! We might have walked right into it!"

"Ridden," Black said. "We haven't been walking. And I've been doing the driving, and I've been watching."

"But … but what would you have done if you *had* seen it?"

"Stopped."

"And *then* what?"

"I hadn't gotten that far."

"Oh, *that's* clever."

"I told you, I thought *you* were ready for it."

"Well, I'm not." Arlian frowned. "But I should be." He looked at Thirif and Shibiel. "They don't know we have magicians with us, do they?"

"How would I know?" Black asked, shrugging.

"Enziet knows you have magicians working for you," Rime said. "He'd assume you might have brought them, but whether he'd tell the others I can't say."

"He wouldn't," Arlian said. "Not if he's leaving them in ambush."

"You probably know him better than I do, but wouldn't he want them to be ready?" Black asked.

Arlian shook his head. "He'd want them confident. He might have told Toribor and Drisheen, but no one else; he wouldn't want them scared."

Rime nodded. "I'd say you're right."

"Then we have surprise on our side." He turned to Thirif. "What can you do to aid us?"

Thirif looked troubled. "You know the nature of magic, my lord."

"I know something of it," Arlian agreed. "Not that much."

Thirif sighed. "Our power is weak here. The dreams are thin and pale, like mist, while the dreams of Arithei are deep water. We cannot create new spells here, but only expend those we brought with us. We have certain magicks I thought might be useful, some of which can be modified; we can work deceptions, or expand the senses, but not much more than that. At home we could shake the earth, draw fire from the sky, summon beasts from the night—but not here. Here we have only the subtle magicks and preparations."

"Sorcery," Rime said. "They've become sorcerers."

Thirif nodded in her direction. "In a way," he agreed. "We still use our own methods—but those are not suited to this place. Lady Rime may be of more help to you than we are."

"But you worked magic in Manfort!"

"We could use the magical things we brought with us," Thirif said, "and we could work minor deceptions and small magics. No more."

"You set up wards."

"We had brought many wards with us; I told you as much."

Arlian knew that was true. "You cast a glamour on me," he said, still hoping for more.

"Also a small magic we had brought with us, and one in those categories I described. Wards are an expansion of the senses, glamour a simple deception. These take no great power. To quickly stroke down a foe—*that* takes great power."

"But who asked you to?" Arlian asked. "I asked what you *can* do, not what you *cannot*."

"Ah." Thirif spread his hands. "We can do here what we could do in Manfort, no more or no less—save that we brought only a few potions and talismans with us, as we did not wish to deplete your stock-in-trade any more than necessary. I have the makings of a dozen wards and a score of glamours, a handful of illusions—nothing more."

"But you have glamours?"

"Of course."

Arlian nodded. "Then disguise us," he said.

Thirif frowned. "We cannot fool the wards Lord Dragon has set."

"We don't need to fool *them,*" Arlian said. "We need to fool *Toribor*. And Drisheen. And the guards they brought with them."

"Ah," Thirif said again. A rare smile appeared on his grim brown face. "I see," he said.

"You think they won't know who we are?" Black asked.

"They're not caravan lords," Arlian said. "They haven't traveled this road often, if at all; how would they know what to expect? If they see five strangers riding in a wagon, will they think it's the people they're waiting for, or will they assume we're just the local traders we'll appear to be? They're probably expecting us to be on horseback, just as they are."

"Are you planning to ride right past them, then?" Rime asked.

"Yes," Arlian said. "And then I mean to find Toribor and Drisheen, and kill them."

Black sighed. "I thought you wanted Enziet."

"I do," Arlian said, "but I want Drisheen, too." The image of Ferret and Sparkle hanging in Drisheen's library loomed large in his memory, and his hand tightened on his mug until his knuckles turned white. "And Toribor—but I want Drisheen more. I believe I might even be willing to let Toribor live if it meant I could kill Drisheen, but I don't think Toribor will agree to that, do you?"

"I doubt the guards will, either," Black remarked dryly.

"And that's *your* job," Arlian said. "Keep them away long enough to give me a chance."

"To kill *both* of them? Skilled swordsmen far older than yourself?" Black threw up his hands. "Why don't the rest of us just turn back now, if you're so determined to die? This whole thing is pointless—I don't know why I came!"

"I'm not determined to die," Arlian said quietly.

"But you're going to give them a chance, aren't you?" Rime said disgustedly. "You won't just cut their throats while they sleep, will you?"

"No, I won't," Arlian admitted. "But I'm not planning on duels, either. They had their chance to meet me honorably. They had their chance to make peace with me, as Nail did. And you're all sure they're planning to ambush me. I intend to kill them both." He bared his teeth in an ugly expression. "I intend to give them a chance—more than they gave Rose, or Sparkle, or Ferret, or the rest—but not an *even* chance."

Black and Rime stared at him, then exchanged glances with one another.

Then Rime smiled.

"That's *better*," she said.

Chapter Fifty-Two

Ambush

"We have just passed a ward," Thirif announced. Arlian looked at him, startled, and was startled anew by the unfamiliar face he found—he had momentarily forgotten the glamour Shibiel had cast on her companion the night before.

They were roughly a day's journey north of Cork Tree, and had made preparations the night before for the ambush they expected to encounter. That was for later, though, perhaps even the next day if they did not reach Cork Tree by nightfall; right now it was early morning, and they had just broken camp half an hour before.

Up until now, Thirif had only sensed wards in towns or at easily remembered landmarks; no such feature was anywhere in sight.

"Out *here?*" Arlian asked.

Thirif nodded.

Black, on the driver's seat, had overheard; he leaned back through the wagon's door. "It's to let them know to ready the ambush," he said.

It was odd for Arlian to hear Black's words coming from the scruffy, long-haired, gray-clad figure that drove the wagon. "But *Enziet* set the wards, didn't he?" Arlian asked. "And he's in the Desolation by now…"

"Drisheen is as practiced a sorcerer as Enziet," Rime pointed out. The glamour had subtracted a dozen years from her already-deceptive appearance and transformed her wooden leg to a clubfoot—the limp could not be hidden, only disguised.

"Oh," Arlian said. "Thirif, how do I look? Is the glamour holding?"

"Of course," Thirif said.

"Good," Arlian said. He looked around at the others.

He would certainly not have recognized them. The Aritheians' exotic southern features had been replaced by utterly ordinary faces; Rime's intensity was hidden beneath a moon-shaped visage and mousy brown hair; Black's distinctive leather clothing and close-cropped black hair had been replaced by homespun wool and shaggy brown locks.

A sorcerer of any talent would be able to see through the disguises, if he were close and made an effort—but why would Drisheen, or even the less-

433

skilled Toribor, bother to look closely?

"Good enough," Arlian said. "Black—I mean, Gall—when do you expect we'll reach them?"

"Midafternoon would be my guess," Black replied, "but I can't be sure."

"Good enough," Arlian repeated. "Drive on."

They stopped to eat lunch and water the oxen at midday, but otherwise pressed on as quickly as they could. "If we arrive sooner than they expect us, they'll be that much more likely to believe our disguises," Arlian explained to Shibiel, who was nervous and unsure just what to expect.

"But they're expecting us on horses," Rime said. "On horseback we'd get there even earlier."

Arlian frowned at that. "But they won't expect us to arrive by *wagon* as soon as we will," he said.

As the day wore on and no ambushers appeared Arlian grew ever more nervous; he began talking compulsively to Rime in an attempt to calm himself. His chatter became sufficiently annoying that the Aritheians got out of the wagon to walk; Rime, with her wooden leg, could not practically avail herself of that option.

She did not seem to mind, however, and when he began to run short of things to say was willing to oblige him with a few stories of her own centuries of life; she had roamed extensively, for more than a century, before finally reaching Manfort and discovering the Dragon Society. She had dozens of anecdotes to tell about those years of wandering.

She told him about being pursued through the streets of Clearpool by a pack of hounds after she cut the throat of Lord Water's son, who had raped her. She described how she came to be snowbound in the Sawtooth, where she smashed her leg in an avalanche and became so desperate for food that she amputated, cooked, and ate the ruined portion, saving the bone as a reminder. Despite his nervousness, she rendered Arlian helpless with laughter with her account of how it had once taken her three days to catch a cat that had stolen her favorite gloves.

During a lull in the conversation, though, Arlian realized that she had not mentioned one incident he was curious about.

"You once said you had your own reasons for wishing Enziet ill," he said. "What are they?"

She glanced sideways at him. "Why do you ask?"

"Mere curiosity," he said, realizing a trifle belatedly that he was being a shade more inquisitive than was entirely polite. "If you would prefer not to say..."

"I generally would," she said, "but today, when we may all die in an ambush at any moment, I find myself willing to speak. You will recall, I trust, that I said I had a husband and four children when a dragon destroyed our village. I told you that my husband died, and let you think that my children died, as well—but in fact, my eldest daughter was not at home. She had married and moved away the year before, and when I had climbed from the well I made my way to her home and threw myself on her mercy. She took me in and cared for me, and I lived there for quite some time—but when her neighbors began to notice that *she* looked older than *I* did, I departed, before accusations of black sorcery arose. Still, I returned anonymously now and then to visit my grandchildren, and my great-grandchildren, and on through the generations." She sighed.

"The family survived, but did not particularly thrive; I have perhaps thirty living descendants today, hardly a large number after four hundred years. I would probably have several more, however, had not one branch of the family fallen into the hands of Lord Enziet's hired slavers."

"But didn't you..." Arlian began.

"Protest?" She shook her head. "By the time I found out what had become of them it was too late—all but one were dead, and the last was mutilated, no longer fit for anything but the life to which Enziet had consigned her. I had told everyone that like the other dragonhearts I had no family, so that no one could use them against me, or gain a hold over me by threatening them, and yet they had died nonetheless; once that had happened, and was over and done, what was the point in admitting my lies? No one would care that Enziet had destroyed half a dozen innocent lives—they were only mortals, whatever their ancestry, and Enziet is the senior member of the Dragon Society."

"I'm sorry," Arlian said.

"You knew the last of them, I think," Rime said. "I believe she was called Rose, and was the Rose you knew."

Arlian sat in stunned silence for a moment, then swallowed. "Oh," he said.

"I don't even remember how many generations lay between us," Rime said. "In truth, I don't suppose she shared any more of my blood than any of a thousand others, and the ties have grown weak over the long years—whether by nature or because the taint in my blood has turned my heart cold, I can't say. Still, I had looked after my family as best I could for

435

a very long time, and from the time I came to Manfort until Enziet's actions, none of them had ever known any real want or serious hardship that wealth or influence might spare them."

"Oh," Arlian said again.

"I'd be glad to see Lord Enziet taught a lesson in arrogance and humility," she said. "I had not thought I would ever be fortunate enough to see it."

"Well, it hasn't happened yet," Arlian said.

"It's begun," Rime insisted. "That he is making his way into the Desolation in pursuit of dragon venom, rather than sitting safely at home plotting the governance of Manfort, is a beginning. You've uncovered his secrets, or at least a taste of them."

"Well, we know that he knows more about the dragons than he's told the Society," Arlian agreed, "but we don't know *what* he knows."

"He can apparently speak to a dragon," Rime said. "We know *that* much. And a black dragon, at that."

"Is there some significance to its color?" Arlian asked.

"Don't you know?" She looked startled. "The black dragons are the eldest, the wisest and most powerful. A dragon's color darkens with age. The youngest ever seen by men were said to be golden, though those were mere striplings by dragon standards, and never ventured out into the open air—they were reported by people who had been down into the caverns in the old days, when the dragons ruled the world. No one has seen one in…well, in a thousand years or more, I would say. The mature dragons are green—it's said the green color appears first at the spine and then spreads until the entire beast is bright green. But then the color continues to darken, until at last the ancients of the dragon realm are utterly black, as black as their monstrous hearts."

"The three who destroyed Obsidian were black," Arlian said. "One still showed a trace of green, I think, but they were black."

"Then they were old," Rime said. She frowned. "That's curious, you know," she added. "The one that destroyed *my* home was very dark, as well, though some green still showed. In all the old tales, though, the beasts that ravaged the countryside or fought against the liberators of humanity were green, and the black ones were said to lurk deep beneath the earth, directing their younger kin from afar."

"Perhaps there *are* no more green dragons," Arlian suggested. "Perhaps only the black ones survive, down there in the dark, and that's why they wearied of the fight and left the surface world to us."

"But what would have become of the young ones?" She shook her head. "I doubt it's anything so simple as that."

"I suppose not." Arlian lapsed into silence, having finally exhausted his urge to babble, and having found things to think about other than the impending ambush.

Just then Black called quietly, "They're in the grove ahead of us, on both sides of the road."

Arlian and Rime exchanged glances; then Arlian turned and clambered toward the front of the wagon, so that he could see out the door.

A big man had just stepped out into the roadway and was holding up his hands, signaling Black to stop. Black reined in the oxen.

"That's Shamble!" Arlian whispered, as he recognized that ugly face.

"Shut up," Rime hissed back.

"What do you want?" Black demanded. "Why are you stopping us?"

"We just want to see who you've got in there," Shamble replied, in his rumbling growl of a voice. As he spoke two other men stepped out of the trees, swords drawn and ready—one of them was Lord Toribor, and the other looked familiar as well.

The two Aritheians, their disguises intact, ambled up beside the oxen, as well—the road was becoming almost crowded.

"We want to get to Cork Tree before dark," Thirif said.

"Then let us look, and we'll let you go," Shamble said.

"Look for what?" Black asked.

"A sorcerer," said the unidentified man, and the voice was the clue Arlian needed—he recognized him now as Stonehand. Three of his enemies stood here before him!

He resisted the temptation to say anything.

"An outlaw sorcerer, fleeing from Manfort," Stonehand elaborated. "He's said to be heading this way. Have you seen him? He looks like a young man, fairly tall and strongly built; he's probably on horseback."

Two more swordsmen had appeared now, but these two were strangers. Arlian could also see archers still more or less in hiding.

"Haven't seen anyone like that," Black said. He asked Thirif, "You seen anyone like that?"

Thirif shook his head.

"Mind if we take a look in your wagon?" Shamble growled.

Black looked at the four drawn swords and shrugged. "I can't stop you," he said.

At that, three of the swordsmen approached the wagon. Shamble stayed where he was, though, and Toribor came more slowly, hanging back behind the others.

Black slid aside to let the three climb aboard.

"Good afternoon," Arlian said, tipping his cap to the first guardsman.

"Anyone else in here?" the intruder demanded, waving the blade of his weapon back and forth across the wagon's interior.

"Just the two of us," Arlian said. "So who is this sorcerer? What did he do?"

"Killed a man," Stonehand said, as he squeezed inside and looked about. "He calls himself Lanair, but he may use other names, as well."

"Who did he kill?" Arlian asked. "Anyone important?"

Stonehand shrugged. "Important enough. A man called Lord Iron. He had the concession to supply equipment and training for the Duke's guards."

"The *Duke* is involved?" Arlian said, trying hard to look impressed.

As they spoke the first swordsman was pawing through the supplies, moving the bundles and boxes about to be sure no one was hiding among them. Now he turned and said, "There's no one here."

Stonehand frowned, and looked at Arlian and Rime. "If you two would be so kind as to step outside, where Lord Belly can have a look at you?"

Arlian glanced at Rime, then shrugged. "Why not?"

Actually, as he climbed out of the wagon he realized why not. If Toribor, who knew at least a little sorcery and knew both Arlian and Rime, stared at them closely enough with his one good eye he might penetrate their disguises.

Arlian couldn't see any way to avoid that risk, however. He dropped to the ground and waited.

Toribor approached cautiously and looked at Arlian and Rime.

"Know them?" Stonehand asked from the wagon door.

Toribor shook his head. "The woman might be a bit familiar," he said, "but it's probably a chance resemblance. Certainly neither of them is Lord Obsidian."

"Who?" Arlian asked—and he immediately regretted it, because the timing of his question had been just slightly too slow, not quite natural.

No one else seemed to notice his slip, however.

"The man we're looking for," Toribor said. "It's none of your concern." He waved a hand in dismissal. "Get back in your wagon and go on."

"Thank you, my lord," Arlian said, doffing his cap and bowing.

A moment later they were rolling again, with Thirif and Shibiel back in the wagon along with Arlian and Rime, while Toribor, Shamble, and the others had stamped back into the trees, out of sight.

No one in the wagon dared speak at first, but when they had put a hundred yards or more between themselves and their enemies Arlian said, "I wonder where Drisheen was?"

"In the trees to the left, I think," Rime replied. "I thought I could sense him. I just hope he couldn't sense *us*—if he felt the presence of sorcery he'd suspect something."

"I hadn't thought of that," Arlian said. He frowned worriedly.

"What could you have done if you *had* thought of it?" Rime asked.

Arlian had no answer for that.

"Should I remove the glamour?" Thirif asked.

"No!" Arlian said. "No, no. We'll need it. After all, we're staying in Cork Tree tonight—and I'm sure *they* are, too."

"Once they give up waiting for Lord Lanair," Rime agreed. She smiled. "This could be very interesting."

Chapter Fifty-Three

The Inn at Cork Tree

There were no rooms at the inn in Cork Tree; Lord Enziet's party had taken them all. Arlian and his companions were allowed to park their wagon in the stableyard, however, and to purchase the ordinary supper. The five travelers had eaten and drunk their fill when the disgruntled ambushers finally came straggling in.

"…sorcery, I tell you," one man in Enziet's livery was saying as he entered.

"It probably was," Lord Toribor agreed wearily. "He probably knew we were there and went around us, and is well on his way to Stonebreak by now."

Arlian turned to look at the new arrivals.

"Shall we go after him?" Stonehand asked.

"I don't know," Toribor said. "I'll need to talk it over with Drisheen. For now, though—innkeeper!"

The innkeeper appeared, a tray ready in his hands. "The ale's still cold," he said, "and I've kept your supper warm, but it may be the worse for the wait."

Arlian looked at his own empty mug. The ale was not exactly *cold*—the innkeeper presumably stored it in a deep cellar, so it was reasonably cool, but it was clear no magic was used, nor even a proper icehouse. It was not cold. It was good enough ale, but it would have been better were it somewhat colder.

Arlian remembered wryly that less than three years ago he had never tasted ale, yet here he was casually passing judgment on the stuff. He thumped the mug down on the table and looked around.

The dining room, which had been mostly empty moments before, was suddenly almost full. Most of the available chairs were occupied. Toribor and Stonehand were side by side at one table; Shamble was at the next. The inn's entire staff—the innkeeper, his wife, and three young people who might have been either his children or hired help—was busily serving out mugs of beer and plates of gravy-soaked ham.

Black belched contentedly, as if the sight of all that ham reminded him

441

of the portion he had eaten himself. He leaned over and said quietly, "I count eleven."

"Not all fighters, though," Arlian muttered in reply—he could see a young boy among the others, and two women who looked too frail to be warriors of any sort. "Where's Drisheen?"

"I don't see him," Rime said.

"Blast it!" Arlian replied. "Where is he, then?"

Just then the door opened again and a guardsman entered, followed by an elaborately dressed lord, a feathered hat in his hand.

"*There* he is," Rime said.

Drisheen paused in the doorway, nose in the air, and surveyed the room. Then he flourished his hat as if waving away an unpleasant odor and stepped inside.

A faint scent reached Arlian, a sweet, cloying scent that was oddly familiar. He frowned, trying to place it.

Then it came back to him, in a sudden wave of memory—falling in through Sweet's window, tumbling onto the floor of a room that stank of perfume, where he had abruptly gone from the cold and empty outside world to the comforting warmth of a woman's arms.

Sweet had opened the window to air out the room, to get rid of the stench of Lord Drisheen's perfume—and Lord Drisheen.

He had smelled it again in Manfort, once or twice—most recently, very faintly, when he had seen Sparkle and Ferret hanging in Drisheen's library.

And that same smell was present now. In Westguard it had been diluted by the scent of powder and cloth and oil and of course Sweet herself, while here it was mixed with beer and bread and smoke and meat and sweat, but it was unmistakably the same smell.

The memory of Sweet's smiling face and cheerful giggle hung there for a moment, then gave way to the sight of her lying pale and still in the bed beside him, eyes closed but mouth slack and open.

He felt his teeth clench, a growl rising in his throat as his eyes followed Drisheen's progress across the room.

"Hush!" Rime hissed.

Arlian caught himself. "Sorry," he said.

Drisheen had reached the table where Toribor and Stonehand sat, and was standing there as they turned to look up at him. Arlian strained to hear what was said.

Thirif, across the table, crushed a tiny blue vial in his hand, and suddenly

Arlian's hearing sharpened.

"I have placed wards on the road, on the trees, and on the entire town," Drisheen said. "If any dragonheart enters this place, we will know it."

Arlian glanced at Rime, who mouthed, "We're already here."

"Good," Toribor said. "Have a seat, my lord, and eat something." He gestured at an empty chair.

"In good time. I would hear, first, whether you have any explanation for the failure of our trap. Do you think your men were so clumsy that he saw us before we saw him, and turned aside therefore?"

Toribor shook his head. "No," he said. "I think he's just cagy. He guessed that we might have set traps upon the high road, and found another route."

Drisheen frowned as he tucked his hat under his arm. "And what do you propose to do about this?"

"I don't know what we *can* do," Toribor said with a shrug. "If you have suggestions I will be delighted to hear and consider them, but left to my own devices I'd say we've missed him, that he chose to bypass us and he's now Enziet's problem."

"And this doesn't trouble you? We were put here to stop him. We have a dozen soldiers; Enziet is alone."

"Alone or not, do you really think he can't handle a stripling like Lanair?" Toribor gestured at the table. "Sit down and have a drink!"

"You sound almost *pleased* to have avoided a fight," Drisheen said, still standing.

"I am—almost. I'd rather have it over with, but that boy has the luck of a dragon. Remember, he killed Iron and Kuruvan. Mishaps can happen anywhere, and even facing a dozen men he might have found a way to do you or me harm before he died."

"Yet you aren't troubled about letting him find Enziet?"

"Enziet has the luck of a *dozen* dragons," Toribor answered.

"Or the skill," Drisheen said.

"Or the skill," Toribor agreed. "Now, I beg you, my lord, do sit down!"

Drisheen reluctantly yielded; he circled around, tossed his hat on the table, and seated himself.

"*Do* you have any suggestions, my lord?" Toribor asked, as Drisheen beckoned to a serving maid.

"Only that we wait here, and send our best men to trail Enziet and warn him, or aid him against Lanair."

Stonehand glanced at Toribor, a motion that Drisheen noticed. "Yes, our best man would be you," he said.

Arlian considered that. It probably meant that Stonehand would be alone on the road …

"Send him alone?" Toribor asked. "And what if Stonehand here happens upon Lord Lanair?"

Drisheen shrugged. "Why would Lanair wish an ordinary soldier ill? I assume Stonehand is capable of discretion and stealth, and can defend himself if pressed."

"We could send another man with him…"

"And another, and another, and before you know it we'll all be on the road, chasing after our murderous lordling, and probably missing him entirely. A man travels fastest when he travels alone."

Toribor frowned. "I suppose that's true."

"I can handle him," Stonehand said.

"That's what Lord Iron thought," Drisheen said. "And Kuruvan before him. No, while you can take your chance if you see it, your first duty is simply to warn Enziet, then return and tell us what, if anything, you saw along the road. We missed the boy in one direction, but perhaps we'll catch him going the other."

"As you say, my lord," Stonehand said, bowing his head in obedience.

"You don't suppose Lanair could have been hidden in that wagon, do you?" Toribor asked.

Drisheen held up his hand and pointed at Arlian, who tried hard to look as if he hadn't been listening; Toribor glanced over his shoulder, then turned back to Drisheen and shrugged.

Drisheen leaned forward and whispered to Toribor, and even with his magically enhanced hearing Arlian could not make out what was said. He turned his attention back to his own party.

"Thank you," he said to Thirif, who nodded a polite acknowledgment.

Arlian resisted the temptation to turn and watch the others as they whispered; it would only draw suspicion.

"What are you planning?" Rime asked quietly.

"Stonehand will be alone on the road for a few days," Arlian said. "I can catch him then, talk things over, and deal with him as seems appropriate. As for Drisheen and Toribor, well, as lords, they won't be sleeping with the others; they'll either have one room apiece, or one room between the two of them, and we'll probably be able to tell which because they'll post a guard at the door. I think I'd like to settle matters with them right here—for Sparkle and Ferret. And Brook and Cricket may be here—if they are, I'd like to free them."

"So you intend to break into Drisheen's room?" Black asked.

Arlian nodded.

"And you'll know which room it is by the guard at the door."

"That's right."

Black nodded. "And how do you plan to get *past* that guard?" he asked.

"I'm working on that," Arlian said wryly. "If you have any suggestions, I'd be pleased to hear them."

"Not a one," Black said.

"You wanted Shamble, too, didn't you?" Rime asked.

Arlian shrugged. "He'll have to wait—which scarcely troubles me, as his crimes are already old, and he holds no hostages. I'd assume he'll be sharing a room with the other henchmen, and we don't want to fight them all."

"Ah, we don't?" Black said. "I'm glad to hear that. And about getting past that guard?"

"Could you find another way into the room?" Rime asked. "A window, perhaps? Or through the roof?"

"The roof's good, sound tile," Arlian said. "I noticed that earlier. How could I get through that? And how would I get to an upstairs window without being seen? How would I get in when it's shuttered?"

"Excellent questions, all of them," Black agreed.

Arlian turned to Thirif. "Do *you* have any suggestions for getting past the guard? Could you put him to sleep, or muffle his cries if he raises an alarm?"

Thirif thought for a moment, then shook his head. "No," he said. "Not with what I've brought."

"Maybe if Thirif got Drisheen involved in a discussion of the finer points of sorcery, you could creep up behind him and stab him in the back," Black suggested sardonically.

"I'm not a mere sorcerer," Thirif said. "I am a *true* magician."

"And how much of a difference is there, really?" Black asked. "You both do your little tricks and petty miracles, waving your jeweled wands about."

Thirif did not deign to respond to that; he simply turned away in disgust.

Arlian, however, looked at Black thoughtfully. "I don't know much about sorcery," he said, "but I suppose most people know even less."

"Probably," Black agreed, startled. "What of it?"

"Well, I think I have a way past Drisheen's guard," Arlian said.

445

"Drisheen's? What about Belly's?"

"Let's take care of the one first, shall we?"

Black shrugged.

Three hours later most of the inn's inhabitants had drifted off to bed. The innkeeper dozed in a chair by the hearth. Arlian and his party had retired to their wagon—but now he reentered the dining room, with Black at his heels.

The innkeeper started awake and stared at him.

Arlian held up a small object that glittered gold in the firelight. "We found this in the stableyard," he said. "I think that lord must have dropped it. The one with the fancy hat."

The innkeeper squinted. "I'll take it," he said.

Arlian clutched the object to his chest. "I don't think so," he said. "*We* found it, and we're honest enough to return it—the reward's *ours.*"

The innkeeper snorted. "Fine, then." He waved at the stairs. "Find your own way." He leaned back.

"I will," Arlian said.

Together, he and Black crossed the room and started up the stairs.

"I saw Thirif give you that," Black whispered, "but what *is* it?"

"I have no idea," Arlian said, "but it looks magical, doesn't it?" He held it up so that it shone in the lamplight on the stairs.

The object was a golden cylinder worked with runes and with a ring of small red stones set around one end; Arlian had chosen it from half a dozen implements in Thirif's collection as looking appropriately sorcerous.

"So you'll tell the guard you want to return Drisheen's trinket, and he'll let you in—but what if he insists we leave our swords outside?"

"Then we'll find other weapons," Arlian said. "Shut up and come on."

They arrived at the top of the stairs and found themselves facing a corridor with three doors on either side, and a door at the far end—and a big man in a guard's uniform was leaning against the frame of that farthest door, eyes closed, arms folded across his chest.

Arlian felt an odd twinge, and the thing in his hand felt suddenly warm, but he dismissed it as imagination brought on by the excitement of approaching danger.

"That's their room," he said. "It must be."

Black didn't bother to answer. The two men advanced down the passageway. At the halfway point Arlian felt another twinge, stronger this time, as if his heart had momentarily twisted in his chest. He stopped, but before he could do anything the guard, presumably alerted by the sound of their footsteps, roused himself and dropped a hand to the hilt of his sword.

"Who are you?" he demanded. "What do you want here?"

Arlian held up his talisman. "We found this," he said. "We think one of your lords must have dropped it."

That twinge troubled him. He had been nervous any number of times—when he was preparing to fight Kuruvan, for one—and he had never felt anything exactly like that before. Usually his hands trembled when he was nervous, but now they were as steady as he might ask.

"Let me see it," the guard demanded.

Arlian snatched his hand away. "*We* found it! And we'll be the ones who collect the reward!"

"You want me to wake Lord Drisheen at this hour of the night?"

"No," Arlian said meekly. "You're right; we'll come back in the morning."

Black looked at him in open astonishment. "We will?"

"Yes," Arlian said. "Run!" He spun on his heel and ran for the stairs.

The door at the end of the corridor slammed open, and Arlian ducked as a bow twanged, sending an arrow over his left shoulder.

He and Black tumbled down the stairs, half running, half falling; behind them Arlian heard several voices shouting, doors slamming, and the clatter of boots, bare feet, and armor.

"What the hell…" Black gasped as they dashed across the dining room.

"Wards," Arlian said. "On the stair and in the hallway. Drisheen knew I was there."

The innkeeper started up from his chair, shouting, "What? What is it?" They ignored him and ran out the front door; Arlian could hear boots coming down the stairs behind them.

When they were outside Arlian turned toward the yard where the wagon waited. The oxen were not hitched up, he remembered—keeping them yoked would have been too suspicious, should anyone happen to look out a window and see them. And of course, no one could seriously attempt escape in an ox-drawn wagon in any case; men or horses could easily catch up with the fastest oxen.

Still, he had to warn Rime and the Aritheians.

Once that was done, though, he intended to make life interesting for his pursuers. Simple escape on foot was impossible—he didn't know the countryside, and he couldn't realistically expect to outrun all his foes—but there were other things he could do.

"See what you can do to protect the others," Arlian gasped as they rounded the corner. He shouted, "Look out!" then ran past the wagon to the stables.

He opened a stall door at random and grabbed at the mane of the horse inside. He was no horseman, but he had learned a few basics to suit his role as Lord Obsidian; he was able to swing himself up on the animal's bare back before the beast was entirely awake.

Startled, the horse bolted out of the stall into the yard, then slowed, confused. Arlian sat up and drew his sword; he hung onto his mount's mane with his left hand.

People were milling about the yard, their faces invisible in the darkness—the inn's two stablehands were probably there somewhere, and Black, and Arlian's other companions might be, as well, but there were others who were undoubtedly some of Enziet's men.

"Light!" someone bellowed. "We need a light!"

"Who's that?" someone else called.

Arlian dug in his heels, and the horse jerked forward, breaking into a canter; shadowy figures scattered out of his way as Arlian rode out of the stableyard onto the high road.

Someone had relit the lanterns by the inn's signboard, and a man stood near the door holding a torch; Arlian was plainly visible to the knot of people there as he rode past, and several voices added cries of, "There he is!" and "Get the horses!" to the mounting din. Lights were beginning to appear in the windows of neighboring houses now, as well.

He prodded the horse into a gallop—which meant clinging desperately with both hands, the blade of his sword waving wildly in front of his face—and glanced back over his shoulder.

People were pouring out of both the inn and the stableyard, shouting and running; some were chasing the fleeing horse while others seemed to be running around totally at random.

Arlian hoped this would be enough distraction for Black and the others to find safety somehow. Then he turned his face forward again and buried his nose in the horse's mane, hanging on for dear life.

The animal slowed to a trot after perhaps two hundred yards, and Arlian raised his eyes. He saw only darkness ahead—a deeper darkness to either side, paler above. As the horse fell into a walk he looked back.

The road had curved; he could see a glow that he knew must be the mob around the inn, but trees and houses hid everything else.

They would undoubtedly be coming after him, though—he could still hear shouting, and it seemed to be coming closer.

Besides, he wasn't interested in mere escape. They might expect him simply to flee, but it was not what he had planned.

He was heading in the right direction to go after Enziet—but that was exactly the course of action Drisheen probably anticipated from him. Arlian was not ready to go after Enziet; he had unfinished business here in Cork Tree.

He slid from the horse's back to the ground, landing awkwardly but scrambling quickly to his feet. He slapped the horse's side, startling it back into a trot; as it continued southward down the high road he turned aside, into the brush beside the road, and once safely out of sight he began working his way back toward the inn.

Chapter Fifty-Four

The Sword of Vengeance

Arlian wished he knew enough sorcery to alter his appearance anew, so that he would have neither his own face nor the one his foes had seen in the wagon and the inn. Unfortunately, he had no prepared spells with him, nor any idea how a glamour was cast, and Thirif and Shibiel were not there to help.

As he walked through gardens and yards, climbing over fences and leaping ditches, he did rearrange his hair—in the wagon he had worn it loose, brushed forward at the sides, after the fashion of the local farmers. Now he combed it back with his fingers, and used his swordbreaker to cut away locks on either side, shaping it into something marginally more like a traditional Manfort style—not that he could see what he was doing, in the dark with no mirror. He removed his homespun tunic, revealing the good linen blouse he had worn underneath—not so much because he anticipated a need to change his appearance as because he preferred the feel of the smoother fabric on his skin, the warmth of an additional layer had been welcome, and in his rushed preparations he hadn't brought any silk undershirts.

He was uncomfortably aware that he did not understand how a glamour worked, and that others might well see him completely differently from how he saw himself, so that these changes might be hidden; still, it was the best he could manage under the circumstances. He hadn't even thought to learn how to remove the glamour.

He stayed well away from the high road, taking cover when hooves drummed past, and again when a knot of yelling men marched by. In one yard a chained watchdog yapped at him, just once, and he froze for a long moment, but the bark was not repeated, no one responded to it, and he finally moved on.

And eventually he arrived in the kitchen garden behind the inn. He had expected to find a guard he would have to circumvent, but the little yard was empty—his enemies had been too disorganized, too unprepared, to post anyone here.

He made his way up the flagstone path to the little wooden stoop, where he pounded on the inn's back door with the hilt of his sword.

The innkeeper's wife, looking puzzled, opened the door and peered out at him. "Yes?"

"There's no one out here," Arlian said brusquely. "Is Lord Drisheen still inside, or has he gone off with the rest of them?"

"Is Drisheen the thin one?" the woman asked uncertainly.

"That's him," Arlian said.

"He's in the dining room. The one-eyed fat one went out after the assassin."

"I need to speak to him," Arlian said, not commenting on her descriptions—he wouldn't have called Lord Toribor *fat,* exactly, though the name "Belly" did suit him well enough. There was a lot of muscle there.

And Drisheen was not really excessively thin, either. Still it was one of several easy ways of distinguishing the two.

The woman hesitated, then stepped aside and let Arlian in. "You go straight through, and don't touch anything," she said.

"Thank you," Arlian said. He obeyed her injunction, marching directly through the generous and cluttered kitchen and out through the swinging door.

Sure enough, Drisheen sat at one of the tables, a boy and a woman occupying two of the other chairs. A single guardsman stood at the front door.

The boy looked up when Arlian entered; the guard at the door was leaning out and peering down the street, while Drisheen and the woman were deep in conversation. The boy clearly had no idea who Arlian was, but the sight of the bare blade in his hand, and the mere fact that he wasn't anyone from Enziet's party, was enough to alarm the child. "My lord," he said, tugging at Drisheen's sleeve.

Arlian wasted no more time; he bellowed, "Get away from him, both of you!" and charged at Drisheen, his sword arm at full extension.

The boy leaped up; the woman turned, startled. Drisheen started to rise, reaching for his sword.

Then Arlian's blade plunged into Drisheen's chest. Because of the furniture in the way, it was not the clean thrust through the heart that Arlian had hoped for, but it was almost certainly a fatal blow.

The woman screamed, and the man at the door finally reacted, turning to see what was happening.

Drisheen looked down at the sword in shock.

"I thought you…" he began, but he was unable to complete the sentence as his mouth filled with bright blood—Arlian's sword had pierced a lung. Red streamed from Drisheen's mouth and nose as he fell back in his chair, eyes wide, right hand tugging at the hilt of his own weapon.

"Fought fair, as I did against Kuruvan and Horim?" Arlian finished for him. "When I can—but against *you,* after what you did to Ferret and Sparkle purely to spite me, I'll settle for butchery." He yanked his blade free.

Drisheen's chest seemed to ripple unnaturally as blood gushed from the wound—Arlian blinked, unsure whether he was really seeing what he thought he was.

Then Drisheen fell forward across the table, into a spreading pool of his own blood, and a thin wisp of smoke spilled from his gaping mouth.

"Sorcery," Arlian muttered. Then he looked up from his dead foe.

The guard at the door was staring, pulling his own sword from its scabbard but making no move to attack. The woman and the boy were unarmed and seemed interested only in getting away.

Behind him, the innkeeper's wife had emerged from the kitchen; now she started screaming. Arlian whirled.

"Shut up, or I'll gut you like a fish," he snarled.

The screams died into a whimper.

The guard took an uncertain step into the room. Arlian spun again, his sword spattering drops of Drisheen's blood across the floor, drops that seemed to glow in the lamplight.

"You want to fight me?" Arlian asked, drawing his swordbreaker. "Drisheen's already dead, and I'm the man who killed Lord Iron—are you *sure* you want to take me on all by yourself?"

The guardsman dropped his sword, turned, and ran out the door.

"Idiot," Arlian said. Then he looked at the woman and the boy. "Get out of here," he said. "Both of you. Right now."

The two of them staggered to their feet and obeyed, following the guard out into the street.

That left the innkeeper's wife. He turned and bowed to her.

"My apologies, madam, for the mess I've made, but this man murdered two friends of mine back in Manfort."

The woman made a strangled noise.

Arlian decided she didn't pose any immediate threat. He could hear shouting in the street, though; at any moment he expected several armed men to burst in, intent on avenging Lord Drisheen.

He didn't want to be here when they arrived.

He could go back out through the kitchen, of course, but if the people out there had any wits at all they would surround the building before making their move—there might already be men moving around to block that exit.

Besides, Cricket and Brook were presumably here somewhere—probably upstairs, in one of the bedrooms. And Black and the others were somewhere, too—if they were still alive. Arlian had too much unfinished business to simply run off into the night.

He sheathed his swordbreaker and picked up the sword the guard had dropped—while he didn't know how to fight with two swords, someone else might need a weapon. He glanced at Drisheen's body.

That hideous, unnatural movement of his chest had stopped, and the flow of blood subsided to a trickle; no more smoke had appeared. He was clearly dead. All the same, Arlian decided not to take *his* sword; the blood on the table and floor had a peculiar, inhuman sheen to it as a reminder that Drisheen had not been an ordinary man. His weapon might be enchanted.

Arlian hefted his two swords and headed for the stairs, clattering up swiftly and swinging around at the landing, noticing as he did that the arrow he had dodged perhaps half an hour before was still stuck in the plaster above his head.

He had hardly reached the top step—encountering no wards this time—when he heard the clamor of armed men entering below. He paused for a fraction of a second, listening and looking.

He could hear the people downstairs shouting about the discovery of Drisheen's death, and boots stamping—men were heading for the stairs after him.

The corridor was unlit—the oil lamp that had illuminated it before had gone out—but Arlian could see that of the seven doorways before him, six stood open—presumably no one had bothered to close them in their rush to pursue him. The seventh—the second on the right—was another matter; it was shut tight.

That was obviously the room he wanted, as his pursuers would know it was occupied and expect him to hide elsewhere. He stepped up and hammered on the door. "Open up!" he called.

"Why? What's going on?" a deep, harsh voice replied—Shamble's voice; Arlian had heard it that afternoon, and recognized it readily.

"Lanair's got an army out here! We need everyone!" Arlian shouted.

"Oh, blood and death," Shamble muttered, barely audible through the wood.

"Hurry!" The first guardsman had turned on the landing and was scarcely twenty feet away, peering up into the darkness.

The door opened, and Arlian charged it, pushing past a startled Shamble before the big man could brace himself. Then he turned and kicked hard, knocking the door out of Shamble's hand and slamming it shut.

Shamble growled and reached for his sword, but Arlian's blade was at his throat.

"Don't try it," Arlian said. "Lock the door."

Shamble snorted. "Not likely," he said.

Arlian pushed, and the tip of his sword drew blood. Shamble growled.

"Lock it or get out of the way," Arlian said.

Shamble backed along the wall, away from the door.

Arlian could hear voices in the hallway, but could not make out the words, as he threw the bolt with the tip of his other sword. He stole a quick glance around the room.

There were four beds, two on either side of a fair-sized room; a shuttered dormer window broke the sloping ceiling opposite the single door. Bundles of baggage were scattered about, sheets and blankets in disarray. An oil lamp burned on a small table.

Two of the beds were occupied—one by Cricket, one by Brook, both women clad in simple nightgowns. They were staring at him, clearly unsure what was going on. Arlian smiled.

"Cricket," he called, "catch!" Then he tossed his extra sword to her and drew his swordbreaker. That felt better, having the proper weapons in both hands again.

She shied away, missing the catch; the sword tumbled off the bed.

Someone was pounding on the door. "Shamble! Open up!"

Shamble growled, but stayed where he was, back against the wall and safely out of reach of the latch. "Move or speak and you're a dead man," Arlian told him conversationally. Then he looked around.

Cricket was scrambling for the sword; Brook was still staring.

"Brook," Arlian said, hoping she would hear but the men outside would not, "tell them Shamble's asleep, dead drunk."

"Shamble! Damn you, man!" the voice called.

"What?" Brook asked.

"Call out! Tell them he's passed out drunk!" Arlian insisted quietly.

Cricket had finally got her hands on the sword; now she held it up triumphantly and shouted, "Shamble's asleep! He drank up all the wine and fell right over!"

Brook looked at her, startled, then smiled and added, "And he stinks! I think he pissed himself!"

Cricket giggled; Shamble started to protest, but Arlian applied warning pressure on the sword.

Arlian could hear a mumbled conference on the other side of the door. He couldn't make out all of it, but it was plain that his pursuers were arguing about whether to believe the women.

"Let us in," someone called.

Cricket and Brook exchanged glances. Brook called, "Do we have to? I hate crawling that far."

"And Shamble's leaning against the door," Cricket added. "We'd have to move him, and he's heavy!"

"And there's a puddle—don't make me crawl through that!" Brook said.

Arlian smiled broadly at them, admiring their quick wit. In a sudden inspiration he sheathed his swordbreaker and undid his trousers. A moment later a malodorous seepage under the door provided added verisimilitude for Brook's tale.

Shamble stared at him with hate-filled eyes, but did not dare move or speak.

That provoked disgusted exclamations from outside, and the pursuit moved on, searching the other rooms vigorously.

"Are you going to kill me?" Shamble asked quietly.

"Should I?" Arlian responded. "Do you deserve to die?"

Shamble growled.

Arlian did not take his eyes off his foe, but called to the others, "Cricket, what do you think? Should I kill him?"

"Please yourself," Cricket said. "I won't weep for him."

"Brook?"

"I don't know," she said. "Who *are* you?"

"That's a good question," Arlian said. "Do *you* know, Shamble?"

"Lord Lanair, I suppose," Shamble said.

"And do you know who Lord Lanair is?"

"A lunatic who's decided to destroy Lord Enziet and his friends, and cast Manfort into chaos."

Arlian nodded. "That's one way of describing the situation," he agreed. "It's not my only one." He shifted the tip of his blade upward an inch, drawing a bloody line on Shamble's throat. "Do you remember looting a village ten years ago, Shamble? Do you remember finding a boy in a cellar there, the lone survivor?"

Shamble's eyes narrowed. "That was *you?*"

Arlian smiled a nasty smile. "Good guess," he said. "Yes, it was. And what happened to that boy?"

"We sold him to the mines at Deep Delving. So you're an escaped slave, dressed up in a lord's shirt."

"Again," Arlian said, "that's one way of looking at it. In fact, I *am* a lord, as I'm sure you know."

"Lord Lanair. That's not your real name."

"Lord Obsidian. Which is as much my name as yours is Shamble. I haven't called myself Lanair since I fled Westguard more than two years ago, and even there it was merely a temporary ruse."

"Lord Dragon calls you Lanair."

"He finds it convenient to do so," Arlian agreed. "He knows my real name, I believe, but chooses not to use it."

Shamble had no answer to that.

Arlian gestured at the women. "They knew me as Triv," he said. "It's short for 'trivial,' because I said my name was unimportant. They don't recognize me because I've used sorcery to change my face temporarily, but they know me."

"We do?" Brook asked.

"Triv?" Cricket said, staring. "It's you?"

"So," Arlian said, not looking at them, "now that we've established who I am, shall we establish who *you* are, and use that to determine whether you live or die?"

Shamble stared angrily back, but did not reply.

"Now," Arlian said, "you helped loot my village when dragons destroyed it. You stood by without protest while I, a freeborn child and heir to much of that ruined village, was sold into slavery. Do those crimes deserve death?"

"No!" Shamble protested. "I didn't hurt anyone."

"You let me be sold."

"It's not the same!"

"Cricket? Brook?"

The women looked at one another.

"I still don't know," Brook said.

Arlian nodded. "I *do* intend to kill Lord Enziet," he said, "as I've killed Kuruvan, Horim, and Drisheen. That's because they were all participants in the ownership of the House of Carnal Society, responsible for maiming the sixteen women who lived there and for the deaths of most of them. Your Lord Dragon ordered the deaths of Rose and three others when that establishment was put to the torch, and later he tortured Dove to death, forcing Sweet to watch." Brook gasped. "He poisoned Sweet, as well—she died in my arms. And he ordered the murder of Seek, who you'd known as Hide. Now, were you involved in any of that? I didn't think to ask Sweet before she perished."

"I did as he told me!" Shamble protested.

"Why?" Arlian demanded.

"Because he paid me!" Shamble said.

"And because you enjoyed it?" He had to struggle not to raise his voice to where it would be heard in the corridor.

"Sometimes," Shamble admitted. "But I wouldn't have hurt Hide if he hadn't betrayed Lord Dragon!"

Arlian gritted his teeth. "But Lord Dragon wanted him dead, so you killed him?"

"I had to!"

"Did it ever occur to you to leave Lord Dragon's employ, as Cover and Hide did?"

"No. He paid well."

"You *never once* considered it?"

"No!"

That was enough; Arlian thrust forward, then slashed. Shamble's hands flew to his ruined throat as he collapsed against the wall and slowly slid to the floor, but he could not cry out.

He fell back and went limp, the light fading from his eyes, hands still clutching his throat as blood poured freely down his chest.

Arlian yanked his sword free.

"You *should* have," he growled.

Chapter Fifty-Five

Out the Window

B rook gasped shudderingly at the sight of Shamble's death; Cricket just nodded, as if she had expected it and was satisfied with what she had seen. "Now what?" she asked, as Arlian wiped his sword clean.

"Now we need a way out of here," Arlian said. He didn't look at the women as he headed for the room's single window; he slid his sword into its sheath as he went.

"But we can't walk," Brook said.

"I know that," Arlian said. "I have a wagon—though getting you to it, and getting it out of here in one piece, won't be easy." He reached for the shutters, then hesitated.

He could see light through the crack between the two shutters—red light. He frowned; it was much too early for dawn, and he had thought this window faced north. Was something burning, perhaps?

He wouldn't find out staring at closed shutters. He lifted the latch.

Red light poured into the room as the shutters swung in—a baleful colored glow like nothing Arlian remembered seeing before. He peered out through the glass cautiously, staying far enough back that he would not be readily visible to an observer on the street.

Something was swirling in the air before him, not down on the ground nor high above, but directly before him, level with the second floor—something red and glowing. For a moment Arlian glimpsed a hideous, inhuman face, and there were definitely claws in the rotating mass. Without conscious decision he found he had drawn his sword again; that *thing* out there resembled a demon—an oddly familiar one.

He heard both women draw in their breath; they did not have the straight line of sight he enjoyed, but both could obviously see something of the monstrosity outside.

Whatever it was came no closer—it was not advancing to attack. Arlian stepped up to the glass, the better to study what he could see.

The window looked out over the stableyard; below the glowing, whirling cloud-thing he could make out the stalls, the mangers and troughs, the tack shed, and his own wagon—and oxen; his draft animals were out of their pen

459

and in front of the wagon.

And standing on the driver's seat of the wagon was a robed figure, waving one hand in the air—Thirif. A lantern hung above the driver's seat, and Arlian could see the magician's face clearly; the glamour was gone and his own features revealed.

Arlian looked at the way the hand moved, and the way the demonic images above it moved, and grinned. He knew now why the "demon" resembled one of the nightmares he had had repeatedly in the Dreaming Mountains on the way north from Arithei. He hoped that none of his enemies down there knew that Aritheian magic could not truly summon demons, but only create illusions.

Arlian had not known that Thirif had brought an illusion like this, but he was very glad to see it. It ought to put a good scare into their enemies.

The rest of the stableyard was almost deserted—almost; it was hard to see clearly, what with the darkness around and below and that seething red vapor in the way, but he was fairly certain he could see Black, still wearing his magical disguise, yoking the oxen. The wagon would be ready to roll in a few minutes, and Thirif's illusion appeared to have frightened away all opposition.

Drisheen wouldn't have been fooled for a moment—but Drisheen was dead.

Arlian frowned. Lord Toribor ought to be enough of a sorcerer to know that the thing was a harmless illusion; where was he?

Well, wherever he was, he didn't appear to be in the yard below. Arlian swung the shutters wide, then unlatched the casement and opened that, as well. He eyed the resulting space critically.

Shamble would never have fit through it, and Arlian wasn't entirely sure he could squeeze himself out that way, but Brook and Cricket were small enough. If he could lower them down…

He turned and began stripping the linens from Cricket's bed. It had worked getting Sweet out of Enziet's house; it ought to work just as well here.

"What are you doing?" Cricket asked. "Can we help?"

"I'm making a rope," Arlian explained. "I have friends down there with a wagon, and I plan to lower you down to them."

Cricket stretched up and tried to peer out the window.

"But…but there's that *monster!*" she said.

"It's just an illusion," Arlian said. "Two of my friends are magicians."

Cricket hesitated—but then she saw that Brook was already pulling the sheets from her bed and knotting them together.

A moment later the rope was ready; Brook went first.

"I don't want to call from up here and let everyone hear me," Arlian told her, as he looped a sheet around her back and under her arms, "so when you're near the ground, call out for Black. That's the man in charge down there."

Brook nodded, and looked back over her shoulder. "The man on the wagon?" she asked.

"No, that's Thirif the magician—don't disturb him! Black's on foot, by the oxen."

"I see him," Brook said. Then she pushed herself over the sill and slid out the window as smoothly as an eel.

Arlian leaned out, watching and listening as he let the rope down, hand over hand; Brook was almost out of sight below him when she called. Arlian could barely hear her, but Black looked up, startled. He spotted the half-clad woman and hurried over to her.

Arlian heard none of their whispered conversation, but he saw Black untie Brook and carry her to the wagon. By the time Arlian had pulled the line of bedclothes back up and hoisted Cricket onto the windowsill Black was waiting at the foot of the wall.

After Cricket was safely down it was his own turn; with the line securely tied in place he turned and began squirming, feet-first, through the window.

He didn't fit as neatly as the women had; the casement slammed back against the dormer, cracking the glass, as he tried to wiggle past it. He had to twist his shoulders up at a steep diagonal to squeeze through.

At last, though, his head emerged from the warm, stuffy air of the inn into the cool crispness of the night, and he half climbed, half slid to the ground.

"Ari!" Black said, slapping him on the back the instant his feet struck the hard-packed earth of the stableyard. "You're safe!"

"Not yet," Arlian replied. "Not until we're out of this town and away from these people."

"Oh, Thirif's put a scare into them," Black said. "We were getting ready to go. They've promised us safe passage." He grimaced, his expression visible even in the eerie red glow. "Only northward, though."

"I'm not going north," Arlian said, as they began walking toward the wagon.

"We could go a few miles, then double back, and go around the town," Black said. "it's only a minor delay."

"There's no decent *road* around Cork Tree," Arlian pointed out. "An ox could break a leg trying to drag us all across underbrush or furrowed fields."

"Well, Lord Belly thinks you're headed south, and he doesn't want us to rejoin you," Black said, as he turned aside toward the stableyard gate. "He agreed to let us go north, but not south."

"You spoke with him?" Arlian asked, following.

Black nodded. "He was commanding the party that went after that horse you stole," he said. "After they found the horse, with you not on it, he sent one group on to the south, while he came back here. He went inside the inn for a little while, and then came out here. When most of them went galloping after you just four men stayed here, keeping an eye on us and blocking the gates so we couldn't get the wagon out; we held them off readily enough while Thirif summoned our friend up there." He pointed at the glowing illusion overhead, then pushed the gate open; the street beyond was dark and mostly quiet, though Arlian could hear shouting somewhere in the distance. "Then Belly and his group got back, just about the time Lord Demon appeared, and he came to discuss matters with us. Some fool came running out of the inn shouting about a madman attacking Lord Drisheen, and Belly said we could go, and everyone went running inside. I hitched up the oxen, but I took my time about it, in hopes you'd be able to join us." He turned back toward the wagon.

Arlian nodded. "Good," he said.

"So you killed Drisheen?" Black asked, as he pulled himself up onto the wagon, forcing Thirif to step aside. Cricket and Brook were inside the boxy body of the wagon but leaning out the door, watching and listening.

"And Shamble," Arlian said. "They'd left him guarding these two." He gestured at the women.

Black glanced at them; Cricket smiled back at him.

"Ah, that's a good night's work, then," he said. "At least, if we can get out of here alive!"

"It'll do," Arlian agreed, "but Lord Toribor still lives, and I wouldn't mind a few words with old Stonehand."

"Oh, you hot-blooded young idiots are never satis…"

"Your pardon," Thirif interrupted, "but I cannot keep this illusion much longer."

"I think it's done its job," Arlian said. "Let it go."

"Thank you," Thirif said, lowering his arm. The demon-image dissipated into fading red smoke, and the lantern over the driver's bench seemed to brighten. Black seated himself comfortably and shook out the reins, signaling the oxen to move. Thirif leaned past him, ducked, and stepped inside the wagon, pushing past the two women, who squeezed aside to make room for him but did not relinquish their place in the door.

"You're heading north?" Arlian asked.

"At least at first," Black said.

"That's fine," Arlian said. "Take the women back to Manfort, where they'll be safe." He jumped down from the seat as the wagon began to roll. "*I'm* going south," he said. "Toribor won't expect me to be behind him."

"Ari, you're mad!" Black said, tugging the reins to halt the oxen before they had gone more than a couple of yards.

"Quite probably," Arlian agreed. "But mad or not, I've sworn to kill Lord Enziet, and he's to the south, not the north."

"How will you *find* him, without the magicians?" Black demanded.

"I don't know," Arlian admitted, "but I'll manage it somehow."

Just then a loud crash sounded above them; Black, Arlian, and the others looked up, startled, as an angry, bearded face appeared in the open window of the inn whence Arlian had escaped.

"Obsidian!" Lord Toribor's voice bellowed. "By the dead gods!"

"Block the gate," Arlian said to Black without looking back. Then he called, "Yes, Lord Toribor—I'm here."

"Hiding behind sorcery," Toribor called back. "Too afraid to show your own face?"

"And you're hiding behind a dozen guards," Arlian shouted back. "Afraid to meet me honorably?"

"So you can butcher me as you did Drisheen and Shamble? Ha!"

"So I can fight you fairly, as I did Iron and Kuruvan," Arlian retorted.

"Fair? You crippled Iron before you killed him!"

"I did nothing of the kind—he was *already* crippled. I merely removed the brace that hid it. And I remind you, *he* challenged *me,* and made no offer to yield!"

"Lies and half-truths!"

"No more than your own!"

Lord Toribor's one good eye glowered down at Arlian for a moment; then he turned and spoke to someone behind him. Arlian took the opportunity to see that Black had started the wagon forward, toward the stableyard gate.

There were lights in the street beyond; Toribor's men were on their way.

"I don't suppose Thirif has any more of those spells…" Arlian said.

"He told me that was the only one he'd brought," Black called back.

Then Toribor was back in the window.

"I'll give you a chance to surrender," he called.

Arlian found himself smiling at that, though he was not entirely sure why. "And I'll return the favor, and allow *you* to surrender," Arlian called. "You tell me your terms, and I'll tell you mine."

"Give yourself up into my custody, disavow your oath to slay me and Lord Enziet, and I'll take you back to Manfort to stand trial before the Duke for Drisheen's murder, and make no further claim on you," Toribor called. "Your friends would be free to go."

Arlian almost laughed. "And the two women? Cricket and Brook?"

Toribor made a disgusted noise. "Oh, fine!" he said, exasperated. "Take them as part of the bargain, if that's what it takes to get you to give yourself up!"

"It's not enough," Arlian called back. "Listen, Lord Belly, to *my* terms. You give me a horse, and your oath not to harm or molest in any way anyone in that wagon until they're safely back to the Old Palace in Manfort, and I'll forestall my vengeance on you—not forgo it entirely, but merely put it off. I'll give you a year before I seek you out to kill you, and you'll be free to try to make your peace with me in that time. I'll be busy hunting Lord Enziet for part of that time—and who knows, maybe he'll kill me and you'll be safe!"

"Are you *mad?*" Toribor roared. "Do you expect me to agree to that?"

"No more than you really expect me to agree to *your* terms!" Arlian shouted back cheerfully.

"Listen, you little fool, you have no idea what you're doing! I can't take any risk that you might kill Enziet!"

"Ari!" Black called, before Arlian could respond.

Arlian turned to find guardsmen with drawn swords standing in the stableyard gate, blocking the oxen. "Thirif! Stand ready!" he called, as he drew his own weapons. Then he bellowed, "Do you men want us to summon the demon anew?"

"There is no demon!" Toribor shouted. "It's all just illusion! Sorcerers can't summon demons!"

"Thirif is no mere sorcerer, Belly!" Arlian retorted. "He's an Arithein mage, from beyond the Dreaming Mountains."

The swordsmen looked at one another uncertainly.

464

Just then Rime thrust her head out of the door; like Thirif, and unlike Black and Arlian, her glamour was gone. She clambered out and stood on the seat beside Black, unsteady on her wooden leg.

Toribor stopped shouting to stare at her, and Arlian turned to look.

"You there!" she said, pointing her trademark bone at the nearest guardsman. "Just what do you think you're doing?"

The guardsman lowered his sword. "Lady Rime?" he asked, baffled.

"Yes, Lady Rime!" she shouted. "Who told you to block my wagon?"

"Ah...*he* did," the soldier replied, pointing up at Toribor.

"And who gave him that authority?"

"Lord Enziet, my lady. He said we were to obey Lord Drisheen and Lord Belly until his return."

"And do you think Lord Enziet meant you to interfere with *me?*"

"No, my lady."

"Then get out of the way!"

"No!" Toribor shouted. "Don't listen to her!"

Rime turned and glared up at him. "And why *not?*" she demanded. "*I* am an adviser to the Duke of Manfort, my Lord Toribor, as you are not!"

"But you're a traitor!" Toribor shouted. "You've been helping Obsidian!"

Rime put her hands on her hips. "*You* dare to call *me* a traitor? *You* fled here and went through all this—setting up ambushes, chasing people about in the middle of the night—because you're too much of a coward to face Lord Obsidian in an honest duel!" She turned back to the soldier. "Did Lord Enziet tell you anything about setting up ambushes? Did he say you were to trap Lord Obsidian?"

"No, my lady; he just said to obey the other lords."

"So you'll just blindly obey any order young Belly gives you?"

"My lady," the guardsman said desperately, pointing at Arlian, "that man, whether he's Lord Obsidian or not, *did* murder Lord Drisheen."

"And what happened before that? Might he have had cause to kill Drisheen in his own defense?"

"I...I don't really know," the soldier admitted.

"He meant to murder us both in our beds!" Toribor shouted.

"I came to speak to you, and someone shot an arrow at me!" Arlian shouted back. He turned to the guard. "See for yourself—it's probably still stuck in the stairway wall!"

The guardsman looked helplessly from Rime to Toribor, saying nothing.

Toribor called, "Rime, stop this! You don't know what's at stake here!"

Rime stared up at him in disbelief. "I don't? Besides your miserable life, you mean?"

"No! It's far more than that!"

"What *is* at stake, then, that's so precious?"

"I...I can't tell you here!"

"And where *could* you tell me? And why haven't you done so before? I seem to recall an agreement to share secrets, Lord Belly."

"I didn't know!"

"And did Lord Enziet? Is this some new lie he's told you, or some secret he's withheld?"

"Rime, you don't understand! Enziet had reasons..."

"I understand enough," she retorted, turning away.

Arlian called up to Toribor, "Listen, Belly—once again, before witnesses, I challenge you to meet me in an honorable duel, to settle all matters between us!"

For a moment Toribor stared down at him in speechless fury; then words exploded from him. "Blast you, Obsidian!" he shouted. "Fine, then! I'll fight you, here and now!"

"In the street in front of the inn!" Arlian called back.

"Done!" Toribor's head vanished from the window.

Arlian smiled, and turned back toward the wagon.

"Good," he said.

"I hope so," Rime said. She looked up at the empty window thoughtfully. "I do hope so."

Chapter Fifty-Six

Crossed Swords

The two opponents faced each other warily, about a dozen feet apart, swords and swordbreakers held ready. The sky was still overcast, the moon and stars hidden, so the only light came from a few windows and the lanterns hung to either side of the inn's signboard; the fighters' shadows stretched out across the street in an elongated tangle of gray and black, arms and blades crisscrossing. Despite the chill in the air Arlian saw sweat gleaming on Lord Toribor's bald head.

The audience consisted of two distinct groups—Toribor's party, clustered in and around the inn's front door or peering from the inn's windows, and Arlian's party, seated in the wagon fifty feet to the north, ready to move out on a moment's notice. The few townspeople who were awake, including all of the inn's staff, had joined Toribor's group, swelling its ranks to perhaps three dozen people.

Black had extinguished the lantern above the driver's seat of the wagon, and Arlian supposed that was to make it easier to slip away into the darkness unnoticed.

"Kill him!" the innkeeper shouted. "I'm *never* going to get all those bloodstains out, and that door upstairs is ruined!"

"We'll pay for the damages," Lady Rime called in reply.

The innkeeper snorted in disbelief.

Arlian watched Toribor closely, looking for some hint of an impending attack, but could see none—perhaps Lord Belly thought that time was on his side, and he intended to wait Arlian out, fight defensively until his opponent tired.

Or perhaps he fought conservatively because of his missing eye—he was blind on his left side, and kept his head cocked at an odd angle to compensate, his right eye angled forward and focused on Arlian's blade.

Arlian tried a quick feint, just to see what would happen; Toribor's blade flashed up to parry, but he made no counter.

Arlian grinned; that suited him fine. He circled to the left, stepped in, feinted, then dodged right and attacked in earnest.

Missing eye or no, Toribor was ready for him and warded off the assault easily—but he still made no riposte, no attack of his own. After a few seconds of clashing steel, Arlian stepped back.

All the light came from the same direction, from the inn; it wasn't bright enough to blind anyone who looked directly at the lanterns, though, so the old sun-in-the-eye trick was no real use. Getting in front of the light might make it harder for his one-eyed foe to see what he was doing, however, so Arlian moved in that direction.

Toribor didn't cooperate; he moved back and to the side, keeping Arlian and the light at an angle.

Arlian considered that. If Toribor kept that up he could be maneuvered pretty much wherever Arlian wanted him; all Arlian had to do was decide where that would be. He looked at Toribor's tilted face, at how he was concentrating on Arlian, staring at him, and he thought he knew.

Toribor had adjusted to his missing eye, but he wasn't comfortable with the darkness; he had probably spent almost his entire waking life in daylight or firelight, and he could not close one eye to keep it adapted for darkness, while the other adjusted to light, as Arlian could. Arlian had both his eyes, and had spent seven years in the mines, with limited supplies of lamp oil; darkness did not trouble him, and he knew a dozen tricks to compensate for low light.

If Toribor would not allow Arlian to block the light, perhaps Arlian could still drive him away from the light entirely. He charged, and in a flurry of steel Toribor retreated.

They were moving away from the inn—and from the observers. As their blades slashed and clanged Toribor said urgently, "Listen, Obsidian—Arlian, Lanair, whatever your name is. You don't know what you're doing!"

"Really?" Arlian laughed. "I thought I was trying to kill you."

"Beyond that!" Toribor said angrily, as he knocked aside another blow and stabbed his swordbreaker blindly at Arlian's midsection.

"I'm trying to kill Enziet, too," Arlian said, as his own swordbreaker blocked the thrust. "Is that what you mean?"

"Yes, blast you!" Toribor said, breaking free. "You can't kill him! You mustn't!"

"Because he's the Duke's chief adviser and the real ruler of Manfort?" Arlian asked, as he waved his sword threateningly. "Because the whole city will be plunged into chaos by his death?" He laughed again. "I think not. The city will survive without him, as it would without any man." He lunged.

Toribor parried and sidestepped and made a tidy riposte, which Arlian turned scarcely an inch from his own sleeve. For a moment the two fought without words, the clash of steel and the mutter of the now-distant crowd the only sound.

"It's not that," Toribor said, as the two men separated and he caught his breath. "You're right, that's nothing; the Duke could have a hundred advisers any time he called for them, and the Dragon Society has a dozen members who might rival Enziet's abilities. But my lord, none of them know—if Enziet dies, the dragons will return."

Arlian had been preparing a fresh attack, but he paused, astonished. "*What?*" he demanded.

Toribor attacked, and Arlian turned it and countered; it had not been a particularly skillful attack, and that, more than anything else, convinced him that Toribor was serious. Had he meant his outrageous claim as a mere distraction he would have followed it with his best, not a halfhearted overhand lunge.

"It's true," Toribor said. "Or at least Enziet swears it is, and showed me evidence. Have you never wondered why the dragons gave up their hegemony seven hundred years ago, when all the fighting to that point only demonstrated that we could not harm them?"

"Of course I've wondered," Arlian said, with a quick little feint.

"It was a bargain they made," Toribor said, barely even bothering to parry. "Humans learned a great secret, and threatened to reveal it, and use it, if the dragons did not depart."

"What secret?" Arlian said, listening.

"I don't know," Toribor admitted. "But *Enziet* does—and he says he's the last man alive who does. When he dies, the pact will be worthless, the secret will be lost, and the dragons will be free to return!"

"And you believe him?" Arlian made a thrust at Toribor's side; he dodged.

"Yes, I do," Toribor said. "He swore to me, by all the gods and by the dragons themselves, that he and he alone knows the secret that drove the dragons into their caverns."

Arlian considered that.

It might even be true, he supposed; Enziet was perfectly capable of lying and breaking his word, Arlian was certain of that, but all the same, it might be true. Enziet was one of the oldest living beings in the world—perhaps *the* oldest, save the dragons themselves—and had certainly been around when the dragons still ruled. If there *were* such a secret, Enziet might well be its sole holder.

But what could such a secret be? And would the dragons truly return when it was lost?

Could the dragons actually return?

And if they did, could a way be found to kill them? Might that perhaps even provide a route to vengeance for Arlian's family and neighbors? If the dragons came to him, rather than if he went searching through endless caverns for them, he might actually accomplish his goal.

That assumed, of course, that he could find a way to kill dragons.

Perhaps *that* was the secret Enziet held, and perhaps he could be convinced to give it up before he died.

"I swore to kill him," Arlian said. "He murdered my friends, looted my home, and sold me into slavery."

"He's done all that and more," Toribor agreed, "but he *keeps the dragons away.* Isn't that more important than vengeance, or justice?"

"He swore to share his secrets with the Society," Arlian said.

"He broke his oath; he admits it. But he had sworn *to the dragons themselves* not to reveal it."

Their duel had slowed as they spoke; now they still stood with weapons ready, but the fight had become a conversation. Arlian risked a quick glance back at the inn.

No one had followed them; the audience still huddled under the lanterns, safe in the light, watching from afar.

"Why hasn't he told anyone else, then?" Arlian asked. "Why take the risk? What if he were killed by thieves, or in a fall from his horse? He'd let the dragons return?"

"I never said Enziet isn't a selfish bastard," Toribor said.

"He deserves to die," Arlian growled.

"He probably does," Toribor agreed. "But we can't afford his death, I tell you!"

"So what do you propose I do about it?"

"Just…just leave him alone, that's all. And me. I don't want to die; I don't even want to kill you. If you'll swear not to kill Enziet, I'll let you escape into the darkness, and I won't pursue."

"I can't swear that," Arlian said. "I will not break my vow, nor forgo my vengeance. Enziet poisoned the woman I love, and she died in the bed beside me, and he will *pay* for that, dragons or no!" He launched a ferocious attack, catching Toribor off guard—but not so off guard he didn't manage to parry at the last instant as he retreated before Arlian's assault.

"You'd rather plunge all humanity back into slavery?" Toribor shouted as he backed away.

"Yes!" Arlian shouted back. "If that's what it takes! I've been a slave, and I survived! We drove the dragons away once, and we can do it again, with or without Enziet!"

"You're insane!" Toribor yelped.

"I'll promise you this much, Lord Belly," Arlian said as he lunged again. "I'll try to learn Enziet's secret before I kill him. I'll *try*. And if there is a secret, and I learn it, I'll use it."

Toribor did not answer. They were well away from the inn now, and Arlian had begun to force Toribor back into the utter darkness of a side street; he was too busy trying to see Arlian's moves in the dark to speak any more.

Arlian, on the other hand, could still see quite well enough to suit him. He had dug and hauled ore in no more light than this any number of times. A sword was nothing like a pick, but both could be used well enough in the dark if one knew how.

He lunged, turned, and jabbed low with his sword-breaker; Toribor started back, and Arlian brought his sword across and down.

It was a glancing blow, but he heard fabric tear and heard Toribor gasp in pain, and Arlian knew he had drawn first blood, cutting a gash in his opponent's leg.

"Blast you!" Toribor said, as he made a wild swing; Arlian ducked under it easily, and took the opportunity to strike again, this time plunging his sword deep into Toribor's thigh.

As he snapped back into position and withdrew the blade Arlian heard the hiss of indrawn breath. "Listen, Obsidian," Toribor said, *"listen* to Enziet when you find him! It's more important than your dead friends, or my life—*listen* to him!"

Arlian paused, and stepped back. Toribor seemed to be conceding the duel; Arlian had not expected that.

And he seemed more concerned with Enziet's life than his own; Arlian had *certainly* not expected that! He moved his sword into a guard position, considering.

Toribor staggered forward, attempting an attack, but his injured leg buckled under him, and he fell sideways in the dirt.

In an instant Arlian had stepped forward and kicked the sword from his hand. He stood over the defenseless Toribor, his own blade at his vanquished foe's throat.

471

There he hesitated.

"Do you want to live?" he asked.

"Of *course* I do, you bloody-handed fool!" Toribor said, through gritted teeth—his wound was obviously painful.

It wasn't fatal, though—Toribor had the heart of the dragon, and if he didn't bleed to death here and now he could recover and heal.

"You're serious about Enziet and the dragons, then?"

"Yes!" Toribor gasped; he had abandoned any pretense and was clutching at his leg with both hands, trying to stanch the flow of blood.

"Then *you* listen to *me,* Lord Toribor," Arlian said. "You have a choice. You can swear to take your men and go back to Manfort and trouble me no more until I return there, and I'll let you live—though it's not over between us, any more than it is between Lord Nail and myself. You both must still make amends for your crimes in Westguard; I'm just delaying the day of reckoning.

"That's *one* option. The other is that you refuse this oath, in which case I'll kill you here and now, regardless of the dishonor in slaying a defenseless foe. You saw what I did to Lord Drisheen; you know I can be ruthless." An afterthought struck him. "Oh, and in either case, I want Drisheen's horse and harness. I'll buy it, or just take it, as you please."

"I'll swear," Toribor said, his voice weakening, "if you'll swear an oath in return."

"I'm not going to let Enziet go," Arlian said.

"Just...swear you'll listen to him, and consider carefully, before you decide whether or not to kill him," Toribor said.

"If he gives me the chance, I'll do it," Arlian said. "I'll swear to listen, if it's not at the risk of my own life."

Toribor nodded. "Then I swear, by the dead gods," he said. "I'll take my men back to Manfort, and you can go on after Enziet, or wherever you please, unhindered.

"And Cricket and Brook stay with me."

Toribor nodded. Then he held up a hand. "I've sworn, and I will keep my word," he said, "but three of Enziet's men are on their way to Stonebreak. I have no way to recall them."

Arlian frowned, then shrugged. "A fair warning, and honorable of you to give it," he said. Then he backed away, out of the alley and into the street, where he turned back toward the inn and bellowed, "You there! Bring bandages! Lord Toribor is bleeding like a fountain!"

Chapter Fifty-Seven

Stonebreak

Arlian was wearing an entirely new face, courtesy of a fresh glamour of Shibiel's making, when he walked into the inn at Stonebreak. He therefore did not worry about being recognized as he took a seat at an adjoining table just behind the three soldiers from Manfort.

He had known they were here by the horses in the stable; no one else in this miserable little town would have had such fine mounts. Arlian had been riding Drisheen's mare hard for days, leaving the wagon and his companions far behind, trying to catch up to these three; obviously the soldiers had not been dawdling themselves.

What puzzled Arlian slightly was the presence of *four* fine northern horses in the stable, not counting his own; Toribor had been specific about saying he had only sent *three* men ahead. Arlian shrugged it aside; he supposed they had brought an extra mount, or perhaps a pack horse.

Certainly, there were only three men in the Duke's livery at the table. One of them was Stonehand—Arlian had suspected as much when he failed to spot his old enemy in Cork Tree after the duel. The other two soldiers he could not recall ever having seen before.

Arlian beckoned to the innkeeper for an ale as he listened, trying to overhear, unnoticed, what the three were saying as they ate.

"I'd heard that the winds blow away tracks in the Desolation in just minutes," one man said, "and that's if the ground isn't too rocky to show tracks in the first place. We'll probably *never* find him up there."

"Well, if we lose the trail, we'll turn back," Stonehand said. He drank deeply from his tankard.

"We *could* just wait here," the third man said.

"Or go back to Cork Tree and tell the lords we missed him," the first said.

"We were sent to find Lord Enziet and warn him that Lanair is on his trail," Stonehand said, thumping his emptied tankard to the table. "We knew he was in the Desolation. We need to at *least* take a look at the top of the cliffs. He can't have gone far yet."

The innkeeper set a mug before Arlian, who accepted it with a nod; the innkeeper frowned, and Arlian fished a half-ducat from his pocket. Clearly, his credit was not good here—but then, he wasn't dressed as a lord, but as a merchant, and that at a time when no caravan was in town.

He had missed part of the conversation at the other table; now, as he drank, he heard the third soldier saying, "...see the point of it. We know Lanair doubled back, he's probably either long dead, or running back to Manfort with his tail between his legs."

"Maybe we should wait here a day or two, in case they sent a messenger to call us back," the first soldier suggested.

"No. We're going up that ravine tomorrow," Stonehand said, brooking no argument. "We are going up to the Desolation, and once we reach it we are going to see whether we can find Lord Enziet's trail."

The other two grumbled, but did not make any further protests.

Arlian drank his ale and studied them, thinking.

They did not know exactly where Enziet had gone; if he simply stayed out of their way they would presumably lose the trail and turn back. Arlian well remembered how barren the Desolation was; did these three even know which route Enziet had taken, east, west, or center? Did they know how the routes were marked?

The Low Road was an actual road for at least part of its length, with markers along the way; perhaps they would follow that, thinking it was Enziet's route, all the way to the Borderlands.

Arlian was fairly sure Enziet would have taken the unmarked Eastern Road.

If these three turned back, or if they took the Low Road, then Arlian could simply let them go on about their business, while he followed Enziet—though he would probably have his own problems in locating Lord Dragon. He would need the magicians' help.

And the magicians were in the wagon, somewhere to the north, and if these three turned back they would meet the wagon on the road, and how would *that* turn out? Arlian frowned.

Did these three know that "Lord Lanair" was associated with the wagon and its occupants?

Whether they did or not, they might well ask to search the wagon, and if they did they would find Brook and Cricket, who they would recognize—even if Thirif and Shibiel had cast yet another glamour, it would not disguise the lack of feet. That might be hidden, if the women were careful, but still ...

There were only three of them, and Black would probably be a match for any of them. If the women and magicians could handle the other two...

But they probably couldn't, if it came to an actual fight. Cricket had that sword Arlian had given her, but how could she use it, even if she knew how, crippled as she was?

And Thirif and Shibiel were running short of magic. They couldn't prepare more in the Lands of Man, where magic was thin and weak, and they didn't know sorcery.

Rime knew a little sorcery, but no sorcery Arlian knew of would be much help.

And besides, Stonehand owed a debt, one ten years old, that Arlian did not want to leave unpaid when he had the man so close at hand.

He couldn't fight all three by himself, though. He knew he was a good swordsman, but he wasn't *that* good. That was probably exactly why Lord Toribor had sent *three* men, instead of the one Lord Drisheen had spoken of—just in case Arlian managed to come after them.

And he had nothing against the other two. Oh, they might well be murderers a dozen times over, they might beat their women and torture kittens, but Arlian didn't *know* it. They might just as well be good sons, faithful husbands, and loving fathers who had taken up the guardsman's trade for lack of a better alternative. His only grudge was against Stonehand.

Perhaps he could make the other two see that. After all, did they know the entire story of just why "Lord Lanair" was pursuing Lord Enziet? Surely they did not—Enziet was a secretive man. In fact, this entire expedition was the result of his desire to keep too many secrets. *He* certainly wouldn't have told the entire party just who their enemy really was.

Shamble had not appeared to know that Lord Lanair was the boy who Lord Dragon had sold into slavery ten years before. Why, then, would Stonehand, or these others?

And Arlian was wearing a new face, courtesy of Shibiel's glamour.

He stood, suddenly inspired, and tapped Stonehand on the shoulder.

Stonehand turned, startled. "Yes?"

"You're called Stonehand, aren't you?" Arlian asked.

Stonehand was suddenly wary. He pushed away from the table and put his hand on his sword-hilt. "Why?" he asked.

"Because I thought I recognized you," Arlian said. He unobtrusively eyed the arrangement of table, chair, and sword, and then, moving as suddenly as he could, punched Stonehand on the jaw.

The guardsman's chair rocked back but did not quite topple over; astonished, his two companions leaped to their feet, as Stonehand clapped a hand to his injured chin and stared up at Arlian.

"You stinking heap of bloody offal," Arlian bellowed. "You sold me as a slave!"

"Hey! Hey! Not in my house!" the innkeeper shouted, waving his hands but standing well clear.

"You stay out of this," Arlian said. "This is just between him and me."

"You have the advantage of me," Stonehand said, still rubbing his jaw. "I don't know what you're talking about."

"Don't you? Ten years ago, on Smoking Mountain?"

Stonehand frowned. "I was on Smoking Mountain once," he admitted. "I don't remember just when."

"Do you remember finding a survivor in the ruins? And what you did with him?"

"I didn't do *anything* with him," Stonehand protested. "He was Lord Dragon's property."

"I was *no one's* property!" Arlian roared. "I was a freeborn child!"

"Well, *I* didn't sell you!" Stonehand roared back. "It was nothing to do with me!"

"You didn't say a word to protest," Arlian said. "You took your share of the loot—my mother's jewels, the neighbors' things, whatever you could find!"

"They were dead!"

"*I* wasn't!"

"And you still aren't! You're free now, aren't you?"

"After seven years in the mines," Arlian said. "You *owe* me for that seven years!"

"Oh, fine," Stonehand said. "What is it you want of me, then?"

"Satisfaction," Arlian said, grabbing the hilt of his sword—but not drawing it.

"A duel?" Stonehand's mouth quirked into a smile. "And if I refuse?"

"Then you're the worthless piece of offal I called you, not a man fit to wear a lord's uniform."

"Oh, now *there's* a fearsome threat!" Stonehand grinned broadly. "A merchant calls me names, and I'm supposed to cower in shame?"

"A *man* tells you you're worth less than a dung heap, and you can take it, and let everyone here see you for the coward you are, or you can fight me

476

to show them I'm wrong."

"I don't want to fight you," Stonehand said. He studied Arlian's face. "You know, I don't remember you very clearly, but your face isn't familiar at all."

"Seven years in the mines will change a man," Arlian said. "Then you're admitting cowardice?"

Stonehand sighed. "I am not admitting anything of the sort," he said. "I am merely reluctant to perforate a mad fool who may have some slight grounds for feeling I may once have inadvertently wronged him."

"'May'? 'Inadvertently'?"

"People are sold into slavery every day, boy. Fate plays with us, and is none too gentle about it."

"And Fate has brought you here, to me, and I demand you fight me!"

"It wouldn't be fair," Stonehand warned. "I'm a soldier; you're a merchant. What do you know about swordplay?"

"Enough," Arlian said. "Then you'll fight me?"

Stonehand glanced at his companions; one shrugged silently, and the other said, "Go ahead. Teach him to mind his own business."

"Fine," Stonehand said. "Outside."

"Of course." Arlian made a formal bow—one suited to a lord, not a mere merchant. Stonehand's smile vanished, and he eyed his foe suspiciously.

He did not say anything, though, and the two men made their way out into the street. They took up guard positions, swords ready, facing each other, Arlian to the north, Stonehand to the south. The sun was below the western rooftops but not yet completely gone.

Arlian drew his swordbreaker; Stonehand was obviously startled by its presence. He had none, but pulled a dagger from his boot for his left hand.

"It's a trick, isn't it?" Stonehand said, gesturing at the swordbreaker. "You're no mere tradesman. You're probably not even that boy from Smoking Mountain."

"I am who I said I was," Arlian said. "But yes, it's a trick—I've studied the sword since I escaped the mines."

"Obsessed with revenge, I suppose?" He smiled. "As I said, Fate plays with us all."

Then he lunged; Arlian parried, made a simple overhand riposte—and skewered Stonehand neatly, running the blade of his sword through Stonehand's chest. Stonehand looked down and said, "I never did get the hang of all those fancy tricks. I always did..."

Then he gasped for breath and crumpled to the ground, pulling free of Arlian's blade, his own sword and dagger falling from his hands, his collapse leaving Arlian staring down at him, astonished with the ease of his victory. The duel had been so brief that the crowd had not even finished forming.

Arlian had expected a much longer contest—but a man called Stonehand would have been named for his fists, not his skill with a blade.

"I wasn't even sure I meant to kill him," Arlian said, as much to himself as anyone else.

"Oh, for…" one of the other soldiers said. His companion was kneeling at Stonehand's side. "*Now* what do we do?"

The kneeling man looked up. "Do *you* want to fight him?" he asked, jerking a thumb in Arlian's direction.

"No," the standing soldier said. "I want to go home."

"That sounds like a fine idea to me," the other replied. "We should take his body, I suppose."

"Is he really dead?" Arlian asked.

"No," the kneeling man admitted, "but he will be soon, I'd say. He's unconscious."

"We'll need to wait here, then, until he dies," the other soldier said.

"He'll be dead by morning, I'd say."

"I'm sorry," Arlian said.

It was the truth, oddly enough. He had sought Lord Dragon's looters for years, with every intention of killing them all, and he had forced this duel knowing perfectly well that he would probably kill Stonehand, but all the same, now that he had done it, he regretted it. There had been little satisfaction in so brief a fight, and while Stonehand had participated in the looting of Obsidian and had served Lord Enziet, he had not been so outrageously cruel as Drisheen, nor so callous as Enziet or the other lords. In the brief conversation leading up to the duel he had shown himself to be a man, not a monster—perhaps under other circumstances, he and Arlian might have been friends. He had done wrong, yes, but he had not been proud of it; he had done as he was told.

And now Arlian had taken something he could never give back. Lord Dragon had taken seven years of Arlian's life, all the years when he should have been growing and learning and finding his path in the world, and Arlian could never get those back, but taking the rest of Stonehand's life did not make up for that. It was simply another theft, not a restoration.

But if he had to do it over again, he could not say he would do anything

478

any differently. And he still had every intention of hunting down and killing Lord Enziet. He was no longer eager to hunt down any of the others, but Enziet, yes—Lord Dragon was a monster, as Stonehand had not been, and must die.

There was nothing more he could do for Stonehand; he wiped his sword, sheathed it, and reentered the inn.

"I don't think I should stay here after all," he told the innkeeper. "I'll find somewhere to camp."

"Please yourself," the man said. "That was quick, I must say."

Arlian ignored the comment. "Before I go, though—I'm looking for a man, Lord Enziet. He would have come through here several days ago, and gone on southward, up the ravine to the Desolation. Do you know who I mean?"

"Oh, the lord with the lamed horse?" The innkeeper nodded. "Those three asked about him, too. He got tired of looking for a new mount and left about three days ago, on foot."

Arlian stared at the innkeeper.

Lamed horse? On foot?

And only three days ago?

His vengeance against Lord Enziet was closer than ever.

"Thank you," he said.

Chapter Fifty-Eight

The End of the Pursuit

The wind on the Desolation was almost cold, not the searing hot blast Arlian remembered, but it blew just as constantly and fiercely as he recalled, and just as dry, sucking the moisture from their mouths and skin.

They left the Eastern Road behind on the fourth day, veering eastward across bare stone, away from the drifting sands, following the glow of Thirif's enchanted crystal. The Aritheian was quite sure that this was the path Lord Enziet had followed.

"He's very close," Thirif assured Arlian. "I think we've gained significantly."

"Why would we be gaining?" Arlian asked. "A man on foot is faster than an ox-drawn wagon."

"If he's hurrying," Black said. "Why would he hurry? He needs to stop for water, just as we do."

Arlian frowned, then shrugged. "I'm going to scout ahead," he said.

This was hardly new; Arlian had been using Drisheen's horse to scout ahead of the wagon regularly. As usual, he found nothing but bare stone.

On the sixth day, while scouting ahead yet again, Arlian thought he could smell salt in the air, and that it was significantly more moist than it had been. His breath no longer dried out his throat every time he inhaled through his mouth. He saw birds in the distance—seabirds, he thought.

He stared at them intently, but could not make out enough detail to be sure—after all, he had never seen the sea or seabirds, except in pictures.

In pictures they usually seemed to have long, oddly shaped wings, though, and these black specks swooping in the distance fit that description.

He was at the point where he would ordinarily have turned back to rejoin the others, but the birds drew his interest; he urged his horse forward, up a slope of broken stone. At the top he paused again, watching.

Then he lowered his gaze and saw the man standing atop a boulder, perhaps two hundred yards away across a broad expanse of water-worn rock—a tall man, dressed in black, with a plumed, broad-brimmed hat on his head and a sword on his belt.

481

Lord Enziet.

And Enziet had paused as well, and had glanced back, and was staring directly at Arlian.

"At last!" Arlian muttered, spurring his mount.

The horse jerked forward and broke into a canter, scattering stones in all directions as it stumbled across the rocky ground. Arlian felt himself losing his seat—he was still far from an expert horseman—and reined the beast in. For a moment he concentrated his attention on not being thrown headlong onto the rocks.

When he had the horse slowed to a comfortable walk he looked up, and Lord Enziet was gone.

"Blood and death," Arlian growled. He rode on, staring ahead, looking for any sign of his quarry.

He saw none.

A few moments later he was alongside the boulder where Enziet had stood; he dismounted, weighted the horse's reins to the ground with a good-sized rock, and looked around.

Enziet was nowhere to be seen; a rough expanse of bare, jagged stone stretched in all directions, hard and cold and alien. Several openings were visible—sinkholes, perhaps, or caves, or just gaps between fallen chunks of rock; Arlian had no way of telling which were which.

He stared at the ground, looking for a trail—and found one; a stone had been turned, exposing a damp underside that had not yet dried in the chill winter wind. He drew a line with his gaze from the boulder to that stone, then extended it straight on—east by southeast, almost the direction they had been heading for the past two days. He drew his sword, patted the horse reassuringly, then began walking that line, slowly and carefully.

A few feet past the turned stone he paused; just to his right was a dark opening between two slabs of stone. He knelt and peered into it.

Something black and powdery clung to the underside of one of the slabs—dead plant life, Arlian supposed, either moss or lichen that had managed to grow there briefly before succumbing to the ghastly conditions of the Desolation.

There were two smears in the black powder—two smears, as if someone's fingers had brushed against it.

"Lord Enziet!" he called into the darkness.

No one replied—but the sound of his voice echoing into the depths told him that this opening was clearly the mouth of a cave, no mere sinkhole.

And it was a cave that Enziet surely knew better than he did, but Arlian had hardly come so far to give up now. There might be another entrance; if he didn't pursue, Enziet might reemerge anywhere, at any time.

Cautiously, his sword ready, he stooped and made his way into the darkness.

The ground sloped down steeply but did not drop out from under him; in fact, after he had gone a dozen feet he found himself on uneven stone steps—whether natural or man-made he could not tell. They wound downward into darkness, the curves shutting out the sun's light.

He paused some thirty feet from the entrance, perhaps ten feet below ground, just before he left the daylight behind entirely. Here he let his eyes adjust and wished he had brought a lantern or lamp, or even just something he could use as a torch. Surely, Enziet could not see down here without some such device!

Of course, if he knew this cave well enough, he wouldn't need to see. He could be waiting at the bottom of the steps, planning to skewer Arlian by sound and feel.

Arlian held his breath and listened intently.

He could hear the wind blowing through the rocks, far behind him—and he could hear something very, very faint ahead, something that might be a person breathing.

"Lord Enziet!" he called. "I know you're there—strike a light, and we'll talk."

"Talk?" Enziet laughed bitterly—and the sound was closer than Arlian had expected. "You want to *talk,* Obsidian? Isn't it too late for that?"

"I'm not sure," Arlian replied, speaking more quietly—and moving as he spoke, sidling to his left, so as not to invite a sword-thrust by sound alone. "Toribor told me I must speak to you before trying to kill you, that there were secrets I should know before I strike you dead, and I swore I would listen if the opportunity arose."

For a long moment Enziet made no reply, and Arlian moved cautiously farther down the steps, as silently as he could. Then that cold voice spoke again.

"Belly got that out of you? I suppose it was his dying wish." He sounded almost regretful—the first time Arlian had heard anything like honest emotion in his enemy's voice.

"I didn't kill him," Arlian said. "Not yet. Drisheen is dead, though, and Shamble, and Stonehand."

"You're a thorough son of a poxy whore, aren't you? Why did you let Belly live?"

"Because with my sword at his throat, he was still more concerned with *your* life than his own," Arlian replied. He was fairly sure, now, of where Enziet stood—the stairs widened out just a foot or two below his own position, and Enziet was to his right at that level.

A sword-thrust at full extension should reach him, but the chance of hitting anything vital was still small—and there were still things to be said.

"You admired his loyalty?"

"Not loyalty," Arlian said. "Shamble was loyal to you with his dying breath, and I cut his throat without a qualm. Belly, though—he was *concerned.* It was compassion, not loyalty, and I couldn't find it in me to kill a man so concerned with the well-being of others."

"Even when *I,* the man you're sworn to kill, am the other?"

"But you aren't," Arlian said. "That's why I'm talking to you, instead of trying to kill you right now. Toribor said you hold secrets, and that when you die the effects will be far more than I could ever guess."

And then Arlian ducked. He was not sure exactly what he had sensed—whether he had heard cloth rustle, or felt the air move, or seen something in the lingering trace of light that reached this far into the earth, but he had somehow known that Enziet was about to strike.

Perhaps it was sorcery, but he *knew,* and he ducked, and therefore he lived; Enziet's blade swished over his head and rapped against the stone wall behind him. He slashed with his own sword, not seriously trying to hit Enziet, but only to force him back.

It worked; he heard the crunch of retreating footsteps, and when Enziet spoke again his voice came from farther away, and a different angle. He had moved deeper into the cave.

"Very good," Enziet said. "You move well, even in the dark."

"So do you, unfortunately," Arlian replied.

"So Belly told you my death will have consequences," Enziet said. "Did he say any more than that?"

"Somewhat," Arlian said. "I prefer not to go into detail, though; I would rather hear your account first, so that I might compare the two."

For a moment Enziet didn't answer; then he said, "Come down here, off the stair."

"Why?"

"Because if I am to tell you my secrets, then only one of us will leave this place alive—at most. I promise you that, my eager young enemy—if I reveal the truth, then at least one of us *must* die. I would much prefer that it be you, but if I speak, and you escape up the stairs before I can slay you, then my own life is forfeit."

"Why?" Arlian demanded.

"Step down away from there, and I'll tell you. And then you'll see why I say one of us must perish, and it's possible you'll choose to die yourself, rather than slay me."

"And what if I come down there, and you flee up the passage?"

"Then the pursuit will continue—but you're young and strong, and I'm a thousand years old, and right now I feel every day of it. And have you no companions aboveground who might apprehend me?"

Arlian considered that.

His companions were probably still miles away, and although they were following him, guided by Thirif's magic, they might never find this place. But why should he tell Enziet any of that? And he had caught up to Enziet this time; he could do it again, if he had to.

"Move away, then, and I'll come down," he said.

He heard the scuffing of boots on stone; Enziet was, indeed, moving back. Arlian stepped down into the chamber and felt his way along the wall.

When he had gone seven or eight feet he stopped.

"Tell me, then, what this dread secret is that you hold, that makes you so important."

"It's simple enough," Enziet said. "I know how the dragons reproduce."

For a moment Arlian stared uncomprehendingly into the featureless darkness. Then he asked, "What?"

"I know how dragons reproduce—and how to stop them from doing so."

"But...but don't they...I mean, the dragons are still animals, are they not?"

"No, they are not," Enziet said calmly. "They are the magic of the Lands of Man made flesh, a primal force drained from the earth and given shape; they only *appear* to us as beasts, as the reptiles we see. That is not what they are."

Arlian took a moment to consider this. He remembered the terrifying image of the dragons above the Smoking Mountain, the sight of that immense face peering into the ruined pantry, all the tales he had ever heard about the dragons.

He remembered Black asking him, long ago, if he knew male from female, or whether dragons laid eggs. He remembered seeing the belly of one dragon as it flew over Obsidian—it had been bare and sexless.

Creatures of sheer magic, like those things in the Dreaming Mountains, but vastly larger and more powerful—it all fit.

"And that's why they can't be killed, then?" he asked.

Enziet snorted. "I don't know whether they can be killed in their mature form," he said. "I think it's possible. I was working on that—for more than six hundred years I've worked on finding a way, and I believe I was very, very near when you came to Manfort and cast my life into chaos. But yes, their true nature is why we have no record that any man has ever killed one."

"Why didn't you *tell* anyone?" Arlian asked. "Why did you conceal this from the Dragon Society? It's so *basic,* so *essential,* yet you hid it for all these years!"

"I had sworn that I would," Enziet said.

"And you swore to the Society that you would *reveal* what you knew about dragons! What oath did you swear that took precedence over that?"

"Haven't you guessed?" Enziet's voice dripped sarcasm. "I thought you were such a *clever* boy!"

"No, blast you, I haven't guessed! Some ancient duke? Your father or mother?"

Enziet laughed. "You're a fool. Why would I care about an oath to someone long dead? No, I swore my oath to a power greater and older than the Dragon Society or anyone in it."

"Some sorcerer, then?"

"Don't be a fool, Arlian," Enziet spat. "I swore to the dragons themselves."

Chapter Fifty-Nine

The Sword of Lord Enziet

For a moment Arlian stared silently into the gloom, wishing he could see Enziet's face—that he could see *anything* other than black emptiness. Then he said, "You mean you swore *by* the dragons."

"No," Enziet said. "I swore an oath *to* the dragons themselves, when I drove them from the Lands of Man and bound them, by *their* oath, into the caverns."

"*You* bound them? You, yourself?"

"I have that honor, yes."

"But they come out sometimes," Arlian said.

"In dragon weather, yes. They're *dragons,* boy—they can't be bound entirely by anything human, not even an oath. But they would speak to me, when the temptation grew strong, and we would agree on what would be permitted them."

"Such as my home and family," Arlian said bitterly.

"Such as that, yes," Enziet agreed. "I chose your village for reasons of my own. I had not intended that anyone would survive, and that error has cost me. I should have known better—dragons are not to be trusted."

"What, you think they left me alive *deliberately?*"

"Yes, boy, I do. I know more about dragons than anyone alive, and yes, I believe they knew you were there, and that they let you live intentionally."

"Why? I've sworn to destroy them!"

For a moment Enziet didn't reply; when he did speak Arlian could hear genuine mirth in his voice. "*Have* you? As you swore to destroy me?"

"Yes! They killed my mother, my father, my grandfather, my brother—if a mortal man *can* destroy a dragon, I will!"

"No dragon would fear your vengeance, Arlian," Enziet said. "They fear no one but me. A boy of ten or twelve, as you were—pah! They'd consider you no more threat than a kitten!" He laughed. "They don't know you as I've come to."

"Can they be killed, then?" Arlian asked eagerly.

"The black dragons? The elders? I don't know. I believe it's possible."

"You said they fear you."

"They do. I know how they reproduce—and I know how to prevent it. Dragons don't live forever, any more than we who they've polluted do. We live centuries, and they live millennia, but we all die in the end, and they want their kind to live after them, as we do. I may not be able to kill a grown dragon, but I can kill their unborn young, and they know it, and fear me in consequence."

"How did you learn this?" Arlian asked. "Did you stumble on it by chance?"

"Does it matter?"

"It might. If you learned it, might others not be aware of it as well, without your knowledge?"

"And then you'd have no compunctions about killing me, eh?" Enziet laughed again. "No dragon has been born in a thousand years, Arlian. How could anyone else have learned what I know?"

"Then you've prevented births?" Arlian asked. "And the dragons permit it?"

"No, Arlian," Enziet said—and Arlian realized his foe's voice had moved closer; he had become so caught up in the conversation he had let his enemy creep closer unnoticed. Now he slashed at empty air and took three quick paces to the side. "It was not I who prevented the creation of new dragons for all those years. The gestation of a dragon takes a millennium, and the first new ones should be arriving within the next century, I would say. Only a very few of them will be born in the next thousand years—but there have been *none* in the thousand just ended."

"Why?" Arlian demanded. "If you're the only one who knows…"

"I was not always the only one who knew the secret," Enziet interrupted. "The Man-Dragon Wars were fought not simply because humans dared to resist draconic rule, but because humanity had discovered the hope of destroying the dragons entirely. The true nature of that knowledge was kept hidden by a secret society, and I was just one member of that original Order of the Dragon. The Dragon Society you know is a sick parody of the Order, Arlian—a parody I created after I betrayed the Order to save my own life. And when the Order was gone, I alone was left in possession of the Order's secret, and was able to do what the Order had not—free humanity of the dragons, not by warfare, but by an exchange of oaths."

"And if you die, the dragons are free of their oath?"

"Of course."

"And they'll emerge and reassert their rule over all the Lands of Man?"

"I don't know what they'll do, Obsidian," Enziet said wearily. "I don't understand them so completely as that. I only know they'll be free of constraint when I'm gone, when the secret of their origins is lost."

"You've told no one? Never written it down?"

"You *are* a naive young fool," Enziet said. "I don't want to die, and I don't care very much what becomes of all the rest of you once I'm dead. There are other reasons, as well—but no, I have told no one, nor have I written down my deepest secrets. There is no one I would trust with this knowledge, and documents can be stolen, or copied, or simply read by the wrong people. So, do you still want to kill me, knowing what you might unleash?"

"You'll die someday in any case," Arlian said.

"Indeed I will," Enziet agreed. "As will you. I might have an hour left to me—less, if you manage to slay me—or I might have a century. Is not the chance of a century's delay in the return of the dragons worth forgoing your revenge?"

"No," Arlian said. "Not when it might be only an hour, and not when you've said we won't both leave this place alive. I don't know that any of what you've told me is true—you could be making it all up to trick me!"

"I swear, by all gods living and dead, that what I have told you is true."

"And I cannot accept your word," Arlian said unhappily. "If it's the truth, you are already forsworn in your oath to the Society."

"The Dragon Society is a sham!" Enziet shouted.

"Yet you swore," Arlian insisted.

"Then you don't believe me," Enziet said.

"No," Arlian said. "If it's true, then tell me your secret, if you want it to survive—because *you* won't survive, if I can prevent it."

"I might kill *you,* instead."

"You're welcome to try. Tell me the secret, then—if you kill me, it won't leave this cave."

There was a long pause before Enziet replied thoughtfully, "I don't think I want to do that. The time may come when you learn for yourself, but I won't tell you."

"Then I won't spare you."

"And I'll do my best to kill you. No quarter asked nor given."

And suddenly Arlian felt a rush of air and sidestepped. He brushed against cloth and swung his own sword, but hit nothing. He turned toward the sound of Enziet's breath, both his blades ready.

"I lived seven years in the mines of Deep Delving," he said. "You won't find me frightened by the dark."

"And I spent two years in the caverns with the dragons, long ago," Enziet replied. "The darkness holds no terrors for me, either."

"Why did you come here?" Arlian asked. "Did you think you could escape me?"

Enziet snorted. "I thought I could bribe Wither," he said. "Bribe Wither, trust Drisheen, talk Nail around, terrify Belly into obedience, and keep my hold on the Dragon Society. I thought you would die on the way here—but I should have known better. Fate clearly has plans for you. I realized that long ago."

"Bribe Wither with what?" Arlian, thinking he sensed movement, thrust even as he spoke, but struck only air. He knew what Wither had demanded of Enziet, but he wanted to keep his opponent talking.

"With venom, of course," Enziet said. "This cave is an entrance to one of the dragons' lairs—five or six of them sleep in a chamber not far below us. Collecting venom that drips from their jaws as they sleep is simple enough; I've done it before, long, long ago." His voice moved as he spoke; he was circling around. Arlian turned, tracking his opponent's movement.

"Wither's been seeking venom for years," Arlian said. "Why are you only doing this now?"

"Because I didn't need Wither's support before, and did not care to see more clean blood tainted by the filth the dragons spew. You should appreciate that—you must have seen what happened to that whore you stole from me."

Arlian leaped and slashed at that, and heard cloth tear, but again he failed to strike flesh, and again he heard footsteps retreating.

He pursued, but after a dozen paces the sound of his own steps and the clattering of the stones he dislodged had drowned out Enziet's, and he lost the trail. He paused, trying to locate Enziet, but once the stones had stopped sliding the cave went utterly silent.

"You *dare* speak of her?" Arlian bellowed.

"Of course," Enziet replied, from somewhere far off to Arlian's left. "I dare anything. I am Lord Dragon, after all; I am he who makes the puppets dance. Human or dragon, free or slave, duke or whore, you all dance when I pull the strings." He laughed bitterly. "Or so I thought; perhaps Fate is pulling *my* strings now. Or perhaps the dragons have all along played a deeper game than I knew."

Light suddenly flared up; Enziet had struck sparks onto tinder. Arlian turned toward the light and hurried toward it, sword raised to strike, but Enziet stepped back and snatched up his own sword.

The tinder smoldered dimly, and clearly would not last long.

"I thought the time had come to get on with it, and settle matters between us," Enziet said. "Let me light a lamp, and we'll have it out properly."

Arlian stopped, and took a step back.

"Do it, then," he said.

Enziet nodded, stepping forward into the fading orange glow. He reached for a pouch on his belt as he knelt.

A moment later Enziet stood, a brass lamp burning in his hand. He placed it upon a ledge on the wall of the cave, then turned to Arlian.

For the first time since climbing down into the cave Arlian could see his surroundings. He could see where he had stood, and where he had run blindly across the cave floor, and he realized how lucky he had been—he had run right by a huge stalactite, and narrowly missed slamming his head into it.

Enziet had undoubtedly known the stalactite was there—but however familiar he might be with this place, he could not have been here for long, and had not been here in years before this visit, so his knowledge of the cave would not be complete.

That was why he had made a light—the cave was almost as dangerous to him as to Arlian. Not only were there stalactites to hit, stalagmites to trip over, and loose stones to stumble on, but there was a black pit to one side that they might have fallen in. The ceiling varied from too low to stand under to too high to see.

"That leads down to the dragons," Enziet said, pointing to the pit. "If you kill me, you might want to go down there to see if you can kill *them*." He smiled unpleasantly, twisting his scarred cheek.

"Are the three that destroyed my home down there?" Arlian asked.

"I don't know," Enziet said. "Quite possibly."

"You know so many secrets—do you know why they chose my village?"

Enziet laughed. "*They* didn't choose it," he said. "*I* did. I had an interest in obtaining a supply of obsidian, and the dragons were eager for a little entertainment—you must remember that summer. The weather had their blood boiling. They told me they were going to strike, but allowed me to name the place, and I thought I would save myself a little expense." He laughed again. "I cost myself far more than I expected. Had I known *you* were there, and what would come of it, I'd have directed them elsewhere and paid for my obsidian in gold." He raised his sword and stepped forward, between

Arlian and the lamp, casting an immense shadow across the cave.

Arlian dodged sideways, then ran and lunged; Enziet dodged, and counter-thrust. Arlian parried, riposted, then broke away.

Enziet stepped down, away from the light, into the shadow of a stone pillar. Arlian circled to the other side of the pillar.

For several minutes the two men maneuvered about the cave, stalking one another, looking for advantageous positions, occasionally exchanging a flurry of blows. Their shadows surged and shrank, twisted and dodged as they moved.

At one point Arlian slipped on a loose sloping stone and went down on one side; before Enziet could take advantage of this Arlian snatched up a handful of dust and pebbles and flung it at his foe's eyes. As Arlian regained his feet Enziet stepped back, wiping at his eyes with his sleeve, knocking his hat off and recovering just in time to meet Arlian's attack.

Swords clashed, and Arlian tried to snag Enziet's blade with his swordbreaker. Enziet dodged, and slashed, drawing a bloody line across Arlian's left forearm.

Arlian gasped and fell back—and Enziet fell into his trap, stepping forward to take advantage of a feigned weakness. Arlian's sword flashed orange in the lamplight as he struck; Enziet parried at the last moment, swinging his swordbreaker up, but the tip of Arlian's blade punched through Enziet's left shoulder, a far more serious wound than the scratch Enziet had inflicted.

Both men retreated, pulling apart; they stood facing one another, swords gleaming. Arlian's blade was tipped with red; Enziet's had a smear of blood diagonally across it.

"The dragons down below," Arlian said, hoping to disrupt Enziet's concentration. "Are they black? Or green?"

"Black," Enziet said. "All the surviving dragons are black."

"Oh? Why?"

"Because they're *old,* Arlian. A newborn dragon is red as blood, but by the time it's a year old that fades to gold. A few decades and it's green as grass, and a few centuries darken that to a black as black as their hearts."

"And are their hearts any blacker than yours, Lord Dragon? Is that why you called yourself that?"

Arlian had expected Enziet to laugh and make some sardonic reply at that, but instead he looked as if he had been struck.

"I have the heart of a dragon," he said bitterly, "as do you, and all the rest of that foolish little society. Yours may still be red, or at least gold, but mine is old and weary and black, just as you say—and as yours will be, one day, if you live that long."

"Never," Arlian said, lowering his sword and launching a fresh assault.

Chapter Sixty

The Final Duel

The fight dragged on; the lamp burned low, and the two men called a brief truce to refill it before resuming their combat. Arlian received a gash across his ribs and another just above one hip, while Enziet's left shoulder was pierced again, and a long gouge cut into his right leg. Blood was smeared across the rocks, on the stalagmites and along the walls. Both men grew tired, but fought on. Neither wasted breath on further speech; the time for talk was past, and both men knew it.

Arlian had no idea how long the fight lasted; in the cave there was no sun moving across the sky to tell him how much time had passed. He could only judge by how tired he was, by how heavy his sword had become.

Finally, though, as they maneuvered around a pillar, Enziet made a thrust, Arlian's parry slammed both swords against the pillar, and Enziet's blade snapped, no more than five inches from the guard.

Enziet reacted quickly, flinging the broken, useless stump at Arlian and running backward, away from his foe, before Arlian could strike him down.

Arlian recovered quickly from his surprise; the hilt of Enziet's sword glanced harmlessly from one ear as he dodged, and then he was in pursuit.

As he fled, Enziet had transferred his swordbreaker from his left hand to his right; now he turned, standing just below the ledge where the lamp sat, and faced Arlian.

Arlian paused. "No quarter, you said," he reminded Lord Dragon breathlessly.

"And I expect none," Enziet replied, gasping. "But on another point, I've reconsidered."

"Oh?"

"You wanted to know the secret of how the dragons reproduce," Enziet said. "I've decided to show you."

"What, you'd play for more time? Lead me down into a trap?" Arlian shook his head. "I don't think so. You'll die right here."

"Indeed I will," Enziet said, "and it's here that you'll see a dragon born." He turned the point of his swordbreaker toward his own chest. "I've felt it coming for months," he said. "I knew it would come in time, however I

495

fought, but I've denied just how close it was."

"What are you talking about?" Arlian asked.

Enziet smiled crookedly. "You thought that when we spoke of dragons in our hearts, we were speaking figuratively. You're about to see just how literal we were."

With that, he plunged the swordbreaker into his own heart, and cut downward convulsively with his dying breath.

Arlian gasped and stepped back in shock.

Blood gushed from Enziet's chest—but it did not spill to the ground as it should have. Instead it expanded and writhed like a snake, curling upward in a solidifying stream. Enziet's chest rippled as Drisheen's had, but the movement did not subside; instead it burst Enziet apart, and a creature, born of Enziet's heart's blood, stepped forth from the ruined corpse and stood upon four crooked, unsteady legs. It raised its blood-red head, opened golden eyes, and glared at Arlian; a mouth appeared and opened, and Arlian saw needle-sharp, gleaming-white teeth spring forth from its jaw. Wings unfolded from the monster's back, and it was a dragon, a bright red dragon, standing man-high, with a twelve-foot wingspan and extending perhaps fifteen feet from its newly formed nose to the tip of the soft red tail it had uncoiled from Enziet's belly.

Arlian stared at it open-mouthed, the sword drooping, forgotten, in his hand.

The dragon stepped toward him, and he scrambled backward, bumping heedlessly against rocks and stalagmites. He dared not take his eyes off the dragon for even an instant. He raised the sword to high guard.

He was suddenly struck by a thought that sent terror through him—what if that thing that had emerged from Enziet's body were to knock the lamp from the ledge, and plunge the cave into darkness? He doubted it needed the light; it could probably *smell* him. Even the slight chance of survival he had would be gone if the light died—unless he could get out, into daylight, before it caught him.

Could it fit up the stairs? Would it pursue him?

It had somehow fit *inside* Enziet, like a chick in an egg; he had to assume that yes, it could fit anywhere it chose to. As Enziet had told him, dragons were magic made flesh.

And there were at least five more dragons asleep in the cavern below, if Enziet had told the truth—and Enziet had certainly proven part of his story to be accurate. What if this newborn monster were to tumble down the pit and wake them?

Enziet had also said that while a mature dragon might be indestructible, he knew how to kill the dragons' unborn young. It was clear to Arlian that he had meant by killing their hosts—and Arlian suddenly realized that in his quest for vengeance he had already slain unborn dragons in Drisheen and Horim—but perhaps a newborn, like this one, was also vulnerable.

If he could kill this dragon he might yet be saved. And every second he waited might be making the thing harder to kill.

With a yell, he raised his sword and charged the thing.

The dragon lowered its head and spat venom at him, but it was a feeble gesture; the spray of venom was thin and weak, falling harmlessly to the stone, and it utterly failed to ignite. A faint wisp of smoke appeared, no more.

Then Arlian jabbed at the dragon's chest, striking as hard as he could—and the sword slipped off, wrenching sideways in his hands. The blood-red hide still looked soft and smooth, but he might as well have tried to pierce an anvil. Cold iron might have power against magic in the Borderlands, but good steel could not cut a dragon's hide.

Before he could recover his balance the dragon struck out with a foreclaw, swatting Arlian aside as if he were a mouse; he slammed against the cave wall, the breath knocked out of him, his back severely bruised.

The dragon stepped away from Enziet's corpse, shaking torn bits of flesh and cloth from its claws; it shook itself out, like a dog shaking off water, then stretched like a cat.

Its claws gouged into solid stone.

Arlian scrambled to his feet, his useless sword still in his hand, and the dragon turned to look at him.

He met its gaze, and a flood of memories came back—of how he had looked into a black dragon's face there in his parents' pantry, ten years before, and had known he would know that face instantly if he ever saw it again; of how he had seen Lord Dragon on horseback, looking down at him as if he were no more than an insect; of how both Black and Wither had looked at his face and told him he had the heart of a dragon; of how the members of the Dragon Society knew one another on sight.

Arlian knew this dragon. He knew those eyes. He had seen them before, in another color and another body. They were different now, larger and inhuman, but they were still, unmistakably, Lord Enziet's eyes.

The dragon smiled at him, a fierce, hungry smile.

Enziet had sworn that only one of them would leave this cave alive—and while he might have cast aside his humanity and his old body, Arlian was quite sure that this dragon was somehow still Enziet.

And it still meant to kill him.

Arlian tried to think what he could do, how he might find a weakness. His sword could not cut that sleek red hide—but what about the black inside the monster's mouth? What of its golden eyes? The thin red membranes of its wings?

He charged it, sword raised, and though it made no sound he thought he could hear Enziet's laughter. It made no move to dodge or counter, but simply stood there as he plunged his sword into its mouth, down its black throat.

Then it bit down.

He barely snatched his hand free as the dragon's teeth shattered his sword; he stepped back, horrified, as it swallowed the fragments and then smiled at him again, Enziet's crooked, sardonic smile.

Arlian dropped the hilt and switched his swordbreaker to his right hand, as Enziet had done. He circled to one side.

The dragon stood where it was, but turned its head, watching him.

Then Arlian suddenly sped up, running wildly across the rough stone floor, scattering shards of stone as he ran; he turned, and ran right up to the monster. He grabbed its serpentine neck to steady himself, and with all his strength plunged the swordbreaker down on one of those great golden eyes.

The blade snapped off with a sudden twang, sending the broken chunk of steel spinning off to the side, and the shock of the impact knocked the hilt from his grip, bruising his fingers; his wrist went numb, and pain shot up his arm.

The dragon shook itself, sending Arlian flying, and he slammed back against the cave wall again, this time hitting sideways. Pain blazed. He heard something crack—probably one of his ribs.

He was injured, perhaps seriously, and unarmed, both his blades broken, and all he had done was amuse the dragon. It wasn't even annoyed, judging by its expression—and a dragon's face, though not as mobile, somehow managed to be at least as expressive as a man's.

Enziet's silent laughter filled Arlian's thoughts as he struggled to his feet.

Even though he knew a steel blade couldn't pierce the dragon's hide, Arlian still wanted one—he felt naked facing an enemy unarmed. Both his own weapons were broken, as was Enziet's sword—but Enziet's swordbreaker was intact.

And, Arlian remembered, that was the blade that had given birth to this abomination; perhaps that would endow it with special potency.

Half running, half staggering, Arlian hurried to Enziet's corpse, behind the dragon. The dragon started to turn, but found itself awkwardly positioned, confined by a stone pillar and a low section of stalactite-encrusted ceiling; Arlian was able to reach the body unhindered.

The swordbreaker was still clutched in Enziet's dead fingers; Arlian started to pry it loose, looking up to see what the dragon was doing.

The monster had disentangled itself and turned, and was advancing, jaws agape.

Arlian, anticipating a spray of venom, ducked—and the venom missed him by inches.

As he moved, Arlian saw something, tangled in Enziet's ruined clothing—the hilt of another knife, a dagger.

That would not have the unique puissance of the sword-breaker, but he snatched for it anyway, and came away with the swordbreaker in one hand, the dagger in the other—just in time to make a rolling dive sideways as the dragon lunged for him.

He rolled away—a painful operation, with his bruises and cracked rib, but he forced himself to ignore the pain, as he had often done in the mines. When he was clear of the dragon's attack he tried to spring to his feet, but instead found himself crouched on one knee as agony laced his side where he had just pulled a muscle right where Enziet's sword had cut him. His eyes closed involuntarily; when he could force them open again he saw the dragon glaring at him.

Now it was annoyed.

He took that as a hopeful sign, and raised the sword-breaker, ready to strike if the dragon lunged.

The monster obliged, raising its head up as its long neck curved into an S, then striking at him like a snake.

Arlian dodged and made a strike of his own, plunging the swordbreaker at the dragon's throat.

It glanced off harmlessly.

"Blood and death," Arlian muttered, as he fell back. He lifted the dagger in a meaningless defensive gesture.

For the first time he saw the dagger's blade, and realized that it was black—not the black of iron or enamel, but the gleaming, glassy black of obsidian.

Enziet had said he had a use for obsidian.

Enziet had thought there might be a way to kill a dragon, or at least so he had said, and he had been researching it.

Enziet had been on his way to steal a dragon's venom—might he have brought something he thought might protect him?

Obsidian had power against fire and darkness, Rime had told him.

Arlian plunged the dagger into the dragon's throat.

The black blade sliced into that impervious red flesh as if the dragon's hide were cheese.

The dragon screamed, an ear-wracking sound like nothing Arlian had ever heard before; it reared back wildly, smashing stalactites to powder with its wings and head, and slashed at Arlian with its foreclaws.

He dodged one, but the other tore strips of flesh from his shoulder; he gasped at the surge of fresh pain, and struck again with the obsidian dagger.

He cut clean through one foreleg, crippling the dragon; the severed claw turned to blood as it fell, and splashed across Arlian's leg.

The dragon screamed again, and Arlian felt something pop in one ear.

The thing was hobbling, not sure how to move on three legs, but its head reared back, then struck at him again.

He met it with the point of the dagger, jamming his hand directly into the dragon's mouth and driving the blade up into its brain—or trying to.

It choked, and spat his arm out in a gush of blood, but it still lived, and was still on the attack.

Just then a faint light appeared where no light had been. The dragon turned to look.

Arlian hacked at its neck, hoping he could do to its head what he had done to its claw, but the blade would not penetrate that far—the obsidian wasn't long enough, and the wound closed once the blade had passed through, leaving an ugly scar but not doing any obvious real damage.

"By the dead gods!" someone called. "Arlian!"

The dragon roared in anger and started toward the steps, trying to separate Arlian from this intruder—but that meant turning its back to Arlian, who seized his opportunity. He rammed the obsidian knife into the dragon's side over and over, his hand rising and falling as quickly as his tired, strained muscles could drive it.

The dragon screamed and writhed, twisting to strike at him, and he felt a spray of venom across one cheek, venom that burned like fire, but he did not stop. Each new blow cut deep, but each cut closed, and no blood flowed.

And then he struck again, one last time, and it was as if a dam had burst—blood was everywhere, and the dragon seemed to dissolve around him.

Then he was lying in a pool of glistening blood, and impaled upon his stolen stone dagger was a human heart.

Enziet's heart.

He stared at it for a long moment, then let go of the dagger's hilt and let his head fall back. Pain and exhaustion boiled up in him, burning the strength from his limbs, and the world vanished in a red and black haze as he lost consciousness.

* * *

After a time he had no way to measure Arlian was vaguely aware of being carried somewhere, and of impossibly bright light; then he was laid upon his back on something hard, the light all around him. He heard voices, but could not be troubled to distinguish words.

Simply breathing was all the effort he could handle.

After what seemed years he realized that the light was daylight, that he was outside the cave. He observed two shadows, and came to see that they were people leaning over him, blocking out that blinding sky. They were speaking to him, saying his name.

"I'm alive," he said, as much to himself as to them, but they understood. One of them fell away, out of his field of vision, and was gone.

The other fell silent, but remained there, looking down at him. Black against the sky, the face was not recognizable.

"Sleep, Ari," the face said at last, and Arlian recognized Black's voice.

"Yes," he said. And he slept.

When he awoke again he was on his cot in the wagon; the sky outside the windows was dark, but a lantern shone comfortingly over the door. He started to sit up, then thought better of it when pain shot through his side.

"He's moving!" a woman's voice called, and he turned his head to see Brook sitting on a trunk at his side.

"Give him water," Rime's voice replied, which struck Arlian as a very fine idea. A moment later Brook held a waterskin to his mouth and he sucked greedily.

He was only awake for a few minutes before dozing off again, but it was enough to assure everyone that he was still alive and intended to stay that way.

After that he recovered quickly. His wounds were painful, but not critical; most of the cuts and gouges were already scabbed over, the bruises already making the transition from purple to golden-yellow. He had not lost any limbs. His right wrist was broken, and at least three ribs were cracked, rather than the one he had thought, but his injuries would heal—except, perhaps, a burn on one cheek that he knew, but did not say, had been left by the newborn dragon's venom.

He would live, and he would heal. He was, as Rime pointed out, a dragonheart.

That reminder sobered Arlian. He lay in silent thought for a long time—by this point he was capable of sitting up, and even walking, but still found it painful.

"Who found me?" he asked. "Who was it who came down into that cave?"

"Black," Rime told him. "I couldn't get down the stairs in time, with my leg. The others stayed in the wagon."

"Just Black?"

"Just Black."

"Bring him here."

"He's driving. We're heading back for Stonebreak, and we need to keep moving if we don't want to run out of water. You can talk to him later."

Arlian accepted that.

"Thirif and Shibiel aren't going on to the south?" he asked, changing the subject.

"No," Rime said. "They decided not to risk it."

Arlian nodded.

That night, when they had made camp, Arlian asked Black, "What did you see down there?"

"In the cave?"

Arlian nodded.

"You were fighting something," Black said. "Something big and red, but I couldn't see it clearly. You were hitting it, or stabbing it, and it was thrashing around, and then all at once it seemed to vanish, and you collapsed. Then I came down and found you lying in a pool of blood, and a few feet away…" He frowned. "What happened to Enziet? *You* didn't cut him up like that, did you?"

Arlian had had time to anticipate that question. "It was sorcery," he said. "Or maybe some other sort of magic. I'm not sure what it was. Enziet made it, but it turned on him, and then when he was dead it attacked me."

"What *was* it?"

"I don't know," Arlian lied. "It had claws and teeth, but it wasn't solid, and when I had cut it enough it vanished."

Black nodded. "Sorcery and illusion," he said.

"I wasn't sure you'd seen it at all," Arlian said. "I'm glad you did, so you can confirm that I'm not mad, and that Enziet is truly dead."

"I saw it. And he's definitely dead."

Arlian smiled grimly at that.

He didn't say anything about dragons, didn't mention Enziet's heart or any ancient secrets. He was not ready to reveal the truth. He was not sure he would *ever* be ready.

After all, he was the one man in all the world who knew the secret of the dragons, the secret Enziet had kept for a thousand years.

And he was a dragonheart, and some day, some far-off day, if he lived long enough, the dragon in his heart would burst forth.

And he hadn't yet decided how he felt about that, or what he intended to do about it.

Three days later he felt well enough to ride up front, in the fresh air, at Black's side as Black drove. Rime sat just inside the door. They had found the edge of the sands and were back on the Eastern Road, headed north, toward Manfort and home.

"So Enziet is absolutely, unquestionably dead?" Rime asked.

"Absolutely and unquestionably," Arlian agreed.

Black snorted. "His heart was ripped out of his chest," he said. "He's *dead.*"

"His heart was ripped out?" Arlian asked.

"You didn't see? It was lying there on the stone, next to a broken dagger."

Arlian nodded. "I wasn't sure *what* I saw," he said.

He wondered whether the dagger had really been broken, or whether Black had not seen its black blade in the darkness. In any case, it had been left behind and was lost forever.

But he knew now that obsidian could be used against dragons, at least sometimes, in some circumstances, against some dragons. That might be very precious knowledge.

He was bound by oath to reveal it to the Dragon Society—but he was unsure just how and when he would inform the Society, or even whether he would keep his word at all in this case. With Enziet dead the entire purpose of the Dragon Society might well be about to change. The dragons might be returning—if they learned that Enziet was dead, and if no one took his place as the keeper of the secret of draconic reproduction. If he could learn how Enziet had communicated with the dragons, Arlian might take that place. He might need to keep that secret, as Enziet had—and if he kept that, why not another?

And the dragons' secret also meant that Arlian saw the Society in a new light—as the dragons' breeding ground, rather than their foes. That changed *everything.* The Dragon Society was not what it believed itself to be.

But he was not yet ready to deal with such weighty matters. He would need to take time to think them through carefully. There would be time enough for his final decisions when he was back in Manfort.

"So you've almost finished your campaign of revenge," Rime said, interrupting his thoughts and providing a welcome distraction. "Just Belly and Nail remain, I believe."

"If I bother with them, yes. And Dagger and Tooth, if I can find them, and perhaps a fellow called Lampspiller," Arlian said. "They're even less important than the lords, though. But even when I've dealt with all of those, my lady, the campaign is just starting."

"Oh? It seems to me you don't have much more to do. You've beaten Belly once, and Nail's an old man, and you don't seem very determined to track down the other three."

"The other three *humans,*" Arlian corrected her. "There are still the dragons—the three that destroyed my village, and the rest of them on general principles."

"The dragons?" Rime asked.

Arlian nodded. "The dragons are my true foes," he said. "I intend to destroy them all." And that almost certainly meant, he realized, that he would have to destroy the Dragon Society itself in time.

And perhaps himself, since he had a dragon growing in his heart.

"That's a lifetime's work, at least," Rime said. "You *do* know that no man has ever killed a dragon, don't you?"

Arlian smiled.

"I'll find a way," he said.

Dragon Weather

About the Author:

Lawrence Watt-Evans has been a full-time writer for more than forty years, with about fifty novels and well over a hundred short stories to his credit, as well as assorted essays, poems, comic books, and so on. His story "Why I Left Harry's All-Night Hamburgers" won the 1988 Hugo for short story, as well as the Asimov's Readers Award. He lives in Bainbridge Island, Washington with his wife.

His website is at www.watt-evans.com.

Made in the USA
Las Vegas, NV
21 June 2023

73703622R00282